ONE
WRONG
WORD

ONE WRONG WORD

HANK PHILLIPPI RYAN

Tor Publishing Group

New York

This is a work of fiction. All of the characters, organizations, and events portrayed in this novel are either products of the author's imagination or are used fictitiously.

ONE WRONG WORD

Copyright © 2024 by Hank Phillippi Ryan

All rights reserved.

A Forge Book
Published by Tom Doherty Associates / Tor Publishing Group
120 Broadway
New York, NY 10271

www.tor-forge.com

Forge® is a registered trademark of Macmillan Publishing Group, LLC.

The Library of Congress Cataloging-in-Publication Data is available upon request.

ISBN 978-1-250-84949-6 (hardcover)
ISBN 978-1-250-84952-6 (ebook)

Our books may be purchased in bulk for promotional, educational, or business use. Please contact your local bookseller or the Macmillan Corporate and Premium Sales Department at 1-800-221-7945, extension 5442, or by email at MacmillanSpecialMarkets@macmillan.com.

First Edition: 2024

Printed in the United States of America

0 9 8 7 6 5 4 3 2 1

For everyone who has a dream.
And yes, you wonderful person reading this, that means you.
You are brave and fabulous and beloved.

And for Jonathan, always always, but he knows that.

ONE
WRONG
WORD

Regret has consumed him, and fear too, and Cordelia wishes she could let her husband know how well she understands his spiraling terror. She's never seen him cry, not like he is now, anguished, head on his knees, taking up all the space on the folding chair in the waiting area off the courtroom. A metal-tipped cord attached to the grimy woven curtains keeps tapping against the window, tap tap *tap,* aggravated by the rattle of the ancient heater. How much sorrow this room has seen, this limbo between guilty and not guilty. Some who sit here, waiting, will go home. Some will not. But no one will ever be the same.

Because regret itself can be lethal. Remorse, too, and the toxic second-guessing that gnaws away the edges of reality. All those "if only" moments. Cordelia knows Ned must be—yet again—replaying that night, over and over, as if somehow he could make it end a different way. But that is impossible. "If only" is now his nightmare.

His coffee, two sugars one cream, sits untouched on the pitted metal table. Nyomi Chang, who'd dramatically defended him, stays silent, staring out a meshed window. The door to the courtroom stays closed. The jury has been out two days and four hours. *Commonwealth v. Bannister.* Three counts. Operating under the influence, reckless driving, and vehicular homicide.

Ned is the defendant, but *her* future is on the line, too. Pip's, too, and Emma's.

"I didn't see him, Dee," Ned says. "I didn't."

"I know, honey." She touches her hand to the back of his navy blazer, feels his shoulders trembling, feels the soft worsted of the too-expensive suit, has a flash of prison orange canvas. Ned is tough, and capable, but he'll never survive. He'd navigated his way up the corporate ladder, now he faces fifteen years in state prison. Where the power structure is terrifyingly different.

"He wasn't supposed to be there. He was trespassing."

"I know, honey."

"And I *wasn't* drunk. I had, maybe, two glasses of champagne. It was a party. But I know drunk. I know myself. I was tired, sure, after all that. But . . ."

She isn't sure who he's explaining it to. Himself, maybe. He'd explained it on the stand, allowed himself to be cross-examined by a gorgon of a DA, admitting he was tired, denying he was drunk. Admitting he was driving fast, *maybe,* but he was the only car in the place, and then repeating those four words, over and over, a refrain of anguish. *I never saw him. I never saw him.* One reporter had actually laughed. The headlines had not been kind. REAL ESTATE EXEC SEZ: WHAT GUY?

Cordelia knows, from the nights he's writhed and tossed in their bed, and as she fails to find any way to comfort him, that he repeats that New Year's Eve moment in his mind as if it were something he could edit, or alter, or hit some cosmic undo button. The curved pavement of the parking garage, Ned's big Mercedes barreling up toward the exit as skateboarder Randall Tennant careens down; the younger man trespassing, certainly, in the private building. Ned had been exactly where he belonged, and Randall Tennant hadn't. But only one had survived. The punishment for trespassing is not—usually—death. Except this time.

She'd been home with Pip and Emma, as she'd told everyone, over and over, and a little angry, she'd admitted that, too, after everyone *kept* asking, to have been left alone with two sniffy whining kids while Ned had lorded it over the bacchanalian fireworks party at his lofty harborview office.

Apparently the champagne had been unending, no matter what Ned said, and now their lives hang in the balance, and that damn jury, ten men and two women who would leave and go back to lives of whatever, have no idea how much power they wield over her future. She tries to imagine that: Ned gone, his pillow empty, his place at the dinner table vacant, Cordelia herself either doomed or free, their children constantly having to explain what happened to their once-revered father. One mistake, one missed turn, one wrong word.

Sometimes we lose the ones we love. And what will she do?

A knock at the door. It opens. A blue-uniformed court officer is framed in the doorway. Cordelia tries to read his expression, but cannot. She stands, almost in tribute, a reflection of the pivotal moment. Nyomi Chang stands, too, the burden of past verdicts, Cordelia imagines, weighing her shoulders. Ned does not budge.

"Mr. Bannister?" the officer says.

PART ONE

1

ARDEN WARD

Hey Warren, how's *your* Friday going?" Arden stood as her boss entered her harbor-front office. She smoothed the sleek wool of her cashmere pants, adjusted the double strand of her trademark vintage pearls, then gestured to the video of the courthouse shown on the wide-screen TV mounted in her bookshelves. "Better than Ned Bannister's, I bet. Time's running out for him. Verdicts always come on Friday. Jurors want to go home."

Warren, tie loosened and bespoke cuffs rolled, carried a crystal rocks glass filled with some dark liquid. Likely bourbon, Arden knew. Fridays at the Vision Group, the drinking started early. *Solving other people's problems was thirsty work,* Warren always said. Whatever tired cliché he chose, he always spoke as if he had originated it.

"They should have called us before the trial, you know?" Now he toasted the television screen, watching the muted video of an earnest reporter stationed outside the gray marble exterior of Boston's Suffolk County Courthouse, the building blending into the November sky.

He took a sip, contemptuous. "Coverage of this debacle's been a total shit show. The Parking Garage Killer." He shook his head. "Pitiful. We'd have nipped that phrase in the bud."

"Agreed." Arden nodded. Of course she agreed with her boss, she understood the balance of power. She'd even stopped what she'd been doing to watch with him. The banner crawling across the bottom of the screen spelled it out: *Jury still deliberating in Bannister drunk drive trial.* "You'd think a guy as connected as Ned Bannister would realize he needed crisis management help."

She paused at Warren's silence. He hadn't arrived in her office to chat about this latest gossip fodder—Boston's elite and powerful partying high above Boston Harbor, the deadly crash, then business exec Bannister publicly branded a careless boozy criminal. It wasn't entirely surprising, she had to admit, Warren often made end-of-the-week visits, the benevolent dictator, to check on Arden's clients, her progress. Her billings.

And sometimes to celebrate. The last time Warren showed up un-announced, he'd bestowed her with a bouquet of white English roses, a wildly extravagant bunch studded with shiny green foliage. The Vision Group had Patterson's Florist as a client, Arden knew, so the pricey flow-ers had not come from Warren's pocket. Still, she'd buried her face in them, deeply inhaling.

"These are spectacular," she'd said. "And you know I love flowers. But what's the occasion?"

"The occasion is your—our—big score. Arthur Swanson is a done deal. And *you* get the Miss Congeniality bouquet."

Arden had rolled her eyes, hidden her derision behind the fragrant roses. *She'd* done all the hard work, getting the pretentious and privileged Arthur Swanson onto the board of Caldecott Hospital. But Vision Group CEO Warren Carmichael was the boss, and he was her lifeline, and he'd taken a chance on hiring her after she'd fled her old life in Allentown.

Not that there was anything left of it; back home the taint of being Governor Porter Ward's daughter wrapped her with a permanent shroud of embarrassment. But in Boston, the name "Ward" was just a name, not a label, and she'd done well here. Maybe bad things sometimes happened for a reason. To allow the good things.

"Arthur Swanson's perfect for the role." Arden had been authentically enthusiastic. "All that money. All that influence. The hospital ate it up. And his wife totally believes it was the result of his merit and her social standing. Patience Swanson seems to live in her own glittery world." Ar-den, daring, could not resist the possibly inappropriate dig. She shook her head. "People."

Now Warren took a sip of his probably-bourbon. Arden could smell it, sweet and smoky.

He'd focused on the television again. "No verdict yet, huh?"

"There's still time," Arden said. "Though Fridays they recess early."

Warren took another sip.

"You okay?" she asked. Might be a little personal, but she thought the Arthur Swanson deal had brought them closer. Warren had been the face of it, and she the supposed "associate." But Warren had no idea that throughout the negotiations Arden had endured—and ignored, or pretended to—Arthur Swanson's advances; the unnecessary touch on her shoulder, the gratuitous hand on her back ostensibly guiding her through a door, the too-personal jokes about her "single-girl" apartment or her weekend plans. The sideways looks, as if they shared some secret, which, indeed, they did not. The dinner à deux invitations she always refused.

In this day and age, she thought. But for men like him, there was only *his* day and age, meaning *now* and *today.* For Warren, too, she had to admit. Who always did whatever was in his own best interest.

"So Arden," Warren began. "About Patience."

"Sit," Arden said. She had a flash of dismay. "Is everything still on? With the deal? Do not tell me she's—"

Warren settled into the butterscotch tweed club chair. "We should talk."

"Sure." Arden calculated the possibilities, speed of light. She hated surprises, *hated* them. *We don't like surprises,* she taught her assistants. *Our job is to stay ahead of the surprises.* Now, surprise, Warren wanted to talk.

"So Patience herself barges in last week, like, loaded for bear."

"And?" Arden heard the bourbon in Warren's voice. Saw his posture wilt. Alcohol always hit him hard, and he'd powered this drink down.

"And she was—pissed."

"What? About what?"

Warren looked at the ice in his glass, the bourbon gone. "So you remember Capital Grille?"

"Sure. . . ." Arden couldn't help but frown.

The week before, the Swansons had invited the two of them, along with Warren's hoity-toity jet-setting peripatetic wife and a group of their friends, to a closed-door celebration of Swanson's not-yet-public new position. Dinner at Capital Grille, in a mahogany-paneled private room with flowing wine and hovering waitstaff. Asparagus, hollandaise, filet, caviar. Food and setting as rich and overstuffed as some of the guests themselves.

Arden had noticed Patience seated her as far away from Arthur as possible, but she'd been grateful for that. She had tolerated enough uncomfortable and insulting moments of removing his hand from her leg. She would never tell Warren, of course. The deal needed to go through, and some things, by necessity, women handled on their own.

"And then she says the weirdest thing," Warren went on.

Warren rarely gossiped with her. She was curious about his new tone, but embraced it. It felt like progress. "What'd she say?"

"'She smells of joy.'" Warren was actually imitating Patience Swanson, that imperious but impossible-to-identify accent that some of her ilk adopted. "I had no idea what she was talking about, you know?"

Arden remembered, in the weird snippets of moments we remember, having sensed a kinship with Warren that night at the Swanson dinner. Feeling she had finally made it as his equal. She'd perceived, with a glimmer of hope and even confidence, that they were a team.

"Joy the perfume?" Arden guessed now. "What 'she'? And why did that matter?"

Warren's face changed. Hardened. He carefully placed his crystal glass, contents diminished to ice, on her side table. Centered it on a copy of *Boston* magazine.

"Yes. Perfume." Warren nodded, once. "And the 'she' is you."

2

Arden took a moment to unpack Warren's words. She stood, uncomfortable in her own office. Then sat in her swivel chair, kept the desk between them.

"I? Me? I smelled of *Joy*? That's kinda random. Well, I guess so. I wear it, sometimes. My mother did, too. It's . . ." She shrugged. "O-G, maybe, but classic. Ask *your* wife."

"Well, seems that's something you and Mrs. Swanson share. Joy. She uses it, too. And she says she recognized it on you at the Capital Grille. That night."

Arden tried to decipher Warren's expression, his growing discomposure. One polished loafer tapped against the steely pile of her office carpeting.

"Okay." Arden took a plastic bottle of water from her bottom desk drawer, twisted off the top. The TV flickered above them. The lower-third crawl repeated the lack of news: *No verdict yet in Bannister case.* "Joy. And?"

"And she is not happy about it."

"About what?"

"More than not happy. Extremely unhappy. Because her husband has a habit of . . . Shit, Arden, she thinks he gave you the perfume. Apparently, this is what he does. Hits on women. Gives them Joy. The perfume I mean. It's like, a pattern."

"What? And—so what?" She stopped. "Oh. Is there some *woman* thing? That we didn't know of? Is the board appointment in jeopardy?" Arden's mind raced with the possibility that their hard work would blow up because of some idiot man's inability to appreciate what he had and stop greedily wanting more. *Perfume?*

Arden stood, came to the front of her desk, team player. "We *warned* him. Told him he needed to tell us everything. That we can't fix what we don't know. We told him we hate surprises. Right?"

Warren actually gulped. She'd never seen his face so ashen.

"Listen, Arden. I don't like this any more than you will. But understand. The Swansons are major clients. Lucrative clients. Company-supporting clients."

"Well, I know. I *brought* them to you. When we met at my Saving Calico childhood leukemia fundraiser. Remember?"

"Oh. Right." Warren picked up his glass, rattled the ice. "I didn't think anything could make this more difficult."

"Make what?"

"So Patience Swanson thinks you and her husband have a . . . thing. That he gave you the Joy."

Arden clapped a palm to her chest. "She's insane."

"Possibly. Probably. But that doesn't change anything. She demands that we let you go."

"She? Demands? You let me go?" Every nerve cell in Arden's brain burst into flames.

"I have no choice."

"Choice? Of course you do." Arden took a step toward him, arms spread in exasperation and disbelief. "Who does she think put her husband where he is today?"

"I'm sorry, Arden. It's a situation. I don't know what to say."

"You don't? Well, I do." She jabbed toward him with a forefinger. "You can say 'she's lost her freaking mind.' You can tell that woman I'm a valuable employee who brings in big bucks, and new clients, and will continue to do so. And who, it goes without saying, is not having some sort of sordid affair with her vile entitled husband who clearly she has problems with. But the 'problems' are not me. A *situation*? It's my *life*!"

"I'm sorry, Arden. Unless you can prove he didn't give you perfume. Unless you can prove he didn't—"

She rolled her eyes to the heavens, then harnessed her outrage. "*I'm* not going to prove one thing on this planet. Ask *him,* right? First of all, I can't prove something that didn't happen, that's through the looking glass, and I cannot believe you're even asking me that. Is that what you think of me? Let me ask *you* that. That this is *true*?"

"No, of course not, no." Warren lurched to his feet, turned away, not looking at her, looking at every place else but her. "He'll deny it. So I can't force him to—"

"Ah. I see. Warren. Look at me. So you believe *her,* not me? Is that what you're saying? Because if that *is* what you're saying, Warren, I could file so many lawsuits it'd make your head spin. Hey. You're a pro. Imagine the headlines. Blame the victim? Or wait, would you paint me the vixen, the temptress? Oh, yeah, do it. *Please* do that. I'd love that. Bring it."

Warren had to know this was bull. "Are you hearing me?" she persisted. "Are you ignoring me? *Look* at me. I know the rules. I know the deal. You cannot do this. I'll go to HR so fast it'll—"

"Be careful, Arden." Warren interrupted her. "Take a beat. If you sue me, well, that's not gonna help you, is it? Suddenly you're . . . a problem employee. A liability. On the defensive. It's not a good look. You know that."

"What I know—and what *you* know—is that it's not true."

"What I *know* is that if the Swansons leave us, if they take their billings, I'd have to fire three other people to make up for it. Do you want to be responsible for that?"

"Oh, no. No. That's not fair." Arden wiped away the space in front of her, erasing Warren's words. "Do not make me feel guilty about people losing their jobs over a lie."

"We won't let this get out," Warren said. "It'll stay between us."

"Right. Between us." She choked down a bitter laugh, focusing her anger. "*And* Patience Swanson. And Arthur Swanson. And whatever gossip mongers and sycophant confidantes and social media jackals—I cannot believe I'm saying this. A *secret*. As if anyone could keep a secret." She drew in a breath, her judgment obliterated by expanding rage. Narrowed her eyes. "Unless they're dead."

"You can say whatever you want about why you're leaving," Warren kept talking, trampling over her words. "That you're on to new opportunities, or . . . and we'll support you. Whatever you want. We'll back you—"

"I don't want anything. What I want—at least until about a minute ago—is to do this work. Where I have changed people's lives for the better." Arden struggled to find the right words. Her vocabulary had vanished, along with her balance and place in the world. "You can't do this, Warren. You can't."

"You'll find another job." He backed toward the door. Watched her, as if she'd change her mind. "You have two weeks. Maybe I can even find you one last client. Go out big. Prove that you left on your own."

"*Bull*," she said. "You want me to lie to protect your lie?"

But he was gone.

Her universe had crashed. Everything she believed in, everything she relied on, everything she cared about. She stood, staring into the empty hallway, set adrift by power. And money. And the power of money.

3

She could still smell Warren's damn bourbon. Arden yanked the cord of the slotted window blinds, letting the wintry late-afternoon glare from the steel-and-ice water of Boston Harbor into her office.

Warren effing Carmichael. She yanked open a desk drawer, dumped it upside down over her wastebasket. Pens and binder clips and ratty packets of Splenda and Band-Aids and yellow stickies tumbled into the metal container. She stood, holding the empty drawer by its aluminum handle.

She considered throwing the most batshit crazy tantrum that anyone in this insane office had ever seen. Because she understood the genesis of fury now. The desperation of the powerless. The rage of the trapped. The crazed unleashed sprawling need to fight back. It had killed her father, the disloyalty of people in power. *The little guys cannot win,* her father had warned her back then. *No matter how we try.* She'd refused to believe him.

But here she was, a bug on a pin.

She closed her eyes, pressed her lips together, physically tried to tamp down her flaming anger. Carefully replaced the empty drawer on its runners.

She'd been screwed, and that's all there was to it. Jerks. She'd never, *ever* have done what they'd accused her of. Never.

Warren clearly knew that. And just as clearly didn't care. How do you prove something didn't happen?

She'd given these people everything they'd wanted: nights and weekends, ideas, success, headlines. Clients, access, money. But in the end, none of it mattered. Warren could do whatever he wanted. Including ruin her. And fighting back would only make it worse.

Severance. Yes, she reassured herself. I get that. *Health insurance!* Her mind screamed at her. That'll run out. Soon. Job hunting. *Shit.* Resumé. Recommendations. What if she *never* found another job? What if Warren spread that lie to everyone?

Deep breaths. Softened vision. Lowered shoulders. Count to ten. She could count to a billion. It wouldn't help.

Warren effing Carmichael. Pretending he wasn't in this up to his neck, his white-collared blue-shirted paisley-tied neck, with that preposterous collar pin, like he was some ad for the Ivy League patriarchy and she was an expendable underling instead of a respected and admired colleague.

Many a beleaguered corporate executive tainted by a lawsuit or families besieged by reporters had relied on her. When people needed their lives back, when they needed guidance, or protection from the relentless questioning and hounding by determined journalists or the violent cancel culture of social media, Arden would run interference. Keep them safe. Advise them what to say.

For the last eight years, she'd helped people. Created their safer reality. Her entire career involved shaping and taming the beast that was public opinion. Now she was a victim of it.

She considered dumping absolutely everything in the office into a trash bin. *Everything.* Just—walk out, head high and trailing animosity. She stood quietly for a moment, hearing the hum of the heater, the soft buzz of the muted television, the footsteps down the hall, contemplating it all.

Lies and secrets, the most powerful forces in the universe. Indelible. Contagious. Lethal.

"Arden? You still here?" Luz Ocasio's voice entered before she did.

It crossed Arden's mind to warn her assistant how the knives-out world they worked in could turn vicious. That the Vision Group would turn on their own if the powers-that-be decided the client was more important. That the gain—*money*—was worth the loss. The loss of an actual human being.

Luz—her colleague for less than a year, hip, smart, ambitious—had no idea what had just transpired.

Luz gestured toward Arden's overflowing wastebasket. "Cleaning up?"

"Sort of. You think he's guilty?" Arden pointed to the TV, changing the subject to the Bannister trial. The reporter, even muted, radiated suspense and drama. *No verdict yet,* the crawl announced. Arden called on all her acting skills, stepping into a precarious pretend-reality. What was she supposed to tell Luz? Or anyone? She pretended, her faux reality, to fuss with the drawer.

She was "looking for new opportunities"? Why would someone so demonstrably successful do that? To take some time to rest? That tele-graphed "rehab," whether from alcohol or drugs or stress. And would raise more nasty questions and vicious gossip than it silenced. Certainly not "to spend more time with her family"—everyone knew her parents were dead and Arden was now unmarried and seemingly permanently unattached. *Married to her work,* she'd heard someone whisper as she left a meeting. What were the vows of business, *till money and power do us part?*

"Doesn't matter what I think." Luz had pushed up the sleeves of her black cashmere sweater and perched on the arm of the visitor's chair. "It only matters what the jury thinks."

"And what the public thinks. That's our job." Arden almost choked on her words. *Was* her job. *Fired.* Her mind would not contain it, that poisonously apocalyptic word.

Now Arden, oh-so-savvy at crisis management, couldn't figure out how to handle a crisis of her own.

And that excruciating irony was almost too much to bear. *Warren eff-ing Carmichael.* And the duplicitous lying Swansons. May they rot in hell.

Words could be as deadly as a gun or a knife. If your reputation gets murdered.

"True, but Ned Bannister's a tough case," Luz was saying. "He *had* to be drunk. The breathalyzer was broken? I mean, please. New Year's Eve? Two A.M.? And behind the wheel of that hulking Mercedes."

She had *some* savings, Arden reminded herself. She owned her town-house. She just didn't have a reason to exist. She'd have to leave town, make another new history for herself, and then a new future. She hated the thought of it. That true bitch Patience—*Patience!*—Swanson and her slavering lying creep of a husband should move. It was their fault, not hers.

As if *she,* Arden Ward, could be seduced by—or try to seduce—that weasel-mouthed, entitled, self-centered . . . Deep breath, count to ten.

"If Bannister hadn't been so—do people say blotto?" Luz was saying. "It might have all ended differently."

"Maybe." Arden tried to engage. At least Ned Bannister had a jury of his peers. Arden had been guillotined by a lie. "Life is strange."

"True. But gotta love that ridiculous Massachusetts law that since he was driving on a private way and not a public street, that even if he *were* drunk, he didn't break the law." Luz rolled her eyes. "Technically."

"Technically is what the law's about, Luz. 'Technically' means 'actually.'"

"Then, Nyomi Chang argues . . ." Luz pursed her lips, maybe remembering. "He never planned to leave the parking garage or drive on a public street. He was going to stop, park again, and call an Uber."

Arden nodded. "So he testified, too. Under oath."

"It's totally believable that he never could have predicted Tennant would be there, though," Luz said. "No one should've been there. Could've happened to anyone."

I know the feeling. She felt like she'd been run over, too. Not flattened on the pavement of a darkened parking garage, but equally powerless.

"They should have called you for advice, Arden. Maybe you could have helped the Bannisters." Luz shrugged. "Or the prosecutor. Whoever contacted you first."

"That's exactly what Warren said. Look." Arden pointed again at the TV. "Jury's gone home for the night. No verdict. Now the Bannisters have the whole weekend to worry."

"I'd drink," Luz said. "What would you do?"

Arden wondered about that. "I'd look for someone else to blame."

4

CORDELIA BANNISTER

This could be his last weekend home, Cordelia thought as she opened the front door of their condo building. Ned stood, back to her, seemed to be fascinated by the traffic on St. John Street, some headlights cutting through the already-darkening evening, slushing through yesterday's snow. The jury is in recess, the court officer had told them. And would reconvene at nine Monday morning. How would she ever make it that far? Cross this chasm of a weekend, watching her hours with Ned evaporate?

"Let's go in, sweetheart," she said.

Ned walked toward her, his collar turned up, his face slack and eyes weary. She scanned the parked cars, hunting for their usual predation of reporters. But so far, no doors opened, no lights flashed, no disgusting questions were shouted at them. *Monday,* she thought. The verdict would certainly come on Monday. Then they'd pounce, feasting on the remains of Ned Bannister.

"My last weekend." Ned echoed her thought, trudging toward her. "Our last weekend."

"Don't be silly, honey." Cordelia reached up to kiss him as he stepped inside. "I'll go get the kiddos," she went on. "I'll bring our usual Friday pizza. We'll have early dinner, together, forget everything." It was a lie, there was no way to forget the weight that hung over them, the knowledge that after two days Ned could be gone.

But the kids. Pip and Emma, poor darling ones, were waiting for her to pick them up at school. She was verging on late, and, secretly, relieved. She'd avoid the moms. After the verdict—praise all that is true and powerful—it would be different. She relied on it. But today, this one more tortured twisting Friday, she needed to avoid them.

The moms. Whose cold eyes and averted postures spoke louder than any harsh condemnations they might have been thinking. Cordelia, enthusiastic newcomer, once the best fairy-cupcake maker at Dunham

School, was now married to a drunk driver, a man who had killed some-one, and the taint of guilt, even *potential* guilt, had transformed Cordelia into an outcast.

The moms had included her, even recruited her, when they'd moved Pip—who'd "totally" outgrown his nickname, just ask him—to Dun-ham Prep and enrolled little Emma in the exclusive preschool's classes. Cordelia had adopted the yoga pants and expensive sneakers, sunglasses dangling from pretty little sweaters, the messy buns. She'd become one of the moms, volunteering, carpooling, mindful of classmates' food al-lergies. Her days were field trips and soccer and the privilege of a happy upscale wife with a handsome successful husband, a cellar full of wine, and monthly book clubs. Whether anyone read the books or not.

And then, after the sneering headlines and the stench of self-righteous suspicion, none of it mattered. After the indictment by Suffolk District Attorney Charles C. Stamoran, the moms had shunned her, every one of them. They'd assumed Ned was guilty, and that meant Cordelia was guilty, too. And the kids.

It wasn't fair, their shifting standards and instant judgments. They *all* drank, their white wine and their husbands' whiskey, and who of them hadn't made a mistake? The rules, Cordelia thought, depended on who created them.

As if that wasn't enough—the constant pretending, and avoiding, and juggling her life and even lying, and protecting Pip and Emma from barely veiled derision—then the trial had started.

And hell got deeper and darker and more inescapable.

The unrelenting reporters. The ubiquitous cameras. The constant phone calls. And finally that jury, twelve random-faced pawns who eyed her with scorn and pity. Suspicious, judgmental. Sometimes they were asleep, or flirting with Ned—juror six especially, she swore it, and how could that be fair? Or maybe, at this one moment in time, it would help.

"I might take a nap," Ned said now. "I'll get up for dinner, but I'm exhausted."

She almost snapped at him. Almost lost it. A "*nap*," she thought, "*ex-hausted*." But it was so Ned. Closing his eyes to things was how that man dealt with the world. If he didn't see it, it didn't exist.

"Whatever you want, honey," she said. The jurors were home now, too, back to their little lives and families and possessing their infinite *in-finite* power. She would pray to them, if she prayed, *please let me go.*

5

Monday morning, after all the waiting, after all the torture and pretend of the weekend, it happened. Their flimsy cardboard cups of coffee had just arrived in the waiting room.

"Verdict," Nyomi Chang had whispered. A benediction.

For a moment, the world stopped.

Cordelia took her assigned seat in the front row of the audience, hands clenched. Staring at her husband's square shoulders, his perfectly straight back. Nyomi patted Ned on the arm. *Hang on,* Cordelia heard her whisper.

Judge Margaret McDonald entered the courtroom, black-robed, a hint of gold necklace showing at her collar, her silver hair sleek and short.

The assistant DA, a Gorgon with dark hair in tight braids and dressed all in gray, flipped open the hard-sided briefcase in front of her on the wooden counsel table, its lid barricading her from the rest of the world.

The jury trooped in. Cordelia had envisioned this moment, had pre-lived it in her mind for almost a year. Pip had finished fifth grade, and Emma had finished first grade, and Ned had been indicted and they'd lived from the Bannister bank account and Cordelia had been in constant anguish. Now the moment was no longer imaginary, or filled with nebulous and haunting possibilities. It was real. Pip and Emma were in school. She'd watched them deflate, during this ordeal, poisoned by the spotlight. After this, the kids might hate Ned forever. Blame him. Blame *her.* They'd never understand.

"Ms. Jury Foreperson, do you have a verdict?" Judge McDonald asked.

"We do, your honor."

"Please hand it to the court clerk."

Judge McDonald accepted the document, read it with a face of granite, and handed it back.

The seats behind the prosecution side of the courtroom were filled with court watchers, maybe freelance reporters, maybe law students. No one from Randall Tennant's family had appeared. Cordelia had asked about that, making sure. The Gorgon DA had made a big tear-jerking deal about it in her closing argument; with a phony catch in her voice had told the twelve rapt faces that "only she" was here "to speak for poor Randall." To "stand up for the victim."

There was no doubt, and Cordelia knew it, that Ned had hit Randall Tennant in the parking garage that night. Run over him. There was no doubt. She knew that. Everyone knew that.

"Will the defendant please rise?"

Cordelia saw only Ned's black wool back, with Nyomi, a head shorter, standing close to his side. Ned adjusted his suit jacket. *Will this be the last time he wears a suit for however many years?* An incongruous question went through her mind. *What will I do with his clothes?*

The district attorney stood too, and Cordelia saw her chin go up, defiant.

"The court clerk will please read the verdict," Judge McDonald said. She touched her necklace with a polished forefinger. Not one juror was looking at Ned.

The clerk, choppy dark hair and two studs in each ear, moved a pair of bright red glasses from the top of her head and onto her face. She opened the folded document.

"We the jury in the above-entitled case, *Commonwealth versus Bannister*," she said, "do find as follows. As to count one, operating under the influence, we find the defendant . . ." She paused.

And Cordelia felt her heart literally stop. *Come on,* she thought, *come the hell on.*

"Not guilty."

Cordelia felt the blood draining from her face, and then rushing back in, and Ned turned to her, an expression she could not read, of infinite shock and tectonic emotion, of regaining the power in his future, the return of control. But it was not over. They knew it wasn't.

Nyomi Chang touched Ned's arm, maybe warning him, her fingers pale against his dark suit. Cordelia saw Nyomi close her eyes, in prayer or supplication. Or fear.

Two more counts. Ned might still be convicted.

This was what she'd prayed about. The end of her troubles. The return of her life.

"As to count two, vehicular homicide, we the jury find the defendant not guilty." The clerk read faster now, no longer dramatic. "As to count three, reckless driving, we find the defendant not guilty."

All the air went out of the room, its space filled with the undercurrent of murmured reaction, a gasp or two, maybe Cordelia's own. The high-heeled reporters clacked toward the courtroom exit, the metal double door squeaked open, the judge's gavel banged.

"Thank you for your service, members of the jury," the judge said, standing. "You are free to go, Mr. Bannister."

The district attorney slammed her briefcase closed. Cordelia could not see her face, but saw her back stiffen. *What should I do?* went through Cordelia's mind. *Wait and see,* she answered herself. *Wait.*

Pip. Emma. They'd gone to school, routine, normal, because Cordelia needed normal as much as the kids did. How much would she need to tell them now? Ned would call his mother, though she'd certainly have heard it on her own—Georgianna Bannister devoured news about the case, debating it with whoever would listen, refusing to believe her precious only son might have done something unforgivable. She'd consider the verdict an affirmation of her own flawless (just ask her) personal judgement.

Now, through the high thick-paned windows flanking the revolving doors of the courthouse, Cordelia saw the reporters and cameras massed in the sunshine, microphones on sticks pointing like battle spears, every lens and eye focused toward Ned's lawyer. Nyomi Chang had ordered her and Ned to wait in the cordoned-off courthouse lobby until the defense attorney herself made a statement on the cobblestone plaza.

"We're supposed to wait for Nyomi's signal," Ned whispered to her. "I love you, sweetheart. Thank you for standing by me."

Cordelia clutched Ned's arm, pressed her body against his. Her husband's entire being felt strong again, as if his substance had returned, his density.

This chapter of her life was over.

"We'll keep the people away from you, ma'am." A security guard, bald and burly in a navy uniform that strained at its buttons, approached them, reassuring, touching the gun on his black leather belt.

That same guard, Cordelia remembered, had eyed her with scorn as they entered this morning. *Dead woman walking,* she'd imagined him thinking. Now, after the verdict, he was Mr. Helpful. And she was "ma'am." It was all about which side you were on when the dust cleared. Her life was about to change again. Finally.

"Cordelia?" Ned put his hand over hers, his black leather glove on her maroon one, and she felt him kiss the top of her head. The man she'd shared so much with, the lies that hovered between them. "No more hiding," he said. "Nothing will stand in our way again."

"Look." Cordelia pointed outside. "You can barely see Nyomi; she's so swarmed by cameras. Wait. She waved."

"Ready?" Ned said.

"I'm afraid," Cordelia said. "How many times have we endured these people, their incessant questions? Asking if our kids know you're the Parking Garage Killer. I can't bear it."

"Don't ever say those words," Ned said. "There's no fear. The jury voted not guilty. Not. Guilty. And that is forever true."

"Right. I know." Cordelia dutifully followed her husband, then stumbled, startled for a beat, as they were separated by the revolving door, each in their glass triangle, the last moment they would have peace.

The midmorning sun hit her, and the harsh November wind, as she took her place in the tableau: gray pavement, the gray buildings, and in the center, Nyomi Chang wearing a red coat, and Ned in his black one. Cordelia imagined the aerial view—Ned, targeted in the center, all eyes and microphones and cameras pointed his way.

She tucked herself in behind him, being there for her husband. Who, the jury had ruled, was *not* the Parking Garage Killer.

"What are your plans?" one reporter called out. "Have you talked to your children?" another said.

Cordelia clasped Ned's hand. She'd pick the kids up in a few hours, as usual, like a usual day. Even though it was far from it.

And Ned. He'd be different tonight. And she'd have to plan for that. With this ordeal over, her husband would be restored to his executive suite and his social standing. He'd expect that their lives faced only happily ever after.

And possibly, possibly, that was true. Cordelia smiled, tentatively, for the camera, and a little bit for herself. Maybe happily ever after could happen.

6

A blast of manufactured heat hit her as she pulled open the oak-carved front door of the Dunham School. This was about to be the best Monday afternoon ever. After a year, a solid sordid year of shunning derision, she was back. She'd be solidly, brilliantly, irrevocably reinstated to her rightful place, just as Ned would be. And no one could ignore it. She might give a party. Yes. A party. A show-stopping party.

A uniformed guard sat at the entrance, incongruous security with his radio clipped to an epaulet, but a pot of russet chrysanthemums on his otherwise empty desk.

"Mrs. Bannister," Hal said.

"Hello, Hal. I'm here for Pip and Emma." This would be the moment. Her life-changing moment. Even Hal looked properly respectful.

The guard pushed a button. The inner door clicked open. To the left, the massive bulletin board, old-fashioned and pockmarked, tacked with notices and sign-up sheets and the casting selections for the middle school winter play, *Frozen*.

To the right, the waiting room, where kids could read or study or play on their phones until parents arrived. Through the glass pane of the door, she saw Pip sitting two chairs apart from Emma, protecting her with his proximity. Pip, in his navy down vest and rambunctious hair, focused on his phone screen, too cool to openly acknowledge his relationship with a little girl. Emma wore those puffy pink boots she'd insisted on, and turned the pages in a glossy picture book while swinging her feet under her too-tall chair.

How did a mother talk to children about something like this? That their father had been acquitted? That he was free. She'd tried to prevent them from watching TV news, but she knew it was futile. She'd approached them about it, tentatively, as the media spotlight focused on them. *It's cool, mom*, Pip had said, *it's fine*. She knew it wasn't true, and

Pip had grown more withdrawn as the days went by. Emma became increasingly clingy, maybe innocently sensing the tension. Her heart broke for them. Today, starting in less than a minute, that would all be over.

As she opened the door, she saw two other kids, Ashley and Max. Their mother was Bethenny, a big deal in the PTO. Great. If those two kids were still waiting, that meant Bethenny was still on the way. Great great *great*. She slicked back her hair, patted her plaid muffler into casual place. Would they make a big deal of her return, or pretend everything was just as before? It didn't matter. She was back. And she could pretend with the best of them.

"Hi, kiddos." She put on her best mommy smile, and stepped into the waiting room. "Hey you all." Max and Ashley almost ignored her, but when they registered who it was, she saw Ashley raise one preadolescent eyebrow in disdain. *Kids.* Then, she remembered. Perhaps they hadn't heard the good news.

Pip and Emma got up, gathered their stuff, and joined her. She kissed each of their heads, Pip writhing away and Emma pasted to her side. "Go get your coats from the coatrack, sweeties. Don't forget boots and mittens. We'll get pad Thai."

For once they obeyed her. "I have news, you two," she went on. But they were yanking on their hats, bickering, and already ignoring her.

Footsteps in the corridor, brisk and determined. And there she was. *Bethenny.* Black jacket, black yoga pants, shiny black tall boots. She'd flirted with Ned, constantly, before she'd turned her designer-clad back on them both. Now things would change.

"Hey, Bethenny." Cordelia kept her voice calm. Now they were equals. Now her husband was not guilty. And now things would be fine. "Love the boots."

"Thanks."

Cordelia pressed on against the surprising silence. "Indoor soccer tomorrow," she said. "And I know I haven't carpooled for a while. And thank you for being so understanding. But now—let's make up for lost time. I'll take the rest of the month, no worries, and my complete pleasure." She was talking too fast, too eagerly, she heard the too-needy edge in her own voice, but she could almost feel it, the anticipation of Bethenny's welcoming hug, restoring Cordelia to her proper place. "I can get them both right from school."

School hallways had a particular sound—the swirl of a sharpening pencil, a closing door, the heating system grumbling. But that all seemed to vanish as Bethenny's expression, awash in skepticism, hit Cordelia harder than the November chill.

Bethenny huffed, dismissive. "I don't think so, Cordelia. We're all set with car pool. And we don't foresee any changes."

"Bethenny, wait, listen. . . ." Maybe she'd misunderstood. Or, *oh*, hadn't heard yet. Cordelia brightened. Anticipating. "Oh, Maybe you don't know. The jury—"

"I do, though," Bethenny said. "Know."

"But Ned is not—"

"He is, though," Bethenny said. "And I will not have my children in that environment."

"In what environment?"

"Are we really having this conversation?"

"Yes," Cordelia said, "yes, we are. I'm trying to, at least. What happened to Ned . . ."

The corridor almost froze with Bethenny's demeanor.

"What *happened*? To *Ned*? What *happened* to *him*?" Both careful eyebrows went up. "It's hardly what happened to him, is it Cordelia? It's what he *did*. Your husband drank, so much he was completely drunk. That did not 'happen' to him. And then he drove his car. That did not 'happen' to him. That was a decision your husband actively made, an imprudent and deadly decision. That poor man in the parking garage, that's who something *happened* to. That poor man could have been any of us."

"The *driver* could have been any of us." Tears were coming to Cordelia's eyes, bitter and baffled, but she could not allow herself to look weak. She had been waiting for this verdict for a year, a solid year, and the jury had said not guilty, and that was certainly, definitely true. Cordelia was sure of it, had always maintained her husband's innocence. Why was Bethenny ignoring the verdict? "And the jury said—"

"Mom?" Pip had come up beside her. Emma stood behind him, clutching her Hello Kitty backpack, her striped muffler dragging on the polished tile floor. Down the hall, a door slammed.

"Hey, kiddo." Had one decision ruined her life? "Ready to hit the road?"

"Be careful, Pip," Bethenny said. "On the road."

"*You* be careful, Bethenny." Cordelia could not stop herself from saying it.

She gathered her children, shepherding them, protecting them from the venom. If Bethenny still loathed her, then everyone loathed her.

The verdict had made no difference.

Her brain burst into flames, then settled, smoldering. There had to be a way to fix this. A way to get her life back. There had to be.

7

ARDEN WARD

Arden looked up from her packing. Footsteps in the hall? She'd snagged some cardboard cartons from the supply room this morning, then tucked them under her desk, planning to stay late and begin packing after everyone left, but she could not wait any longer. She had tried, tried to pretend through this whole ridiculous Monday. But no way she could do this for two more miserable weeks.

Today? She should win the Academy Award for her performance. Acting like everything was normal-fine-perfect. Coddling the organizers of the Polar Bear harbor swim—she'd helped them when the city threatened to stop their storied event. She'd reassured the caterers of an on-again off-again wedding between two old-line Massachusetts families that the nuptials were indeed on, never divulging that the bride's estranged mother had not only been instructed, but actually paid off to stay away from the rehearsal dinner.

How are you? someone had asked. *Oh, fine,* she'd said, lying. Luz had puttered through, oblivious, and Lois the receptionist had brought her a box of Girl Scout Thin Mints. Normal normal normal. Except it wasn't. She'd been fired. Over a lie. A lie about *herself.* For all her public relations savvy, now she felt as if her skills only worked in some other world.

She pulled an orange plastic dispenser from her bottom drawer. *Tape your boxes,* she instructed herself. *Keep at it.* She scrabbled with a fingernail to find the end of the clear packing tape. She always told her clients not to panic, and now endeavored to take her own advice.

The footsteps came closer.

Warren effing Carmichael appeared in her doorway again. The ghost of firings past.

In that moment, that ridiculous moment where our optimistic brains scour the universe for hope, the moment convicts on death row dream of the governor's clemency call, or drowning victims imagine that mermaids are real and will save them from the darkness, her silly mind presented the possibilities to her: reprieve, regret, remorse. *Pretend it never happened,* Warren would say. *I was wrong.*

She looked up, tape dispenser in hand. Didn't trust herself to say anything. Didn't trust whether she'd be enraged or in tears.

If he was not going to apologize, beg for mercy, maybe tell her Patience Swanson was a lying bitch, then she didn't want to hear from him. Still, for now, he was the boss. Her stomach curdled at it. *Walk out,* she told herself. *Go.*

But she didn't move, frozen in transition.

"This is awkward," Warren began. "But—"

"Did Patience admit she made it up?" Arden couldn't hold it in. "You're here to apologize? That's the only reason I'd be willing to talk to you, Warren. All due respect. You being my boss and all for the next—" She looked at her watch, dramatic. "Nine business days."

She would not cry. She would not give him one instant of satisfaction.

"I need a favor."

He was asking for a favor? In the universe of power dynamics, this was impossible. The laws of workplace physics precluded it, the laws of civility made it laughable. Warren didn't even look embarrassed.

Arden searched for language, almost failed. "A what? Favor?"

"Or an assignment, if you want to look at it that way," Warren went on. "Like I told you. I succeeded in finding you one last client. One last job. I cannot keep you, Arden, the company would fail. But I *can* send you out with big billings. And a big payoff. And a big reference."

He looked her square in the eye, confident as only Warren could be. He wanted what he wanted, and assumed everyone would do it. Had he ever been worried, or wrong, or disappointed? Or betrayed?

"You up for it?"

She did not have the moral wherewithal, not right now, or the emotional bandwidth, to make such a choice. She picked at the elusive edge of the packing tape. You didn't have to like your boss. Even respect him. And wouldn't doing Warren's "favor" be better for her? But no. *No.*

"Too late for that. As you can see." She brandished the tape dispenser. "You fired me. I can't."

"Of course you can." Warren actually sounded enthusiastic. "Think of it as my parting gift. You can help a person who desperately needs you. In a worse position than you are. And make some bucks."

"Are you honestly saying that?" *I'm in the Twilight Zone,* Arden thought. Or in business world. Or maybe those were the same.

"I know you're upset." Warren took a step closer to her, engaging, or predatory. "You've made a powerful person unhappy. And nothing I can do about that. But *I* still respect you. And I'm trying to help. *Big* bucks, Arden. It's security."

She blinked at him. *Respect. Security.* What did those words even mean? A raggedy pigeon landed on her windowsill, observed them with beady baffled eyes, then leaped off into the nothingness of the dark sky. Did it know where it was going? Does anyone?

"Fine if you say no," Warren said, interrupting her thoughts.

"Good. No." What was he gonna do, fire her?

But she didn't like the look on Warren's face. He could take her down, even further, she knew that. With one carefully placed wrong word. A viral hashtag. He was brilliant at it. One of the best.

"You need this, Arden. Trust me, I'm doing it for you." Warren sighed, maybe acknowledging her contempt. "I know, it's tough, it's unfair, and again, I'm sorry. But this could help you. And they insist they want you, only you, and I could not dissuade them."

"Who?"

"Will you do it?"

She mustered the sweetest ingenue expression she could. "I'm well aware if I refuse, that might affect whatever recommendation you might give me. So, of course. Thank you. Whatever you say."

"Don't be like that, Arden."

"Be like what? A person with a spine?"

"You know this is out of my control."

"Is it?"

"But I do control the money," Warren went on, ignoring her mockery. "And your severance. Which will—if you succeed—double."

Health insurance, her brain shrieked at her again. *Don't let your anger destroy you.*

She didn't trust herself to speak.

"Good. Smart." Warren nodded, approving. "Here's the deal."

8

Today Warren's "favor" would arrive at her office. She was as prepared as anyone could be. She'd do this "favor," sure, because
Warren held her career in his weaselly paws, and she was utterly trapped. And it was better than staying home and breaking things.
Which is what she actually felt like doing.

She puffed the dust from the edge of the last book on the top book-
shelf. She'd packed several boxes yesterday, and another two already today, greeting the inevitable, box by box. As her office got emptier, she
would physically watch her life here become shorter; her vanishing possessions an hourglass, marking the days until she left.

A favor.

What she hated most, though, was how curious she was about this.
She checked her watch, 8:15. One more box.

She used the knife edge of the dispenser to tear the tape, then pressed
it onto the flaps, smoothing it flat, sealing the cardboard. Sealing in her
past. She thought about the memories inside—of people who had come to
her for help; miserable, defiant and defensive, inexperienced and besieged.
Misguided, or misunderstood. Sometimes they'd made a mistake, a wrong
decision, an inappropriate comment on an open mic, an unfortunate photo.
I didn't mean it. It was a mistake. And sometimes that was true. *I'm only
human,* some would say and Arden, with that, would agree. People were
fallible. And not all of them deserved to be canceled by the juggernaut of
public opinion.

She worked her magic, and those people went back to their lives, whole
again. Safe again. She'd helped them succeed, or given them back their
reputation. And their privacy.

Now Arden had to fix her own life. There was no rule book for that.

"Happy Tuesday! Are you off to someplace glamorous?"

Arden looked up as Luz entered. Put the tape dispenser on her wrist,
a bracelet. "Glamorous?"

"I'm faking it now," Luz was saying. "My enthusiasm. I'm actually devastated." She pouted. "Warren told me you were quitting."

"What? That was out of line, Loo. I was going to tell you." *After I decided what to say.* Warren should have at least allowed Arden to create the narrative.

"I sure hope you're off on some fabulous adventure," Luz continued. "I know, it's hush-hush. Warren said it was a secret. I'll truly miss you, you know. You've taught me so much." She gestured at the packing box. "Why don't you have someone else do that? I could, even. Though that tape dispenser bracelet is an elegant accessory."

"It's a look." Arden put the dispenser back in the drawer, then held up her hands. "I've got to go wash these," she said. It was almost nine. "Quitting is a dirty job. I'll be right back."

"No wait," Luz said. "Don't go out there."

"Out there?"

"There's someone waiting for you in the lobby. I told her you were appointment only, but she insisted."

"You have a terrible poker face. Skip to the big finish, Luz." Arden popped a cleansing wipe from a plastic container on her desk. Slid the fragrant tissue over her hands. Warren had told her to act surprised. The meeting was supposed to appear unpremeditated, a spur-of-the-moment decision. "Who's 'someone'?"

"Guess."

Arden tossed the wipe into a metal wastebasket. "Seriously?"

"Cordelia Bannister."

"Does she look . . ." Arden paused again, calculating. "Happy? Angry?"

"She looks . . . sad?" Luz finally said. "To me at least. Tired. Defeated."

Arden checked her hair in the enamel-handled mirror she kept tucked in her top desk drawer. Hair fine, no book dust on her white shirt, no corrugated box lint on her black skirt. Good enough, she thought, for 9:00 A.M. and a person with no appointment.

"Her husband's not here?"

"Nope. I suppose he could be parking."

"I wonder if anyone will ever be able to talk to him about parking again. Or say the word 'garage,' or 'skateboard.'"

"Ouch," Luz said. "True."

"Could I step over the line and ask you to bring us coffee?" Arden craved it, and hers was gone. This was Warren's favor. Cordelia Bannister. They'd discussed the Bannisters last week before the verdict, Arden remembered. Maybe Warren actually had reached out to them?

"There are no lines between us." Luz smiled. "Should I ask our visitor, too?"

"Sure. Thanks. Bring her in. And take her coat so she knows I accept that she's staying."

It was those little things, that instant creation of a relationship, that Arden knew made her who she was. Understanding what a client wanted, or how to find out at least, and how to make them comfortable telling you. When their world was falling apart, people sometimes had trouble asking for help. *Ha*, Arden thought. *Look who's talking.*

Because there was absolutely no one to help her. She'd kept potential friends away, all these years in Boston. Once people burrowed into her life, into her past, she'd inevitably be outed as Governor Ward's daughter. The former defense attorney and once-respected politician who'd furloughed the convicted killer. Furloughed the criminal who—after forty years behind bars—had then walked out the prison gates and murdered a little girl. "We can only try our best for mercy," her father had tried to explain, and shouldered the blame when it was actually the crashing dominoes of systemic failures. He'd even cried on live television. But Arden's dad had a fatal heart attack even before the second edition of the Harrisburg *Patriot-News*. The unfairness of it, the tragedy, imprinted on her soul. He'd had no one to help him, either.

Arden was sure her mother had died of the humiliation. Back then, Arden's brand-new husband, an up-and-coming politico, couldn't handle the constant battering attention or the ugly vitriol, much less protect her from it. He'd fled. End of story.

Cordelia Bannister now stood in the doorway, top to toe in black cashmere, tawny hair in a tight bun. Stick thin, whether from dieting or depression, tired around the eyes.

"Did I interrupt something? Ms. Ward?" A tentative voice, but persistent.

"It's Arden. Please." She gestured. "Have a seat."

"And you know who I am." Cordelia Bannister lowered herself into the visitor's chair, fussing with the thin wool scarf she'd looped around her neck, a fluttery pink thing that would not seem to settle into place over all the black.

Arden catalogued the nervous set of her berry-tinted lips, how she fidgeted with her gold wedding band and its accompanying rock of a diamond solitaire, sliding both rings around with her thumb. She'd bitten at her cuticles, Arden saw.

"I do, Mrs. Bannister," Arden said. She tried to sound friendly. Not judgmental. Not hostile about being pressured into this. "How are you?"

Cordelia laughed, out loud, and Arden could not tell whether it was from humor or bitterness.

"I'm so sorry." Cordelia dabbed a careful fingertip under each eye, then shrugged. "'How are you' should be an easy question, I know. But it's impossible."

"I understand, as much as anyone can. Maybe let's start with why you're here."

"My husband," she began. Then looked up at Arden.

Arden nodded, encouraging.

"Well, you know the story. Everyone knows the story."

Arden nodded again.

"And I know the jury verdict is the final verdict, but in the real world, a verdict doesn't matter."

A tap on the door. Arden wondered if Luz had been listening from the hallway.

"Come in," Arden called out. "Here's the coffee. Thanks, Luz."

As Luz closed the door again, Cordelia took a sip of coffee. Put the white ceramic cup on the glass table beside her. "I'm sorry, I've had a tough—year, I guess you would say, and my skills have crashed, just like my brain has, and just like my life has. But you protect people, don't you?"

"If I can."

"I know you can. I know it. And you're the perfect person to help me. Us, really, help *us*. My poor family is—it's awful."

Arden waited. Tried to imagine what Cordelia Bannister was going through, the headlines and the accusations, the life-twisting reality of a public trial. The end of privacy. The drumbeating public question of *what if* . . . her privileged actually-guilty husband had "gotten off"? Arden had seen it before—the illusion that when a jury acquitted, their "not guilty" decision became reality. Hardly ever true.

And without help, the results for families in crisis were often depression, divorce, division. Disaster. Arden knew that firsthand. And it was why she'd started in this work. Saving lives, she sometimes called it. She wished someone had saved her father's.

Maybe Warren was trying to save hers. Maybe.

"Does your husband know you're here? Should we all talk?"

"Ouch. You're good. He tried to stop me, actually," Cordelia said. "I told him that *I* needed help, that *he* needed help. That *we* needed help. And that I'd heard about you. And . . . can this be confidential?"

"Sure," Arden said. "As long as it's not illegal."

"Good. Well. He told me not to come to you. That he—we—didn't need you. But I knew you were the best. I looked up stories about you, what you did for that man who won the lottery, the one who was inundated with people pretending to be relatives. And for that little boy whose parents were accused of faking his cancer—but turned out he was truly horribly sick and they'd always told the truth. I hear you didn't even charge them."

"Journalists can be relentless," Arden had to say. "And once the rumor steamroller gets underway, it can be difficult to stop it. Public opinion is an irresistible force, gathering momentum as it goes. People prefer to believe the worst."

"People *do*! They're *terrible*!" Cordelia's eyes welled. "I knew you'd understand. Anyway, I told Ned I could talk to whoever I wanted, and finally he said, whatever, go. So yes, he knows."

"And he's okay with that." Arden leaned back in her swivel chair, rotating gently as she waited for the answer. Why hadn't Warren taken this high-profile case himself? Easy answer. Because Arden would be leaving the firm. Which meant the repercussions would leave with her. Maybe Warren had *offered* her up, that was the likely scenario. Arden, the clean-up crew. The short-timer. If she failed, the blame was all on her.

"He's got to be okay," Cordelia said. "He knows how worried I am."

"So you're interested in having me try to . . . rehabilitate his reputation?" Arden sipped her coffee. "Even though, as the jury said, he's not guilty of anything."

"Yes," Cordelia said. "We need you. I need you, Arden. His family needs you."

9

CORDELIA BANNISTER

Maybe I should leave well enough alone, Cordelia thought again. Time would go by. People would forget. She'd move on. But so far, her life—their lives—had been wretched in every way. She had to continue.

"So, if I hire you, do we have confidentiality?" She picked up the white cup and saucer the pretty assistant had brought in. "Like lawyers do? Or reporters?"

Arden was tapping buttons on her desk phone. "Let me just postpone something."

Arden Ward was chic enough, Cordelia assessed, as Arden swiveled away from her. And she recognized that white cotton Akris blouse; Cordelia owned one herself. Apple Watch on one wrist, Peretti bangle on the other. Edgy, her look was, and shrewd. Still relatable though, the way a few wisps of dark brown filtered the layers of her hair, as if the honey color had started to grow out and Arden hadn't bothered to keep up. But that seemingly-casual haircut, artfully windblown, did not come cheap. The woman knew what she was doing. She was still on the phone, low-voiced.

Arden was the one. It would work. Their lives would change, and it would all be worth it. Sometimes the world presented obstacles. You just had to get over them.

Soon enough it would be New Year's Eve again, a chilling anniversary.

"I apologize," Arden said as she hung up. Cordelia saw her check the time. "You asked about confidentiality. What we say here is in the bubble, based on trust. But there's no absolute privilege like a doctor, or lawyer."

"But you could refuse to answer."

"For a while, I suppose." Arden gestured, admitting.

"Can you help us?" Cordelia asked. It was a risk, this visit, in every conceivable imaginable way it was a risk.

She'd taken so many of those in her life. Her mother had called her

Calamity Jane; always enticing the younger kids to take dares, being the first to risk a dive into the lake behind their family's summer house, the first to try the fraying old rope swing, once even taking a tentative snow-booted step onto tiny Calliope Pond, then hearing the crack of the ice and seeing jagged fissures shooting out from under her boot. Falling forward. Losing her footing. Throwing herself back onto the snow behind her. Laughing at her luck, and staring through the bare branches, while her soggy boot, sheened with pond water, froze almost instantly. She remembered a scarlet cardinal had landed in the scraggly branches of whatever tree was above her; *pretty pretty pretty,* it cried at her.

"Well, I hope I can help. Tell me what you need."

"Thank you. Here's the thing. I know my husband was acquitted," she said, "but the rest of the world—they don't care. Our lives are still miserable."

"It's only been, what, one day? Maybe—"

"No. No." Cordelia felt her fists clench. Was she being dismissed? "It's been a year. A year! I'm afraid, Arden. My husband runs a high-echelon commercial real estate business, beyond reproach, there's never been a glimmer of impropriety. In business, at least. But he's packing this away like last season's slipcovers. Stashing it in some emotional lockbox. *That's* what I can't live with. His denial. Oh, not of the accident, he admits that. But of the reality. Our lives will never be normal again. He thinks they will."

Arden fiddled with one chunky gold earring. "You want me to make your husband feel guiltier?"

"Of course not. I want him to see reality. That I'm not 'oversensitive.' That the world thinks he's guilty. Persuade Ned. Convince him we need help. Arden. Please. The reporters. The constant phone calls. The hideous questions. It's so merciless—last night I even said we should move! I truly did. And Ned said no, absolutely refused. *The reporters will go away,* he insisted. *My business is here.* In that Ned voice."

Arden had pushed back her chair, walked to the window. "That's your husband's office, right?" She pointed across the harbor. "And they were watching fireworks."

"Were you, too? I'd wondered about that."

"No." Arden turned to face her. "Look. There'll be people who think that because your husband is extremely successful, that he 'got away' with it. That people 'like' him, rich and powerful, and connected, can do anything they want. Nyomi Chang has a reputation for handling those cases. I know you're aware of her price tag. You and your husband paid it."

"Exactly my point." Cordelia felt her heart wrench, this was so important. "Even if my husband is not in prison, maybe there are things that are worse than that." She took a deep breath, collecting her emotions. "He needs your help. *I* need your help. We all need your help."

Arden probably thought she was overdramatizing. And that's how she felt sometimes, as if life was spinning out of control and only she could stop it.

"And may I tell you something?"

"Sure." Arden sat in the chair next to hers, turned her body to listen.

Cordelia lowered her eyes, seeming to picture it. "Pip, my darling son, is . . . changed. He tries, he pretends, but all the joy has evaporated from him. Even today, after yesterday's verdict, I dropped him at school, and his classmates *physically* moved away from him. Poor kid, he walked in alone. Me, I can handle it, of course, but even this morning, even after the verdict, nothing changed. I expected hugs, and reassurances, and connecting with other moms who had, I don't know, faced disaster and survived. But none of that happened! I thought a not-guilty verdict would give me my life back. But no. I'm *still* an outcast. My children are outcasts. It's even worse now, if that's possible."

"Maybe the moms didn't know? About the verdict?"

"Impossible. It was like being back in high school hell, the mean girls. Look. The jury doesn't matter. It only matters what the public believes. Truth is only what someone *believes*. Or can be convinced to believe." She smiled, rueful. "I suppose you know that. Actually, I'm relying on it."

"I've often said that very thing."

"Now I see that the public *is* a jury. A never-ending endlessly scrutinizing infinitely judging jury. Those memes, on Insta or whatever, they will never die. Social media *thrives* on sorrow and pain." Cordelia put her hands over her eyes for a beat. "I don't mean to be melodramatic. But it's . . . relentless. Destructive."

"Well, we can . . ."

"Arden. Face it. You know Ned will always be the Parking Garage Killer and I will always be the Parking Garage Killer's wife, and I could change my name until forever and someone would always find out. And someday Pip, and then Emma, will have to write a college application essay. Or endure a 'bring your father to school' day. I cannot *cannot*—"

Arden handed her a flowered box of tissues. Cordelia dabbed her eyes with one of them as she went on.

"He looks like a bad person, don't you see? He's like poison. And all of us are infected by him. I cry every day."

Arden leaned forward, the pearls of her long necklace clinking, and reached out, briefly, as if she'd wanted to touch Cordelia's shoulder, then decided not to. "Has he ever threatened you?"

"Not . . . really." Cordelia, surprised, tried to be careful here. *Had he?*

"Have you gone to couples counseling?" Arden was keeping her eyes locked with Cordelia's. "It sounds like you have some issues."

"Oh, we have issues, all right. That's why I'm here."

"But maybe you and your husband should work this out. Privately."

"Arden. It's you and me now, and I feel safe with you. If we women don't stand up for each other, who's going to?"

Two short buzzes came from Arden's desk phone. She held up a finger, picked up the receiver. "I know," she said. And hung up.

"Please. Listen." Cordelia felt like crying, she really did. "Our marriage will be a disaster. The kids will be miserable. People hate us. It has to stop, or I will . . . die. I will just—die."

She saw Arden respond to this. "Arden? Have you been married?"

"Long ago." Arden looked down at her desk for a beat.

"So you know. Whatever the wife says, it doesn't matter." Cordelia paused, gauging.

"It is a truth universally accepted that husbands don't listen," Arden said. "But maybe go home, Cordelia. Maybe count your blessings. Maybe help *make* them blessings. You've been through a horrible ordeal. You've won. Now persevere. Time will heal things."

Arden's phone buzzed again.

She couldn't let Arden say no. "The kids and I—we didn't do anything. And yet, we're paying for it."

Arden was standing now, scanning her almost-empty bookshelves, and Cordelia saw a stack of flattened cardboard boxes.

"Do you know what it's like to have the rug pulled out from under you?" Cordelia softened her voice. "To have the life you once relied on simply—vanish? Through no fault of your own?"

Arden's expression had changed.

"Here's my card," Arden finally said, taking one from the crystal holder on her desk. "It has my cell. Give my assistant, Luz, your contact information for an appointment. Tomorrow?"

"Thank you. Yes." *Thank you,* she thought. "I will. And I'll do my best, for the sake of the kids."

Arden nodded, and Cordelia felt her sympathy and understanding, as Cordelia hoped she would. She tucked the business card into her tote bag, looped the strap over her shoulder, then turned to go.

"And Arden?" She turned back. She'd risk one more thing.

"Yes?"

"I—" *No.* She couldn't. Not now, at least. "Never mind, it's nothing."

"Nothing is nothing," Arden said. "If we're working together, I cannot allow any surprises. That is my absolute rule. I have to know everything about everything. Truth is our only weapon. I can't neutralize potential obstacles if I'm not prepared. So, no matter how minor it seems, you should tell me."

Cordelia spooled out a breath. "It's really nothing."

"What's nothing?"

"Really, no. I would tell you. I would."

"Cordelia?"

"I know a verdict is a verdict," Cordelia began, carefully. "But I know men, and I know my husband, and I think . . . I think he's hiding something from me."

10

She knew exactly what pleased him. For all of Ned's faults, Cordelia thought as she pulled the tight black turtleneck camisole over her head, then yanked the scrunchy from her hair and allowed the softened waves to fall across her bare shoulders, he wasn't persnickety about the house, or particular about his food, or . . . selfish in bed. She stared at herself in the bathroom mirror, assessing, dabbing a bit of flaked mascara from under one eye, then twisted around to reassure herself about the fit of her jeans. *Not bad for forty-three,* she thought. *Or, four.* Sometimes she honestly lost count.

But her parents had taught her, starting when she'd stolen a quarter from the top of her father's dresser—he'd put it there to tempt her, she'd later learned—that taking responsibility for one's actions was the only path.

Now Pip and Emma were headed for Vermont, having a pretend-vacation week with Ned's mother in the Green Mountains. Cordelia had confided in Georgianna Bannister—another risk—and asked her to take them. "School is worthless this time of year," she'd explained. "Ned and I just need a little . . . private time. We're trying to protect our kids, and our marriage, but poor Ned is all at loose ends . . ."

"It's vacation when I say it is," Georgianna had proclaimed, as if it was her own idea, and had even sent a car service to pick them up. The kids loved her, and her goofy dog, Bartok, and the woods surrounding what she called "my cabin in Dorset." Ned had gone right along with it. He always listened to his mother. *She* was *always* right.

Cordelia snapped off the bathroom lights and headed into their bedroom, the skylight a rectangle of stars and darkness in the November night.

That New Year's Eve, the skylight view had been magical, an array of constellations, the universe twinkling its possibilities. And earlier, there was Ned, leaving. She'd urged him to stay home, she reminded herself.

She sat on the edge of the pristinely white Frette comforter, near its matching pillows and shams and accent puffs, remembering. She could hear his voice now, that New Year's Eve, picturing him as he adjusted his black bow tie and slipped into his sleek tuxedo jacket. *My responsibility is to pay the bills,* he'd retorted. My responsibility is to my clients. My responsibility is to be there for guests I invited.

He never listened to *her.* Never ever ever. And turned out, it became one of those moments that changed their lives.

If he *had* listened to her, if he had stayed home that night, none of this would've happened. Randall Tennant would be someone else's problem.

But now he was *their* problem. No matter what the jury said.

She chose a pair of pale pink suede boots, an extravagantly ridiculous purchase, but Ned loved them. She'd even cooked, and the aromatic boeuf bourguignon simply needed to be reheated, the baguette toasted, and the salad mixed. Ned would be content, and that's all that mattered. Just ask him.

Cordelia sat on the black velvet tufted stool in the closet, reflected and reflected by the ceiling-high mirrors surrounding her. But even all of those multiple Cordelias could not put their marriage back together again. It had ended before New Year's Eve, she knew it, but there was Pip and Emma and it all had to be worked out. Now, after everything, it still had to be worked out.

When Cordelia met Ned, she'd felt her future unfold. Marrying one of her father's real estate rivals had seemed impetuously daring and potentially romantic, like something out of a competitors-to-lovers rom-com with an adorably happy ending. Her father had been all for it. "We'll merge the dynasties," he'd told her, but her mother had pulled her aside, whispering about the drawbacks of "younger men." Possibly true. She zipped the other boot, smoothed her hair, changed her posture.

The front door has opened, the alarm's robotic voice announced. She'd set it so she'd be alerted to Ned's arrival.

Now, two hours later, she watched him soak up the winey sauce from the beef with a chunk of perfectly toasted baguette, and heard more stories about his triumphant return to the office. He always said it that way, *The Office,* as if it had capital letters.

"They were amazing, honey," he said. "Edwina brought champagne, and Hakim put up one of those letters on strings things, you know? That said 'Welcome Back.'"

"Very festive." Her husband was drinking expensive wine. She supposed that's what one did, having avoided a hefty stint in prison.

"And then what?" She smiled, encouraging.

"It appears we haven't lost any of the deals," he was saying. "So all in all . . ." He held up his wineglass, toasting her. "I have my life back, and I have my business back, and I have this delicious dinner, and a bottle of Opus One, and I have you. What more could anyone want? And Pip and Emma of course. How are they? Did you hear from Mother?"

Ned's list of priorities always put Ned first. Did he even hear himself? "Pip texted that they'd arrived."

"So I see we're on our own." Ned had leered at her, crumpling his white cloth napkin. She remembered what that exact same look had meant, early on, and she'd looked at him the same way. Those cheekbones, and the way his hair was always *almost* too long, his sometimes-hazel eyes. She'd felt that she was teaching him things, about business and about pleasure, though he was only three years younger.

"I've been neglecting you, I know," Ned said. "Why don't you get yourself upstairs and . . . get ready. I'll take the dishes to the kitchen. You've been patient, Dee. I appreciate it."

This would all be worth it, she decided. She'd think of the future. Whatever that would bring.

"Is that your phone or mine?" Ned pushed his chair back from the table, patted his pockets.

"Yours," she said, thanking the phone gods for the interruption. "Mine's upst—"

"Hang on," he told her, holding up his cell. "Nyomi."

"Why is she calling you?"

Ned rolled his eyes at her, as if to say *how the hell do I know?* He picked up his wineglass, and turned his back, intent on the call. Cordelia gathered the dishes. She heard Ned say *"what?"* in a tone she couldn't decode.

Nyomi had been ruthless in court. She'd made that cop admit that Ned had never been driving on a *public* street, and no matter the breathalyzer results, under Massachusetts's quirky law, it was not illegal to operate a vehicle on a *private* way, even if possibly impaired. She'd also elicited his reluctantly honest testimony about how upset Ned had been as he tried CPR on Randall Tennant.

"Was Mr. Bannister crying?" Nyomi had asked.

"He appeared to be," the cop said.

"'*Appeared*'?" Nyomi pushed him.

"Okay. He was crying," the cop said.

"Did he leave the scene?"

"No, he called 911. Even tried to get into the ambulance as it drove away."

The prosecutor had objected, but the judge let it in. Poor sympathetic Ned.

Ned appeared at the kitchen door, his face flushed with anger or wine or both, and for a moment she wondered if he was about to throw his half-full wineglass against the wall. Or at her.

"Ned? Is something wrong?"

"It's fine." Ned's chest rose and fell, and his eyes, gone gray and murky, seemed to stare straight through her. "I'm sure. Nyomi says it's not even confirmed yet."

Cordelia felt her heart beating faster. An acquittal was an acquittal, and for that to change there would have to be something of staggering importance. Impossible. "What? The trial is over."

"Exactly." Ned took a sip of his wine. "And Nyomi says not to worry."

"Ned? About what?"

"Never mind," he said. "It won't matter. Nothing can matter."

11

ARDEN WARD

As the jouncing Uber passed the corner of Cambridge and Bowdoin Streets, Arden scrolled her phone, speed-reading. BANNISTER SKATES, one newspaper headline sneered. A scathing editorial cartoon showed a boozy Ned Bannister caricature on a skateboard, money dripping from his coat pockets. She saw it all through Cordelia's eyes, the vicious aftermath of an unpopular decision. One TV reporter had staked out the jury foreperson's house in Allston, and harassed her so relentlessly she'd called the police. "We were following the law!" the juror yelled, before slamming the front door in the reporter's face. The clip, showing the woman's terror and the reporter smirking and Ned's postverdict grin, garnered hundreds of retweets, all with #skated. She wondered if young Pip had Twitter, whether he'd seen the hashtag, or the juror clips, or understood the publicity barrage. *Cordelia was right,* Arden thought. That family needed help.

The golden dome of the Massachusetts statehouse glowed under soft lighting, illuminating the sleet into twinkling fairy dust against a dark sky muddled with thick gray clouds. *November,* she thought as she stared out the window, heavy with the promise of the winter sure to come. Mushy pellets splattered on the car's windshield, and the floor beneath her was a shallow puddle of melt left by the previous passenger's shoes. And where would she be when November was over?

"This the place?" The driver pulled to the curb, the car tires slushing. "Two Mt. Vernon? With the flowers?"

Arden opened her car door, confused. "Flowers?" Then she saw what he meant. At the top of the three redbrick front steps, and tucked under the narrow brick overhang, a container wrapped in clear plastic. Under the slush-dotted beams of her lantern-shaped porch light, Arden could make out something yellow. Flowers.

As the car pulled away, a list of possibilities presented itself. A gift from Luz, as an early farewell? Maybe.

Sleet hit the back of her neck as she bent to look. A card on a plastic stick, labeled Patterson's, was stabbed amid a bouquet of golden sunflowers in a bright blue vase. *Thank you. I'll call tomorrow.* A droplet landed on the handwritten card, blurring the word "tomorrow."

"That's helpful," she said out loud. She tucked the vase under one arm, readjusted her tote bag, dug into a side pocket to pull out her keys. Getting flowers was not an unusual occurrence; her life included people trying to persuade her, too. Potential clients, or vendors wooing her, trying to convince her to buy a product or use a service or have an affiliation. And too late now to call the florist, but Patterson's, a Boston legend, was a client of theirs, and buddy-buddy with Warren. Tomorrow she could easily find out.

Warren. Yes. Warren "I need a favor" Carmichael. Only he could get flowers delivered this late. She should toss them. She didn't need Warren's pitiful flowers.

She opened the front door, and stomping her boots on the raffia mat, briefly imagined Warren's head underfoot. She'd almost discarded the bottle of Joy from her dresser top this morning, but it was her mother's bottle, brought home from a Paris honeymoon so many years ago, a treasure Arden kept refilling. It was certainly not an inappropriate gift from some sleazy and predatory client. And why should she throw away a memento because of a lie? She'd *worn* the perfume instead. Screw them.

Dumping her tote bag on the entryway side table, she tapped the code for the inner door, and had that moment, as she always did as she entered her living room, of safety and comfort. The fragrance of last night's fire in the brick fireplace lingered. Maybe she'd make a new one tonight. Read, have a glass of wine. Start building a new life. She'd done it after the divorce, she could do it again.

"Hey, fish," she said to the blue glow. She considered where to put the cello-wrapped flowers. In the kitchen maybe, on the round yellow breakfast table. Or on the fireplace mantel. Or on the dining room table, centered between Grandmother's silver candlesticks. She tried it there, golden against the polished cherry table. She wouldn't toss them until she confirmed they were from Warren. Maybe there was a more palatable explanation.

She'd positioned a massive and extravagant tropical fish tank as a makeshift divider between the living room and dining room. The entire first floor, living-dining-kitchen, was an open plan, surprisingly more modern than the circa 1875 exterior. Up a metal spiral staircase were four bedrooms; one, judging from the wall-to-wall mirror and the smooth wooden barre, had been used as a ballet practice room. Her grandparents, who'd owned the house and bequeathed it to her, had made it a guest room, reluctant to take down the mirror, hesitant to live with it. Arden did not have many guests, but the ballet room closet was valuable space. Her own bedroom overlooked the tiny Mt. Vernon Square, a massive old elm in the center, the hobbit tree, she called it, random tulips in the spring. The biggest bedroom, once her grandparents', was now her office. Arden had loved the house the moment she saw it, her first day in Boston as a kid, decades ago.

It was too big for just her and the fish, of course. So she rented the third floor to the Dellacortes, Olen and Mariah. Her tenants were neighborly pals, and good fish-sitters, and vacationing in their Kiawah Island place until after New Year's.

Now she tapped flakes of food into the hiss and burble of the fish tank, studying the turquoise water, the floaty ferns, and the enigmatic creatures that inhabited it, neon tetras and angelfish, and one combative firemouth she'd named Bella.

Fish-Bella and the others sprinted to the top of the tank, their little mouths gulping the flakes. *Cause and effect,* she thought. Offer someone what they want, and they'll do anything to get it.

From the depths of her tote bag, her cell phone rang.

"Hello?" she answered. Pretty late to call.

"I see you're already on the job." A woman's voice.

"Hello?" Arden said again. "Cordelia?"

"Who else would it be?"

She heard Cordelia laugh.

"I'm so—" Arden paused. She wasn't sorry, she was baffled. "Are you all right? I'm surprised to hear from you."

"Oh, because the card said I'd call tomorrow? I didn't sign the flowers, to protect your privacy. In case anyone read it. I hope I'm not bothering you."

Arden watched the fish flutter back and forth, following some fish instinct.

"The flowers are lovely. But—" She looked at the card again. "The card says thank you. For what?" She paused, rewinding. "And what do you mean, 'I see you're already on the job.' Isn't that what you said when you called?"

"Well you are, aren't you? On the job?" Cordelia's voice was almost a whisper. Almost gossipy.

"Cordelia? I don't understand."

"I don't know how you did it, but Ned's already concerned. Because something, and I don't know what, has happened. He got a phone call a little while ago from Nyomi Chang. His defense lawyer, you know?"

Arden blinked at the fish, unseeing. Nyomi Chang. "What did she say?"

"Well, I don't *know*. That's why I'm calling *you*." Cordelia's whisper had turned testy. "I'm on my cell inside my closet, now, because I don't want Ned to hear. He was so angry or so upset or so distressed—I'm not sure which—at whatever Nyomi said that he decided he had to take a shower. And that gave me a chance to call you. I'll try to find out. Still, I instantly put two and two together, and figured this was your fine hand."

Arden lowered herself to her couch and toed off her boots, then tucked her legs under her, settling into the soft navy-blue leather. She pulled a throw pillow onto her lap. "Figured? Why?"

"Well, I offered to hire you—to make Ned understand that what he did had consequences. And to change his ways. And barely twelve hours later, voilà, he's most definitely changed, that's for sure. I assumed that was the Arden Ward magic."

"Not at all," Arden said. "We haven't even agreed—"

"Hang on," Cordelia was saying. "I'm getting a text."

"Sure."

"Sorry. You still there?" Cordelia's voice. Still a whisper. "I'm in my bathroom now. I have the water running so he doesn't hear me."

"I'm here. You sure you're okay?"

"I'll be fine." Cordelia's voice lowered even more. "Look, you can say whatever you want, but I know this was you. Whatever Nyomi told Ned. It was *you*. That's what the flowers are for."

"No, I—and how did you get them delivered so late?"

"I love how you're not taking credit," Cordelia said. "It means you're good at this. I'll call your assistant and make an appointment. I'll try to find out why Ned's upset. I told you he was hiding something."

"I—"

"And Arden. The text I just got? Ah—never mind."

"What text? I told you, if we're working together . . ." Arden realized there was no question about that anymore. "If it's about what happened, you have to tell me."

"He's coming. Got to go."

"Cordelia. No surprises. What does the text say?"

She heard a breath, a sigh, maybe. A hesitation.

"It's that hashtag. It says '#skated.'"

"Do you recognize the phone number it came from?"

"No. Arden, I have to go, I have to. Talk tomorrow. Don't worry. I'll be careful."

Careful? Arden clicked off the phone, stretched her legs the length of the couch, wondered why she'd chosen a job where the stated purpose was to meddle in people's lives. Because she was doing a good thing, most often at least, and guiding people though a life crisis seemed benevolent and valuable.

She closed her eyes, listened to the gurgle of the fish tank. She understood Cordelia's distress, shunned by the women at her children's school, embarrassed about what happened to her little boy. Her fear of the future with a privileged and dismissive—and reviled—husband. Cordelia had a point: a jury's verdict was a legal decision, but not necessarily transferable to the rest of the world.

Cordelia had chosen a life as a wife and a mom, opposite of Arden. But both had exactly the same experience. They'd been unfairly rejected. Abandoned. Thrown out of their comfortable existence by the biased and selfish actions of someone who had control over them. People who were once their friends—their colleagues—had turned against them. They'd each had no choice. They were each trying their best to live with it. Cordelia obviously felt powerless. But Arden did not. She most certainly did not.

What's more—something destructive, something mysterious, was going on in that marriage. *He's hiding something,* Cordelia had insisted. Had he #skated?

And maybe Arden, in her final assignment, should find out.

Help change someone else's life. And then try to fix her own.

12

CORDELIA BANNISTER

It wasn't fair that sex could do that to people. Cordelia threw off the flowery comforter, and lay, languidly naked, on their bed. Her husband, dead to the world, snored, spent, beside her. No matter what, Ned always managed to make her forget everything about everything.

"I love you, Dee," he'd whispered moments ago.

"I—" she'd begun. But Ned simply flopped over, his back to her, zonked.

So certain of what I'll say, Cordelia had thought, *that he doesn't even need to hear it.*

Ned murmured, adjusted position, throwing a possessive arm across her bare chest. She'd look at the bright side. If Ned was content, sated, comfortable—she could ask him anything.

"Honey?" she whispered. "You awake?"

"Too soon." He moved closer to her, his breath on her. "You're a beast."

In the soft darkness, he couldn't see her expression.

"*You're* a beast," she supplied her half of their longtime call-and-response. It had been true, once. Maybe it still was, although in a different way. A siren wailed by outside their window, a reminder that people died, and that sometimes, other people caused their deaths. An ambulance with a siren just like that had screamed into Ned's parking garage that night, Cordelia could almost hear it. "But honey?"

Ned sighed, opened one eye, relinquishing only half of his attention. "Yeah? I'm really tired, babe. This whole thing has been a lot. It's like—I keep forgetting everything is okay now."

"Can I ask you something?"

"Something other than that?"

"Ha ha." Another tired joke. "Seriously. Just making sure we still agree about—Ned?"

Silence.

"Honey?" She turned over, facing him, poking his shoulder seemingly playfully, to get his attention. She twisted her hair down one shoulder, letting it fall over her chest. "Seriously. Focus. I need to know. What did Nyomi say?"

He propped his head on one hand, elbow on the bed.

"Okay." He rubbed a palm over one eye, as if trying to wake himself up. "Nyomi said hi, then asked how I was, then said something came up, and she wanted to 'confirm that neither you nor I had previous contact with Randall Tennant.' You know how she talks. I said no. Of course."

"What?" she said. "Whether *I*—we've been over this." It was impossible, she thought, why would Nyomi ask *that*? "And then what did she say?"

"That's all, babe. Don't you think I *asked* her? I'll follow up later this week. During the *day*."

"I'm just worrying about you, darling," she said.

"She said to let it go," Ned said. "Let's let it go." He closed his eyes, flopped onto his back.

How many times had she seen him like this, she thought, running her eyes down his body and back to his face. She loved him, she remembered that.

"I'm just trying to remember how it feels to be free," Ned said to the ceiling. "Isn't that a song?"

"I think so." Cordelia lay parallel to him, his legs stretching out past hers. She pulled the comforter over herself, hiding in the flowers. "Are you still okay with me going on the retreat?"

"Going . . . ?"

"I know, it probably slipped your mind, but remember I told you about the sorority thing?"

"What time is it?" Ned asked. "Got to be the middle of the night. Can we talk about this tomorrow?"

"Sure, of course." She adjusted her pillow, leaned closer to his ear. "But the sorority thing. Later this week. I'm supposed to go to Palm Beach with the Chi Os. Remember?"

Ned yawned, a massive yawn. "Palm Beach?"

"Exactly. I don't want to leave you alone," she went on. "Since the kids are at Georgianna's. And I don't want people to think I'm deserting you, honey. But they made all the reservations . . . and they're so sweet, they said they wanted to take my mind off things."

She moved closer, lining up herself against him, then propped her chin on her elbow. "But I cannot sleep for thinking about it. I'm so torn, and I know this is our time, and I don't want to make you unhappy, so I'm just wondering . . ."

No answer from Ned. Was he asleep?

"It's fine." She sighed, resigned. "I'll stay here. I'd rather be here, with you, honestly, I would. They'll understand."

Ned reached out a hand, slid his forefinger along her collarbone. "Huh-uh, no," he said. "Go. We have all the time in the world now, and what happened shouldn't get in the way of your life. Any more than it already has."

"No," she said. "My place is here with you."

"I insist. We can't let those people run our lives. We can't be afraid. If we're going back to normal, we're going back to fully, completely normal."

"I suppose," she said. "I'll only go if you tell me to. If you insist."

"You know I'm a beast," he said, "and you know I insist. And I'll even meet with your Arden Ward. Now—go to sleep. And then go live your life. Just come back to me."

"You *are* a beast," she said. "And I will do whatever you say."

"I know you will," Ned told her. "Now go to sleep."

He touched her cheek with one finger. It felt hot, like a brand.

13

ARDEN WARD

I'm sorry your wife couldn't join us," Arden lied. She selected a flour-dusted breadstick from the wicker basket on their dinner table, broke it in half. She'd texted Ned Bannister that she'd be late to the restaurant, hoping he'd order a drink. He had.

She'd spent the day multitasking. Packing her office and throwing memories in the trash and all the while touching base with reporters, calling back the ones who'd continued to pursue Ned and Cordelia. Gauging what they wanted, stalling them with vague promises about future interviews. There were no new #skated posts anywhere on social media she could find, only ones about actual skating. She'd worried that reporters had gotten mysterious texts, too, or any other suspicious communications. It was impossible to ask without giving it away—but no journalists had even alluded to such a thing. Maybe in this case, no news was good news. Had Cordelia told Ned about the text? It meant someone knew her phone number—but that was out there, certainly, judging from the reporter calls she'd received. Arden had texted her, and called several times, to find out. But no answer.

Now Bannister fidgeted with his stubby glass, rattling the melting ice cubes. "Cordelia told me to be here, so here I am." Bannister looked at her, amused, or maybe lying, too. "I put her through a lot, and I'm hoping to make it up to her. She's getting ready for a sorority thing, girls' weekend away. It's fine. I just want her to be happy."

It had been easy for Arden to get reservations at Salazar, a place where she often took clients when she wanted to gauge the public reaction to them. Not that Bannister knew that. And Arden hadn't even needed to ask Eduardo to make Ned's drink strong, though it did not seem that Bannister noticed. His second one, now, and Arden could tell no difference in his demeanor. Still, she would not choose to be in his path in a dark parking garage. Especially not careening down on a skateboard, with him, drunk, or not, behind the wheel of a two-ton vehicle.

Tennant's body had been . . . Arden put that thought from her mind. She did not want to imagine that horrendous level of injury. Even the news coverage had avoided it, apparently deciding there's only so much graphic human destruction that's appropriate. If she had to, at some point, she could probably get the police report, but dead was dead.

"Cordelia—I call her Dee—told me she wanted to hire you," Bannister was saying. "I told her not to." He grimaced, as if he had broken some social rule. "Don't take that the wrong way. I told her not to hire anyone."

Arden took a bite of breadstick, then a sip of the Malbec she'd ordered, making it impossible for her to answer so Bannister would keep talking. The rustic-walled restaurant was filling with customers, hip tattooed twentysomethings in graphic T-shirts, a scattering of awkward-looking couples, and a pack of chattering young women, one of them wearing a beauty-queen sash that said BRIDE-TO-BE. Classical guitar, Arden recognized the Segovia, played in the background.

"I know what you do, and I don't need that," Bannister was saying. "Again, I'm only here at her behest. And I hear the tequila shrimp are life-changing. Better than my own cooking, right? Or carryout? Even though the kids love it, there's only so much pizza a person can eat."

"I'm not sure about that." Arden smiled, trying to forge a connection. "It would be fun to experiment. But your kids?"

"At my mother's. For the week." Bannister finished the last of his drink, held up his glass, and a waiter in a black bolero soon arrived with another.

"Are you happy about that?" Arden tested the waters. "Your children being away?"

Bannister took a sip, signaled to the waiter that it was fine. "The kids are great. Pip is a trooper, and as Cordelia always tells me, not a bit like his father. And Emma is a rock star. She's five, going on Taylor Swift. And yes, I do miss them. I want them to have a normal life," he said. "Even though . . ."

He looked away from her, seemed to be staring at a vibrant mural across the room. "I don't know." His voice softened. "They're fine. I hope. Kids are resilient."

"So I hear," Arden said.

"You don't have any?"

"Not yet." He was making small talk, Arden reminded herself. "Shall we look at the specials? I don't want to keep you late."

"Like I said, nowhere to go." Bannister picked up his red leather–covered menu.

Arden studied him over the top of her own red folder. When she'd watched a video of Bannister after the verdict, he'd looked positively haggard, dark circles and tension lines around his mouth. Now he looked like he'd gotten some sleep. *Could a person ever get over it?* That moment when the jury comes back, but before the judge reveals their decision. Where your entire life depends on what happens next. Or maybe that's what happens every day, to everyone. Decisions get made, decisions of timing and proximity and coincidence, decisions we aren't aware of, moments that propel us into the future.

"You said you wanted your kids to have a normal life." Arden picked up the talking point. "And your wife."

Bannister lowered his menu. "Good try, Ms. Ward," he said. "I'm a salesperson too, and you're good, Arden, if I may call you that. But like I said. I'm here for Cordelia. Pitch away, I'll have the tequila shrimp and the asparagus, and then we'll call it a night. Agreed?"

"I'm here for Cordelia, too." Arden smiled. "So we have that in common. And the shrimp and asparagus, too." She held up her red wine, toasted him. "And call me Arden. I hope we can agree on the chocolate cinnamon soufflé."

"Sure." Ned sipped his drink. "I'm Ned." The background guitar continued, and the sound of laughter from across the room. "So," he said. "You called me, invited me to dinner. Any other situation, I would think you had an ulterior motive. But my wife's hired you, I know that. I'm happy to pay you, but I don't need you. And I say that with all due respect."

Arden laughed, an honest laugh this time. "Isn't that the most fraught phrase in the world? One of those—is there a word for it? A figure of speech describing something that means exactly the opposite of what you say?"

"I think that word you're searching for is 'lie,'" Ned said. He leaned forward, chin on laced fingers. "What can I help you with, Arden? My life is an open book. As I'm sure you heard during my trial."

Cagey, Arden thought. Confident enough to come to dinner, but savvy enough to be on the polite defensive.

"That must have been exhausting," she said.

"As you can see, I'm a free man now. I would have done anything, have gone through *anything*, to make that happen. You know what's been hard? Besides hanging up on all the damn reporters? Driving. Funny. Or not. Things change you, in ways you don't expect."

"I never thought about that. Like some sort of PTSD."

Ned drained the last of his drink. "I'll get over it." He put his glass down, the ice rattling.

Newcomers, two women in quilted silver vests and black turtlenecks, passed by their table, and in a few seconds, Arden saw one of them stop, turn, and stare at them. The woman turned away, then whispered to her companion.

"Someone you know?" Ned asked.

"Someone *you* know?" Arden replied.

"Nope."

"But you saw that." Arden gestured toward the women.

"Sure," he said. "It was pretty obvious. As I said, I thought they were friends of yours."

"Can you do an experiment with me?"

"A what?"

The waiter reappeared, carrying two brightly colored ceramic plates, each with thin stalks of luminously green asparagus and two skewers of grilled pink shrimp. A mound of brown rice on the side was dotted with a sprig of fresh parsley.

"The shrimp and the shrimp. And two glasses of rosé. Chef's compliments." The waiter set the dishes down in front of them, the fragrance of butter and pungent seasoning mouthwateringly intoxicating. "Is there anything else I can get you now?"

"Thank you," Arden said. "This is lovely."

As the waiter turned away, Arden picked up her fork so Ned would begin. "Looks good, right?"

"So." Ned held up his rosé, toasting her. "Here's to freedom."

"A nice thought," she said, not quite clinking his glass.

Ned took a sip, nodded approval, then said, "You were asking about an experiment."

"Yes. Definitely. Are you game for it?"

"Right now?"

"Right now."

14

m *I* the experiment? Or are you?"

"Both of us." Arden scanned the restaurant. Almost every table was full. The decibel level in the room had increased, and the music, now more salsa than Segovia, created a party atmosphere. The bride's table was doing the Macarena in their seats, their hilarity taking up more than its share of space. Perfect.

"Don't look now, okay?"

"Okay." Ned drew out the word. Amused. Held up a piece of shrimp on his fork. "Can I still eat?"

She ignored his question. "In a minute, turn to your right. Two tables away, two couples in that low red banquette, a table for four. One of them older, guy with the gray beard. The other couple younger, possibly . . . son and daughter-in-law?" She saw Ned start to look. Touched his arm to stop him, and widened her eyes. "Not *now*. Let me tell you first."

Ned twinkled at her, the only word that she could use to describe it, as he looked down at her hand, and she noticed, no matter what criminally ugly secrets he was hiding, he was attractive in an off-kilter kind of way. And he was clearly smart, too. She erased that from her brain. She had a job to do.

"Anyway. They have not taken their eyes off of you, and all four have their phones out."

Ned put down his fork. "Everyone has their phones out. You do, I do."

She nodded. "Yes. But those four are waiting for the right moment to take your photo. They've almost done it. The daughter-in-law as I call her, is especially fascinated with you, but then they chicken out."

"So?"

"So?" Arden repeated. "What do you think they're saying about you?" She cut into her last shrimp, and as she chewed, she could almost see Ned's mind working. Then, just as quickly, she saw it shut off.

"Frankly, Arden, I don't give a damn," he finally said. "If I may be so bold. So that's your experiment?"

"Nope. But let me ask you, since you don't care, is it your opinion that they're thinking: 'There's that super-nice guy who was wrongly accused of driving while utterly plastered and killing a trespassing skateboarding kid?'"

"He wasn't a kid." Ned put a hand on his drink glass, now only melted ice and a soggy wedge of lime.

Arden saw the reaction, the reflex toward alcohol, noted it. "Fine. Although not the point. What would *you* speculate is the way they describe you? Why they're so riveted by watching you? What they're whispering about? Why you think the 'damn reporters,' as you call them, are hounding you?"

The restaurant noise swirled around them. The waiter walked by, and Ned held up his glass. Never taking his eyes off of Arden.

"And who do you think those people think *I* am?" Arden pushed him harder. "They've seen Cordelia on TV. They know I'm not Cordelia. Do you figure they've decided you're out with a pal? While your wife is—I don't know, like she said she was that night? At home with two sniffy kids?"

"I see. The experiment is you seeing how inappropriate you can be before I walk out of here." Ned's face darkened. His new drink arrived. He ignored it. "You're close, Arden. Damn close."

"Ned. Mr. Bannister." Perfect. She'd learned she could ruffle him, and it didn't take much. The "accident" was still tender to the touch. "I'm sorry," she lied again. "You're right. I was inappropriate. But I'm only trying to show you the real world. Unless you leave town, change your name, become an entirely different person—"

"I'm not going to do that."

"Okay, then. But in that case—"

"Did Cordelia tell you to suggest that?" Ned leaned across the table. Eyes narrowed. "Is *that* what this is about? She wants me—us—me—to leave town? Hell no. Hell. No. And if she wants to discuss that again, or anything for that matter, she should just talk to me. She doesn't need to hire you. For you to 'rehabilitate' my 'reputation.' Protect me. Manage my crisis. I know that's what you two are conspiring to do. But, as I said, even before the shrimp and wine. I don't need you."

"Ned—" Arden glanced at the couples at the banquette. The daughter-in-law caught her eye, quickly looked away. "They're still eyeing you. This public scrutiny, this judgment, is what you'll face every time you go out. Cordelia, too. Your children, too."

"The only judgment that matters is from the jury."

Ned chewed his last shrimp as he spoke. Almost viciously, Arden thought.

"Well, that's naïve," she said.

Ned cocked his head toward the banquette. "Those people couldn't care less about me."

"You think? Before the wine, you had three gin and tonics—or vodka tonics, who knows—just during the time I've been here," she said. "And everyone is watching."

"Gin and tonics?"

"Or straight gin, or vodka, or whatever is in those glasses. You think people aren't noticing that? Counting?"

Ned picked up his glass, rattled the ice remnants. "It was tonic water," he said. "With lime. You think I'm that naïve? To have three—" He toasted her with the icy glass. "Drinks in public?"

Arden tried to hide her surprise, but Ned wasn't as clever as he thought.

"Very savvy," she said. "But if *I* thought it was a G and T, what do you think *they*"—she tilted her head toward the foursome—"what do you think *they* thought? To any observer, you're pounding down alcohol. It's only about how it looks, not about reality. That's why I'm here."

Ned put down his glass. "Okay. But they still don't care. I'm nobody, and anyway, I didn't do anything wrong. No one is judging."

"Ha." Arden smiled then, challenging. "So. Here's the experiment. I'm going to walk over to the maître d's station and pretend I'm waiting for him to come back."

Ned blinked at her. Skeptical.

"You take out your phone. Pretend to be absolutely engrossed in the screen. Do *not* look up."

"This is what you get paid for?"

"Ned. Just do that. Trust me."

"Right." But Ned picked up his phone.

"Now. Nod at me, as if the food was terrific, and point to the maître d' station. Then focus on the phone."

"This is so much fun."

"Trust me." Arden grabbed her own phone, stood, and walked past the banquette, never making eye contact with the occupants, as if she were on a mission. The minute the banquette was behind her, she turned and snapped a photo. At the maître d' station, she took two more. As Eduardo returned to his podium, she thanked him for their table, and the wine, and then, tapping on her cell phone, returned to Ned.

Handed him her cell.

"See that?" She sat, tucking her skirt underneath her. Scooted closer to the table. "Three photos. Swipe."

Ned looked at the screen. Used two fingers to expand it. Then swiped. And again. And again.

"They're taking selfies. So?"

"I predict they won't turn out to be very good ones of *them*," Arden said. "Because they're not really trying to get photos of themselves. They're taking pictures *of you*."

She watched Ned swipe her screen again. His chest rising and falling, his face a countenance of reality, or realization, or defeat. This was the moment, Arden had seen it so many times, when rationalization no longer worked. Ned, like her other clients, eventually had to own his notoriety. How the public, without a moment of compassion, viewed people like him as fodder, as a social media post, as currency for their own status and access. Ned was now a commodity. And in this moment, he knew it. Arden had revealed it to him in three snapshotted phony selfies.

"How many surreptitious photos," she asked gently, "do you think have been taken of your children? Of your wife? Of yourself? How many of your clients do you think will be proud to introduce you as their real estate adviser?"

Ned handed back her phone. "Assholes."

"I agree," Arden said. Her phone vibrated. A text. She looked at her screen, flinched at what had silently pinged in. A screenshot. And a message. She tried to stay focused. Cordelia had instructed her not to tell Ned about this. Maybe she wanted to tell him herself. Or . . . not. To protect him, somehow.

"Still, I assume you know there's a Twitter hashtag about you? #Skated? You think your son hasn't see that?"

"Like I said, assholes."

"Fine. That's why I'm here. Let's make all that go away."

"I'd do anything for the kids, and Dee, but . . ." Ned's shoulders sagged. "What *can* I do?"

"You can order dessert," she said. "And then you can listen to me. And do what I say from now on."

Ned took a sip of wine, and Arden sneaked a look at that text again. From Cordelia. *Another one,* the message said, clearly referencing the text Cordelia had mentioned last night. *Freaking out. Don't say anything to Ned.* And then the screenshot.

Ned knew Randall Tennant. We can prove it. #skated.

PART TWO

15

ARDEN WARD

Y ou got my screenshot? Of the text?" Cordelia, bundled in dark
wool, her sunglasses reflecting the morning glare, stood on the
bustling sidewalk outside Arden's office building. Admitted
she'd been waiting for Arden's arrival. "I didn't want anyone to see us in
your office," she explained as Arden walked toward her. "I thought out
here we'd look like everyone else going to work, no one would notice me.
But Arden, I'm so afraid."

Her words had puffed into the cold, like ghost words. Like an incan-
tation.

"You knew I was with Ned at the restaurant last night," Arden said,
off balance at Cordelia's unexpected visit. And the disturbing text she'd
sent. "You knew I couldn't answer you. I called when I got home but—"

"I know I know, I'm so sorry." Cordelia's words tumbled over each
other. "I took a pill, because I had to sleep, and then I was embarrassed,
because I knew you would worry, and then . . ." She shook her head, lazy
snowflakes dotting her eyelashes. "I saw you called. Thank you. But now
I'm so frightened about texts and, oh, I don't know."

"The latest text you got said—"

"Ned knew Randall Tennant." Cordelia dabbed a finger under one
eye, then the other. Looked at the sidewalk. "Yes."

"Is that true?"

"Of course not!"

"What did Ned say about them? The texts?"

"Oh. I could never tell him."

"Why not? Your goal is for him to take this seriously. This is serious.
They're from the same number, right?"

"What if it's true? I love my husband, but he's hiding something. And
if I ask him, he'll tell me I'm hysterical. He'd say—*how many times do I
have to tell you I don't know that man?* That's why *you* have to. Ask him.
Who would send that to me? Why?"

Arden took a deep breath as they stood in the powdery snow, her carry-in coffee steaming into the cold air, the conversation giving her chills. A few latecomers, coffees in hand and coats flapping, trotted into the building. "Someone angry about the verdict?"

"Maybe. Or who knows something I don't."

"But certainly the police would have discovered a connection."

"The police? Oh, my god, I have no idea about the police. But what if they find out now? What if *they're* getting the same texts?" Cordelia said. "We have to keep this quiet, Arden. We do. I *cannot* take it. Can you imagine? The whole thing blows up in our faces *again*?"

Arden nodded, weighing the options. "Here's the dilemma. I've talked to reporters, felt them out, and they don't seem to know anything about it. I mean—if someone is being nasty, harassing you, and I'm so sorry, but if we poke the bear, and it's not true, it could make things worse."

Cordelia's eyes widened, as if envisioning that. "Oh. I see. Yes. Yes. I completely agree. We ignore it."

Arden fiddled with the plastic lid of her coffee, playing it out. "On the other hand, Cordelia, if there *is* something, I have to know. I've told you. It's infinitely important. No surprises. Is there anyone who might want to hurt you?"

"Arden, Ned is a—he has his fingers in every real estate pie in this city. In the state! He's at the center of power. I have no idea if he has enemies. I assume he does, right? But let's just—listen. I should never have mentioned it."

"Of course you should have," Arden began. "You have to tell me everything. It's crucial that you—"

"And I want to hear about last night with Ned, too. What happened?"

"He's on board, Cordelia. And—"

"Great. All I need to know. Now. You go decide what to do about the texts. That's more important. Tonight *I* need to have dinner with Ned, like everything is fine. It probably *is* fine. I can't risk the phone to tell you about it, I'm worried he might be listening. Come for coffee tomorrow morning. He'll be at the office. We'll have privacy. And no snow." Cordelia clutched at her arm. "Please. I'm so lost."

"Again. Let me think."

She *had* thought about it, as she packed the last of her boxes, and taped up the contents of a vanishing part of her life. Thought about truth, and fairness, and families, and how one wrong word could ruin so many people. How the right words could sometimes—sometimes—remedy that. Or even better, prevent the damage in the first place.

And she'd picked up the phone.

.   .   .

"I appreciate this," Arden said. "Thanks for meeting me here. We can just walk on into the garage. Should be pretty empty." She and Assistant District Attorney Monelle Churchwood, the lead counsel on Ned's prosecution, had arrived at the metal gateway that blocked the entrance to the Bannister Building's parking garage. The scene of what the jury said wasn't a crime, almost as gloomy as the evening outside, with only ceiling lights struggling from overhead fluorescents. The glass-walled booth at the entryway was unattended. She hoped they weren't trespassing, but Ned and Cordelia would vouch for her if need be.

"I don't mean to seem mysterious," she told Monelle. "The Bannisters have hired me, that's no secret. And now I'm trying to understand some things."

"Sure, nothing I love more than reliving an acquittal. My favorite." Monelle, wearing a white cashmere coat and a white hat and muffler, followed Arden, edging herself between the grimy stanchion and the equally grubby concrete wall. She checked her coat for smudges, then seemed satisfied. "But half the stuff you read is not true, and who knows what lies the Bannisters are telling you. I have fifteen minutes. Happy to set you straight. But hang on." Monelle began checking her phone, scrolling through screens.

"Thank you." Arden was almost lying to the assistant district attorney—omission was lying—but she was still apprehensive about getting involved. She kept telling herself this was just one conversation, simply research, but that wasn't true. If the text Cordelia had shown her this morning was correct, Monelle might go crazy. Arden wouldn't tell her specifically about it, of course, but she had to know what—if anything—might change if the text were true. She didn't like surprises.

"All set. Fifteen minutes starts now," Monelle said, stashing the phone in her coat pocket.

"You okay to walk down with me instead of taking the elevator?" Arden pointed to her own chunky boots. "I want to get a feel for it."

"Sure. Whatever. And my boots?" She lifted a foot, displaying. "They're tough. Too damn cold for pretty. Fashion's got to wait until spring."

"I hear you. And yes, fifteen minutes. Thanks, Monelle."

They walked side by side down the incline, deeper into the parking garage, thin tubes of light above them fighting through the gloom, barely showing the way as they descended, their booted footsteps squishing on the damp pavement.

Monelle drew her coat closer. "I forgot this place isn't heated. Just to reiterate—I'm prohibited from talking to you about anything that wasn't in evidence."

"I know, and I'm not asking."

Arden couldn't help but imagine it, the moment in time gone tragically wrong. Now, almost a year later, the place felt deserted, the yellow-striped parking spaces, each one numbered, empty. Arden had arrived at five, and watched a stream of drivers insert their parking cards into the machine; their cars, single file, exiting one at a time, and heading out into the darkness.

As the place emptied and Monelle Churchwood did not arrive, Arden began to expect a phone call, cancelling the meeting. She almost hoped for it. It would be easier, or logical, or smarter, every word like that, for Arden to stay out of it.

But that text. And what it might mean. Haunted her. And as a result, Arden had invited the prosecutor who had tried to put Ned Bannister in prison back to the scene of the accident. The not-crime. The verdict might have been different if Ned *knew* Randall Tennant. But the police—and Monelle Churchwood—would have discovered that. Wouldn't they? This was one way to find out. And maybe Churchwood was getting the same texts. She could find that out, too. Maybe.

Now, as they walked, the gradual uninterrupted downward spiral of the garage unspooled in front of them like a smooth concrete river. Arden snapped a few shots on her cell. "Do you skateboard?" she asked.

"Are you serious?"

"Me either. But I guess—if you know what you're doing—this is a ready-made skateboard park."

"People do what they do," Monelle said. "Look, Arden, anytime you want to tell me why we're here, I'd appreciate it. My kids need dinner, and if I'm late, my wife will flip, and I'll spend the rest of the night apologizing."

"Okay, question one. And listen, thanks for your patience. Why would Ned Bannister park his car on the lowest level, not the top?"

"He testified he wanted to leave the good spots for clients."

"Okay." Arden saw the pavement allowed two narrow lanes between the rows of spaces; one lane up, and one lane down.

"That's a video camera, right?" Arden pointed to a black box mounted high above her in the corner. "Newspaper says one's on every floor."

"Happy to show you all of them, if you like." Monelle gestured at the ceiling. "It won't make any of them have worked that night."

"That's peculiar," Arden said.

"Well, it's not as if it's impossible, but this time it did seem . . . convenient. 'Intermittent' was the word they kept using. 'Glitchy.' Other nights, it worked." The lawyer stopped, rolled her eyes. "Blah blah, the security guard had taken the holiday week off, so allegedly, no one knew they were off until Bannister mowed Randall down in that monster of a car. The man got away with vehicular homicide, I know it. And it sticks in my craw."

"But there's no way to prove what actually took place."

"Well, there sure as hell is, forgive my language, Ned murdering Bannister could tell us. Which he did not, on the stand, raising his hand to take his oath like a choirboy, lying through those whitened teeth. I mean, come on. Only two people in this parking garage. One of them stupid-drunk—"

"Which you couldn't prove because of the breathalyzer thing."

"Don't even remind me about that." Monelle put up two palms, cutting her off. "I felt like the goddess of justice had turned against me. The uncertified breathalyzer, the out-of-commission video surveillance system, ten freaking *men* on the jury. And no witnesses, you know? Only one rich guy, and one dead guy. One dead guy who was trespassing. One random trespassing dead guy, with no family to rabble-rouse the media. How do you think that's going to come out?"

"Well—"

"Shit. Sorry. Language." Monelle shook her head, her white wool cap low over her forehead, her braids underneath swinging with the motion. "Look. I thought I could win. Even ignoring the outdated and ridiculous 'private way' element of the law, Ned Bannister ran him down and killed him. Guilty as charged. But in this case the law protected the guilty more than it protected the innocent."

"It's supposed to protect everyone," Arden said. "Hear that? Is that a car?"

"Move," Monelle said.

Arden stepped to her right and between the yellow lines of an empty parking spot, gesturing Monelle to follow, just as a set of headlights glared into view around the tight corner, the engine sound unmistakable. The car whooshed by; a four-door, some dark color, one person inside.

"We heard that car. We moved." Arden thought about their instant reaction. "We got out of the way."

"Tennant caromed down and around the corner just as Bannister was accelerating up. Do your homework, Arden." But she smiled as she said it, and took out her phone. Held it up. "And now you have seven minutes."

Maybe Tennant had thought the parking garage was empty, Arden mused. Figured he'd be alone. He was trespassing, so his goal would be that no one saw him.

"Two more questions. First, why was Randall Tennant skateboarding down in the up lane? Why couldn't Ned avoid him?"

"Only one person knows," Monelle said, "and he's not talking. But apparently they were painting new lines, and they'd blocked off one lane."

"But how did Tennant even know about this place?"

"Add that to the list of unanswered questions, sister," Monelle said. "And if you want the rest of the list while we walk: Why did he come to Boston. Why doesn't anyone seem to know him. Why was his phone a burner. Everywhere we checked was a dead end. And no, I cannot tell you where those places were. But the jury ruled. So none of that matters anymore. One more floor."

Arden could almost hear Monelle thinking as they continued down.

"Right here." Monelle had stopped, her white coat incongruous in the grimy garage darkness, a strip of florescent light above. "After the turn."

Arden saw the tight curve. The restrictive angle. Imagined it as one lane. She could almost hear the sickening impact. She took another photo, then put her phone away, embarrassed.

The two women stood in silence, as if they'd agreed on taking a moment to grieve, or at least remember. Tears came to Arden's eyes, something about the power of the place, as if it housed determined ghosts in an atmosphere forever changed; this corner of an ordinary parking garage seemed haunted with unanswered questions, with the specter of injustice or indifference.

Indifference seemed the most cynical of emotions, the most destructive.

If anything, Arden knew her flaw was caring too much. If there was a way to regain an equilibrium, or justice, Arden should help. Anyone would help.

"Monelle? Last question. And just a thought. Would it matter if you found out Ned Bannister had known Randall Tennant?"

16

rden. Thank god. I haven't slept. Not at all." Cordelia hadn't even completely opened the front door to her Brookline condo as she began talking. "What did you decide? What do we do?"

"Did something *else* happen?" Arden took in Cordelia's disheveled hair, the mascara smudges under her eyes, the fraying black T-shirt, pilling yoga pants. "Did Ned—"

"Ned's at work. I'm not sure I could have stood it another minute." Cordelia stepped back and gestured Arden into a shockingly modern living room, softened by the winter noontime sun from a rectangular skylight. "Give me your coat."

A sleek black leather couch, curved and inviting, dominated the room, and two claret-red upholstered wing chairs flanked a ceiling-high black marble fireplace. A faceted French press pot, two red ceramic mugs and matching coffee service were arranged on a molded lacquer tray atop the glass-and-chrome coffee table.

"Sit." Cordelia placed Arden's coat on one crimson chair, settled into a spot on the couch near the coffeepot, and then patted the sleek cushion beside her. "Sit. And Arden, the reporters. They're—constant. Thank you, so much, for handling the calls. Like you told me, I send them to you and your assistant, then I hang up. Arden, you can't believe—I'm about to lose it. I'm so relieved the kids are away."

"We'll take care of the press," Arden said. "I've put off the interview requests, told them you all need privacy, and time to recover. And I told them if they keep showing up at your house, or calling you, or run negative articles, they're off the list. They get it. So have you gotten more texts? Has Ned?"

"Ned. Right. Tell me about your dinner. Tell me everything. And no, no more texts. Not yet, at least." Cordelia picked up the red pitcher from the coffee service. "Cream?"

"Yes, cream." Arden frowned, remembering. "Your husband said—you were going out of town?"

Cordelia poured, and the fragrance of the dark roast mixed with far-away chocolate. "I am. Palm Beach. With my sorority sisters. Where it's safe and anonymous. *They* still love me, at least. But leaving makes me feel awful, disloyal, like the public will think—" She handed Arden a mug. "Will they?"

"It's a long-standing engagement? Planned before? I could handle that."

"It is. Truly. It is, and Ned wants me to go." She made a skeptical face, a fleeting microexpression Arden wasn't sure she was meant to see. "He wants me to be happy, just ask him."

"He *does* want you to be happy," Arden had to say. There was no reason for her to defend Ned Bannister. Still, there was something about him. "At dinner, he spoke of you with true affection. Concern. And your children, too; he softened when he described them."

"What did he say? About them?"

Arden pursed her lips, trying to remember precisely. "That they were . . . I don't know, some word like 'troopers.' He said he missed them." She shrugged. "It was mostly an impression, more than the actual words."

"What did he tell you about Pip?"

"Nothing, really." Arden took a sip of the rich creamy coffee. She could read people, their expressions, the emotional clouds that shadowed their faces. If Cordelia was afraid, or nervous, or even in danger—and sometimes Arden got that vibe from her—maybe the children were in danger, too. Maybe that was the real reason Cordelia had sent them away. "Why? Is something wrong?"

"The kids? Are fine. Wait, we have brownies. I'll get them from the kitchen." Cordelia stood. "And then tell me what we should do. About Ned and Randall Tennant. Which is not fine."

As Cordelia walked away, Arden knew the time for decision-making was over. In a few minutes she'd have to tell Cordelia something perplexing. Difficult. And life-changing.

17

Arden tilted her head, listening. Cordelia had said she was getting brownies. But she was clearly talking. Maybe on the phone?

No matter what, Arden could not avoid revealing, any minute now, the bombshell Monelle Churchwood had presented yesterday as they'd left the Bannister Building parking garage.

The lawyer had spooled out a foggy breath in the crystalline cold, traffic on Atlantic Avenue picking up, the colored lights of the Zakim Bridge in the far distance shining purple in honor of something. *Would it matter if Ned Bannister had known Randall Tennant?* Arden had asked her. Something like that.

"Do you have information that he did?" Monelle had pounced.

"I—" She'd known it would be thin ice. But she had to find out. If it was true, they had to get ahead of it. No surprises. "No. I was just wondering."

"Wondering." Monelle nodded. Infinitely skeptical. "Sure."

"Really. Just asking."

But then, Monelle had answered.

"Since you're 'wondering'?" she'd said. "Even if there turned out to be a *video* of Ned Bannister threatening to kill Randall Tennant. Or a menacing letter. Or a text. Even if there's a snapshot of them together, proof they knew each other. Name your evidence. It wouldn't matter."

"It wouldn't matter?" Arden had tried to get her head around that.

"Nope."

So what was that text all about? Arden risked it, pushed again. "Why?"

"In order to prove murder, you have to prove—" Monelle had put her gloved hands to her face, covering her eyes briefly as if to block out distractions. "Let me make it easy. When Bannister was acquitted of vehicular homicide, he was found not guilty of causing the death of the victim."

"Yeah, so?"

"So the law says he cannot be tried *again* for that. That would be double jeopardy. And we could not get a murder conviction without the element that he *caused* the death of the victim."

A huge truck rattled by, three massive pink flamingoes painted on the side.

"Are you actually telling me—"

"Yup." Monelle nodded. "I know you're just 'wondering,' but Ned Bannister could shout to the rooftops *I ran him down on purpose ha ha*—not that he would—but theoretically he could. And it would not matter."

"That's justice?"

"That's the law. We're done with Ned Bannister. And I have to learn to live with it."

"I—" Arden had looked up at the winter constellations, playing it out. So it wouldn't matter if that text was true. Maybe this was good news? For Ned Bannister, at least. "What if—"

"Trust me, sister, nothing I'd like better than to see that man rot in prison. But it's not going to happen. I'm trying to get over it, and you should too."

"I cannot believe it."

"Believe it. Are we done? The family calls." She stuffed her hands into her pockets, cocked her head, inquiring. "Unless there's something you're not telling me? I'm just . . . wondering."

"Nope, nope," Arden said. "I wanted to make sure I know all the facts. Just wanted to see this through your eyes."

"Sure. I've enjoyed this oh so much."

"Thanks, Monelle," Arden had called out to Monelle's departing back. But the lawyer had lifted one acknowledging hand, and kept walking away.

Cordelia now carried a silver tray through the dining room, the shiny oval piled with more brownies than two people could ever eat. She set the tray on the coffee table, handed Arden a square white linen napkin, and sat on the couch.

"Eat one of these while I tell you the plan."

"The plan?"

"Yes. So. When I'm out of town, you find out what those texts mean. If Ned was actually acquainted with Randall Tennant. Then we can decide how to handle it."

"Cordelia? Before you continue. There's something you need to know."

"Oh, Arden." Cordelia looked apologetic. Or maybe embarrassed. Her shoulders drooped. "I am so sorry. Was Ned . . . unprofessional? At dinner? Did he hit on you?"

Arden put a hand to her throat, tried not to choke at this non sequitur while searching for emphatic enough words. What was it with this idiotic suspicious wife thing? Patience Swanson. Now Cordelia. *All* she needed.

"No, not in any realm of the imagination. No," she went on. "Not at all."

"It's just that it's his . . . way." Cordelia tapped a brownie crumb from her lips. "I think it's part of how he does business, you know, that he comes across, well, a little personal. Intimate. I know some of his clients, women, have gotten the wrong impression. Because he seems so harmless, you know? Like he needs you to take *care* of him. Feel sorry for him. And some women—I've seen it, I truly have—actually take it seriously. I don't *think* he ever follows through, but sometimes I worry . . . well, anyway. *Men.* Sorry. I'm babbling. I should have warned you, maybe. About him and women. That's how he rolls."

"There was no rolling, Cordelia. It's not about Ned 'hitting' on me. We're here to talk about Randall Tennant. I did—some research." She parsed her words, deciding how much to say. "And I must tell you that in the *law* . . ."

Cordelia waved off what Arden was about to say. "Are you kidding me? I don't care about the *law*. We're not talking about the *law*. If you're about to tell me about some double jeopardy thing, don't you think I looked into that?"

"But—"

"No. No buts. A lawyer friend told me about . . ." Cordelia paused, as if trying to remember. "Whatever. I just need the truth. So my life—and the kids'—can go on. There are prison sentences that aren't served in prison itself. You know that as well as I do."

"But your husband was acquitted. That's a good thing."

"Arden, I don't mean to be annoying. But if one person knows something, someone else is going to find out, don't you see? We have *kids*, and our lives are already—"

Arden's phone pinged in her handbag, but she ignored it.

"Ten million dollars that's Ned."

The phone rang again.

"I dare you. Look at the caller ID."

Arden opened the drawstrings of her leather bag, pulled out her cell phone. Stared at the screen.

Cordelia crossed her arms over her chest, victorious. "Told you. Don't answer. We need to talk."

"I don't want to ignore him," Arden said. "I asked him to call. *You* wanted him to." But she didn't answer, since she'd either have to say where she was, or not, and either way was awkward. After one more ring, she tucked it into her bag, letting it go to voice mail.

"Thank you, Arden. Listen." Cordelia's face changed. "We can't ignore it. Because—I got another text. Like the other one. That's why I couldn't sleep. Why I look like this."

Arden stopped, a brownie midway to her mouth. "Another text? What did it say?"

Cordelia picked up her cell phone from the coffee table. Scrolled through it. Held up the screen. "Look."

We know ur husband knew Randall Tennant. From barber shop. #skated

"What? What barbershop? Did you try to find out who sent it?"

"Of course I did. But my reply went nowhere. So now, it's out of control. It's only going to get worse. *Worse!*"

"Okay, let's think." Barbershop? What was the point of this? "Look, why don't you simply ask Ned? Say—'look at this weird thing.' I mean, you don't know everyone who goes to your salon, do you? I certainly don't."

"Ned will just lie! He's insisted all this time he doesn't know him."

"But maybe he doesn't realize he knows him."

"I mean," Cordelia kept talking. "There was no reason for the cops to ask where Ned got his hair cut, was there? I mean, is that a thing?"

Arden made a face. *How would I know?*

"Now I worry, now I am *overwhelmed* by worry," Cordelia went on, "that something . . ." She shook her head. "What if this is true? And someone actually knows something about Ned? Like, a scary thing. And what if Ned's involved? In the scary thing?" Her eyes widened. "What if he still is? What if they tell everyone? What about me? And the kids? They have my cell number!"

"Why would you think—or who—"

Footsteps. A willowy young woman in a beige canvas apron and blue jeans hovered at the entryway to the living room. "Y'all fine with the brownies?" she asked.

Arden heard the accent, theorized Mississippi.

"Perfect." Cordelia smoothed her hair, lifted her chin. "Thank you, Megan. Feel free to take off, and I'll be out of town for the weekend."

"And Mr. Bannister?" Megan said.

"Just leave him a casserole," Cordelia said. "You know he'll eat anything."

"Will do, Ms. B. As always." Megan untied her apron, slipped it over her head. "Safe travels," she said, and turned toward what Arden assumed was the kitchen.

Something went through Arden's mind. Something that didn't match.

"She's your cook?"

"Yes, majoring in culinary arts at Boston University. Comes in a few times a week, she's a dream; she was kinda famous, at some point, Miss Alabama or something. Megan LePlavy? It's risky, with Ned around; like I told you before, he's a charmer, but you can't fire someone because they're too pretty. Plus she's a genius in the kitchen."

"She cooks. For you. And your family."

"That's what cooks do."

There's only so much pizza a person can eat, Ned Bannister had said. He'd talked about carryout, and definitely, *definitely,* had never indicated that anyone cooked for him while Cordelia was gone. They'd discussed this very topic. Arden tried to decide whether that was—well, what was it?

Easy answer. It was a lie.

18

Cordelia lifted the coffeepot, offering. When Arden declined, she poured more for herself, a few brown droplets splashing onto the red tray. "A look crossed your face. Are you wondering whether Ned's having an affair with the cook?"

"Of course not." Arden tried to appear as if that were true. "Just thinking about that new text. And what it means."

"What it means? What it means is that this is not over. Listen," Cordelia said. "We, you and I, need to plan. While I'm out of town, you help him. Keep wrangling those reporters. Kill the ugly tweets. I hate #skated."

"I do, too. And I'm on it, as you know. You'll be seeing some #just-ice4Ned hashtags, too. All part of the service. Leveling the playing field, swaying public opinion. But it has to be subtle, feel organic, to work." It's what she'd been hired to do. *For the next week at least,* she remembered. Warren Carmichael. Arthur Swanson. Ned Bannister. *Men.*

Cordelia held up a finger, continuing, "And find out about Randall Tennant. It may be risky for me. I know. But I cannot live without the truth."

"But that's almost—" *Self-destructive,* Arden stopped herself from saying. "Look. If it turns out Ned was connected with Randall Tennant, forgive me, wouldn't that leave you in a much worse position? And your children? Why not just be grateful for the acquittal? Leave well enough alone?"

"Because we have to know. Or it will never stop. Just like you always say, I don't like surprises. I'd always be looking over my shoulder. So would all of us. And Ned."

Arden's phone rang again.

"Speak of the devil."

"If it *is* Ned, he's calling me because you wanted him to. Getting my guidance was your idea. Right?"

"Right. Okay. Yes. But there's not much time. You're quitting, right? Leaving?" The phone rang again.

"I didn't tell you that."

"Come on, Arden. Your office is full of boxes, and your person who brought me in, Lucy? She said you weren't working there much longer."

"She did?" Arden frowned, calculating the wisdom of that. Maybe Luz was trying to protect her. Warren crossed her mind; another possible way Cordelia could know. The phone rang again. Arden let it go. It went silent.

"Did you speak with Warren Carmichael about—" she began, but Cordelia kept talking.

"Arden? Are you saying now—ignore the texts? Leave well enough alone?" Cordelia's face turned hopeful, tears welling. She held up her phone, showing Arden the screen. "Maybe this will go away, and we'll go on with our lives? Should I delete them? Double-delete them?"

Arden looked at Cordelia's screen, and those blocky words that might change this woman's life. And her husband's. It was her job, Arden's, to help them. For another week, at least.

"Cordelia, I'm sorry. Here's what I think. You could delete the texts, but that won't delete the reality. No surprises, exactly. First we find the truth, then we can decide how to handle it."

The room went silent for a moment, the fragrance of the chocolatey brownies mixed with the pungent coffee. Arden watched Cordelia thinking, the woman's chest rising and falling. She'd picked up a gold-framed photograph from an end table. Stared at it.

"Amalfi Coast," Cordelia said, showing it. "Our first trip."

Arden nodded. Cordelia had kept the photo on display. It meant—didn't it?—they'd been happy.

"Arden? What happens to people? I'm trying so hard." Cordelia's words had turned halting, and she took a deep breath, seemed to steel herself. "But it seems like everything I thought was true—" She put the photograph back. "Anyway. If everything is a lie, and someone else knows it, too, that puts me and the kids in the middle."

"I understand. But—"

Cordelia's eyes glittered with tears. "He's happy!" she whispered. "I cannot remember the last time I was happy. Laughter. I can't even remember laughter."

Arden felt her heart break with the irony. Of course Ned Bannister was happy. He was free. His wife wasn't.

"Cordelia, I need to ask you. Flat out. A hard question. Do you think there's any legitimacy to these messages? Do you think your husband hit Randall Tennant? On purpose?"

"Oh." Cordelia sat up. Bolt straight. "Absolutely not. No. No. Ned would never hurt anyone. No. It's just that . . . who knows what he's involved in? I mean, maybe, he might not even be aware."

"So he's not dangerous. I'm not helping a murderer."

"No. Of course not. No. Be careful, though. Really." Cordelia leaned forward. "Doesn't it seem like someone's warning me? Might even be watching me? Or Ned. If I got this text, there's something going on." She held it up again. "Maybe someone wants to ruin him. And they're not giving up. And that puts all of us in danger."

"But who—?"

Cordelia nodded. "Yes. You're so right. We have to find out. Thank you."

As they stood at the door, she grabbed one of Arden's arms, her expression openly pleading, tears once again welling. "I don't mean to be heavy handed, but Pip and Emma, they deserve a champion, and I've failed them. But *I'm* not embarrassed to ask you for help. Ask him where he gets his hair cut. See how he reacts."

Ned did have a champion, Arden silently thought. Nyomi Chang. And *she* clearly had not failed. "And you're definitely going out of town?"

"They're my only friends now," Cordelia said. "Besides you. I'll let you know when I'm back."

"I'll try, but—" Arden felt Cordelia's grip tighten.

"Arden. There's no one but you, now. No one but you."

19

There was nowhere in Boston colder than the waterfront—the late afternoon wind knifed through Arden's coat and wormed its way through the smallest gaps in her knit cap and muffler, and her feet would never be the same. But she needed to understand Ned Bannister, and who better to help her than the person Ned would have confided in most. His own lawyer.

And there was Nyomi Chang, hustling toward her on the curved path leading away from the redbrick edifice of the new federal courthouse. The not-quite-skyscrapers of the financial district were silhouetted in the almost-sunset. The wind, now spiking over Boston Harbor, threatened to topple the defense attorney, who was at least a head shorter than Arden.

"Kidding me with this?" Nyomi wore bright green mohair mittens, a flash of contrast to her sleek black coat, black boots, and a black muffler twisted around her neck. "You ever heard of inside? It's like, fifty degrees warmer."

"Very funny." Arden used one hand to clutch her coat closer, and the other to shake Nyomi Chang's emerald mitten. "You have a hard day in court?"

"It's always a hard day for a defense attorney." Nyomi tucked her arm through Arden's, pulled her toward the building. "What's up? Can we at least go inside? Late cases are still on."

"Happy to, if you're not afraid to be seen with me," Arden told her as they walked. "That's why I didn't ask to come to your office. Give us deniability."

"Do we need deniability?" Nyomi asked. "Yow. Look at those crazy people."

They paused, watching a two-masted sailboat race across the harbor water, three figures in neon yellow slickers hauling lines and leaning against the wind. "Death wish, right?" Nyomi asked. "Can you imagine how cold that water is?"

"Spare me," Arden said. They hurried toward the courthouse. "Of all the Boston things I love, sailing is not one. Anyway. I need five minutes. You're still floating, right? Happy with your Bannister verdict?"

"Always a pleasure to hold the Commonwealth's feet to the fire." Nyomi gave a thumbs-up in one emerald mitten. "Even better to win."

"Well, you're the best." Arden pushed them through the revolving glass doors and into the vestibule, and to the metal bench along one wall. "It's a strange place to be discreet," Arden said, as they sat, "but I guess we'd both have reasons for being here. I just need a tiny bit of information."

"What's all the hush-hush?" Nyomi had burrowed into her fluffy muffler, wrapped her arms around herself. A rackety heater attempted to warm the entryway. "Is everything okay at work?" She leaned closer, whispering. "That's why you wanted privacy? Can I help?"

Arden shook her head. "No, all good." She smiled through the lie. Nyomi didn't know she was leaving. And certainly not why. "It's about Ned Bannister. And I needed to speak to you as soon as I could."

The revolving door whooshed behind Arden, and two men in bulky overcoats, each carrying a newspaper and smelling of cigarettes, bustled past into the darkening afternoon.

"I can't talk about Ned Bannister." Nyomi shifted on the bench. "You know that. Only what was in the papers."

"Agreed." Arden nodded. "Do you like him?"

Nyomi's eyes narrowed, and Arden knew she was calculating. She was a terror in the courtroom. Now that legal mind was going full speed.

"Huh. Okay, Arden. Without breaching any confidentiality, Ned Bannister was acquitted, fair and square, by a jury of twelve brilliant people. End of story."

"I know. But Nyomi? Did Ned Bannister know Randall Tennant? Did his wife?"

"There was nothing in evidence about that."

"Come *on*. It's me. The vault. Do *you* know if there was a connection?"

"Look. Arden." Nyomi seemed to flip an emotional switch. "We've been pals ever since the O'Riorden case, and I'm grateful for the help you gave our firm in that. If we ever need crisis management skills again, you'll be the first we hire. But—for Ned Bannister, there's no crisis. He's a free man. And just talking generally, you think that if there were a case where someone was killed and the person accused of doing it, or even connected with them, may have known the victim . . ." She raised an eyebrow, as if Arden was a slow learner. "Don't you think the DA would have pounced? Looked for a murder charge?"

"But if you kill a person you know, and if it truly *is* an accident, that wouldn't make it murder."

"Exactly. Murder is about intent, Arden. And it doesn't have to be an elaborate conspiratorial enterprise, or require complicated or specific planning. Intent can be split second. The moment you decide, there's no more accident."

"Okay. So—and I'm just thinking out loud here."

Nyomi nodded.

"If Randall Tennant had *not* been *randomly* skateboarding—"

"Trespassing. Okay."

"In a *random* deserted office parking garage—"

"Which was not a public way."

"On what happened to be New Year's Eve, then he'd have been there on *purpose*. Maybe. . . ." Arden paused.

Nyomi's phone buzzed. She looked at the screen. "Hmm," she said. "Got to take this." She moved her muffler to clamp the phone to her ear. "This is Nyomi Chang."

Arden was glad for the interruption. Glad to stop her snowballing conjecture. She was *fired*. She'd hand the complicated Cordelia Bannister and her complicated marriage back to Warren, or Luz, or another person in the firm, it didn't matter. She'd write a novel. Take French. Work on her beloved kickboxing, which she'd been ignoring. Forget about telling people how to think and what to feel and who to believe.

"No. It's important," Nyomi, low-voiced, was saying into her cell. "I've now confirmed it in the records. I'll show you."

But what if there was more to the Bannister case? Arden couldn't help but think about that. What if Cordelia Bannister's intuition—or those texts—were correct? What had Nyomi told Ned on the phone last night, the thing Cordelia said made him upset?

Shut up, *Arden,* she told herself. *Turn off your imagination.*

"Sorry, Arden." Nyomi put her phone in her coat pocket. "A client. You were saying, 'maybe'? 'Maybe' what? It's really cold, Arden. Good thing I like you."

"Would you have to tell the prosecution something incriminating that *you* knew, but didn't want *them* to know?"

"What're you getting at? The trial's over."

Arden put up her palms, acquiescing.

"Now. My turn to ask a question." Nyomi leaned closer, whispering. "Who's hired you?"

It took Arden a minute, maybe two; first to elicit a promise of confidentiality, and then to bullet-point what she'd heard from Cordelia.

She watched Nyomi's eyes get wider and wider, as Arden continued her recitation. Not about the texts, she'd keep those to herself for now, but of Cordelia Bannister's raw emotion, her feeling that Ned was not taking responsibility, the hurtful snubs of her PTO moms, her vulnerable children, and finally the idea that Ned was hiding something. At that, the lawyer burst out laughing, the sound bouncing off the glass walls of the vestibule.

"You're looking for dirt on Ned? From *me*?" She clapped her hands to her face, *Home Alone*. "First of all, that's entirely nuts. He *should* be happy. He's a free and innocent man."

"You're *laughing*?"

"Didn't you? Laugh? I mean—Can you believe it?" Nyomi stood, adjusting her coat and scarf. "First, I'm not gonna tell you one thing about my client. Full stop. But maybe you could make a whole new career of this. 'Make Your Spouse Regret What He Did, Incorporated.' Here's your motto: *No partner too difficult, no transgression too minor.* You could make a mint. Retire, even."

Arden stood, too, evaluating the lawyer's reaction. First, *was* there something to tell about Ned? Nyomi had been cagey about that.

"She's serious, Nyomi. I think she believes Ned's involved with something. And that since you called him after the verdict, and told him something that made him angry—"

"Did he tell her what I said?"

"I have no idea. She didn't say so. But Cordelia thinks the phone call means you are both covering up whatever it is. And putting her and the kids in danger."

"And that's why they call me a criminal lawyer, ha ha?" Nyomi did not look amused. "Because I'm a criminal?"

A blue-uniformed court officer tapped on the other side of the glass door, pointed to Nyomi, pointed to his watch.

Nyomi winced. Pantomimed her understanding. "They're closing."

This was not going well. "Of course, I don't think you're a crim—"

"They call that 'zealous defense,' Arden." Nyomi's expression had darkened. "They call that 'following the rules.' Did I help him quote-quote get away with something? Hell no. I made the prosecution try to prove their case, and they couldn't. That's my job. No matter what happens, that case is closed."

"Of course. But you know me and surprises. That I hate them. Cordelia Bannister is upset, and—"

"She was a situation from day one, that woman. And *that* I can ethically tell you, since *she's* not my client. *Her* life is not my concern. Not now, at least."

"Does she love her husband, do you think?" Arden asked the question, before she even thought about it.

"That's a strange question."

"Which you don't want to answer."

"I have nothing for you, Arden. I'm celebrating my victory."

"Call me if you change your mind."

"You never give up, do you? That's why you're so good. Love you, kiddo. No matter what." Nyomi poked her in the shoulder. She cocked her head toward the lobby, where the lights were clicking off. "Def closing time. And, speaking of strange questions, I have an important meeting to get to now. And I cannot be late. But hey, if things go bad in court someday, maybe I'll hire you for your future occupation. Could you make judges miserable, too?"

20

Hey, Lois." Arden unbuttoned her coat as she walked into the Vision Group reception area. Lois Reibach's desk, a broad semi-circle of pale oak dotted with terra-cotta pots of aloe, blocked the entrance to the main offices. Lois wore state-of-the-art black telephone headphones, and seemed to wince at Arden's greeting.

"What's wrong?" Then Arden realized. Whispered. "Oh, are you on the phone?"

Lois put up a blue-polished fingernail. "Hang on," she mouthed.

Arden pointed to her own chest, questioning. "Are you talking to me?"

She'd wait until Lo was finished. Arden's tote bag still bulged with cellophane-wrapped brownies, Cordelia's insistent gift, and she needed to stash them in the breakroom. If she took them home, she'd eat every one.

"Certainly, no problem," Lois was saying into her headphone mic. "Hold on," she mouthed.

"I'll just go on back." Arden pointed.

Lois stood, her black sweater dress demure but chic. "Wait," she said. "I'll tell Luz you're here."

"No need," Arden said. "I'm heading to the breakroom. I've got some irresistible brownies, which will be gone in two seconds. Want one now before you lose your chance?"

"The breakroom?" Lois seemed to hesitate.

Arden looked at her, defending her decision. "I know, I'll put them in the fridge. I promise they won't get left out overnight."

"I'll take them." Lois came from behind her desk, held out her hands. "I'll put a note saying they're from you. You just go to your office."

"Lo, thanks, but I can handle brownies." Arden headed toward the frosted glass door to the interior office.

At that, Lois darted in front of her and stood, blocking the way. "Arden. You can't go in there. Trust me on this."

"Did something happen?" Arden frowned, calculating. "Who's in there?" *Ned Bannister,* she thought. Cordelia Bannister. Or—both of them. Monelle Churchwood. Randall Tennant's family. Nyomi Chang. Oh. *The Swansons.* She'd worn Joy again, just to flaunt it, and now, in a heartbeat, regretted the possibly imprudent decision. "Tell me."

"No no no." Lois wore an expression Arden had never seen.

"Lois. Tell me."

Lois pulled Arden out of reception and into the carpeted hallway by the elevators. "They're going to kill me," she said. "But—"

"Who? What are you talking about?"

"Oh, I don't mean *kill me* kill me. Figuratively. Look, go back down the elevator. Then come up again. Pretend we didn't see each other."

"What?"

Lois gave a deep sigh.

"Warren arranged a surprise party for you. To celebrate your new life, he says? Everyone stayed for it, waiting for you. They figure you have a whole nother week, so you'd never guess. It's all set up in the breakroom. So now you finally show up, and where are you headed? Straight to the breakroom."

"Well, that's great. Right? I would've been surprised." *Word sure got around,* she thought. Whatever. Done was done. Who cared.

"They would have, too, been surprised. That's the thing. They'd planned to get there first, pop out at you. With funny hats, and all that. Cupcakes. And champagne."

"Champagne? Whose idea was that?"

"Warren. He said to alert him when you came in, but I was on the phone, and . . ."

"You're so kind, Lo. I'll miss you." She hoisted the brownie-filled tote bag onto her shoulder. "Okay. This never happened. We never talked. You say I called to check on something, whatever, and told you I'd be back in five minutes."

"You saved my life," Lois said.

"Hardly." As Lois scurried away, Arden pushed the button for the elevator. Waited in the hallway, juggling emotions. She'd loved this job, and every time she thought about how she'd been discarded, she got even more outraged.

It was as if she'd changed places with her clients. Now she was the one victimized by a flashfire of lies. And the duplicitous venal Warren—the man who she'd once trusted but who'd chosen client over comrade—was audacious enough to initiate a charade of a farewell party, which made it all the more unbearable. He'd actually wear a funny *hat*? She imagined it, to her disgust. Maybe he'd make some sort of phony we'll-miss-you speech? Which would entail flat-out lying to his own employees.

She made a sound, dismissive. Maybe she was lucky to leave. Maybe this was the best thing that ever happened to her. Somehow.

How many people had she helped over the years? She stabbed the elevator button again. How many calls in the middle of the night after a career-ending tweet, how many frantic texts from clients who had been "misquoted," how many tantrums from entitled celebrities incensed when magazines used an unflattering photo? Families protected from reporters pounding at their doors and calling at ridiculous hours.

Public opinion was a beast to be controlled.

But that was one of the things that bothered her most. Arden had never seen the approach of her own demise. The swift sword of a jealous wife, as ridiculously clichéd as any story could be, but here Arden was, having to pretend to be delighted by a surprise party hosted by an emotional traitor who'd sacrificed her for money, and attended by people who had no idea she'd been tarred and feathered with lies. Talk about a surprise. They'd all be surprised if they knew the truth.

The elevator door slid open, and she was relieved to see the empty car. She saw her haggard face reflected in the shiny brushed aluminum walls, and hoped that the sorrow lines etched around her eyes were a distortion of reality. *I hate surprises,* she thought as the doors closed her into the tiny cube, but knew the secret preparations, from everyone but Warren, were a gesture of affection. She'd miss these people, her colleagues, and their work together was often for the good. Was what Cordelia Bannister wanted for the good?

The door opened, redepositing her on the building's first parking level. She imagined, again, that skateboarder in the Bannister garage careening around the corner. The disoriented Ned Bannister squinting, baffled, confused. The squeal of brakes. And then, possibly, for one hideous moment, silence.

When Arden's phone rang, she winced. Jangled back to reality. So unsettled she actually looked to see if a car was coming. "Chill, girl," she muttered.

The phone rang again. She had a few minutes before she could go back upstairs.

Ned.

The third time in the last hour or so. He was either ridiculously persistent, or incredibly demanding. Or he'd realized he needed her.

"Hello, Ned," she said.

"Arden, for god's sake." Ned's voice seemed shaky, or maybe he had a bad connection.

"Excuse me?"

"You need to answer your phone. I've been trying to call you. Listen, you know Nyomi Chang."

"Your lawyer. Yes." *We're work friends,* she didn't say. *We just talked about you, and your wife. And Randall Tennant.* She didn't say that, either.

"It's bad, Arden. The worst. Nyomi's been hit by a car."

21

rden's phone pinged a message. *All clear here Lois.* The party. She had to ignore it for a minute. The garage held the faint scent of gasoline, and oil, and burned rubber. Rows of salt-stained parked cars with empty spaces between, like gapped dirty teeth, lined the concrete walls. In a few minutes, the place would be full of commuters, the five-thirty traffic, headlights popping on and engines revving. *Nyomi Chang.* Who'd engineered Ned Bannister's acquittal in a vehicular homicide. Who she'd just sat with, teasing, and asking questions. Barely an hour ago.

"Ned? Is she okay?" she said into the phone. "Hit by a car? How, when, where?"

Arden heard Ned breathing, but nothing else on his end of the line. Then she heard a rumble, and headlights shone around the corner. Heart pounding, she retreated a step, moving closer to the elevator door, against the concrete wall and out of sight. Out of the way.

"Ned? Tell me. Where did it happen? How is she?"

"I don't know," he said. "They don't know. She's at Mass General. I don't know. No one knows. It's a hit-and-run."

"How'd you find out?" Arden's mind raced, she needed every detail, everything. *Another* car accident?

"She was on her way to see me," Ned was saying. "She was late. She's never late. Then her paralegal called. And told me."

I have an important meeting, Nyomi had told her. *I cannot be late.* And now . . . Arden jabbed the elevator button to go back upstairs, back to her office, back to quiet. Then remembered. Quiet was the last thing that awaited her.

"Where are you, Ned?"

"I'm in my office. Where, in case you were wondering, I have been all day."

Arden *had* been wondering.

"There's no way out of this," Ned was saying. "The reporters are going to be—"

"Hold on," she said.

"But—the other lines are already—"

"I said hold on. Please. One second. Do not answer the phone." Arden texted Lois, saying she'd gotten an important call. *All fine, but can't come up now. Thank you for handling.*

K. The answer came instantly.

Whatever that meant, she thought, but she didn't have time to ask for clarification. She did allow herself, though, a moment to let her heart break, recognizing that decision she'd instantly made, choosing between a client and the colleagues who sincerely cared about her. But they of all people, Luz and the rest of them, especially Warren, would understand. They'd have done the same thing. Warren already had, right? As a result, here she was in another clammy parking garage, a bag of brownies on her shoulder. Talking to a client who might be about to hit a minefield.

"I'm back," she said. Did anything connect Ned to the accident? No matter what, right now Ned Bannister was an innocent man. "Look, reporters will pounce when they hear about this. They'll call you."

"I told you. They're already calling! I see it on the caller ID. They'll show up here, for sure. Crap. And all my staff is gone."

"That's why you have me. Don't answer the phone unless you know who it is. Reporters will soon learn to call my office. Hear me?"

Silence on the other end.

"Now. Is there a back way out?" Arden had to ask.

"Yes," he said. "But only one exit from the parking garage. If they're staking me out . . ."

Arden leaned against the cold concrete of the garage wall, felt the whir of the machinery behind her even through her thick wool coat. Heard the clank of gears as the elevator moved.

"Listen," she said. "Don't drive. Don't try to hide. Go out the back. Just confidently leave. Can you do that?"

"My car, though, that's a good thing. It's in the garage. They'll be able to tell by the gate that I never left the building. Isn't that right? I didn't do this. I *couldn't* have done it."

"Done it?" Arden asked, realizing the leap Ned had made. "What? Why would anyone think you're involved? If they hound you, it's just for comments. It's a terrible ironic coincidence."

"Hey. You of all people know it doesn't matter what really happened. You know everyone thinks I killed Randall Tennant. And now someone else has been killed in a car accident."

"Wait. Is Nyomi *dead*? You said killed."

"I don't know, I don't *know*."

Arden heard the tension in Ned's voice. She imagined him in some fancy leather swivel chair, glass-topped captain-of-industry desk, a row of unused fountain pens on the top, and a bottle of bourbon hidden in a drawer. A wall of Ned photographed with famous people, or maybe of Ned in front of important buildings. And that panoramic view out over the harbor, where they had all watched the fireworks that New Year's Eve.

"The police must be investigating, Ned, calm down. It'll be fine. You were in your office. If Nyomi is still alive she'll be able to tell them exactly—"

Arden stopped herself midsentence, remembered she was talking about Nyomi, a friend, *a woman she'd just talked to,* as if she weren't a real person. An image of Nyomi in a hospital bed, bandaged or hooked up to a machine or IVs, white-coated doctors hovering, filled her mind, and almost brought her to tears. She'd just questioned her, tried to extract information from her, and maybe even lied to her. And now here Arden was, finagling a way to get her client out of the line of media fire. Because Nyomi had been hit by a car.

"That's what I'm hoping for," Ned said. "She'll explain. But what's gonna happen until then? Crap."

"One step at a time. The police haven't called you, correct? Nothing like that?"

"Not yet. But Arden—she was on her way to my office. The reporters will tear me to shreds. I did nothing. *Nothing!* But that hashtag, *#skated,* is still out there. And the bullshit articles are still—you were right at the restaurant. Everywhere I go, people whisper. I am so screwed."

The elevator door swished open beside her, and Arden stepped away, hoping it wasn't anyone from her office. A twentysomething in a mohair hoodie trotted by, brandishing a car door clicker like a magic wand, paying her no attention. Headlights flashed on across the grimy asphalt pavement.

If Ned hadn't done anything, and she had no reason to believe he had, this was the most wretched coincidence that had ever happened. And wasn't it her job to protect him?

Nyomi was a criminal defense attorney. She probably had legions of people who hated her, crime victims maybe, who thought she'd helped bad guys get away. It was simply bad luck for Ned that this happened now.

"Arden, you there?"

"Have you called your wife?"

"She's on a plane," Ned said. "To Palm Beach with her sorority friends. She'll go berserk when she hears this. Explode. Probably leave me. Take the kids. She's already on the edge. This'll push her over."

Now she pictured him alone, hiding in a darkened office. A fugitive of coincidence. She remembered his contemplative and sometimes even reflective tone in Salazar—a dinner that seemed much longer ago than it was. "What time does she land?"

The elevator behind her rattled.

"No idea," he said. "Dee always calls me. I almost don't want to talk to her. But she cannot hear about this from anyone else."

"I know. I'm so sorry." Ned sounded on the verge of panic, and she needed to head that off. Panic would only make it worse—and cause everyone to make unfortunate decisions. "Look. Let's meet. I'm in a . . ." She paused. *Parking garage* seemed cruel. "Not in my office. Or yours. So, ah . . ."

An entire Rolodex of places spun through her mind, but all were wrong. Anywhere public was a huge risk. She herself had proved how recognizable Ned was. Certainly not a hotel. She couldn't go to his office, he couldn't come to hers. And not his house. Some wild-ass reporters might have already heard about this, would be staking it out. Hiding behind a news car's darkened windows, photographer with camera at the ready.

"Come to my house," Arden was deciding even as she said it. "Leave the building, go out the back way. I'll pick you up. Just tell me where."

22

Did you see those news trucks?" Ned yanked the car door open, his words puffing angrily at her. "Outside my building?"

Arden had gotten lucky, hit the red light at Atlantic, and had pulled up alongside the parking lot of the James Hook lobster place. Hook's was always a crush of people in season, but now sat deserted, an empty square of pavement on Atlantic Avenue, its ramshackle cabin topped with a trademark massive lobster. A place for pedestrians to pass quickly, perilously situated in the wind tunnel from Boston Harbor, and a haven for aggressive seagulls scavenging whatever they could find. She'd seen Ned from a block away, pacing, his shoulders hunched, and wearing a black coat and muffler, a dark knit cap pulled over his head. Hands stuffed in his pockets.

Ned threw himself into the passenger seat. Just as the light turned green.

Arden pulled away, and he dragged his seat belt across his chest, yanked off his hat. Scrabbled at his hair. "Assholes," he said. "How did they freaking find me so freaking quickly?"

"Hospitals have leaks, you know that. You're a local celebrity, Ned, and so is Nyomi Chang. Have you heard anything, by the way? How is she?"

"Nothing." Ned put his gloved hand over his eyes, rubbed his forehead. "I told her paralegal to call me, but she hasn't."

"The privacy laws won't let the hospital confirm how she is, or even if she's actually there," Arden said. "I suppose we could go see. She's your lawyer after all. You have a relationship." Arden stopped at the light at Causeway Street, turned toward Beacon Hill.

"Great. This is the way to Mass General."

"It's also the way to my place," Arden said. "Mount Vernon Square."

Ned looked at her, one eyebrow raised. "Nice."

"My grandparents owned it, and willed it to me. It's a bit—surprising inside," she said, though he'd see soon enough. "I think a ballerina lived there once. I rent out the top. It's too big for just me."

"Probably worth a fortune," Ned said.

Arden pulled into the intersection. "Are we talking about real estate now?"

"Sorry." He shrugged. "Can't help it."

"Ned?" She had to ask. "Could there be anything that links you to this?"

"How could there be? But how could there not be? She just got me acquitted of vehicular homicide. Now *she's* hit by a car."

"It's a tough coincidence, that's for sure. But we'll handle it." Arden wished she could pat his arm or something, comfort him, what any human being would do for another worried soul, but talk about inappropriate. An ambulance screamed by them on Cambridge Street, and then another, one of the perils of living on Beacon Hill. If you needed it, though, the proximity of the revered Mass General Hospital would be a benefit.

"Coincidence. Tell me about it." Ned's voice had turned bitter. "I'm trapped by this damn thing. I'm trapped by my face, and by people's, I don't know, voyeuristic interest in me. Like I'm some serial killer. I heard a radio talk show just now that even called me that. Me!"

"So here's the deal." Arden had to stop him from spiraling. She pulled alongside a black Audi parked on the street, then backed into her parking spot.

"Don't tell me you have a parking place."

"Came with the house." She shifted into park. "What can I tell you?"

"Millions," Ned muttered. "This one you?"

She saw him looking out the passenger side window to the redbrick building across the blue-salted sidewalk. "Yeah. You going to Zillow me?"

"Zillow? They get their info from *me*, Arden. Sorry," he said. "Anyway, you were about to tell me?"

She turned off the ignition. "We need to focus. Create a strategy. At some point, people will swarm to their next trending topic, and you'll be forgotten. But for now—"

"If nothing happens," Ned interrupted. "*If.* If Nyomi Chang is alive, and can tell the police what happened. And even then, if—"

"Ned. One step at a time. And the first step is to go inside." Ned was smart, but Arden was more experienced at situations like this. It may well be that Nyomi Chang had no idea what happened, poor thing, and it was disturbing that her lack of specificity might make everything worse. If whatever she might say wasn't a slam dunk to save Ned Bannister. If she was still alive. If she wasn't—Arden decided not to think about that right now.

She pictured the lawyer, vibrant and passionate and powerfully alive, only a few hours ago, wearing those green mittens, pantomiming with the helpful court officer, triumphant about holding the prosecution's feet to the fire, proud of her victory.

Arden got out of the car, signaling Ned to do the same.

"Watch the door doesn't bang into the streetlight," she said.

"They're not real gaslights." Ned had gone closer to it, examining it, the orange glow ruddying his face.

"It's all an illusion," she said. *Just like most things,* she didn't say.

This was a moment to juggle. Cordelia had instructed her to see if there was a connection between her husband and Randall Tennant. To-night's accident, this probably-a-coincidence, might give her a chance to do that. The texts Cordelia got might be harassment. Or might be true. According to Monelle, it wouldn't matter.

Is Ned dangerous? Am I helping a murderer? Arden had asked Cordelia. Cordelia had said no.

She felt his presence behind her, closer now, in the dark November night. Snow had just begun, tentative, hesitant.

"Terrific neighborhood." Ned gestured toward the Beacon Hill, a nar-row winding ribbon of neighborhood created in colonial times, where brownstones had plaques proclaiming their Revolutionary War–era birthdays, and some of the lavender-tinted glass in their leaded windows was original. "A gold mine."

"The Otis family lived around here, and the Copleys and Grays. When I was a little girl we came to visit," she went on, pointing to the townhouse, three stories, nine windows fronting the street, three cobblestone steps to the bright red front door with the old lion's-head knocker. "My father told me stories of Sam Adams and Paul Revere's ride. He—"

"Got elected governor, eventually, right? Pennsylvania?"

"You looked me up?"

"Goes without saying." Ned stuffed his knit cap into his pocket. "No wonder you moved away."

Arden fumbled in her tote bag to cover her thoughts. Touched her phone.

Her phone. She'd never called the office. A guilty vision flashed through her mind, almost a video, of Lois telling Warren that Arden was not coming back tonight. Arden imagined sugary cupcakes waiting in a white cardboard box. Maybe one of her colleagues would take the cupcakes home.

And the party would be over.

Her house key slipped into the lock, and the key turned. "Come in," she said.

23

"Are you getting more calls or texts?" Arden asked as they entered her front hall. Had Cordelia's mysterious message gone to Ned, too? The blue light from the fish illuminated the apartment beyond, as always, and Arden heard the burbling of the tank, constant, reassuring. Fish life goes on. "Social media?"

"Surely you're joking. Incessantly. Look at this tweet." Ned held up his phone, read from the screen. "*Did you kill again, Mr. Big Shot?* it says. Then it has *#skated*." He hit a button. "Blocked him. Jerk. But there's nothing from Nyomi's paralegal. She has my cell. And I've told my office to hold all my business calls until further notice. It's the weekend, anyway."

Ned was unbuttoning his coat, and she gestured to the curved cast iron coat rack against the hallway mirror. "What's the blue light?" Ned draped his coat over the only empty hook. A plaid muffler and a red knit cap took up the other spots, a furled umbrella dangling at the ready.

"Fish. Could you call her? The paralegal?"

"The kids are always asking for fish." Ned pointed toward the blue. "When I was a kid, mine would always die, and my mother would flush them. I'd have won them at the county fair."

"What county?" Arden hung her coat next to Ned's, covering his muffler.

"Bennington," Ned said.

"Vermont. Nice." Arden started toward the living room. Imagined little Ned skiing the White Mountains, or hiking the national forest, winning fish at a ping-pong ball toss. How'd he wind up in Boston real estate?

"Follow me," she said. Arden kept envisioning Nyomi Chang in the hospital, her tiny body swathed in white up to her chin, bandaged, and fragile. And oblivious.

"Tea?" Arden went on. Seemed like alcohol was not a prudent thing to offer. But maybe she was overthinking. "Or . . . beer?" Arden inventoried her kitchen. *Or the brownies from your wife and your sexy college-student cook that're in my bag,* she didn't say. "I have chips, I think. Maybe salsa."

Ned had stopped at the entryway to the living room. Stared at his phone.

"What?" she asked. "Who? *Nyomi?*" She waited, hand clapped to her instantly revving heart, but he shook his head.

"The kids," he said. "Shit. I forgot. I forgot I'm supposed to FaceTime them. I set a reminder, since my life is always chaos. I hate to miss it tonight."

"Call them," Arden said. "Take the couch, I'll be right back. Unless you need privacy?"

"I can show them your fish. I'll say I'm at a friend's house. That's true enough. I'll show them the sunflowers, too."

Arden held back a smile, wondering how Ned would react if he knew the provenance of the sunflowers. *True enough,* he'd said. As if there were levels of truth. "Thanks. I'll go up to my office, and text me when you're done?"

"It's just the kids." He lifted his phone as if they were inside it. "I don't mind if you hear, but I hope you're interested in Minecraft. Pip hardly knows where he is half the time, he lives in Minecraft world. And Emma loves whatever Pip loves."

Arden felt a buzz in her blazer pocket. A text. She closed her eyes, wondering about priorities. Security? Justice? Truth? Loyalty—that was a tough call. But this visit was her job. For now.

Ned was scrolling through his phone. "I should check the office voice mail—"

"No. Ned. Listen. It's almost eight P.M., you're done for the day. You are not available twenty-four seven. I am, though, if you want me to be."

Ned gave her a look, not quite a smile, not quite over the line. *Did he hit on you?* Cordelia had asked. She'd been suspicious of that cook, too. Maybe Cordelia's distrust of Ned was justified. Or maybe Cordelia was paranoid.

She did not return his smile. "You'll let me know if they call, right? Have you heard from your wife? You should tell her about this, not any-one else."

"Right," Ned said. "I'll text her to call me. She might not love that I'm here, though. Alone with you."

"Why not? Isn't that my job?"

"Cordelia's a little touchy about women. She has this idea that . . . Whatever. Just so you know." Ned gestured with his phone, sat on one end of the couch, fish tank nearby. He leaned back, crossed his legs. "Let me talk to the kids, then we can discuss it. And in answer to your question, a beer is great. Thanks."

"Sure." So she was right about Cordelia's jealousy. Suspicious wives. To be avoided at all costs. She deposited her bag on the dining room table and headed for the kitchen. As she opened the fridge door, she remembered the text she'd gotten a minute ago. Took her cell from her jacket pocket.

Cordelia.

Here, the message said. *What's latest?*

Arden stared at the words, one hand still on the fridge door handle, the cold air hitting her. Why would Cordelia contact her, but not Ned? She heard Ned's voice, a murmur from the living room, then laughter. Luckily she'd taken the card out of the sunflowers, not that it was signed.

Another message pinged. Luz.

Her words popped up. *What the hell?*

Sorry. Arden closed the fridge door with one foot as she typed back. *I know you wanted to*

But Luz was still typing. Arden watched the moving dots, realizing she'd almost given away that she knew about the surprise. Luz's dots vanished.

Nyomi Chang critical? Luz's words appeared. *Hit and run ax? You know this?*

Arden deleted her unsent message. Typed as fast as she could. *Yes but did not know critical. Any info?*

No, but on it

LMK

OK

Cordelia's message remained, the one line of white letters in a blue bubble. She would not know whether Arden had read it. Arden did not need to reply, nor did she need to tell Ned. But she couldn't unknow that Cordelia had contacted her before her own husband.

Arden found a beer on the lowest shelf, then another behind a container of yogurt. No salsa. Found her chunky-handled beer mugs, and then some blue corn chips, and bit the edge of the bag to open it. Ned was blustery, and privileged, but did not seem threatening, she thought, dumping chips into an earthenware bowl. Still, Cordelia and Ned—after how many years of marriage?—had a history. Arden had known him for one day.

More laughter from the living room. She tucked the beers under her arm, slipped one hand through both handles of the beer mugs, grabbed the bowl with the other hand, and headed toward her guest.

Her guest. Who had been acquitted of killing a stranger with his car. But his wife was receiving messages saying they were *not* strangers. Now Ned's own defense attorney had been a victim of exactly the same kind of accident. *No,* she corrected herself. She had no idea if it was exactly the same.

Ned was aiming his phone at the fish tank, and Arden could hear two young-sounding voices, laughing and calling out to the fish.

"I don't know what their names are," Ned was saying. "What would you name them?" He looked up as Arden entered the room, pointed to the fish, gave her a thumbs-up.

Arden set everything on the coffee table, sliding wicker coasters under the cool damp beer bottles. Ned, discussing fish names with his two children, did not seem like a criminal mastermind. But his car had hit Randall Tennant. And killed him. And if they knew each other . . .

"Love you too, kiddos," Ned was saying. "But no promises about fish." He held up one finger to Arden, *almost done.* "And we'll talk tomorrow, same bat channel. Give your grandmother a big hug from me, and you each get two hugs. Each."

They know each other from the barbershop. That's what the text had meant. But how was she supposed to casually work that into a conversation? What if it was a wacky conspiracy theory type? Or some justice-seeking #skated zealot? Plus, the police were certainly working on Nyomi's case right now. They'd have answers soon.

"Love you more," Ned was saying. "Sleep tight."

Arden's phone pinged again, and she hoped it was Luz. With news of Nyomi. Good news. *Please be okay,* she sent her prayers skyward, and toward Mass General.

24

nswer your door, the text message said. No name, an unfamiliar phone number. So, someone Arden hadn't texted with before. Ned, still on the couch, poured his beer into one of the mugs.

Who's this, Arden typed back.

Then the unmistakable sound of the lions-head door knocker.

Ned stood as she looked at her phone screen. "Are you expecting—"

"Of course not." She showed Ned her phone. "No name, but they know my cell number. And they're saying to answer the door."

You need to tell me who this is, she typed.

Monelle Churchwood, the message came back. *Didn't want to surprise you if you're not presentable.*

Arden held up the phone, watched Ned's face change as he read it. She put one finger to her lips, then pointed to his beer, and the glass, then the chips, then to the spiral staircase to the second floor. Gestured up. "My office." She mouthed the words. Then repeated, whispering, "My office. Top of the stairs. *Go.* Sit. Don't walk around up there, it's creaky," she managed to say as Ned, food and drink in arms, hurried toward the staircase.

"Coat!" she remembered, pointed, and then grabbed it, laying it over his shoulder. "Stay quiet," she whispered.

"Got this," he said, and headed up the stairs.

Arden had taken off her boots when she came in, but now she took her hair out of its twist, and mussed it a bit. Unbuttoned a button on her blouse, newly home and getting comfy. Carried her beer to the door. Just another solitary Friday night. That at least, would be believable. Not that Monelle knew about her life.

"This is a surprise," she said, opening the front door. The cold blasted in, the dark of the night, a few wisps of clouds over a crescent moon.

Monelle was backlit by the orange streetlamps, wrapped in her coat and wearing that cap pulled low over her braids. White flakes sparkled in the lights behind her, as if she were in the middle of a snow globe. But there was nothing pretty about the expression on her face.

"I know this is an intrusion." Monelle stomped her feet, as if to remind Arden it was snowing. "I won't take up much of your time. I hope."

Arden envisioned Ned upstairs, sitting at her desk in her office, maybe, maybe snooping into the ballet room, or even her bedroom. But she'd ordered him not to walk around. The two-hundred-year-old floors complained at the slightest step. His presence felt heavy above her, a deception, but she had no choice here. If Monelle was looking for Ned—why? She didn't like surprises.

"What's this about?"

"It's like, a blizzard out here, Arden," Monelle said.

"Sorry, sorry, of course. Come in." Arden decided to risk it. There'd be no reason for Monelle to suspect Arden was hiding anything. Or anyone. "I got home a bit ago, and I'm just, feeding the fish. Getting ready to turn in after a long ridiculous day. But sure. Come in."

Ned would be equally interested to know why Monelle was here. And no reason for the assistant district attorney to know the man she'd failed to send to prison was hiding ten feet above her. Hidden by Arden herself. Was she protecting Ned because she was being paid? Too late now. And he was innocent until proven guilty.

Monelle closed the door behind her, wiped her boots on the woven mat, then seemed to notice the beer bottle in Arden's hand.

"I'm sorry again," Arden said. "I'm out of beer."

"Not gonna stay long enough for that, thanks, got to hurry home."

"Your kids," Arden remembered.

"Exactly. They keep needing dinner, every day, who knew. And I have wet feet, probably, so I'll stay here in the hall."

Good, Arden thought. She watched Monelle's expression darken.

"Are you aware that Nyomi Chang is in the hospital?"

Was she supposed to know this? Arden tried to calculate. How would she have known this?

"What happened?"

Monelle tapped one finger, tonight gloved in magenta leather, to her lips.

"Arden Ward. You brought me to that parking garage. We discussed what must've happened that night. And you know how pissed off I am that the drunken liar that is Ned Bannister is now walking the streets, driving, a free man. And now when I bring what clearly is *not* news about his own defense attorney being injured in a hit-and-run tonight, you act like you're baffled. Nyomi was on her way to see Ned. We know that. She never got there."

"Yes, I heard." Arden decided to own it, since it proved nothing. "And it's so awful. How is she?" Arden desperately wanted to take a sip of beer, but that seemed inappropriate. "Do you have any leads?"

"Leads? *Leads?* Arden? *You're* the lead. *You* work for the Bannisters. And we retraced Ms. Chang's steps today. Turns out *you* were seen in the courthouse this afternoon, just before closing, talking to her."

"I—"

"Don't even try to deny it. In fact, given the timeline, it's likely you were the last person to speak with her. Why were you together? What did you tell her? What did you ask her? What did she tell you? Did she give you any indication that she was afraid of Ned Bannister?"

"You don't think *I*—do you think *he* hit her?" She'd face it, show no fear. See what she could find out.

"Why would you think that?" Monelle emanated a chill, not only from the cold air she'd brought inside, but from her glacial expression. "Why would you even ask that?"

"Come on, get real." This was happening pretty fast. Unless, somehow, the cops had him dead to rights. The man upstairs. "Am I a suspect? Is he a suspect? Do you have any actual evidence that you think points to . . . either of us?"

"Your office alibied you, Arden. Don't look so shocked. It's what we do. But Mr. Bannister? That's another story. Which I cannot discuss."

"Got to ask you, Monelle, why would Ned Bannister mow down his own defense attorney? The one, forgive me, the one who got him acquitted?"

"Mow down?"

"Whatever happened."

"Arden. Do you know exactly where Ned Bannister is? We'd like to talk with him."

"No, I don't know. Exactly where he is." *True enough,* she thought. "You know, come on in. Your feet are fine." She gestured inside, trying to change the tone of the conversation. Again, risky, but possibly a way to get the prosecutor to open up. Ned would understand. Even approve. And

Cordelia had *hired* her to find the truth. She could only do her job if she knew the facts. Now she had a chance to get them.

"Briefly," Monelle said. "I'll leave my coat on. I have just one more question."

25

Monelle pulled off her gloves, stuffed them into her coat pocket. "Arden? You asked me at the garage whether it would matter if Ned Bannister knew Randall Tennant."

Deep trouble. Deep deep trouble. Arden could hear her father's voice, the words he'd intone whenever teenage Arden had transgressed. She remembered a few times, coming home late, or smelling of weed. Her father always knew, always. Now, as they walked toward the couch, Arden checked to see if Ned had left an indentation in the navy leather.

"I was only wondering," Arden said. "And you said it wouldn't. Matter."

"And now *I'm* 'only wondering' . . . did Nyomi Chang know that the two of them were connected? Did she tell you? Or did you 'wonder' to her? It's important."

Monelle sat in the exact same spot where Ned had been not ten minutes before. Crossed her legs, black slacks showing in the opening of her cashmere-looking coat. Looked at Arden expectantly, chin up. Arden sat as far away from Monelle as politely acceptable.

She was curious, she had to admit, whether Nyomi *had* known that. Cordelia said Ned had been "upset" by a phone call from his lawyer. Maybe that's what Nyomi had asked him about. Maybe she'd gotten a text, too.

Arden risked a sip of her beer. Then with one quick move, stacked Ned's wicker coaster on top of hers, hoping Monelle hadn't noticed there were two on the table.

"Arden? Are you trying to come up with a story?"

"No, just thinking about Nyomi. And who could have . . ." She took a deep breath, deciding "who" wasn't the best choice of words. "I mean *what* could possibly have happened."

"That's not for you to investigate, is it? Your responsibility is to tell me who else is aware that Bannister might not be a stranger to Randall Tennant."

"Um. . . ." Arden's brain was not working fast enough.

"'Um.' Interesting response. Look. The accident reconstruction team is now at the corner of Boylston and Mass Ave. Where Nyomi Chang was hit on her way to Bannister's office. Right after meeting with *you*. I don't believe in coincidences."

Arden knew Ned, upstairs, could not hear their conversation—as a curious kid, she had often tucked into a wallpapered curve at the top of the stairs, trying to eavesdrop on the grown-ups' discussions in this very living room. She had never succeeded.

"Arden, who did you tell about a possible Tennant-Bannister connection? Ned? Cordelia?"

"What're you thinking? I mean—are they in danger?"

"Danger? Of course, danger. I thought the Bannister case was over, miscarriage of justice that it was. But now—" Monelle sighed. "If someone is angry about the verdict, about Bannister's freedom—what would be destructive to Ned Bannister? To kill him in retribution? Or his wife? Or his children? Or . . . his lawyer?" She nodded, seeming to agree with herself. "Or—even his PR mouthpiece?"

This was Arden's last moment to decide what to do. She had planned on checking the barbershop connection on her own. But she was not equipped to do that. Or authorized. Monelle was. And if it turned out to be pivotal, and it turned out that Arden had kept this information a secret . . .

Monelle was looking at her, waiting her out.

"Can I trust you?" Arden asked.

"I'm an officer of the court."

"That's not an answer."

Monelle gathered her muffler. "Arden, here's *why* to trust me. I can make your life miserable."

Arden felt her shoulders sag in defeat. There was no virtue in hiding this. And "danger" was not a word she wanted to hear. Or "miserable." Her life was miserable enough.

"Fine. I know that. Yes," she said. "Cordelia got an anonymous text about Randall Tennant and Ned. And then another one. But I *didn't* tell that to Nyomi. I didn't."

"I see. Good." Monelle yanked at her coat belt. "Now. Between you and me. If you're not still hiding something, what did the texts say?"

"That they knew each other. That they got their hair cut at the same place." Arden blurted out the words. "I don't know where that is. I honestly don't. Cordelia said I should ask Ned. And I haven't done that. And as for Nyomi—I did *not* tell her that. Did not."

"Haircuts." Monelle nodded, and sat, silent, for a beat or two. Bella ducked under the ceramic-ivy-covered arch, and appeared on the other side, feathery fins undulating in the clear water.

"Cordelia Bannister," Monelle finally said. "I watched her in court, with that attitude, and the jewelry. She looked at me, every day, as if *I* were the problem. Does she still have the texts?"

"I don't know."

Monelle paused, then looked at her Fitbit. "Got to go," she said. "Unless you have more to tell me? Nyomi is my priority. But you're number two."

"Me?"

"You. And your client Ned Bannister. And the impossibility of coincidence. If you're hooked up with him—"

"Hooked up?" Arden interrupted. Frowned, defensive. There was no sex involved in her professional life, never had been, and yet Monelle glibly assumed it was possible. Warren, too, for that matter, but he was a man. "What d'you mean by that?" She narrowed her eyes. "What if I asked *you* that?"

"Hey. *Professionally.* Whatever you people do. Look." She paused. "There's more to this. You know that. Be careful, Arden. I've had enough surprises."

A creaking above them—one instant there, the next, gone. Both of them had looked up at the sound.

"Did you hear that?" Monelle stood, cocked an ear. "Upstairs?"

"What?" Arden said. *Damn it, Ned,* she thought.

The hum and burble from the fish tank underscored the silence as Arden tried to decide what to say. She could lie, or she could tell the truth, and either one was equally dangerous.

26

I told her it was the heater," Arden said, "these old buildings, blah blah. She bought it. I think. And she had to go, so maybe that's why she didn't pursue it. But she's looking for you, Ned. And I don't like lying."

He'd taken his shoes off, and held them under his arm as he walked down the spiral staircase in his stocking feet. The gold toes of his socks reminded Arden of her father.

"Lying? Isn't that what you do for a living?" Ned had peeled the label from his beer, she saw as he held it out to her, and had poked the shiny shredded paper into the empty brown bottle.

"Hey. You want my help or not?" She didn't take the bottle, annoyed enough after her testy encounter with Monelle. Let him take care of his own trash.

"Wouldn't it be more important for you to tell me what Monelle Churchwood said?" His shirt had come untucked, and he'd loosened his tie. "Why she was here? And thinking about it, I would have been perfectly happy to stay down and talk to her."

"Would you?" Arden took the bottle, a reluctant hostess with a difficult guest. "And what, you would have been 'perfectly happy' to answer her questions about where you were tonight, and why Nyomi Chang was on her way to your office when she was so brutally interrupted, and how you would have known the route she would take?"

They stood eye to eye in Arden's dining room, a standoff, her purse full of brownies still on the oval table. Awkward, with Ned's dishabille and her own mussed hair and slouching blouse. She'd asked Ned to come over so they could strategize about his potential pursuit by reporters—and worst case, the police. But so far, because of Monelle's arrival and Ned's FaceTime with his children, they'd gotten nowhere. And she could not tell Ned about her meeting this afternoon with Nyomi. He'd ask why, and what would she say?

"Should we sit down again?" Ned asked. "But first, I need the bathroom. Flushing would have been a problem."

"True. But if you can wait a sec, have you heard from Nyomi Chang's paralegal?"

"Nope. Here's my phone," Ned said, pulling it from his pocket. "I have nothing to hide from you. All you'll see is nonstop texts from reporters, who apparently will never give up." He tapped the screen as he talked. "Scroll through my messages. Feel free to handle them. Or delete 'em if you want."

"Really?"

"Sure." Ned shrugged, and turned away.

Well that was a first, Arden thought. And pretty confident, to hand over his phone like that. He had it opened to the text message screen, a series of grayed-out circles with generic white silhouettes. She recognized some names instantly, reporters, and call letters of four TV stations, a radio station, and two newspapers. And Cordelia, she saw. But no, that was yesterday.

"Any questions?" Ned had stopped halfway up the stairs, looked back at her over the wrought iron railing.

"Go," she said. "Let me think."

"If you want to look at my pictures, that's fine too," he said, as he headed up. "Why don't you do that, in fact. Get to know me better." And then he disappeared from sight.

It touched her, the innocence of that gesture, the openness. The vulnerability. Sometimes it seemed like the river of time was racing ahead, swirling her up in events and responsibilities, with her a lifeguard, helping people swim against the current of public opinion, rescuing them. Some people hated her, she knew that: the public was cynical of public relations—*flack catchers and spinners*, they thought they all were. *Lying? Isn't that what you do for a living?* Ned had asked.

She poised her finger over the multicolored logo for Ned's photos, wondering if she should intrude into his world.

If someone opened her photos, what would they see? Receipts, certainly. A few random shots of the snow, sparkling in her neighborhood streetlights, taken when she'd tried to slow down and be present in the world instead of in her head. And she'd taken a photo of her office at the Vision Group before she started to disassemble it. She had no trophy shots, no photos with name brand clients, that's not what she cared about. In her album labeled *Favorites* she kept pictures of her parents, one of her dad and mom on the white marble steps of the statehouse, smiling and looking triumphant. She had it framed on her nightstand, too. Sometimes, seeing photos of her mother, Arden saw her own face.

There'd also be the photos at Salazar, proving the feral bandwagon was hot on Ned's trail. And of course, the shots of the Bannister Building parking garage. The crime scene.

Arden heard the toilet flush, and quickly opened Ned's photos. *My Albums,* the screen said. *Recents. Properties. Kids.* The photo marking the "kids" album showed two grinning children—that ridiculous kid-grin when an adult demands that you smile—standing in front of a door; an awkward-looking boy with Cordelia's face, a shock of dark hair, hands shoved into khaki pants pockets. And beside him, a full head shorter, a curly haired little girl, like a baby Cordelia, also in khaki pants and polo shirt, holding the paw of a scraggly . . . she fingered open the photo. Tiger.

"See anything you like?" Ned was saying. He came up beside her. "Oh, that's Pip and Emma. At my mother's in Vermont. And Roo."

"Roo is a tiger? Isn't it—Tigger?" She couldn't believe they were having this conversation. She handed the phone back. She should have looked at more pictures. Too late now.

"What can I say. It's her Roo. Could I ask you for another beer? And look, I'm, uh, starving. Can we get some kind of food while we figure out what to do? We could order in."

Did he hit on you? Arden was haunted by Cordelia's question.

"Cordelia hasn't called?"

"She did, in fact. When Churchwood was here. I'd put the phone on silent. And I jammed one of your love seat cushions over my head to muffle the sound while we talked. For all of ten seconds."

"And?"

Ned pointed to the couch, toward the aquarium, toward Arden's beer bottle she had left on the two stacked coasters. "I told her about Nyomi. She's horrified, end of call. Can we order? DoorDash it? Then talk more? Plus, I left the chips and my mug upstairs, I'll go get them."

She had to eat, she thought, and so did Ned. She thought of poor Nyomi, in that bleak hospital bed and Monelle in the heat of investigation. Getting food would not make any difference. Maybe it would help.

"Sure."

"Sushi?"

"No eel," she said. "Otherwise great. But Cordelia is safely in Palm Beach?"

"So she says."

Arden had headed toward the kitchen, and now turned back. "What's that supposed to mean?"

She saw Ned take a deep breath, look at the ceiling. Then back at her. "Nothing is supposed to mean anything. Look, Arden, I don't mean to joust with you. I'm on edge, I'm cranky, I'm worried. And I'm hungry. Cordelia—she's been through a lot. I don't mean to sound suspicious. Or critical. I should be happy, I'm a free man, but gotta say, as of tonight, I don't feel free. Not anymore."

"I understand," Arden said.

"What the hell happened? First, Monelle. And if the cops come after me—"

"Yeah." Arden nodded, the specter of Nyomi between them. And Tennant. And Cordelia. "Why was Nyomi coming to your office, anyway?"

"I'll tell you everything. Let me order first."

Moments later, Arden brought in another beer for Ned and a glass of red wine for herself. Whatever they decided, she reassured herself, he wasn't going to drive.

"I probably got too much," he said, putting his phone on her stack of to-be-read New Yorkers. "Never order food while you're hungry."

"When else would you order it?" Arden couldn't help asking.

Ned's eyes crinkled with amusement. "Fifteen minutes," he said. "So they say."

"So, let's see how many questions you can answer before they arrive. First. Why was Nyomi on her way to you?"

"I don't know exactly why. Something about records." Ned unstacked the coasters, put his beer on one of them, and slid the other toward her. "That's what haunts me. I can't think it was something good, or she would've told me on the phone."

"Maybe." Arden remembered that from the courthouse, Nyomi talking about records. So Ned had been the 'client' who'd called. Nyomi had kept quite the poker face. "And forgive me, but confirming—you never left your office."

Ned nodded, his fingers to his lips, his wedding ring illuminated by the blue light of the fish tank. "Never."

"Okay," Arden said. "I'm thinking about your reporter calls. It's often better to take the hit—just let them say 'Ned Bannister did not return our phone calls or emails.' If you go on camera, even be recorded, they'll describe you, characterize you, choose loaded adjectives like 'beleaguered' or 'controversial' or 'newly acquitted.' Stay out of it." Arden took a sip of wine. "As long as you can."

"Why would I be *in* it?" Ned started peeling his beer bottle label again, pulling the paper from the glass.

"Because Nyomi's paralegal, Heather Bellwin, knows she was on her way to you. And if a cop or reporter asks, and she tells the truth, *that's* when you're in it."

"Shit." Ned brushed his hair from his forehead. Then covered his eyes with both hands. "How the hell did this happen? It was New Year's Eve. A celebration."

"That's over, Ned."

"Is it?"

"Yes. Legally, it is." Arden nodded. That she knew. "Emotionally of course, publicly, it's still raw. Like I showed you in Salazar. But what happened today—this is different. And it's still early in the investigation. So I can prepare, tell me about you and Nyomi Chang. Would she walk to your office?"

"Good question. I don't know."

If Nyomi were walking, Arden couldn't help theorizing, it might mean she knew she wouldn't need a car later. Because someone else would be driving her. Someone like Ned. Whose wife had just gone out of town. Nyomi had *not* told Arden she was going to meet Ned. Why?

"You two—was there anything in your relationship I should know? Anything personal? I know she's not married. But you are. And you were together through an intense drama. Life-and-death stakes. Your future was in her hands."

"Is everything sex? Is that how you see the world? You're just like Dee." Ned sat up straight, placed his beer on the table with more force than it needed. "I can't have a business relationship? Christ, aren't I allowed to hire a female lawyer without it being fraught?" He tilted his head, as if disappointed. "I would've thought otherwise of you, Arden. Plus, and I don't even know why I'm telling you this, but if we were—how do I say it politely—screwing, would she have told her paralegal Heather where she was going?"

"Sorry. Yeah. I'm sorry." She put up a palm, honestly contrite. Moments ago, she had mentally criticized Monelle for thinking the same way about her, now she was equally guilty. "I didn't mean to—never mind. Yeah. My bad. Truce?"

Ned's muted phone signaled a message, the vibrations moving it across the glass coffee table. "Probably the sushi," Ned said. "And hey. You're not just like Dee."

Then Arden's phone pinged, too. Arden saw Ned tap his screen, and she did the same thing on hers.

Arden's message was from Luz.

Nyomi awake. Briefly. Not now. She talked.

Three dots bounced on the screen. Luz was still typing. Arden waited. There was no way to make the words appear any faster.

"What the—?" Ned began.

Arden looked at him, saw the expression on his face. His eyes glued to his own screen. *Not the sushi,* she thought. "What?"

"Heather Bellwin," he said, not looking at her. "She says Nyomi's awake. Or, she was."

"So she's recovering? Talking?" Luz had messaged the same thing, *awake.* Which had to be better than not awake.

The dots on Luz's end repeated, taunting her.

Arden saw Ned's chest rise and fall, saw him staring into the middle distance, into nowhere, or maybe into Nyomi Chang's hospital room.

"She said one word." Ned's voice was leaden.

"What? What word?" She looked down at her own cell phone screen. No more dots. Luz had typed the answer.

She said Ned.

27

Because she was on the way to see me. Because she expected to be in my office." Ned stood, and paced toward the dining room, then pivoted, pacing back to her, eating up the jewel-toned carpet in long strides. Talking almost to himself. "A million reasons she might have said my name."

"Ned—" Arden began, but he was pacing again. Some of those excuses—reasons—had crossed her mind, too, in addition to a few others. Others that were not so benign. "She might have also thought you were in danger. Wanted to warn you."

"Maybe she was worrying about me. Maybe she wanted me to come see her." He shook his head. "But those people won't care. They've been out to get me from the moment of that verdict. They'll think she was accusing me."

He was right, Arden didn't say. Monelle was already on Ned's tail. She might have even known what Nyomi said. And she'd kept that from her, even as she'd told Arden to trust her.

"It's not enough," Arden tried to reassure Ned, no reason for him to panic. Even though he was right about Monelle. And reporters wouldn't care what was true, they just wanted a story. They'd "fix mistakes in the follow-up," how many times had she heard that? "If they don't have more evidence than that," she went on, "it's the delirious ranting of an injured and medicated person. Maybe she said 'bed.' Or 'head,' maybe her head hurts."

Ned stopped, pursed his lips, nodded. "True."

"Her paralegal told you?"

"Yeah, Heather Bellwin. She knows everything Nyomi does."

"But was Heather there? Or who told *her* that?"

"I have no idea." Ned scratched at his ear, almost viciously. "I'll text her back. But do I go to the hospital? What if she's asking for me? I should go."

"Sure. If you want to take your life in your hands," Arden said. "I would advise against that. Monelle was on the way there. So I say we sit tight."

Ned pointed to Arden's phone. "Speaking of which. Hey, who told *you*?"

"My assistant, Luz Ocasio. She's got a whole network of resources, probably heard from them. And her fiancé is a doctor at MGH." She let out a deep breath. "We're about to get even more deluged, Ned. As soon as any reporter hears what Nyomi said. They'll want reaction from you, pretending to be solicitous. But they won't stop, and they'll push like hell. Insinuate. And things may get worse for a bit. But they'll never track you here. Let's just see. Which reminds me. Cordelia."

"Happily blissfully, and, apparently, drunkenly in Palm Beach, from the sound of her voice," Ned said. "I'm glad she's away from this." Ned's gesture seemed to include everything in the world. "She's been through enough."

"Did she know about this? Before you told her?"

"She didn't. I hated to do it. Ruin her day as much as mine is ruined."

"You know, Ned . . ." Arden looked at the fish tank, trying to retrieve a thought, as if an elusive answer were hidden amidst the fish and ferns. "I was thinking of something like—why doesn't what happened to Nyomi, whatever it was, mean you're *less* guilty? *Less* a suspect? Why would you hit-and-run your own defense attorney?"

"I wouldn't. Someone must hate me. Or Nyomi. Or both of us."

"A person who doesn't like what she did. In your trial. Or a different trial, more likely. I keep thinking—"

The doorbell rang, *bing-bong,* and she saw the raw fear on Ned's face "It's the sushi," she said.

Ned half laughed. "Oh, right."

He pulled out his wallet as he sat back down on the couch, selected a black credit card, and offered it to her. "Thank god."

She shook her head, waved it off. "Nope. I'll get it. No eel, right? My credit card's in my bag. No need to have your purchase linked to my address."

"Oh, good call," he said. "And you can bill me for it."

"What I'm thinking is," Arden went on as she walked toward the dining room, "let's change tactics. Answer the reporters head-on. You have no idea what happened. And now your thoughts and prayers are with your brilliant and accomplished lawyer. End. Done. Goodbye."

She turned to Ned, who'd put his feet up on the coffee table, and stretched out his arms behind him. His tie was off now, draped over the back of the couch.

"Agreed?" She nodded at him, confident. "I like it."

"Sushi first," he said. "Then you're the boss."

The doorbell rang again.

"Coming!" she called out. She felt better, more in control for the moment at least, as she dug in her purse for her wallet. She and Ned would have this carryout food, and then—*carryout*. What did that remind her of? Her wallet was underneath something. Oh, she thought, the brownies.

She stopped. Stared at the clear plastic baggie in her purse. The brownies. Ned had lied about always eating carryout food. Ned had lied about the cook. And that proved Ned was a liar. And she, stupid *stupid* Arden, had fallen for it. Every single specific thing Cordelia had warned her about—his engaging attitude, the sympathy ploy, his posture as loving family man. The crinkly eyes. Now the sushi was here, and Arden needed to remember reality. Whatever that was.

Credit card at the ready, she put her hand on the doorknob.

Opened the door.

"Monelle," she said.

28

This is the worst idea imaginable. The thought roiled so insistently through Arden's mind that she wasn't quite sure if she was actually saying the words out loud. *The. Worst.* And yet here she was, and Ned, too, and Monelle.

Sitting in a row, still wearing their snow-dotted overcoats, on a low chocolate leather couch in the hallway of the Atherton Wing of Mass General Hospital. Facing the closed door of Nyomi Chang's private room.

"We're leaving," Arden now said for the billionth time.

"No way," Ned said. He crossed his arms over his chest, lifted his chin. Obdurate, and immovable. "She said my name. I want to find out why."

"Thank you for being cooperative," Monelle said. She'd kept her voice low, they all had, in deference and respect.

"I'm not being cooperative. I'm being—"

"Ned. Please," Arden interrupted. She still wasn't wholeheartedly committed to helping Ned, though Cordelia had hired her, and Warren had strong-armed her to, and certainly in her career she'd had to shepherd people she felt even more ambiguous about. But now she felt out of equilibrium, as if circumstances were moving faster than her skill could manage or forecast.

Monelle, on the other hand, seemed obsessive. Hell-bent. Thirty minutes ago, showing up again at Arden's front door. Seeing Arden, blouse askew, hair jumbled, credit card in hand. Seeing Ned, coat off, tie off, shoes off, shirt untucked, who'd looked as relaxed as a satisfied lion, sprawled on her couch.

Arden knew what it had looked like. Intimacy, seduction, lust, everything unprofessional there could possibly be. Monelle's demeanor had stiffened as Arden tried to explain. And Arden knew whatever she said only sounded like an excuse. She was damn tired of trying to convince people—Warren, Patience Swanson—she wasn't a . . . whatever it would be. And now Monelle certainly had the same misguided impression of her.

"Well, well." Ned's voice had come from behind her.

Arden turned, trying to pantomime *no, stay away*, but Ned ignored her.

He'd stood, squared his shoulders, and strode toward them. "Monelle Churchwood," he said. Apparently cordial, welcoming, as if she were his best friend and not the prosecutor who'd tried to put him in prison for years. Underneath, though, Arden still sensed a predatory jungle creature, padding closer to its chosen quarry. "What brings you here?"

"Let *me* ask, Monelle," Arden had interrupted, this time shooting a *shut up* glance at Ned. "Is Nyomi—?"

"First let *me* ask Ned." Monelle looked Ned up and down. "How long have you been here?"

"Why does that matter?" Arden tried to step between them.

"Arden?" Monelle looked at Ned but had directed her words to Arden. "Does this mean . . ." She paused, as the entryway space filled with her suspicion. "Does this mean that Mr. Bannister was here when I came earlier? Kidding me? *That* was the noise upstairs?" She looked past Arden and past Ned and into the blue light. "The 'ancient heating system,' I remember you told me."

"It was a private—" Arden began.

Monelle had seemed to be relishing the moment. The cover-up it implied. "I knew there was something wrong." At this, Monelle actually looked amused. "I cannot even believe—"

"I need to interrupt you, Monelle." Arden had to cool this. Why was this woman here?

Words like "arrest warrant" and "probable cause," came to mind, but Arden had nothing to hide. And Ned might not be thinking straight at this moment. That was part of Arden's job, thinking straight under intense pressure. *Put the ball in the other guy's court,* she reminded herself. *That gives you time to think.*

"The better question is what can we do for you." Arden kept her tone as pleasant as she could. "This is a private home. Whether I have visitors is, forgive me, not any of your business."

"I see." Monelle stood, framed in the open front door, snow glittering in the streetlights. Another car went by, headlights briefly flaring, then another. Arden saw a dark sedan double-parked outside, blinkers flashing.

"So," Arden began. "What can—"

"What can you do for me? Easy. Ms. Chang is out of ICU. And spoke. That's good news. And why I came to talk to Arden in person. However, all good. Now I know where you are, Mr. Bannister. So you can come with me. Right now. To Mass General Hospital."

"Monelle, no," Arden answered, and felt Ned, behind her, take a step closer. Nyomi was out of ICU. Such reassuring news. But for Ned? "No. Ned needs a lawyer. This is—"

"I'll decide that." Ned's voice, a harsh whisper. He'd stood next to her, his arm almost touching hers. "A lawyer? My *lawyer* is in that hospital room, isn't she? And she asked for me."

Arden saw Monelle roll her eyes. Arden pretended to ignore it. A gust of dark wind had huffed in behind them, aggressive and insistent.

"Ah. 'Asked for you.' If you say so. But it does mean you are indeed aware of the general situation, Mr. Bannister. Excellent," Monelle said. "That will expedite matters. I can skip the explanation of this evening's unpleasant but certainly intriguing series of events. We'll take my car. And I'll arrange for transportation home. . . ." Monelle looked over Arden's shoulder, into the living room. "Or wherever you decide to go. If events progress that way. If not—"

"Hey." Arden had frowned, put up a stop-sign palm. This was bull, and Monelle's obsession combined with Ned's stubbornness was a volatile combination. Monelle hated Ned, she'd used those very words to her, or very near, in the Bannister Building garage. Ned hated the prosecutor equally as much.

"I'll get my coat," Ned had said, and turned away.

"Mr. Bannister?" Monelle called after him. "Better get your shoes, too."

Arden looked silently at Monelle, trying to connect. "What the hell," she finally whispered.

"Your client," Monelle said, "if that's what he is, must be connected to what happened to Nyomi Chang. Look. Truth. We have video of a car leaving the scene, a car very like Ned Bannister's black Mercedes."

"'Very like' a 'black Mercedes'? That's hardly conclusive."

"Arden?" Monelle had continued. "Ms. Chang said one word. 'Ned.' Do you think she was talking about another Ned?"

"I have no idea what that means," Arden began. "Nor do you. Did you hear her? You personally?"

"That is not being made public right now."

"I'm not the *public*." Arden could not keep the anger from her voice. She imagined Ned putting on his shoes, deciding what to do. She'd been surprised by his hasty acceptance of Monelle's demand. She'd have thought a businessperson—hell, a defendant recently acquitted of homicide—would be more careful. Now this was all in her lap.

"How do you know she even said 'Ned'?" Arden went on. "There are countless other words she might have said. Or meant. *If* she said anything at all. Isn't she injured? Medicated? Ned needs a lawyer. And you know it."

"He doesn't seem to think so," Monelle said.

She looked like she was about to say something else, trying to restrain herself.

"What?" Arden had challenged her.

"I'm just thinking—if you're coming with us, possibly you should put on *your* shoes as well. And I'm wondering, too, by the way, if Cordelia Bannister knows where her husband is."

Outside, another set of headlights moved slowly toward Arden's house. Inched past Monelle's car, double-parked in front of it.

"Reinforcements?" Arden asked.

"Not for me," Monelle said. "Are *you* expecting anyone?"

Outside, the car's door opened, then slammed closed, and a slender silhouette strode toward them. In the amber of the streetlight, Arden saw a dark hoodie, dark pants, boots. And a paper bag. And a ball cap with a recognizable logo.

"*Dammit,*" Arden had whispered.

"You ordered from Sushi Girl?" Monelle's voice had been a mixture of scorn and disappointment as the delivery approached. "You are too much, Arden Ward. People are dead." She paused, had seemed to consider. "Put away your damn sushi. I'll meet you both in the car."

Now, they sat in the hallway of this opulent wing of MGH, reserved for private payers or big shots or philanthropists. It looked more like an elegant hotel than a hospital—soft indirect lighting instead of buzzing fluorescents, polished Italian-tiled walls tastefully showing peaceful landscapes; the Hudson River, the Atlantic Ocean, an array of olive trees, full and voluptuous and healthy. A gleaming not-quite-marble floor. The surroundings sent the subtle message that a stay here would be brief. Safe. Healing. And in this case especially, private.

Two obvious cops, failing to be inconspicuous in tired tweed jackets and white shirts, stood sentinel on either side of Nyomi's door. They stared at the walls, pretending the three visitors did not exist. Heather, Nyomi's paralegal, who Ned had theorized "must be there," was nowhere in sight.

"When can I talk to Nyomi?" Ned asked. He'd shrugged off his coat, left it against the back of the couch. "When can I talk to a doctor?"

A nurse emerged from Nyomi's room. Lowered the protective blue mask from her face. The three of them stood, in one motion.

"Zuhrah?" Monelle asked. "What?"

"Ms. Chang is conscious," the nurse said. "She's sleeping now, but aware. She could be awakened. She's asked for ice slivers, and took some. Closed her eyes again."

Arden took in the Pooh tunic, the blue-striped drawstring pants, the worn-in white sneakers. The clipboard, holding a stack of papers. Zuhrah wore a wedding ring, and her hair in a white-banded ponytail.

"I need to talk to her." Ned took a step forward.

"No, *I* do." Monelle came up next to him.

"No visitors," Zuhrah said. "She's too fragile."

"I'm from the district attorney's office, and—"

"One person," Zuhrah said. "One. For one minute."

The nurse turned, peered through Nyomi's meshed window, then faced the three of them again, holding up a forefinger. "One."

29

e." Ned took another step forward, advancing. "You have to let me talk to her."

Arden saw the cop-watchdogs shift position, then glance at Monelle, maybe looking for direction. From down the corridor, Arden heard the insistent pings of an alarm, then a voice, muffled, over a gentle PA system.

"No." Monelle clamped a hand on to Ned's shoulder, stopping him.

When he turned to reply, Arden saw an expression cross his face; angry, or protective. Or determined.

Monelle must have registered it, too. She removed her hand, even took a step back, out of his force field. "Both of us, then."

Arden tried to calculate, move the chess pieces on the board. She peeled off her coat, buying some time. Monelle could not be allowed into that room alone, who knew what damning statement she'd concoct and then decide to call probable cause. Not Ned alone, either, not without a witness. No matter what he reported, Monelle would never believe it. Maybe . . .

"One person," Zuhrah repeated. The nurse had planted herself in front of Nyomi's door, sneakers wide apart, making herself big. "More is too dangerous. She might be overwhelmed. One wrong word could set her back—who knows how far."

"I'll go," Arden said. "I'll record it on my phone." She looked at the nurse, inquiring. Noting her name. "Or you could come with me, Zuhrah. I won't frighten her. She knows me. She trusts me."

More alarm pings from down the hallway.

"I'm not sure how long she'll be . . . available," Zuhrah said. "And if you all can't decide what to—"

"Fine. Do it, Arden," Monelle interrupted. "Go. But you have to take this with you." She pulled out a cell phone, tapped at it, handed it to Arden. "Record it on *my* phone. Ask her what happened. That's all. No funny stuff, no secret signals. If you screw up, I'll never believe it wasn't on purpose. I'll know you're covering up. Start recording now. Let me see."

Arden held up the phone. And for one, two, three, they watched the seconds advance. Zuhrah moved away from the door, a gatekeeper relinquishing her post.

"Do not say a word while I'm in there, Ned," Arden instructed him. "Do not answer anything she tries to ask you. Not anything, no matter how benign it seems. And now *that's* been recorded too, Monelle."

Arden took a step toward the room. Reached her hand out to the door. The unfamiliar phone vibrated like a living creature in her hand, she could almost feel the weight of its import. Whatever Nyomi said—and there was utterly no way to predict—could ruin Ned's life, or save it. Or be so ambiguous that it would make the situation even more complicated. But again, it would be truth. Some kind of truth. More seconds ticked by.

"You going?" Ned's voice.

"Arden?" Monelle's.

"No." Arden turned back to them, one hand still on the doorknob. "Ned. Nyomi is your lawyer, right?"

"Yes."

"And your communications are privileged. Confidential."

"Of course."

Arden felt the doorknob warm to her touch. Saw Monelle narrow her eyes. Calculating.

"This is—no. We're not doing this," Arden said. "Nyomi is in no condition to make any decisions, and she might, under the influence of drugs or pain or lack of judgment, inadvertently say something that might breach that confidentiality. She might say something to hurt you, Ned."

"What would that be?" Monelle asked, a lizard snapping up her prey.

"There's nothing—"

"Stop talking, Ned." Arden steeled herself, made up her mind. Hoped she wasn't destroying the possibility that Nyomi would say something that indisputably blamed someone else, or at least took the spotlight from Ned. She held up the recording phone like a shield. Fewer than two minutes had passed. "No one is going into that room, especially not you, Monelle, or anyone affiliated with you or law enforcement. You brought Ned here. You put him in this position. Now, no one in law enforcement talks to Nyomi Chang until Ned gets a new lawyer."

Monelle took a silent step toward her. "But don't you see? This may be our only chance. Who knows, forgive me, when—or even if—Nyomi will recover? Who knows what might happen to her? This is a crucial moment for—"

"Who knows what might happen to *Ned*?" Forgive me, Nyomi, Arden thought. She lowered Monelle's phone, kept it recording, for what it was worth. Monelle could simply erase it. But the nurse had heard the conversation, and the cops, too, not that they were reliably honest. "Ned? The Commonwealth of Massachusetts most certainly thinks you're involved with this. Did Monelle here tell you they now have video of a car that looks like yours at the scene?" She saw him wince. "No, right? They brought you here to keep an eye on you. We're leaving."

Monelle drew herself up taller, her shoulders squaring. "I didn't force him to come here. He agreed."

"Bull," Arden said. She thought of tonight's unexpected knock at the door, the double-parked car, the explicit demand that they—Ned—come to the hospital. "Look. Ned. Nyomi, your lawyer, who I have to figure is the *last* person you'd want to harm—is in the most vulnerable position imaginable. She is not in control of her faculties, let alone her critical judgment. If you have ever, *ever*, told her anything you might not want her to divulge—"

She saw Ned's eyes widen. Considering, perhaps replaying past conversations. She hoped she was right about this—she was taking this stand partly from common sense, partly from having a defense lawyer turned politician for a father. But she couldn't allow Monelle to go in alone. Ned, certainly not. And she, Arden, could not put herself in a position where Ned was in legal jeopardy, or not, depending on the medically undependable statements of a person fighting for her life. Ned's life was at stake, too.

She imagined Nyomi, just feet away behind that closed door, IV tubes stabbed into her arm and taped into place, wires attached to chest and forefinger, monitors beeping, electronic graphs changing with her every breath, her every heartbeat. She pictured Nyomi's eyes closed, the once-articulate lawyer now floating in a distant and indecipherable world of her own.

"Nyomi—she's in no position to protect you now, Ned. She may say something that might be misinterpreted, might harm you, might not even be true. I understand you want answers. We all do. But what if—"

"Right," Ned said. "I see. Yeah."

"So there *is* something," Monelle said. "I knew it."

Zuhrah had listened to this exchange, arms folded across her Pooh tunic, back against the corridor wall, unmoving. The two officers guarding Nyomi's room had inched even closer. Watching, silent, wary.

"Zuhrah?" Arden tried to keep her voice pleasant. "Can you please contact your supervisor? The hospital's legal department needs to ensure this patient is protected. She is the hospital's responsibility. No one in law enforcement is allowed to communicate with Nyomi Chang until Mr. Bannister has an attorney who can advise him. Hospital security should be alerted to implement that."

"Contact them right now?"

"Whenever you think your supervisor would be happiest to hear it. Be clear that we can handle it the simple way right now, or we can go to court." Arden gathered her coat, gestured to Ned to do the same. This was mostly bluff, but based on a client she'd helped years ago. And her father had always threatened court, a useful deterrent to the litigation-wary.

Most important, Monelle did not have Ned's best interests at heart. Arden did. "We're leaving. And Monelle, if you need us, you'll have to go through Ned's new lawyer." *Whoever that'll be,* she thought. But once Nyomi spoke, it could not be undone. It was her one word, "Ned," that had brought them here in the first place.

"But . . . ," Monelle began. Arden watched her expression change. "What if Nyomi says something that is completely exonerating? Do you want to abandon that possibility? Ned? Arden here, for all her talents . . ." She indicated Arden with a flip of one hand. "Is not a lawyer. And *she's* most assuredly going home to sushi. I'm not as certain about you."

"Well—" Ned began.

Arden saw, literally saw, Ned's mind at work. "No, Ned."

"What if, Ned," Monelle kept talking, angling her body toward Ned. "What if Nyomi tells us she knows exactly what happened. Describes a driver who is not you. Maybe she'd tell us she said your name because she was worried about you, wanted you to know why she was late for your appointment."

"I'm sure that's what she meant," Ned was saying. "She hated to be late."

He stood beside Arden now, close enough to peer through the small wire-meshed window on Nyomi's door. Monelle didn't try to stop him.

"I can't see in there, not a thing." He turned to her, and Arden saw the worry lines in his face. "Arden, listen. I didn't have anything to do with it. Whatever it was. I'm not afraid. Maybe we should let her talk."

"Agreed," Monelle almost purred. "And then you'll get sushi, too."

"Ned. Stop." Arden eased between Ned and the hospital room door. Hoping she was not about to ruin Ned's life by playing lawyer. But her job—her life—was about making sure her clients were treated fairly. "I told you. No."

"Give me back my phone," Monelle said. "You had your chance. And you'll be sorry you blew it."

30

The Mass General ladies' room, pungent with the sharp tang of disinfectant, was deserted this time of night, after midnight and now officially Saturday, no other feet showing under the scratched once-maroon walls. Arden's phone rang, the sound vibrating through the tote bag she'd draped on the hook of her stall's metal door. Her coat hung underneath it, dangling by the loop of its label.

"Who on earth?" she muttered. Arden had to let the phone ring once more as she rearranged herself, dug it from the bag, and saw the caller ID.

"Cordelia," she said. "Are you okay?"

Ned was in the basement cafeteria getting carryout coffees and any food he could scrounge. They'd agreed to walk back to Arden's, the coffees serving as both handwarmers and caffeine. Even pushing one in the morning, her Beacon Hill neighborhood was as safe as any part of Boston could be.

But Cordelia. To call at this hour meant something either very very good or very very bad.

"I heard about Nyomi," Cordelia said.

"It's awful, I know. She's still . . . iffy." Arden held the phone between her shoulder and cheek, then pulled back the warped latch of the stall door. A line of white porcelain sinks gleamed under a long mirror. She saw her reflection, her skin garish from the fluorescent lighting. She needed a shower. She needed sleep. She slid one arm into her coat sleeve, shrugged it on.

"Cordelia? Where are you? Did you hear me about Nyomi? Are you okay?"

"Am I okay? Am I *okay*? Want to know what I just got on my phone?"

"Cordelia, please. Calm down. What? Another text?" Arden thought she heard laughter in the background, maybe music. A sorority trip to

Palm Beach, drinking and gossiping with college classmates. She must have graduated what, twenty years ago? It seemed odd that she would choose her sorority sisters, no matter how beloved, over her husband and children. But Ned had urged her to go, Arden remembered. And now that she herself was tired and cranky and worried, she was taking it out on Cordelia. Cordelia, who'd struggled over the last year, and who had said, in a wistfully poignant voice, that she didn't remember laughter. Pain, and fear, could make people do strange things.

"Well, hell yes, a text. With a video. It's hard to see, but they say it's *Ned's* car at the scene. Or, leaving it, I should say. Arden? Do they think *Ned* hit her? I'm living on the edge here."

"Who sent it?" That was fast, Arden thought. Had to be Monelle. Or one of her goons. *Monelle.* Arden had outplayed her, so Monelle had raised the stakes. "And yes, I know about it, but it hardly sounds conclusive. Does it look like Ned's car to you?"

"It looks like a black and blurry nothing. *How* can this be—"

"Cordelia. It'll be okay. This is a coincidence. A sad and terrible co-incidence."

She paused, but Cordelia said nothing.

"So you don't know who sent the video?" Arden went on. "Can you forward it to me?"

"No, of course not. And no. I deleted. Double-deleted. It's—whatever. No. It's gone."

Silence then, in a shiny-walled bathroom, where Arden felt as if she were in another world, a midnight porcelain limbo with one friend on the brink of life and death and a client under suspicion of causing her grave injuries. Cordelia must have put her hand over the microphone, blocking the sound, as all Arden heard was an opaque absence.

"Sorry," Cordelia's voice came back. "But you were saying a coincidence. Is it? I keep thinking—and I know it's awful. What if they find out Nyomi told him something that night on the phone, something so ruinous that—oh. No. I can't even think that. Poor Ned."

Had Cordelia known Nyomi was on the way to Ned's? Had Ned told her that? "I completely understand why you're upset, and I am, too, but I'm sure—"

Cordelia kept talking. "I *keep* thinking, though. I told you he was upset after he talked to her that night. And maybe—"

"Cordelia, listen. What may seem like cause and effect is not always cause and effect. Sometimes one thing doesn't have anything to do with another thing."

"I should come home to the kids. Right now." Cordelia's voice was a whisper, and Arden strained to hear. "Arden. How can this not be connected?"

Arden shifted the phone to the other shoulder, put her hands under one of the faucets. Nothing happened. She rolled her eyes, moved to the next sink. Nothing. "So stupid," she said out loud.

"What?" Cordelia said.

"Oh, sorry, not you." Arden turned the faucet with her free hand. "I'm in a bathroom, and I thought the sink was automatic, but it wasn't."

"Huh? Where are you? I assumed you were home."

Arden looked at the line of fancy metal hand dryers, imagined the noise, grabbed a wad of toilet paper and dried her hands. Tossed the damp clump into the wastebasket.

"Arden." Cordelia hadn't waited for an answer. "Please tell me he has an alibi."

Arden saw herself in the mirror again, the reflection of her confusion. Whatever happiness the Bannisters once shared, it seemed to have shattered, as irrevocably as this mirror might, into a million shards of dangerous impossibility. They had children, and Ned seemed genuinely fond of them, more than fond. But Cordelia had sent them away. To get rid of them? Or to protect them?

"Let me ask you, Arden." Cordelia was still talking. Arden listened for slurred words; any sign of the alcohol Ned had mentioned earlier. "Oh, hold on. Can you?"

The line went silent. Arden opened the bathroom door and peered out into the softly lit corridor, the hospital noises, pings and beeps and distant padded footsteps surrounding her. Life and death, at every moment, on every floor of this building. Hospitals were a place of transition, not only for the patients like Nyomi whose physical futures hung in the balance, but for their loved ones, the ones who could only wait and hope. And the nurses, like Zuhrah, were as much life guides as medical practitioners.

"You still there?" Cordelia's voice over the cell phone.

"Yup." Arden entered the elevator, pushed the button marked Cafeteria. "I'm in an elevator now. If I lose you, I'll call you back."

"An elevator? Are you in a . . . hotel? Wait, are you with Ned? It's so late. . . ."

"No." She did not need to tell Cordelia where she was. Arden could only imagine the absurdity of another angry wife complaining to Warren.

The elevator doors rumbled open, directly into the cafeteria. The wide, white-walled room smelled of steam and salt, the rows of long tables seating a scatter of white coats and blue surgical scrubs, and a few civilians. Each of them, heads lowered in defeat or exhaustion or fear, stared at paper cups or at the empty plastic tabletops.

Ned stood on the far side of the room, carrying a cardboard tray with two cups and what looked like brown bags of plain M&M's, waiting behind three other people for the only cashier on duty. He hadn't noticed Arden.

"Arden?" Cordelia was still talking. "You there?"

"Yes. Sorry, I got distracted." Arden had two minutes, at most, to finish this.

"I'm just saying," Cordelia went on. "What if the police show up with that hideous video? Will you be able to help him deal with that? Listen, when Ned contacts you, tell me what he says."

"Well, I think . . ."

"It's horrible," Cordelia was saying. "At least the kids are safe with Georgianna."

Ned had seen her. He waved. Oblivious.

"Cordelia? Does Ned have another lawyer? Not for real estate, but anyone he consults?"

"Nope, only Nyomi." Cordelia paused. "Oh. Does he need one?"

"Maybe."

"Don't forget about Randall Tennant," Cordelia said. "Did you ask about the haircut?"

"Not yet. I'm not forgetting." Arden watched Ned walking toward her. "Take care, Cordelia. I'm sure Ned will call you."

"He'd better," Cordelia said. And she hung up.

Arden looked at her black phone screen. "Bye," she said to no one.

"Sustenance." Ned held up one of the brown M&M's bags. Waved it toward Arden's phone. Then frowned. "Who was that? Was it about Nyomi?"

31

O h, no, nothing new on Nyomi," Arden said. "I was checking my messages," she lied, stashing her phone in a coat pocket. She thought about the origins of the incriminating video Cordelia had received. Monelle's tactics with it. "Did you get any? Messages? Not counting reporters. They're still working, probably. Like vampire bats."

"Yeah, Pip and Emma." Ned set the cardboard carrier of coffees on a long linoleum-topped table, then buttoned his coat. Adjusted his muffler. Pulled on his gloves. "I had silenced my phone for the hospital, and didn't hear their voice mails kick in."

"Are they okay? They're in Vermont?" She looked at her watch. "Isn't it pretty late for them?" The elevator lights showed the car on floor 11, high above them.

"It is, although when it comes to bedtime, it's no holds barred with their grandmother. They were upset, because Cordelia missed her Face-Time with them. Like I have mine, she has one, too. If she's out of town. She had promised to show them palm trees. But she didn't call, and didn't answer when they called her. So they called me. Have you talked with her?"

She looked at the elevator indicator, watching it come closer.

When Arden was a teenager, when her father had first started to think about running for office, he'd given her some advice, advice she'd relied on ever since. *Use your conscience as your north star,* he'd said. And you'll know what's right, no matter how you try to talk yourself out of it. Remember there are at least two sides to every story.

What would he think of what she was doing now?

"No, I haven't called her." Arden, ignoring her north star, answered a question Ned hadn't asked. "Oh, the elevator. Finally."

The elevator doors slid open into the lobby, a gloomy expanse of almost-empty rows of vinyl plastic chairs, with a few people huddled in coats and slumped into themselves, seated, Arden thought, as far as

possible from one another. The atmosphere had a sense of bleak desperation; in the early hours of a Saturday morning, nothing good could have
happened to bring these people here. No one carried flowers or presents,
no one even looked up. Arden, with Nyomi in mind, tried to remember
that hospitals were places of hope as well as despair.

"And now it's too late for me even to call Mother. Poor kids," Ned said.
He pushed open the hospital's thick glass front door into the dark night
and moved aside to let Arden go through first. "They must feel abandoned. And confused. Gotta tell you, I know the feeling."

"If they had stayed home, though," Arden said. "Who'd be taking
care of them? You were at my house to avoid reporters. But they—and
Monelle—would have found you at home. Might have been a real mess."
It felt bizarre to comfort him with an it-could-have-been-worse situation,
but sometimes it was all relative. And no reporters were staking out the
hospital, not that Arden could see. They'd arrive in the morning, most
likely. She wondered if Monelle had sent *them* the video.

A blast of cold air surrounded them, and she was grateful for the comforting heat of the coffee cup through her gloves. Thick white clouds
obscured most of the stars, though a few still twinkled stalwartly in the
inky sky. The random neon signs and darkened storefronts of Cambridge Street were in front of them, and past that, the steep strips of
narrow side streets up Beacon Hill.

"I feel so guilty," Ned was saying. "First their mom didn't call, and
then I didn't answer them. Mother will take care of the kids, she's great
with them. But I tried Cordelia from the cafeteria, and she didn't pick
up. Now I'm worried about her, too. I know she and her friends are
having fun, but she's usually attentive to her phone. What if something
happened to her?"

"If something happened, you would have gotten a call. She's fine."
Arden tried to ignore her own guilt, knowing she could make Ned feel
halfway better by telling him Cordelia hadn't answered because the two
of *them* had been on the phone. Which meant his wife had preferred to
talk to Arden than to him. Who had sent Cordelia that video? If it was
Monelle, why? "Maybe try her when we get to my house?" *Without telling
her where you are,* Arden didn't say.

Arden heard him sigh as they walked side by side past the hospital's
darkened parking garage. She'd never see a garage like that again without
thinking of what happened to Randall Tennant. And to Ned, and to his

family. It was unsettling to realize they still didn't know exactly what took place that New Year's Eve. Or to Nyomi. An ambulance, siren wailing at full blast, careened past them, on the way to someone else's disaster.

"Yeah. I guess. It's so late, though, I don't want to scare her. These were supposed to be happier times. It's been a long year, and I hoped for some peace."

"It's late, it's dark, you're exhausted," she reminded him. "And you've had disturbing news. Monelle Churchwood is a tyrant, and bitter about the acquittal. No one's more righteous than a crusading prosecutor, and I know you thought she was out of your life. We'll sort it out. Things will be better when the sun comes up."

She could not believe her own facile pseudo-philosophy, but she had to say something that sounded positive. Nyomi haunted her, and Cordelia, too.

"Sun up?" Ned glanced at the sky. "I wish. This night has been hellish."

"I know," Arden agreed.

They trudged up to the corner of Cambridge Street, their soft damp footsteps the only sound on the snow-dusted pavement. Though the street was deserted, they both waited for the light at the zebra-striped crosswalk. The pavement glimmered with a sheen of melted snow, traffic lights shining red and green on the shiny surface.

"The kids must be okay," Ned finally said, "or Mother would have called."

"Totally right," Arden said as they reached the other side. "She handled you as a kid, she can handle them, too." She pointed. "This way."

Not a car passed them until they turned onto Mt. Vernon Street, when a dark SUV, headed the opposite direction, shushed by. They continued, their breath puffing white, and Arden had almost tricked her body into ignoring her lack of sleep. The night was gorgeously still, the three-hundred-year-old landscape with its redbrick townhouses and wrought iron railings, the gaslight of the streetlamps, transported them, as if they walked in another time, or their own separate universe. Ned crushed his empty coffee cup and looked for a place to toss it. "Trash cans?" he asked.

"Nope," Arden said. "They took them away after the marathon bombing. We're almost there, though."

The atmosphere seemed to change as they neared Charles Street, the widest of the Beacon Hill thoroughfares, lined with chic boutiques and antique shops, trendy restaurants and some shabby but popular bars. This time of night on the hill, most everything was closed. But the light felt different, and the sound.

"Lots of cars on your block." Ned had stashed the cup in his pocket. Pointed. "Look at those brake lights. All those people live there?"

"Stop." Arden clamped a gloved hand on Ned's arm. "Don't take one more step."

32

"N ed. Come with me." Arden kept her hand on Ned's arm, physically turned him around. "We need to go *this* way," she said. The statehouse lights shone in front of them as she dragged him away from her home.

"What?" Ned said. "Aren't we—?"

"Those cars in front of my house? Not neighbors. News cars. Reporters. And no question who sent them."

"Monelle," Ned said. "I knew it."

"Exactly." Arden's mind raced. She recognized the profound irony of turning away from her own home, a refuge that was now completely barred to her, in the middle of the night in the darkened city of Boston, where nothing was open and nothing was available and there was no place for them to hide.

"You'd think she'd do that, sic reporters on us?"

"Without a second thought. Remember she said 'you'll be sorry'? I bet she picked up her phone and dialed every reporter in town. Told them about Nyomi, told them about you, told them about me, told them where I lived. Maybe even leaked that stupid surveillance video she conveniently avoided telling you about. I'm not even sure that's . . . legal? Ethical? It's certainly not fair."

"Crap. What a—nothing is fair," he said. "Seems like that's the only thing I know for sure. Does that woman have utterly no boundaries? Does anyone?"

"I need to think." The temperature had plummeted. Their options were few. "We can't go to your place," she said, "they'll be staked out there, too. What if—I go home by myself, and you go to a hotel?"

"You mean, I hide. And you face the reporters alone. If Monelle has spun some ugly story, it'll be tough for you to get them to leave."

"I'll walk past them. Not say a word." Arden put her nose in the air, pantomiming. "I'll go inside, close the door, lock it, and turn off the lights. They'll give up. It's not the most fun idea, but I don't see an option."

"I hate to leave you with that," he said. "Making yourself a human decoy to save me."

"Again, part of the deal. That's what you Bannisters are paying me for. To protect you and your family from the onslaught." Arden rubbed her arms, trying to keep warm, failing. "Plus, we've got to do *something* besides standing on the street, starving and freezing."

"I feel like we should laugh," Ned said. "This is ridiculous."

If Ned saw humor in this, it was better than him being despondent. Arden watched the snowflakes intensifying, dancing in front of the nearest streetlight. All the feeling in her toes had disappeared. "Just another day in public relations world," she said. "Right?"

But Ned, staring into the dark distance, no longer looked amused. "Nyomi Chang is in the hospital, and I have no idea what happened. Yet the full weight of the district attorney's office is focused on hammering me. *Me.* There are countless black Mercedes in Boston. My wife has gone out of town, my children are unhappy, I'm an innocent man, and all I feel is guilt. I did nothing. We should make them prove I did. Right? I should just turn myself in."

"Turn yourself in to what? To who? Why? Listen. Ned. I know it seems like the world is crashing down, but let's take this one step at a time." Arden nodded, deciding. "There's a hotel on the corner of Cambridge and something street, I forget the name, but people stay there when they have family at the hospital. They're probably used to people showing up at all hours. It's an easy walk, three blocks. Go, check in, let me know. I'll handle the reporters."

Arden's phone rang, and even though muffled by her tote bag, it seemed louder than usual. *Nyomi,* she thought. *Get better.*

"Who is it?" Ned said.

Arden saw the caller ID. "Monelle."

"Something's happened to Nyomi," Ned said.

"Hello?" Arden said at the same time.

"Just checking to make sure you got home safely," Monelle said.

"You're checking to see if I got home safely?" Arden repeated for Ned's benefit. "In fact, I'm not going home."

"You're going to Ned Bannister's?"

Arden heard the disbelief in Monelle's voice. "It's none of your business where I'm going." She cocked an eyebrow at Ned. "Or Mr. Bannister, either."

Monelle had obviously called to revel in Ned's and Arden's discomfort with the barrage of reporters, maybe even say *I told you so*, and Arden had denied her that. "What can I help you with, Monelle? How is Nyomi?"

"There's no change with Nyomi, according to Zuhrah. I'm not allowed into the room, remember? The hospital's attorney is named Lisa Thurau-Gray." Monelle spelled it. "She was not happy with being called at this hour."

"Well, no matter what time it was, *we*'re not happy with Nyomi's lawyer-client confidentiality with Mr. Bannister being breached." She rolled her eyes. Maybe she was more tired than she realized. "So we're clear? No one in law enforcement is to go into that room. Not even to say how are you."

Ned nodded, listening to her approvingly.

"You people are all alike," Monelle said.

"You people . . . ," Arden repeated. "Should not be giving out addresses of private citizens. Or releasing videos."

"What?"

"You heard me." Arden's breath puffed white, and she thought there might be the beginnings of dawn in the changing sky. "Shall we expect a call from Ms. Thurau-Gray"—she spelled it again to prove she'd heard it, and to be annoying—"in the morning? And she'll call *me*, correct? Not Mr. Bannister."

Ned's phone rang, then, sounding like an old-fashioned landline.

He tapped on his phone, held it to his ear, turned his back and took a few steps away, standing under a wrought iron streetlight. His "Hello?" was faint, and she heard nothing more.

"Monelle, I think we've accomplished all we're going to accomplish in this call."

Arden could almost hear Monelle calculating what to say. "We'll see what happens tomorrow."

"Indeed," Arden said. But Monelle had already disconnected. Arden looked at her phone, made a face.

Half a block away now, Ned was still deep into murmured conversation, gesturing with one hand as he talked. Arden took a few steps closer, brazenly eavesdropping, but could not hear anything.

Middle of the night, she thought. Had to be Cordelia. She turned away, giving him some privacy, trying to decide how to handle the staked-out reporters. She could not believe Monelle had sent them, it was so nasty, and so hostile; such a tactic. If she'd leaked that video, it could be all over social media any minute. Monelle had considerable power, enough to cause even more upheaval in Ned's life. And Cordelia's. Arden took a deep disapproving breath, wondering about justice.

She tried to create a movie in her mind, envision the events, as she aways did when tackling a problem. Some car hits pedestrian Nyomi Chang. Someone calls the police. Does that someone see the car? Do they take video? Meanwhile, the police and the medics come to the accident scene, get Nyomi's ID, then call her office? And then—what?

The sound changed again on the street beyond. Arden pivoted, assessing, listening. Then stepped closer to Ned, and even though he was still talking, grabbed his arm and pulled him into the shadows, in the lee of a lavender-windowed three-story brownstone.

"What?" He pointed to his phone, shook his head. *Still talking.*

Arden jabbed a finger away from them, toward the dark sedan that was pulling out of Mt. Vernon Street and in the direction of downtown Boston. Within seconds, another four-door followed it, then another.

Ned watched, his eyes widening. He nodded. *Whoa.*

"Good, honey," he said into the phone. "I miss you, too. It's very late, you go to sleep, and . . ."

Not Cordelia, Arden thought. Unless she was drunk and being difficult.

"We'll talk in the morning." Ned paused. Listening. "Maybe. I'll try. You do what Grandmother says. And be nice to your brother." A pause. "Yes, he *is,* honey. I know. But he loves you, too."

Ned looked concerned, Arden saw, and wondered if there were actually tears in his eyes, or whether his face was misty from melting snow.

"You have your Roo? Then sweetest of dreams. Yes, Roo, too." He clicked off the call.

"Poor Emma," he said. "Those the reporters leaving?"

"Gotta think so." Arden looked across the street at the now-silent, now-empty intersection. "And pretty interesting how quickly that happened after I told Monelle we weren't there."

"Is it politically correct for me to call her a bitch?" Ned scratched his head, fingers under his watch cap.

"It's totally correct," Arden said. "Now we can go to my house without being under siege. I must admit I was not looking forward to running *that* gauntlet." She let out a breath, pointed. "Anyway, you can take the guest room. You can't go near your home. Or your office. Monelle is—"

"Arden?"

A clunky old MBTA bus wheezed up Charles Street, interior lights dimmed and anemic. Arden saw only the silhouetted heads of its passengers, many propped against the wide windows, either going home after a night shift or headed off to the early shift. Soon the lights of the storefronts would begin to pop on, and another day would begin in earnest.

"I have to go to Vermont," Ned said.

33

W e'll need to get gas," Arden said, reading the gauge. "Whoever rented this car before we did apparently didn't fill it. I hooked up my phone to the Bluetooth, just in case. Anything else?"

"Let's get farther out of town," Ned told her. "I'll feel safer."

Safer, Arden noted the word. From the reporters, and from the police. She'd left her car in front of her apartment, so it would appear she was home. She'd put this rental on the Bannister expense tab, that was for sure. She eased into the fast lane, propelling them north toward the Massachusetts border. "I'll drive the whole way, you navigate. Okay?" she said, thinking of Ned's apprehensiveness. "But not the Mass Pike. People are maniacs."

"You don't take the Pike to Dorset," Ned said. "It's Route 2, the scenic route, if you're a fan of unrepaired infrastructure. I'll tell you as we go. Gotta say, I've never been out here at six thirty in the morning. At least I have clothes there. Your guest room and shower saved me, but this suit has seen better days."

A rusty once-white truck clattered past them on the right, and Arden flinched, swerving to her left.

"Shoot," she said. "Sorry."

"Are you sure you're awake enough to drive?"

"Huh? That truck? *I'm* fine. *He's* the one who can't drive."

The highway itself, Route 2, was like time traveling to the fifties, its too-narrow lanes pocked and dotted with potholes, and apparently a magnet for ramshackle gas stations. A steep hill led to a treacherous rotary, and on the left, the razor wire and a formidable fence securing MCI-Concord, a Dickensian fortress housing a medium-security state prison. Where, under less fortunate circumstances, if they *were* fortunate and not a travesty of justice, Ned Bannister might have resided. Instead, he was sitting in the front seat with her on his way to see his children.

"Luckily I'm not in there," Ned said, echoing her thoughts. "I can't tell you how often I woke up in the middle of the night, petrified by the prospect."

"I bet," she said. "Cordelia, too."

"She never said so. I think she was trying not to show how frightened she was. And we didn't want the kids to hear us worry about it, of course."

Arden eased to a stop at a traffic signal that seemed to pop out of nowhere. "What a ridiculous place for a light," she said.

"Welcome to Route 2," Ned said. "Listen, thanks for driving. I'll be fine, at some point, but . . . anyway. Thank you. Emma is so unhappy, and I don't know what to do except go see her in person. It's probably indulgent, or bad parenting."

"She's been through a lot, too, even if it's just seeing you and your wife being—tense," Arden decided on the word. The traffic light went green, and she heard the obligatory horn from the driver behind her, in case she hadn't noticed that. "Does your mother know we're coming, though? That *I'm* coming? That could be a surprise. Who am I going to be?"

"What do you think's going on at the hospital?" Ned asked, ignoring her question. "I wish I could call my office. But it's Saturday. No one will be there."

Saturday, Arden thought. She wondered again about cupcakes, and Warren, and Luz. Lois, waiting yesterday at the reception desk. Fuming, or baffled. They'd probably think she'd chickened out, avoiding emotional goodbyes. But she'd deal with the office when she could. *Warren*, she thought. This was his stupid fault.

"Can you grab my phone? In the pocket of that black bag." She gestured to the space between them on the vinyl seat. "I need to see if the hospital attorney has contacted me." She pointed at a not-too-run-down gas station with an adjacent fast-food drive-through. Wished she hadn't left Cordelia's brownies at home. "Let's get coffee, and anything with carbohydrates. Dorset's four hours away. I'm starving."

"Your fish," Ned said. "Won't *they* starve if you're gone?"

"You're so funny," she said. "But nice of you to think about it. I texted Luz from my office. She has a key, and she'll come feed them. I'll get her maple syrup as a thank-you."

"I'll do the gas," Ned said. "And you grab the food."

"Sure," Arden began. "No. Don't use a credit card. Let's be careful."

"It feels like we're on the run. It's so unfair." He handed her the phone he had pulled from her tote bag. "Because I shouldn't have to be running *from* anything. I'm running to see my children. But I suppose it's wise that we're covering my tracks. Outrageous as it is."

"Well, it gives us time to plan. Without you being hounded." Arden tucked the phone into her jacket pocket and made the right turn into the gas station. She bumped over a curb and pulled up to one of the pumps. A tentative sun struggled through gathering clouds. Massachusetts, where the weather forecast didn't matter. The weather did whatever it wanted.

"I'll get the gas." Arden unclipped her seat belt. "You get food. An assortment of carbs. Pay cash."

"Coffee black, if I remember from the hospital?"

"Thanks. And those yellow peanut butter crackers."

As Ned walked away, she flipped open the gas tank, unscrewed the cap, and shoved in the nozzle. Ned was right. They weren't running away. They were taking care of Ned's children, and she and Ned were a phone call away from the hospital lawyer. And from Monelle.

She was about to check her messages when the phone jangled in her pocket. A dilapidated clock on the outside of the gas station service bay, with giant numbers and windshield wipers as hands, said ten after seven. Who would be awake at this hour, and feel it was proper to call? The hospital. Arden caught her breath, her eyes welling with the dread of possibility. She pulled out the phone, knowing she could not ignore it, that whatever this was, whoever, it was business. Part of her job. She needed to know.

She saw the caller ID. Cordelia.

34

ello?" Arden watched the numbers on the gas pump click up and up and up, a faint ping with every gallon.

"Me," Cordelia said. "Where are you?"

"Where are *you*?" Arden asked. "What's happened, is everything okay? It's pretty early."

"Everything is not going to be 'okay' for a very long time," Cordelia said. "I'm terrified to think what horrible text may come next. What accusations. What—oh, I don't know, I don't know *anything*, Arden. That's why I'm calling you."

Another car, a massive white minivan, turned into the gas station. The bell dinged announcing the car's arrival. The driver got out, slammed the door. Then the van's side door slid open and three gangly boys clambered to the pavement, chattering and arguing.

"And honestly, where are you? It sounds like you're at a circus."

"Getting gas," Arden had to say. Cordelia might be relieved she was with Ned, doing her job. But this time of the morning might seem suspicious. Cordelia didn't need to know everything about every minute. Arden would simply avoid it. For now.

"I can't get the hospital to tell me anything about Nyomi Chang. Oh, hang on, sorry. Don't leave."

Cordelia did this every time. Her sorority pals demanding attention, Arden decided. It was good she was away, it meant she was safe. After the tank was full and nozzle stashed, Arden stayed outside the car waiting for Ned to return; zipping up her puffy black vest with one hand, holding the phone with the other. At least she'd gotten to change clothes when she and Ned risked a trip back to her—reporter-free—house. In defiance, she'd spritzed on a tiny bit of Joy. She'd started using it as a sort of armor, a scented reminder of how unfair the world could be. And not only unfair to *her*. To Nyomi, certainly. Cordelia. And maybe even to Ned.

"I'm back. So, Nyomi?"

"It's a privacy thing," Arden explained. "The law. That's why they won't tell you. But no, I haven't heard anything either. When the phone rang, that's who I figured this was. Have you talked to your husband?"

"I tried to call him a few minutes ago, but he didn't answer," she said. "He's probably fast asleep somewhere. Who knows. Maybe with the cook, ha ha. But what if—do you think he's all right? What if he's not?"

"I'm sure he's fine, Cordelia." That was true at least. And the cook? Cordelia, even now, seemed unable to hide her jealous suspicions. All Arden needed, another aggrieved wife. "You're right, he's probably asleep. And you know, actually, I told him to turn off his phone overnight. Yesterday was difficult. He'll call you, I'm sure."

No sign of Ned coming from the convenience store.

"Arden? Are you on the way home? I could call you there instead."

Arden thought of something. "Cordelia, you wanted me to help with the aftermath of the Randall Tennant case. And with—the texts. But now this—Nyomi—is a different situation."

"Oh, does it matter? It's all the same. It's all Ned, who must be hiding something. Surely you see that."

"Look, Cordelia? Could I ask . . . why you came to Warren? Who sent you to Warren?"

Arden heard Cordelia laugh.

"Everyone knows Warren Carmichael, and everyone knows you, Arden Ward. And, oh, my dear friend Linnea Mortimer, her son was the puppy rescue boy you helped? She absolutely adores you. Not that she's talking to me now, of course. But you know exactly why I called. Have you asked Ned about the barbershop?"

The pack of arguing little boys crawled back into the rear of the van, and their mother got back behind the wheel. The van pulled away, and as it moved, Arden saw Ned, paper bag in one hand and a cardboard coffee carrier in the other, emerge from the store. She waited until she knew he could see her clearly, then pointed to the phone with one finger, shook her head, then put her finger to her lips. *Be quiet.*

Ned came closer, nodding. Listening.

"Not yet," Arden said. "Oh, I'm so sorry," she pretended to talk to someone else. "Sure, one second. Cordelia, I have to go, someone's asking me to move. I'll call you when I know anything. And you call me. Everything will be fine."

"I rely on that," Cordelia said.

"I have some errands this morning, so I'll be out of pocket for a couple of hours. But if I hear anything about Nyomi, I'll call no matter what."

"Or about Ned."

"Of course. Talk soon." She hung up, before Cordelia could give her more instructions. Or ask any more questions.

She looked at the ridiculous windshield wiper clock again. Almost seven thirty.

"Cordelia?" Ned said.

"Yup." Arden opened the door and slid behind the wheel. "We should go."

"What'd she want?" Ned placed one of the cups in each of the cup holders on the console, then tossed the carrier onto the floor in the back.

"She wondered about Nyomi."

"Did you ask Dee why she missed the FaceTime?"

"Ned? How would I have known about that?"

"Oh, right." He scratched his forehead. "Hard to keep everything straight."

Got that right. Arden put her tote bag on the backseat and patted the place between them. "The food can go here. Thanks for the coffee."

"She's incredibly suspicious of me. Jealous. For absolutely no reason. She'd probably be unhappy that you and I are together."

"Which is . . ." Arden searched for a word. "Puzzling, I mean, that's what she hired me to do. Be with you."

"Even so." Ned flipped open the perforated flap of his coffee cup. "It's bizarre."

"Careful," Arden said, "there's a bump when I pull out. What's bizarre? Cordelia's jealousy?"

"Well, that, but I meant Nyomi. She could be awake now. And could have said something by now, a whole raft of somethings, and who knows if anyone heard her. That nurse, Zuhrah? Maybe Monelle, maybe those cops outside the door. Zuhrah could have left the door open. Those people ignore the rules, we know that. And they hate me."

"Exactly," Arden said. "And precisely why you need a lawyer. A good, hard-ass criminal lawyer. You need to be protected. More than I can do without a law degree."

"Nyomi Chang is my lawyer," Ned said.

"And she'd be the first person to tell you to hire a new one." Arden adjusted her rearview mirror, flipped on her blinker, and eased into the fast lane. Saturday traffic, impossible to predict. "How about getting a partner in her firm? If it's her colleague, then whatever you've already told Nyomi is fair game for the new lawyer. The same confidentiality. The same lawyer-client privilege. It's like having Nyomi. Until she's ready to come back."

Arden heard a rustling beside her. Ned had pulled out a turquoise minibag and flapped it in her peripheral vision. "Pretzels?" he said. "Think of them as toast strips."

"Seriously, Ned."

"Fine. I hear you. Agreed. I'll call when it's a reasonable time." Ned held out the open bag as they approached yet another traffic light. "She has a partner, Jean, something. Trout something. I'll find out. Here."

Arden took a few pretzels, white salt scattering on the black front seat. "Jean Trounstine, I know that name. She's supposed to be terrific."

He was silent for a beat. "Lawyers."

"Well," Arden began. "Sometimes it's good to have one."

"Especially if you're the fall guy," Ned said.

Arden risked a quick glance at him as the highway hooked westward. "That's a strange thing to say. Fall guy?"

"I don't know," Ned said. "But I mean, how could this have happened? Churchwood says she has video of a black Mercedes. And she decides it's *my* car? Like I said. She hates me. Maybe she's so enraged with the verdict that she's setting me up. But I just—I gotta say, even for her, that seems excessive. But something's going on. Or I might just be losing it."

"Might you want to talk with a therapist about this?" Arden began. "This is such a difficult—"

"I'm fine, Arden. All good. Just processing. Next topic."

She felt him shut down, close his body language, turn away, and look out the window.

"You know, Arden." He crumpled the empty pretzel bag. "Not everyone would be comfortable being in a car with me."

Arden raised her eyebrows. *Processing,* he'd said. "C'mon, Ned."

"Well, it's true enough," he said. "Even though it was not my car that hit Nyomi Chang. And even though Randall Tennant had no business being in our garage."

It was as if the universe was forcing her to ask. He'd brought Tennant up. *She* hadn't. They were alone, and this could be as private as any conversation could be. She needed to know the truth about this. No surprises.

She could almost hear Cordelia's voice. *Ask him where he gets his hair cut.* And here on rural Route 2 in a rented beige four-door, there was no way for him to leave if he didn't want to answer.

She felt a jab of conscience. The poor man wanted to see his children. But Cordelia had told her that Ned was a good liar. That he made people feel sorry for him. Arden kept forgetting that. And forgetting one part of her job. To find out whether there was more to the Randall Tennent story.

And whether poor Nyomi Chang, now on the cusp of life and death, was caught up in the same—whatever it was. They'd crossed over Route 495, the outer band of highway around Boston. When you drive past 495, everyone said, you were headed away from civilization. But civilization had done Ned no favors recently, so maybe this was a good idea. LANCASTER, one road sign announced. DEVENS. LEOMINSTER.

"Ned?" Arden began.

Ned's phone rang, then, that old-fashioned ring.

Arden flinched. "Is it Monelle? You do not answer Monelle. Under any circumstances. I told her to call *me*. Or is it some reporter? Do not answer. Do *not*."

"It's Cordelia," Ned said.

35

Arden kept her eyes on the pavement unspooling in front of her, but it was impossible not to overhear Ned's conversation with his wife. She could only hear Ned's half of it, and couldn't resist trying to fill in the other half.

"Hey, how are you?" Ned asked.

And then silence.

"Because the kids said you missed the FaceTime."

Silence. Cordelia must be explaining.

"Asleep? You were asleep?"

Silence. She'd heard Ned's skepticism, and implied criticism of her answer.

"It's fine, Dee, it's fine. I know you're tired, and we all are, and worried about Nyomi. Have you heard anything?"

Silence. He'd had to placate her, so she must be defending herself.

"Yes, I'm in a car. I rented one. I'm . . ."

Arden glanced at him in the space of this hesitation, and he was looking at her. "Like I said. I'm on my way to Vermont. Emma is super upset, because—"

Cordelia must have interrupted him. And he hadn't mentioned that Arden was with him. Arden couldn't ever mention it either, now, without causing a problem.

She'd called Arden less than half an hour ago, and Arden had said she was at a gas station. Cordelia might wonder why her employee—publicist? consultant?—and her husband were both up so early, and both already on the road.

What a disaster. She could just imagine it, Cordelia complaining to Warren about Arden and Ned. She could imagine, too, Warren's derision. How it would intensify his misguided belief that Patience Swanson was right. The final miserable fabricated nail in Arden's professional coffin.

"*Yes,* Dee. Of course I tried to explain that you were busy, and that you loved her, and Pip, too, and that you'd talk to her in the morning. She has Roo."

Silence. Longer silence. Cordelia should be thanking him, Arden decided. But from the sour look on Ned's face, she wasn't.

"Because she *called* me, Dee, at least my mother called, and put Emmie on the phone. She wanted to hear one of our voices. I called you, too, last night, but you didn't answer. So what was I supposed to—"

This conversation, with its baiting animosity, should have been private, and Arden felt as if she were being intrusive, but he'd opted to create the illusion he was alone, now he had to deal with it. And allow Arden to be privy to their raw exchange.

"I was worried, what can I say? Is that a bad thing? Should I not be worried when I can't reach my wife? Cordelia—"

Silence. Arden saw Ned's shoulders sag. The landscape spun by, flat and listlessly barren, trees without leaves stabbing their branches into a graying sky. Thick blackbirds perched like predators, watching the humans whoosh beneath them in their metal machines. Arden was driving in a direction she had not planned, could never have planned, with a person who was suddenly her charge. Then again, maybe Ned was in charge.

It crossed her mind, as clouds made of dark cotton filled the horizon ahead of them, that she was trapped right now. But Ned was, too.

"It's fine, Dee. It is. I'm *happy* to go to Dorset. My office is closed for the weekend. I can come back to the city if need be. But the kids need reassuring, and—"

Silence. Ned's voice had lost its sarcasm, and it almost sounded as if he were pleading with his wife. Maybe calming her. Arden heard him take a deep breath, then let out a sigh.

"Mother is perfectly capable of taking care of them, Cordelia, let's not argue. It's simply—they miss me. And you. They're kids."

Arden glanced at him again, trying to telegraph, in one expression, that she understood, that she commiserated, that she was uncomfortable hearing all this, that she wouldn't hold it against him. Ned winced. *Sorry,* he mouthed.

"So Dee, have you heard anything about Nyomi? Has anyone called you? Her paralegal, Heather Bellwin, or anyone? No?"

Arden heard him alter his tone, changing the subject, and knew he'd repeated Cordelia's "No" answers for her benefit. She nodded, held up crossed fingers. No news was good news, her new mantra.

WARWICK. The green highway sign spelled out the town name in bold white letters. Then, with an arrow pointing right, ROUTE 91 NORTH TO BRATTLEBORO. Arden patted the seat beside her with her hand, trying to get Ned's attention.

He noticed the noise, looked at her. She pointed at the sign, pantomiming, *go that way?*

Yes, he gestured to the right, nodding, *yes, take that.*

"Nothing," he said into the phone. "I had to make the turn onto 91. Should I call you when we get there? Could you FaceTime?"

Arden's phone rang. The unmistakable trill, feeling foghorn loud, came through the speakers of the Bluetooth. Her heart raced faster than the car. She looked at Ned, eyes wide. He hit the red button on his phone, hanging up on Cordelia.

"I'll say we were cut off," he said. "We're on the highway, I'll say I hit a dead zone."

"I'm so sorry," Arden said. "I understood you didn't want her to know I was with you, right? That's fine, but I couldn't get to it fast en—"

Her phone rang again. The traffic had picked up, as it sometimes mysteriously did, and she tried to keep track to the left and right, ahead and behind, steer safely, and remember how to accept a phone call on the unfamiliar car's Bluetooth.

"Nothing you could have done," Ned was saying. "But see who that is. Cordelia's going to call me back, if I don't call first, and she would hear you. Yeah, maybe should've told her I was with you, but no way to know how she would react. Crap."

Arden finally hit the right button. She held up one finger, *hang on.*

She didn't recognize the number on the caller ID. Area code 617. Boston.

"Arden Ward," she said. Ned was looking at her, inquiring. She shrugged. *No idea.*

"Lisa . . . ?" She listened, trying to decode the name. "Oh. Yes. I'm in the car, it's noisy. You're with Mass General legal department, correct? Again, sorry, it's chaotic, Saturday mornings, you know." She paused. "No, it's fine, let's talk right now."

Arden could almost feel Ned's concentrated attention as they listened to the hospital's lawyer begin to say something about a meeting

"Excuse me, Ms. Thurau-Gray? Okay, Lisa. And I'm Arden. You're on speaker, so you know. Since I'm in a car." Arden hoped Lisa would not ask whether she was alone. That would be a lie she did not want to tell.

The faint buzz of the Bluetooth speakerphone filled the car again. She felt as if she were in the midst of a professional firestorm, protecting people's lives. Cordelia's, and Ned's, and Nyomi's. And her own.

"Sure," Lisa said. "I can wait until you get to your destination."

Ned's phone rang. He clapped a palm to his forehead, and Arden saw him decline the call. Cordelia was not going to be happy.

"Now is good," Arden said, hoping Lisa hadn't noticed. "Let me ask you though, first. Is Nyomi Chang awake? Is she improving? How is she?"

"Well, that's precisely the situation."

Situation? She tried to keep her eyes on the road, and her mind on the staticky voice.

"Federal privacy rules prevent us from giving you information about a patient who may or may not be at the hospital."

"What? 'May or may not be'?" She stuck out her tongue at the Bluetooth speaker, grateful this Lisa Thurau-Gray could not see her.

"Come on, Lisa," she went on. *Calm down,* she instructed herself. *Negotiate.* "I don't think we need to handle it this way, we really don't. I'm sure you understand I was simply trying to protect Mr. Bannister, as well as your patient, from inadvertently breaching the lawyer-client confidentiality."

"And we're simply following the law."

"She's his *lawyer.* The district attorney is waiting to pounce, to charge him with god knows what. You're a lawyer, Lisa, you see the danger. If he were your client, you'd want to protect him, too."

Silence.

"Lisa?"

"I cannot say one more word about a patient who may or may not be here."

Arden could hear the satisfaction in her voice. The woman was smart. Zealously advocating for the hospital. But one wrong word from Nyomi Chang, and Ned and his family were back in the ugly spotlight. And the public would revel in gloating about Ned Bannister, the Parking Garage Killer, who had plowed down another pedestrian.

She took a deep breath, at sixty-five miles an hour, trying to figure out her next move. "Fine. And you confirm that no one from law enforcement talks to Ms. Chang until Mr. Bannister is represented."

"Agreed," the lawyer finally said. "But who's his new lawyer?"

"We'll let you know soon. Today."

"Fine."

Ned gave a thumbs-up, mouthed the words *thank you*.

"But Arden?" Lisa's voice came from the speaker again. "One more thing."

"Yes?" Arden frowned. When people said *one more thing,* it was never a good thing.

"You might want to hurry."

36

addy, Daddy!" Arden watched Emma Bannister, thin as a five-year-old blond whisper in rubber boots, a pink tulle tutu, and a pink puffer jacket, and wearing a pink knit cap with what Arden decided must be tiny mouse ears, clamber down the three wide wooden steps in front of Georgianna Bannister's sprawling colonial house. *The cabin,* Ned had called it. Classic New England understatement, Arden thought, three lofty redbrick and white wood stories topped with two tall redbrick chimneys, mullioned dormer windows and carved cornices, a pinecone wreath on the forest-green front door. A sprawling farmer's porch, chairless now, for the winter, Arden figured, but she imagined a row of rocking Adirondacks as soon as spring arrived. Every square inch of surface area was coated with snow, except for the newly shoveled front steps and long paved front walk.

Ned had called his mother when they were thirty minutes away. It had taken much longer than expected; the combination of eager weekend skiers and gawking out-of-staters making traffic a constant snarl. "I want to give her a heads-up, but not too much time," Ned had explained. "She has a landline so we don't have to worry about service."

"Cell service is—" *All* she needed. Or maybe it'd be a relief. Depending on who wanted her. Them.

"Usually fine. Iffy, but we're used to it. That's why the landline."

Cordelia had called back, suddenly "too busy," as Ned reported with a Cordelia voice, to talk any further. At one minute after nine, he'd also left a message for Nyomi's law partner Jean Trounstine. Saturday, so voice mail was the only option.

The phone, Arden thought. It ran their lives. Although she preferred to know things as soon as possible rather than wait and worry. Not a word yet from Monelle, speaking of worry.

"What are your plans for this encounter?" Arden had asked. "Do you know whether your wife has mentioned me to your mother?" Arden

winced, unpacking that sentence. It sounded like something from a melodramatic soap opera.

"Good question. We'll play it by ear."

Arden had taken the turnoff for Dorset, and the road narrowed almost
immediately. She had to slow down, and as they neared the end of the
journey, the enforced delay made the prospect of what was to come next
even more suspenseful.

She understood why Ned had covered up about Arden being in the
car. Cordelia's mercurial jealousy must be difficult to live with. Arden
had worried about that, too. Still, she was only doing the job Cordelia
had hired her to do.

Job. She had one more week.

"Play it by ear? What ear?" Arden had asked. "Am I your publicist,
your consultant, your Uber driver? What if your mother mentions it to
Cordelia? Your mother supports you, doesn't she?"

"Is there someone you know who doesn't?" Ned said. "Other than the
rest of the world? Has Cordelia said something to you? She hired you
to—" He made a dismissive sound. "Rehabilitate me. How's that going,
by the way?"

"It's lucky she did, Ned. Or you'd be on your own. Probably arrested
by now."

Arden brushed pretzel crumbs from her lap, assessing. Cordelia had
wanted her to ask Ned about Randall Tennant. But the moment she did,
their trust would be broken. He'd never deal with her the same way. But
who was sending Cordelia those harassing texts? And what if they were
true? It might not matter legally. But it might mean that Ned had put
them all in danger.

Every time she started to trust this man, the name *Cordelia* came up,
and she was reminded of her tightrope reality.

"Cordelia loves you. And is trying to help you. She—and the kids—
have had a difficult time. I'm just trying to plan," Arden said. "I suppose
I could be a friend who's bringing you to Vermont because you don't like
driving. But if your mother tells Cordelia—"

"They took my license, you know," Ned interrupted. "For forty-five
days. Nyomi got the results thrown out; those breathalyzers are crap.
But the whole thing just—dragged on. They can punish you even if you
didn't do anything wrong."

Arden nodded. "The law protects everyone," she said. "An innocent person goes through the same process as a guilty one—it's only the end that's different."

They'd ridden in silence, then, passing stands of snow-topped cedars and lengths of rustic fences, no billboards in this part of the world; only the unsuccessfully disguised cell phone towers intruded on the pristine and rural landscape. Then the atmosphere changed; a lifting of weight, a distance.

"Turn here," Ned had said, pointing. "That's our driveway." He gestured in front of them. "We're in the Green Mountains," he said. "That's Owls Head. Up there ahead. You a hiker?"

She made a face.

"I see. Maybe not," he said.

They'd rattled up the crushed gravel driveway, lined with columns of spiny evergreens, and the sun seemed to be burning the clouds off the mountains beyond. Owls Head, Ned had called it. *Hiking. As if.* Her kickboxing was all the exercise she wanted, and that was indoors. Arden had parked the rental car in the horseshoe turn around in front of the house, and hung back, trying to be invisible, as Ned hurried to meet his daughter.

Georgianna Bannister, must be, had positioned herself at the top step, stationed in front of the lacquered front door. A sentry, or a welcoming committee. Steely gray hair, black turtleneck over black leggings, sturdy-looking black boots. A border collie, maybe, seated but with tail wagging furiously, waited obediently by her side.

"Hello, sweetheart," Georgianna called. "What a treat!"

Ned had trotted the last three steps toward his daughter, and swooped her up in his arms, twirling her around.

"A ballerina in the snow? You're a ballerina in the snow, Emmie!" Arden heard him say; his voice had become enthusiastic. Loving.

"Like that snow globe you gave me, Daddy. Yes! I'm a . . ." She lifted her arms over her head, posing. "A ballerina in the snow."

"And you are beautiful and perfect," Ned said. In the stillness, Arden could hear every word. "Maybe later we can come out and dance in the snow, but aren't you very very cold? We should go inside."

Carrying his daughter, he climbed to the porch and wrapped his free arm around his mother. Arden saw her lean into him, for a fraction of a second. Then step back, looking him up and down.

"Have you had breakfast? Lunch?"

"Hey, Mom," he said. "I can always have more of either." He gave her a quick peck on the cheek, and the dog snuffled around Ned's legs. "Hey Bartok." He skritched the dog's calico ear, and the dog almost fainted with delight. Mother, son, granddaughter, dog, and the picturesque Vermont farmhouse in the snow. A postcard of happiness, Arden thought, but nothing could be further from the truth.

Arden had a moment of wondering whether she should just get in the car and drive away. Pretend to be an Uber driver, something like that.

But now Ned was waving her toward them, encouraging her.

"Thanks for being flexible, Mom. Is Pip around?" Ned turned, gesturing. "And Mom, that's—"

"Arden Ward," Georgianna said.

"Arden Ward," Ned repeated. "How did you—?"

"Welcome, Arden." Georgianna waved, greeting her. "Never a dull moment around here. I rely on it. Pip is upstairs, Minecrafting. Boys will be boys. As I learned the hard way. I'm glad you're home, dear." She stood on tiptoe, gave Ned a kiss on the cheek.

"We're making lunch pancakes for you, Daddy! In shapes!" Emma said. She'd wrapped her booted legs around her father's waist; a contented, comfortable position she'd clearly taken many times. Ned carried her as if she were weightless.

"Shapes of what?" Ned asked her. "Should we go bother your brother?"

Feeling the three sets of eyes on her, Arden hurried up a damp gray front walk mounded on either side by snow-covered chrysanthemums, a hint of their coppery yellow peeking through on some of them, their green leaves persisting under the snow. Arden had no one, not even her parents, and sometimes, looking at a tableau like this, she wondered why she had chosen career over family. Any number of times she could have gotten married, did, even, that once, disastrously. Now it might be too late for her. There would never be a farmhouse like this, or a grandmother like this, or children like this.

She rarely regretted it, but soon she'd go home to no job and no family and no anything, just some fish. Times like these she'd still dredge her memory for advice from her mother or father, but right now she couldn't think of anything consoling. Here in this snow-covered Vermont moment, she was alone.

Ned was making a show of shifting Emma's position, and the little girl giggled with delight.

"You are getting too big for this, Em! Arden," he went on, introducing, as she approached. "This is my mother, Georgianna."

"Lovely to meet you," Arden said, that thing you say even in the worst of situations. It wasn't lovely, none of this was, it was simply a father's desire to make his children feel safe and happy. But at the other end of the highway, back in Boston, a situation might be unfolding that would make her father very *un*happy.

"Daddy, can we go in?" Emma, still clinging, began tugging at Ned's jacket. There was not a hint of whining in her voice, Arden heard, only a little girl who wanted her father's attention. "I am way too cold. Aren't you way too cold? Grammy, aren't you way too cold? Way. Too. Cold," she repeated.

"Of course, petunia," Ned said. "But first say hello to my friend Ms. Ward. She's probably cold, too."

Emma put her thumb into her mouth. Then she laid her head on her father's shoulder, curling up into him, looking at Arden from under her eyelashes.

"Hi, Emma," Arden said. "I love your tutu."

Arden felt the little girl's curious scrutiny. The thumb came out. "Hi." She turned back to her father. Held him even more urgently. "See? Mommy was wrong. You're still here."

"Wrong?"

Arden saw the confusion on Ned's face.

Emma nodded, infinitely serious. "She told me you might be going away. For a very long time."

PART THREE

37

MONELLE CHURCHWOOD

Four hours of sleep. *Four.* Monelle walked the hospital corridor, groggy and still undercaffeinated, counting 142 steps from one end to the other. At the portrait of a sour-faced white guy, probably a hospital donor, she pivoted again, powered by her own frustration and animosity.

Would Nyomi wake up? When? And what would she say? The morning had ticked by, offering nothing but speculation.

Monelle strode past the chiaroscuro photograph of some Italian village, then the fake impressionist wheatfields. Nyomi had to know something about what happened. Had to. If Nyomi implicated Ned Bannister, in any way whatsoever, that'd be sufficient for probable cause to arrest him. But yesterday, Arden Ward had almost dragged Bannister bodily out of here. And that pushy woman had prevented everyone in law enforcement—everyone meaning Monelle—from hearing what Nyomi Chang might say.

And to seal the deal, to totally keep the lid on, the hospital had sent a Valkyrie in a black turtleneck to join the waiting party. She'd introduced herself as "Kath Sundstrom. MGH security" and now she sat on the bench, staring at Nyomi's door as if daring it to open. Today's plain-clothes team had also arrived; an up-and-comer called PJ Noonan, and Detective Josiah Owulu, PJ's savvy mentor. The two had bonded over their obsession with the daily *Globe* crossword puzzle and now sat, heads down, pens in hand, muttering. Unless, of course, some non-hospital person approached Nyomi Chang's room. Then they had weapons mightier than their pens. *They'd* apparently all slept as usual.

She hadn't. Four hours of sleep.

Monelle herself had staked out the sedated Nyomi as long as she could, then finally taken a saggy Uber home, hoping Nolah and the kids would not wake up. But Nolah had been staking *her* out, sitting in her big blue reading chair, a mug on the table beside her, the tea bag tag hanging out.

She was up to her chin in a plaid blanket, and dead asleep. Monelle had tiptoed up to the mug of tea and put her hand around it. Stone cold.

"Don't think you can ease on by me." Nolah had not opened her eyes as she spoke. "I can see you through my eyelids, and I can smell the sneaky on you, sister. You know I'm bionic when it comes to you." She'd opened her eyes, by then, thrown the blanket around her shoulders like a shawl, given Monelle a welcoming kiss. "News?"

"Nyomi Chang is still out of it," Monelle had said. "They won't let me question her, won't allow *any* law enforcement in. They're assigning hospital security to guard her. Believe that? It's obstruction of justice, and—"

"And there's not one thing you can do about it at four in the morning. Go to sleep, get up, it'll be a new dawning day and things will be better."

Now she hoped Nolah's "things will be better" prediction would soon come true. Cops were scouting for witnesses. Scrounging for store surveillance. They had that one lousy cell phone video snippet, taken by a quick-fingered bystander, showing a maybe-black maybe-Mercedes. Like Ned's. Maybe. Better than nothing. Their video team was trying to enhance it, *a fifty-fifty chance*, they'd whined. The witness who'd shot it had refused to give his name, said he didn't see anything, and told the police "I was looking at my phone, right?" Ridiculously, the city's closed-circuit traffic cam feeds were not recorded, some legal thing that some goody-good defense attorneys had finagled.

Monelle's brain accelerated along with her walking speed. Wonder how they would feel now, those goody-good *lawyers*, now that one of their own was on the precipice of death, maybe, and Monelle—simply doing her job for justice—could not discover who had harmed her because of their misguided zeal.

"*I*—" She jabbed a finger into her own chest, incensed, grumbling to herself. "I actually went with Arden Ward to that garage. I told her about the—"

"You okay?" PJ asked.

"Fine. Fine as anyone could be in this situation." She stopped, spun to face him. "The witness to a crime, the actual victim, might be able to tell us exactly what happened. But no, of *course* not, some attorney comes in and impedes the entire process of justice."

"*You're* an attorney." Owulu looked up from his crossword. "If I may remind you."

"What's a five-letter word for wise guy?" Monelle said. But she laughed as she continued her hallway march.

Things had to change today. The DA was counting on her.

If there was such a thing as speed dial, Charles C. Stamoran, Suffolk County district attorney, had her on it. And she knew CCS, as they called him, was as bitter about Ned Bannister, and all he stood for, as she was.

"Him and his money. Because he owns half the city, he thinks he owns the justice system, too. He's a damn white privilege asshat," Stamoran had said on Friday, right after they'd heard what happened to Nyomi Chang. Both had been on the verge of leaving the office—Monelle actually buttoning her coat, and preparing a *see I'm not late this time* speech for Nolah—when the police call came in.

Monelle had bitten her tongue at Stamoran's white privilege line, and Bannister hardly owned half the city, but point well-taken. And she'd learned when to shut up. She'd had a case once where the DUI defendant had screamed at her in court, yelling "you can't do this to me, I have white privilege!" *People unclear on the concept,* Monelle had told Nolah. The woman got twenty-three months, and it was Monelle's privilege to tell her so.

Stamoran had kept her standing in front of him like a misbehaving student in the principal's office. Swiveling behind his battered wooden desk, rolling a fat black pen between his thumb and forefinger, Stamoran had the bespoke demeanor of a patrician Brahmin, but underneath he was battle-scarred and brutally ambitious. Monelle knew he had come from a hardscrabble background, done his best to polish off his rough edges, but his vocabulary disintegrated when he got angry. That's what made him good, she had to admit. He could succeed in two worlds. Street fighting, or cocktail party schmoozing. She knew he had higher ambitions. She did too.

"And it is still difficult, Ms. Churchwood," he had said, his eyebrows, gray and trimmed, lifting for a sarcastic moment, "difficult for me not to blame you personally."

She had opened her mouth to protest, but he'd lifted one palm as a barrier.

"I know, I know. Not a public way, screwed up Breathalyzer, no surveillance. And now he's out there, driving again. And what does the flippin' moron do? This time we will not let him go. *You* will not."

"Why would a person run over his own lawyer?" Monelle pursed her lips, thinking.

"She knew something. She was about to tell. He needed to stop her. A whole goddam list of reasons. He's an idiot, though. Might have chosen a more subtle method. But I suppose you take the opportunities you can get."

"We're going to need more than—"

"Then get it," Stamoran had ordered her. "Get 'more than.' You blew the first case. Now the gods have given you another try. And by the gods, I mean me."

Monelle's eyes had widened at that, but Stamoran had turned on the charm.

"Joking," he said. "Now go forth and nail the bastard."

"On it," Monelle had said.

Now, Saturday just past noon, standing in the hospital corridor with a silent witness legally barricaded behind a guarded door, Monelle was so deep in thought that when the phone rang in her blazer pocket, she almost didn't recognize what it was.

CCS, the caller ID said. Monelle's Spidey sense shifted into high. Charles Stamoran. There must be news. Something must have happened.

38

ARDEN WARD

The Bannister home was a postcard, but sitting in Georgianna Bannister's kitchen was a page from a glossy aspirational magazine. An array of nubby gourds, the color of autumn leaves and sprigged with bittersweet branches, scattered expansively across the white cloth covering the kitchen table. The place smelled of coffee and bacon and pancakes, and Arden wondered how someone selfish and manipulative could have grown up in all this homey warmth.

She sat, empty chairs around her, feeling like she must look. A solitary person in a world where she was not connected to anyone. Emma had taken Ned upstairs to see some new treasure. Georgianna, wearing a green canvas apron with a linen towel draped over the drawstrings, had bustled off to drag Pip from his games.

"That boy," she'd said, affectionate and exasperated, the perfect TV mom.

Arden took out her cell phone, and placed it on the white tablecloth. Her cell phone, her companion, her lifeline.

She took another sip of the coffee, chocolatey and subtle, and wondered how rude it would be to call Warren. *Where are you?* he'd ask. *I'm trapped in a Currier & Ives etching,* she'd have to say. She hoped she wasn't actually trapped. She touched the car key fob in her pocket. *Nyomi,* Arden thought. *What happened to you?*

She heard a noise. An odd scratching. A clattering. She tensed, waiting.

The dog paused at the entryway to the kitchen, cocked his head at her.

Bartok, she remembered his name was. And she, Arden, was an idiot.

"Good puppy," she said. "Hi, Bartok." He wagged his plumy tail, still tentative. And then, behind Bartok, footsteps. Ned. And Emma. She could hear them chatting before they arrived at the dining room archway.

"Hey, Arden. Emmie showed me where she wants to put her new fish," Ned said. He'd changed into a flannel shirt, *of course,* Arden thought, and jeans, and tan moccasins with tassels. But the two of them were cute together, the little ballerina and her Ralph Lauren father. He seemed far from the vilified real estate exec who mowed down innocent people. But again, what do bad guys look like?

"She did, huh? Fish?" Arden had only fuzzy memories of being Emma's age. She'd felt safe, and loved at least, so long ago, with a beagle named Pepper. And goldfish. "Emma, so you're thinking about fish. What kind of fish?" Arden spread her hands wide apart. "Like that big? The kind you get fishing?"

Emma apparently did not think that was funny, and tucked herself behind her father. Looked at Arden as if she were from another planet.

"She's teasing, Emmo," Ned said.

"She's silly," Emma whispered. Bartok had plopped himself down by Emma's side, his head just reaching the edges of her pink tutu.

"I love to be silly," Arden lied. "Don't you?"

"Yes!" Emma said, and deigned to reveal her full tulled self again. "Do you have fish?"

Ned's eyes widened. But she didn't need his signals.

"I did when I was little," Arden said, happy not to lie. "Named Merry and Pippin."

"I'll read you that book someday," Ned said. "We'll read it together. Your mom can read it with us, too. Now what did you say about pancakes?"

Arden wondered how Ned could seem so at ease, so unworried by the potentially devastating chaos that awaited him in Boston. Here in the serene protection of his childhood home, where no one could find him, maybe he felt safe. Safety would be brief, she predicted. All hell would certainly break loose very soon.

Bartok suddenly pivoted and trotted away. And a second later, Georgianna appeared with a stocky mop-haired boy at her side.

"Phillip, say hello to Miss Ward," Georgianna instructed.

"Hi," the boy said. "Nice to meet you." It came out one word, *nicetomeechu*.

"Hi Phillip," Arden said. "Nice to meet you, too."

Arden felt like she had entered a movie where everyone had lines, and everyone knew them except for her, and she had to improvise, guess, try to fit in. When Georgianna Bannister recognized her, out on the front steps, Arden had been surprised. But as they walked inside, Georgianna had explained how Cordelia had mentioned hiring Arden.

"If you can make my son's life more . . . pleasant," she'd said, "I'd be grateful. It appears much of the public has very little brain, and certainly no compassion. Ned has suffered quite a bit through this. It's the first time I've been relieved his father is not here to experience it." She put a palm to her chest, fiddled with her turtleneck. "And of course the children are affected. And Cordelia."

"What do you think about that? About it all?" Arden had said, gently probing. "Cordelia doesn't know I'm here, in fact."

"I understand." Georgianna nodded. "But I only want what's best for my son. Thank you for driving him, too."

Georgianna's voice had dropped to a whisper as they walked up the hall. She pointed to a row of brass coat hooks on the wall, some hung with nylon jackets and a rainbow of striped scarves, then gestured to Arden's puffer. "I'm reassured that he admitted he didn't feel comfortable driving," she said, as Arden hung her vest. "It means he trusts you, and that's good enough for me."

Arden almost burst into tears at that, Georgianna's declaration of trust in her. And at Georgianna's faith in Ned. In this setting, Ned didn't seem even close to deceptive or nefarious or dangerous. And the jury had deemed him—legally—not guilty. If that was *actually* true, then something else was going on.

But Nyomi Chang. Those two events, Randall Tennant and Nyomi Chang—two car "accidents"—could not be unconnected. The texts. The video. Nyomi being hit right after meeting Arden.

There could never be that much coincidence.

39

MONELLE CHURCHWOOD

onelle Churchwood." She'd answered the phone even before the second ring. Turning her back on PJ and Owulu, keeping her conversation private from the two cops who were certainly listening. And from the Valkyrie. Charles Stamoran was calling. Wheels were in motion.

"You at the hospital?"

"In the hall, outside Nyomi Chang's room."

"Anything?"

"No." Monelle turned, as if the door might have opened in the twenty seconds they'd been talking. "Hospital security has landed, such as she is."

"Visitors?"

"Nope. And nothing from any new lawyer Bannister may have hired. Unless they've called you?"

"Hardly," Stamoran said. "Plus, you're point person. All roads lead to you. Unless there's a pivotal decision. Then all roads lead to me."

Monelle, times like these, was ready to turn off her phone and stalk away down the hospital corridor one final time. Stamoran could hire a new flunky. The way he ordered her around. The whipsaw changes in his attitude. Letting out the line and giving her responsibility. Blaming her when something went wrong, taking credit when something went right. She didn't need this. But she was under the gun after the Bannister verdict. She'd been so certain of that, damn it. Stamoran had, too. And now she was paying. Plus if she ever wanted a new job, she needed his approval.

"Absolutely," she told him now, trying to keep any of what he would probably call 'attitude' out of her voice. "Speaking of which," she went on, "any word on the bystander video?"

"I'll handle that," Stamoran said. "But Nyomi Chang is the ballgame. She's a material witness. And a victim. If need be, we'll get a search warrant for her room. At some point, my patience will run out."

Owulu had materialized by her side. He cocked his head down the hall, pointed to his ear. *Listen.*

"Hold on, can you?" Monelle said into the phone. She put her hand over the receiver. *What?* She mouthed the word.

But by this time she heard what Owulu meant.

Footsteps. Hard and determined, clearly high heels on the hospital linoleum. The shoulders on the two women marching toward her were squared and straight, both wore black pencil skirts not quite matching their jackets and not quite high heels. Modest, confident, one with slicked-back gray hair, the other in braids not unlike Monelle's own.

"Lawyers incoming," Monelle told Stamoran on the phone, keeping her voice low.

"What lawyers?"

"Hard to tell. I'd guess one of them is Ned Bannister's new hire."

"Maybe Nyomi Chang's relatives?"

"I don't think this is them," Monelle said.

"Can you leave the line open as they talk to you?"

"Is that legal?" she asked.

"Legal?" She could almost hear his eyes rolling. *"Legal."*

"Miss Churchwood?" The shorter woman held out a hand as she approached. "I'm Lisa Thurau-Gray. The hospital's legal team. Call me Lisa."

Monelle lowered the phone to her side, reached out her other hand to shake. "Monelle."

"And I'm Jean Trounstine," the tall one said. "Jean. Nyomi Chang's law partner."

"How is she?" Monelle asked. "Is she awake?"

"I'm not going to discuss that with you," Lisa told her.

Monelle could almost feel Stamoran yelling on the other end of the phone.

"What? Not discuss?" She must have looked utterly perplexed. "This is a hospital, you're the hospital lawyer. I'm asking: How is your patient? Surely you can tell me that."

"I agree, Ms. Churchwood." Jean Trounstine was nodding. "I came here first thing this morning, but the reception desk called Miss Gray here, who explained that no one in law enforcement could go in until Mr. Bannister gets a lawyer. Very prudent. But I'm not law enforcement."

This time Monelle could definitely hear buzzing on Stamoran's end of the phone. Her boss, yelling. No way to disguise it.

She put the phone to her ear. "Oh, hello," she said, innocent and apologetic. "Let me call you back." She paused as Stamoran roared his disapproval. No one told Charles Stamoran they'd call him back.

"Who's—?" Lisa began to ask.

"Can I have two minutes?" Monelle tried to placate Stamoran, then sent up a silent prayer for absolution. Then she clicked off the call, and turned to the two women. "Where were we?" She nodded, remembering. "Right. No law enforcement goes in. Ridiculous as it is."

"But again, I'm not law—" Jean began.

"The hospital is also keeping her closed to *other* visitors," Lisa said. "For her safety. And ours."

Jean hoisted her tote bag higher on her shoulder. "Very good. But. I'm her lawyer. You need to let me in."

"What? Jean, no, you're not her lawyer," Monelle protested. "When did she hire—"

"I don't need to tell you that."

"Show me the paperwork."

"Will do, Monelle. And if anything happens to Nyomi Chang in the meantime, Lisa—" Jean pointed a forefinger at the hospital attorney. "*You* are responsible."

"Give me a br—" Lisa was almost sputtering.

"*Completely* responsible." Jean had pointed again, emphatic. Her parting shot came as she strode away. "And that is on the record."

"My brain is exploding," Monelle said. "Does *everyone* want to get in the way of justice?"

"Poor Ms. Chang." Lisa shrugged. "We're doing all we can."

Monelle's heart dropped. "What do you mean 'poor'? 'Doing' what? Why?"

"I'm sorry." Lisa looked at the floor.

"You're—?"

"We'll be in touch. I need to get back. It's going to be a long day."

"Got that right," Owulu said. The detective had come up beside her as they watched the lawyer go.

"Cluster, huh?" Monelle muttered. "She's in there, we're out here, and the bad guy's getting away. You hear anything in there? Alarms, beeps, voices?" Monelle asked. "Phone?"

"Would have told you," Owulu said.

Monelle's cell rang. She held up the caller ID to the cops. *CCS*. Made a face like, *here goes*.

"What the hell," Stamoran began before Monelle could say anything. "You hung up on me."

"I'd never do that," she said. "The connection must have dropped. But listen." She told him what had transpired. "And we have no idea where Ned Bannister is anyway," she ended her story. "My last conversation with Arden Ward, she wouldn't say where they were. Or going. So we have no eyes on him."

"That's where you're wrong," Stamoran said.

40

ARDEN WARD

Arden waited for her second coffee to cool, wondering how quickly she could extricate herself and Ned from this family gathering. How could he just casually chitchat over brunch with his mother and kids? He needed to get a lawyer. They'd listened to the news on the radio as they drove here, Nyomi not the top headline, but close. Stories full of legally careful allusions describing Nyomi as "the lawyer for the acquitted so-called Garage Killer." "Clinging to life." Couched and qualified, tiptoeing, devastating. Reporters must not have the video yet, or any texts, but Arden predicted it was only a matter of time. Monelle held that video time bomb in her hands. She'd unleash it when she was ready. Arden was sure of that.

She stirred her coffee, half hearing the conversation around her, watching the dark liquid swirling in her mug. A tiny vortex, turning in on itself.

Arden and Ned had been together for almost twenty-four solid hours now, in such a pressure cooker of emotions—fear, and sorrow, and suspicion—that it felt like time had made its own rules for them. Intensified, and contracted. Everything in their lives depended on what someone else said or did or wanted. But Arden still did not know Ned Bannister at all.

She looked up at him, sitting across the table from her. He was looking at her, too.

"What?" she said.

"Nothing." He turned his attention to his son. Pip held a ceramic pitcher shaped like a maple tree and was dumping fragrant maple syrup over his towering stack of pancakes.

"Hey, buddy," Ned told him. "Save some for next time."

Pip didn't look up as he continued. "It's good this way."

"I bet," Ned said.

"Let him be," Georgianna Bannister said from her place at the stainless-steel stove. "Growing boy." She poured more pancake batter into a loved-looking cast-iron pan. Emma, perched on a three-step kitchen stool, watched intently, naming shapes.

"Mickey Mouse," she said. "That's three circles. Make an *E* for Emma, Gramma," she instructed.

Make an S for screwed, Arden thought. They were hiding here in postcard land, but Monelle Churchwood and her band of investigators were probably scanning traffic videos. Finding witnesses. Building a case.

Wake up, Nyomi, Arden sent a silent prayer. One right word, exactly the right words, from Nyomi could eliminate the sword over Ned's head. It wouldn't solve everything, but one step at a time.

When did Ned know Randall Tennant, and how did he know him, went through Arden's mind. The minute they were alone, she'd just ask him about the barbershop. Could she do that? *Why do you ask?* he'd say. And then how would she answer? He would never trust her again. And she kept wondering—for all her explanations, why hadn't Cordelia told him about the texts? And moreover, why did Warren send the Bannisters to Arden specifically? She'd call him, right now.

"May I use your bathroom?"

"Where we hung your coat," Georgianna said. "The door next to that."

"Thanks." She put a hand on top of her cup. "My coffee's perfect, and I'll finish it when I get back, okay?"

Emma and her grandmother were negotiating whether the little girl could use the spatula to flip the pancakes as Arden left the room, passing a living room bursting with plaid couches and strewn magazines, a LEGO set with its blocky colored pieces scattered across a braided rug. Arden found the bathroom light, closed the door. Locked it.

She stared at herself in the medicine cabinet mirror, saw her tousled hair and ineffective mascara and lack of lipstick, and wished she had some aspirin or ibuprofen or anything that could relieve the headache she felt rumbling behind her eyes.

She lifted her hand to open the medicine cabinet, then put it down, feeling intrusive.

It's the powder room, she reminded herself. It's *for* guests.

The bathroom was painted a matte barn red, and white hand towels with embroidered golden wheat hung on a brass towel rack, folded precisely. A faceted crystal dispenser held liquid orange soap, and Arden imagined persimmon, or tangerine. Across one wall, a gallery of black-framed photographs of a goofy golden retriever and a little boy, romping in a bucolic springtime meadow. She came closer to the photographs, examining the boy's face, looking for Ned. She saw the Bannister house in the background of one of the photos, bathed in golden sunlight, a patch of a swath of lavender growing along a pathway. Was this the childhood of a liar? Of a drunken self-centered philandering business executive? Every psychology book would say no, but who knew what happened to people. Money happened. And pressure, and ambition. Jealousy. Greed.

Funny, little boy Ned did not look like Pip at all, she thought, examining the photographs. Even at that age, young Ned was lanky and tall, with cheekbones even then, and a sense of presence. Pip was the opposite; rounder, stockier, curves instead of angles. Maybe Pip had gotten Cordelia's genes. While Emma got her father's.

Cordelia. The girl had not mentioned her mother again, so maybe Ned's visit had done the trick. Maybe they could leave.

Although why was she in a hurry? Ned would be hounded wherever he went. It was safer to stay right here.

"Ha," she said out loud. These days, she had no idea what safe even meant.

Advil. She needed it. And, though she knew she was reciting the predictable mantra of everyone who snooped in a medicine cabinet, no one would ever know.

She opened the rectangular medicine cabinet to reveal a polished-mirrored interior. She could see herself again, and the photographs behind her, and the deep red wall. There was a white plastic container of Advil, and one of aspirin, and a tiny tube of toothpaste and a navy-blue toothbrush, brand new, still pristine in sealed plastic. And next to that, a miniature brandy snifter filled with multicolored perfume samples. Each one seemed different, and expensive, and doubled in volume by the mirrors. Classics, Arden saw, Shalimar, and L'Air du Temps. She risked putting a forefinger into the jar, shifting the minuscule bottles. Caleche, and Chanel, and Miss Dior. Nina Ricci. *Old-school,* she thought, no Gaultier or Opium or Poison for Georgianna Bannister. It was pretty when the lights from the wall sconces hit the jewel-like bottles, each one a special fragrance, as beautiful outside as inside.

Hurry up, she instructed herself. And as she reached for the Advil bottle, and looked at the perfume container from a different angle, she saw it. A tiny clear tube filled with amber liquid, and on the outside the name of the perfume. *Joy.*

"It's a *coincidence*." She actually said the words out loud. "And only proves how common the stupid perfume is," she muttered. She shook out two pills, then a third, turned on the water and, realizing there were no bathroom cups, lowered her head and drank from the faucet. Slugged the pills down.

Joy. Of all the incongruous names. It was *Joy* that had brought her here, in a way, and now there it was in Ned's own house, taunting her.

But it meant nothing. It meant absolutely nothing.

She fussed with her hair, a losing battle, and flushed the toilet so they knew she had not been lying. Then she washed her hands, so they would hear the water running. She had to stop worrying about her blazingly unfair treatment from the malevolent Swansons and from her own boss. Warren had decided what was important to him. Money, not loyalty. Not Arden. And now there was no time to privately call him.

By the time she got back to the kitchen, Emma and Georgianna had joined Ned at the table. Emma sat as close as possible to her father, shoulder to shoulder.

Pip, slouched, had his elbows on the table, chin in his hands.

Georgianna reached over and ruffled Pip's unruly hair.

"Come *on*." Pip squirmed away from her touch, half batted his grandmother's hand away. "Gimme a break."

"Pip," Ned began.

"You need a haircut, young man," Georgianna said. "Doesn't your mother take you to the barber?"

"Mommy?" Emma alerted at the name.

"Pancakes, Emmo," Ned said, pointing.

Arden almost missed the seat of her chair as she tried to sit. She knew she must have looked surprised, hearing Georgianna Bannister's random question about haircuts, and coughed to cover it up.

Georgianna was still talking. "Ned, darling," she said. "Why don't you take this young man to that place you go to in Boston? What's it called?"

41

MONELLE CHURCHWOOD

"Do you have a warrant?" The attendant in the booth at the entrance to the Bannister parking garage had opened a yellow-filmed plexiglass window, removing the barrier between him and Owulu. The attendant wore a pale blue work shirt, with a black plastic nametag pinned over the chest pocket. ORVATH WELLING, BANNISTER GARAGE. Welling's battered green cap did not seem regulation, and his long fingers were yellowed with nicotine stains. A metal ashtray set in a black beanbag, filled with stubbed-out filters and gray ashes, sat next to him on the counter. A brown plastic radio muttered an unintelligible talk show.

"And yeah," Welling went on as if gaining confidence. "Do you have some identification?"

Monelle stood behind the police detective, watching this unfold. Yes, they did have a warrant, but she'd let Owulu have the fun of telling this guy so. *Little victories,* she thought.

A car's horn beeped, a BMW driver in the exit lane impatient with the woman in front of him fumbling with her exit card. No cars were entering the garage at 4:00 P.M. on a dreary Saturday afternoon, but the exit lane was bumper to bumper, salt-spattered Audi and Avalon exhausts pluming into the musty chill. Weekend for them, Monelle thought, but workday for her and Detective Owulu.

"Yes, sir, Mr. Welling." Owulu was using his polite voice. He'd been on the accident reconstruction team at one point and had asked to be assigned to this investigation.

"Can I *see* it?" The attendant turned the radio down, and seemed unnecessarily suspicious, but then again, no one liked dealing with cops. Unless they needed one.

Owulu flipped open his badge wallet, showed it, put it back in his pocket. Then pulled out a folded piece of paper. Plainclothes cops never liked to wear overcoats, and Monelle could never figure out how they stayed warm in Boston winters with only tweed jackets. Cops looked at it as a badge of honor, *we don't need no stinkin' coats*.

Monelle wrapped her arms around herself to keep warm, happy she hadn't worn her good white coat, like when she'd been here with Arden Ward. She shook her head, remembering. Arden Ward. *What a liar.* She watched the attendant squint, concentrating, as he read the warrant.

"How are we getting a warrant?" Monelle had asked Charles Stamoran ninety minutes or so ago. He'd called her to his office, gestured her to a black leather visitor's chair. He'd remained behind his desk. "What probable cause do we have to search Ned Bannister's car? Why don't you pick him up, if you know where he is?"

"Can of worms," Stamoran said. "He'll come home, he has to. And if he goes elsewhere, I'll know."

"How?"

Stamoran had kept talking. "And the probable cause for a warrant is that I want one. And I can get said warrant, from a few judges at least, simply by saying please. Even on a Saturday afternoon."

Monelle had fidgeted at that, shifting in the slick chair. She'd experienced the fragility of such "favors," the possibility some defense attorney could fight it, and win, and evidence the warrant unearthed would be declared "fruit of the poisonous tree," and thrown out. *Some defense attorney,* she thought. Like Nyomi. Who was still in the hospital and still out of reach and still either talking or not, Schrödinger's patient, no way to know until she knew.

It was Arden Ward's fault. And now the woman was clearly on the run with her client. Or whatever he was to her. She flashed on Arden's disheveled blouse and mussed hair. The beer. The couch cushions in disarray. Arden's discomfort. Her lies, and her omissions about his whereabouts— that he had been upstairs in her very house. And Arden might have been the last person to talk to Nyomi.

"Reasons for the warrant?" Stamoran had used his fingers to count off his points. "Like I told Judge Kelly. One. Ned Bannister has a history of vehicular homicide. Two, that video. Three, he's fled the jurisdiction. Four. His, whatever she is, bodyguard, has put a damn monkey wrench into our interviewing the victim—consciousness of guilt. And five, Nyomi Chang was his—"

"—lawyer," Monelle had finished his sentence. "And the one who, I hesitate to remind you, got him acquitted of said charge. There is utterly no reason for him to be involved in this."

"Nyomi Chang is a menace." Stamoran had leaned forward, elbows on his massive wooden desk, and jabbed at her with a forefinger. "And I told you, Bannister's trying to shut her up about something. She'd clearly threatened him, and was on her way to see him, and safer to let her have it during rush hour than in the confines of his office, where anyone could have seen them. Do the math."

The math hadn't added up to Monelle at all, and seemed completely backward. Why hit Nyomi on purpose in public? *Ned Bannister is smarter than that,* she thought, then wondered about her own definition of smart.

But Stamoran was the boss. The DA had sent an intern to scout the garage and make sure Bannister's car was there. Then, true to his word, had gotten the search warrant from the compliant judge.

And here they were, now, serving it.

"I guess it'll do." Welling handed the warrant back to Owulu, and Monelle saw a tattooed bracelet of blue barbed wire around the man's wrist.

Within minutes they'd taken a creaky unreliable-sounding elevator to the lowest floor of the parking garage, where Ned Bannister's chunky black Mercedes sat parked, a solitary metal hulk surrounded by empty parking places. Even though there were no windows, Monelle could feel the November chill from outside, and the desolate emptiness of a place where people had once been, but were no longer. Fluorescent lights, and the distant hum of a heating system that did not work well enough. Nolah and the kids would have dinner without her again. But Nolah loved justice just as much as Monelle did. And choices had to be made.

"How are we going to get inside this thing?" Monelle asked again. There were all kinds of specific legal rules about searching cars, lots of exceptions and caveats. "You keep saying it'll be fine."

"Nothing more powerful than a screwdriver and a warrant, Mo," Owulu said. "But if all goes as planned, we won't need to get inside."

Monelle thought about that as they approached the car. "Right. Because when a car hits someone—"

"There'll be evidence on the outside of the vehicle."

"If they haven't removed it. Fixed it. Whoever they is."

"There's fixing it and fixing it." Owulu pointed. "And we may be in luck."

The black car sat illuminated by a spluttering fluorescent light above it, its wheel covers salt spattered, and the hubcaps crusty with white residue.

"No damage. I can see. Huh. How is that lucky? And it's coated with road salt," Monelle said.

"That's the luck," Owulu said. "Don't touch anything."

The detective pulled out a cell phone, clicked on the flashlight. Played it, inch after inch, across the front of the car.

Monelle watched, imagining what might have happened. She calculated the height of the bumper, of the side panel. Remembered the petite Nyomi, who'd stood beside her in court. She thought about the heavy car, and the gravity of Nyomi's injuries. What she must have felt when it—

"Look." Owulu aimed his light.

Monelle stepped closer. Saw what he meant. "No salt. I mean, there's one place where the salt is—smudged off."

"Bingo." Owulu was clicking at his phone, and now aimed it at the side panel, taking photos.

"Let's get Nyomi's coat," Monelle said. "And then let's get Ned Bannister."

42

ARDEN WARD

Ned hadn't reacted, Arden noticed, when his mother mentioned taking Pip to the barber. He hadn't glanced at her. Or looked uncomfortable.

Arden pretended to sip her coffee, waiting for the answer she so deeply wanted. It would solve everything if he would say the name of the barbershop. Then she wouldn't have to ask him, and she could simply go there and ask a few questions.

An electronic beep sounded from somewhere.

"The surveillance monitor? Who's here?" Georgianna asked. "Ned, darling? Is someone else coming?"

"Mommy?" Emma said.

"No, Emmie," Ned said, but this time he *did* look at Arden. "*We're* not expecting anyone. Are *you*?"

Arden shook her head, imagining all the possibilities. Cordelia at the head of the list.

"Can you check the video monitor, please, dear?"

Ned went into the hallway, Bartok padding after him.

"It's at the end of the driveway," Georgianna said, explaining. "It's too far away to see from here, and you probably didn't notice the camera in the pillar. But anyone who turns into our driveway is either lost or invited."

"Maybe it's a delivery truck," Pip said. "We always get deliveries."

"I know," Georgianna said. "But up here, visitors are few and far between, sweetheart."

Ned returned, shaking his head. "Taillights," he said. "They must have turned in the driveway, then backed out and pulled away. Lost, I guess. Going over the river to grandmother's house for Thanksgiving, maybe. Took a wrong turn."

Bartok curled up at Georgianna's feet.

But Ned looked distressed, Arden thought. She risked a questioning glance at him, but he'd turned back to his children.

"Pip, why don't you show Miss Ward your tree house?" he said. "Your grandmother and I need to talk, and you should have a little outside time. Wouldn't you like to see the tree house, Arden? It has a great view, you can see a long way away, but even in winter, you're completely out of sight."

Pip frowned, failing to hide his unhappiness with this suggestion.

"I'd love to see it," Arden said, hoping she was picking up on Ned's cue. She'd put together that he'd seen something—or someone—in the home surveillance video, and was signaling that she could check it without being seen.

"That's very nice of you, Pip," Georgianna said. "Miss Ward, you can use any of the mudroom boots that fit you. Take any scarf and hat you fancy. Ned and I will chat, and we'll make hot chocolate when you get back."

Emma clambered onto her father's lap, cuddled up against him. "Don't *you* go, Daddy," she almost-pleaded, already understanding the power of a pout.

"Scout's honor," Ned told her, holding up a two-finger salute. "But we came all the way here to give you a big hug, or fifty hugs, and then I'll need to go back to Boston. And you'll come home too, soon."

"And Mommy?"

"She'll be there, too," Ned said. "And now you stay right here on my lap. Pip? You'll guard Miss Ward?"

Even the stubborn Pip apparently could not resist that role. He stood a little taller, and a moment of enthusiasm crossed his face, then quickly disappeared. "I guess so," he said. "If she wants."

"I wouldn't want to go alone," Arden said. "I don't even know where it is, and you might have to show me how to climb up into it."

"It's kind of hard," Pip said.

"I'll do my best," Arden said, and was rewarded to see Georgianna Bannister wink at her.

"Have fun," Ned said. "Thanks, bud."

"And you'll make your phone calls, correct?" Arden pushed him.

"As I told you I would."

Georgianna Bannister glanced between them, as if she had picked up on their telegraphed communication. "Anything I need to know?"

"All good," Ned said.

A few moments later, she and Pip were crunching down the driveway,

Arden bundled in a borrowed parka over her vest, muffler, and mittens, with one of Georgianna's Swedish knit caps pulled over her hair, the braided dangling earflaps making her feel like a beagle. Pip had unzipped his yellow parka the minute they got outside, and had refused to wear gloves. Their elongated shadows, Arden's much taller, glided beside them as they walked in the waning afternoon, surrounded on all sides by an expanse of snow, footprintless and sparkling in what remained of the sun. Lofty pine trees, their thick branches coated in white, were turning green, branch by branch, as the snow melted from them. She heard it plop onto the ground, the only sound except for the insistent call-and-response of some far-off birds.

"Do you ice-skate or ski?" Arden tried for conversation as they trudged. The driveway was long, and curved, and kept the house out of sight from the road. She hoped it kept them out of sight, too. Ned must not have thought it was dangerous, since he'd sent his son out with her. But it was distressing enough, she calculated, that he did not want to risk being seen himself.

"Nope," Pip said.

So much for conversation. "I saw your T-shirt says 'Minecraft.' Your father says you're an expert."

"Yeah."

They walked in silence for a minute or two. Making small talk with an eleven-year-old boy was tougher than she'd predicted.

"How's school?" she tried. Then remembered how Cordelia had explained the difficulties at Dunham.

"Fine."

"That's good," Arden said. And then she thought of something else to ask, something that she did not want to ask, but that might seem logical to an eleven-year-old. And not suspicious or threatening, like it might to his savvier father.

"So *do* you get haircuts with your dad? Like your grandmother said? What's the name of the haircut place again?"

"Huh?" Pip said.

Good try, Arden thought. But she couldn't push it any further. Besides, grilling a kid about his father's activity was pretty much over the line. Except—what was the price of justice? Her own father used to quote Socrates to her; "Nothing is to be preferred before justice."

Unless it put this boy's father in prison.

Or kept him out.

"We're almost at the tree house," Pip was saying. "If you still wanna see it. It's like two more bends in the driveway. It's kind of high."

"Your dad seemed proud of it," Arden said. "Did he play there when he was your age? Or did he build it for you?"

Pip kept walking, his eyes straight ahead, and did not answer. More snow splatted onto the ground, and though Arden could not see the street yet, she picked out a wooden structure balanced in a massive bare-branched tree.

"Is that it?" She pointed. "That's pretty cool and you're right, it's high. How far can you see from up there?"

Pip tilted his head, thinking. "You can see the street. And like, the lake way out there. Once I saw a hawk. And a fox. You have to be really really quiet. They don't like people."

"There must be lots of cool animals here," she said, happy for common ground. "Do you and your dad come and look at them?"

Arden saw Pip's chin go up. He wiped his nose on his parka sleeve.

"He's not my dad," Pip said.

43

MONELLE CHURCHWOOD

Stamoran had actually come to his feet when Monelle arrived at the door of his office, a wolf sniffing prey. Or smelling victory.

Owulu had airdropped all the photos to her, and had stayed behind in the garage, in case anyone—Ned—came to retrieve the car. Or wash it.

"Here's the car." Monelle handed her phone to the DA. "We need a warrant for Nyomi Chang's coat."

Stamoran used two fingers to enlarge the photo.

"If I may." Monelle gently took the phone back. Swiped to the left. "Here's a closer shot." She swiped again. "And here you can really see the smudge. I think—and Owulu thinks—this would reach about thigh-high on Nyomi Chang."

"Told you. Bring me that coat. Now. And I predict what's not on the fender of Bannister's car is now on her coat."

"Locard's principle," Monelle said. "With contact between two items, there will be an exchange."

"Whatever you call it. It's evidence. And indisputable. We couldn't get Bannister for Randall Tennant—*you* couldn't—but if this salt matches, we'll nail him for this." Stamoran went back behind his desk, and Monelle half expected him to prop his feet on top of it, already victorious.

"Justice may be slow, sometimes," he said. "But justice never gives up. And neither do I."

"So you'll call your judge?" This was actual probable cause, and she—and Owulu—had found it. And then she thought of something. "No, well, wait. We'd still have to prove Ned Bannister was driving."

"His own car? And parked in his own private garage? Who else would be driving it? I predict he'll cave."

"Or maybe Nyomi herself will be able to tell us what happened." Nyomi Chang was the bane of the DA's office, scoring too many wins. But no one deserved to be mauled by a two-ton car. Maybe Stamoran was right. Maybe Nyomi did have information that Ned Bannister wanted to keep quiet. Who knew what could push a person to that level of violence—rage, or fear. Jealousy. Or power. Money, certainly. Or all of the above.

"Get the coat, Monelle. It's probably in the closet of that hospital room right now, waiting for you to bring it to me."

Monelle pictured that; going to the hospital, entering the room, opening the closet door. She shook her head, weary for the time and weary for the delay and weary for her failure and the impossibility of anything happening quickly. Hearing the clock ticking on her career. Sometimes the law was a damned obstacle.

"But she's not capable of giving us permission to get it. And if it's in her room, we can't even ask, because we can't go in there." Telling Charles Stamoran about the *Alice in Wonderland* rules was the last thing she, or anyone, wanted to do. "We'd need a warrant. Not sure even *your* judges would—"

"I know you're talking," Stamoran said. "But I am not hearing you. Are you hearing me? This is not a warrant situation. It's Saturday afternoon. The big guns are out-of-pocket. The hospital would fight it, time would tick by. That's why I can't hear anything from you except 'hello, Mr. District Attorney, here's the coat you wanted.'" Stamoran looked at her again, with those wolfish eyes. "Am I clear?"

I quit, Monelle didn't say. She clenched every muscle in her body, holding back her scorn and her disgust, holding back years of being dismissed and ordered and instructed. He'd even mocked her voice.

"I'll do my best," Monelle said.

"You might want to do better than that." Stamoran wasn't even looking at her anymore, but had picked up a letter opener and was slitting open a manila envelope.

Monelle turned and left, before the letter opener got too tempting.

She wondered if she could do it. Quit. Wondered whether she'd ever get another job.

The Uber back to the hospital, an evergreen-scented Prius, had a clear plastic bag of mini Butterfingers hanging from the front seat. *Thank u,* a handprinted sign said. *Take One (1).*

She resisted the candy. And texted Owulu.

ANYTHING?

NADA

She dialed his number. In a moving car, it was more efficient to talk. In ten minutes she'd be at MGH.

"Hey. Wu. While you're there. Do you see security cameras?" she asked. "Working, I mean. They're in every corner. Can you tell if they're on, like a red light?"

"Better if I go ask our friend Mr. Ex-Con Welling," Owulu said.

"No, no." Monelle pictured the scene. "Don't leave that spot. The security video won't disappear if we wait."

"You hope," Owulu said.

"Pray for Nyomi Chang," Monelle said. "I'm on my way to the hospital to get her coat."

"You have the warrant?"

"Don't talk to me about that, okay? Let's see what happens."

The Uber had pulled onto Cambridge Street, two blocks now from Mass General. But then stopped. The Saturday afternoon traffic had begun in earnest, with ambulances screaming to and from the hospital making the congestion even worse, and Boston drivers, never hesitant to honk their horns, adding to the chaos.

"The heating system in here sucks, by the way."

Monelle restrained herself from making a crack about Owulu's lack of outerwear.

"Okay. You want to get the car and drive back in?"

"I suppose so." Owulu's voice sounded reluctant. "Yeah. Sure. No need for me to freeze to death."

"And ask Welling about the security system, if you're going out that way." The Uber hadn't moved, the intersection now choked in textbook gridlock. A faint ghostly moon shown over the top of Beacon Hill, over Arden Ward's house, too, where Arden Ward was not. Why had they run away? Bannister was clearly scared.

"Keep me posted," she said. "And hey. Thanks."

"No big," he said. "Let me know."

44

ARDEN WARD

Arden tried not to visibly react to Pip's revelation. Ned was not his father? He hadn't seemed sad when he said "he's not my dad." Now she had about ten thousand questions to ask, and it felt as if the universe had shifted. Cordelia had never mentioned this. Neither had Ned. Maybe it didn't matter. Maybe it did.

"Oh," she said, "I get it."

Their crunching footsteps began to match. In sync, she hoped. "My parents are both dead," she said.

Pip glanced at her, briefly searching. "Sucks," he said.

"It does," Arden said. Figuring he was trying out the word on her. See if she reacted to it, or criticized him. "Do you see your biological dad, ever?"

"No. He was gone when I was little."

"Oh." Arden took a deep breath, knowing it wasn't only the snow that was treacherous footing at this point. The tree house was in sight now, the snow-lined wooden ladder that led to it leaning against a thick tree trunk. It looked simple and solid, with open rectangles for door and windows. Its maroon paint peeled in spots, its slanted roof dark-shingled and splotched with snow. Sturdy bare branches cradled it, and it seemed sturdy and reliable. Seemed.

"But Ned's *Emma's* biological dad," she said, hoping he understood that. What did an eleven-year-old understand?

"Yeah." He eyed her, up and down, looking dubious. "You want me to go up first?"

"Sure," she said. "You're the expert."

She tried to see whether the road was visible from up there, but couldn't tell. She'd almost forgotten the reason they were out here: because Ned had seen something on their home surveillance system. She had her phone tucked in her parka pocket and Ned would text if there was any new information.

She thought of something. "Do texts work out here?"

"Sometimes," Pip said.

She watched Pip clamber, bare-handed, up the rustic wooden rungs. Her almost middle-aged concerns began to burble to the surface: What if the wood was rotten, what if the full floor fell through, what if Pip fell, what if she did.

"I'm here." Pip looked down at her through the open rectangular entryway, barely taller than he was. "You coming or what?"

"Absolutely," she said, trying to sound enthusiastic. Pip had no idea of her actual mission, but his father—*not* his father, Ned—had described how they could see the end of the driveway.

Mitten over borrowed mitten, she toiled up one wooden rung at a time, tentative, and then more secure as the rungs did not wobble or creak beneath her. She stooped her way inside the tree house. Place was bigger than it looked from below.

Pip had his finger in his mouth. And looked unhappy.

"You okay?" she asked.

"Splinter," he said. "It's a little bleedy."

"Let's see." She took his hand. "Easy one," she said. She took off one mitten, picked out the splinter, dabbed the place with a tissue from her vest pocket. "There. Gone. Better? Good. So—do you hang out up here?"

"Thanks," he said. "Yeah. In the summer. The leaves cover everything, but now it's just kinda open."

"It's high." She looked in the direction of the street, stuffed the tissue and splinter back into her pocket. The view was unobstructed because of the bare-branched trees, but the end of the driveway was not quite in sight. She stepped closer to the window, felt the chill of the wood through her mittens, the cold air on her face harsher than it had been below. She squinted, searching the far distance, even leaned out the window space, her head in the branches, holding on to the sides of the opening. All she needed, to fall out of this thing.

Now she could see some of the narrow pitted road she and Ned had travelled a few hours ago, but the light was fading, and it was harder to distinguish shapes.

"It's a better view from this side," Pip said.

"Thanks," she said, and pulled herself inside. She heard a strange sound, and turned to Pip, quizzical.

"Woodpecker," he said.

What a city girl. Out the side window, though trees spiked through her line of sight, she saw the street, and the end of the driveway with two brick pillars on either side. To the right of one pillar, a car.

A car. She pulled out her phone. Hoping to get a shot of it at least, though she couldn't see the license plate.

"Pip? Do you know about cars?"

"Like what?"

"See the car out there?"

He stood next to her, his puffy jacket against hers. She pointed.

"Brown," he said. "Light brown."

"Agreed," she said. She snapped the best pictures she could, in case the driver decided to leave. Its headlights were off. And impossible to tell whether anyone was inside. "Do you know what kind of a car, though?"

"Four doors," he said. "Like a . . ." Pip leaned farther out the window, and Arden resisted the urge to grab his parka and pull him back. "Buick? Like in the commercial."

"A tan Buick four-door," Arden repeated. "I agree." She checked her photos, but expanding a fuzzy photograph only made it fuzzier. But a car was a car, and it was there, and it was not moving.

"Maybe they're lost," Pip said. "Or hurt. Maybe we should go see."

True, Arden thought, they could be lost or sleeping or looking at a map. If people still used maps. But Pip had no idea of the other possibilities.

It could be the district attorney's office following Ned. But they had no jurisdiction here.

It could be the same people who hurt Nyomi Chang.

Or someone angry about Randall Tennant.

Or someone who wanted to punish Ned. Or the children.

Or her.

She exhaled, assessing, her thoughts turning white in the chilly Vermont air.

If she and preteen Pip sauntered down to the end of the driveway, all helpful Vermont housewife and curious little boy, could they pull off that ruse?

Or would whoever was in that car recognize her? That surveillance camera meant Ned might see what happened, but it didn't matter. Ned could never get to the end of the driveway in time.

45

MONELLE CHURCHWOOD

An ambulance had just careened into the driveway of the emergency room entrance. Monelle darted toward it, looked both ways in the gathering darkness, past headlights and turn signals, and arrived just as the ambulance driver hopped down from the front seat. His colleagues had already jumped out the back and into the emergency room lobby, the automatic doors sliding to allow them in. The ambulance driver stood by his open door, arms crossed.

"Are you on an emergency run?" she asked. "Do you have thirty seconds?"

"What can I help you with, ma'am?" He seemed too young to have a driver's license, gangly in a bright orange zippered jacket with a blue-and-white EMT patch on one arm.

"Oh, thank you. I'm . . ." If she said who she really was and what she was actually doing, this kid would clam up in one second. Probably rat her out to someone.

"A friend of mine was in a car accident the other day, and she had, like . . ." Monelle thought about how specific to be. "Stuff with her. And it's not in her hospital room."

"You'll have to go to lost and found, ma'am."

"Oh, good idea." She smiled, as if embarrassed. "But it wasn't lost. I mean, it was with her. So what would you all have done with it, generally? Or would you . . . toss it?"

"No, ma'am; it belongs to the patient." The kid frowned, maybe reciting something from the ambulance driver rule book.

"I see, terrific," she reassured him, "and I'm sorry to be pushy about my friend's stuff. Would it be in like . . ." She was leaning in hard on the ditzy woman act, but sometimes you did what you had to do. "In her hospital room? Or in . . ." She shrugged prettily. "Some holding room?"

A microphone speaker clipped to the driver's shoulder squawked, and he gave it his full attention. No voices followed.

"That's the two-minute signal," he said. "Look, ma'am, there's different things that could happen. We have plastic patient belonging bags, when we put things in those, it goes on the stretcher with the patient into the hospital."

"And then what?"

The driver lifted an orange shoulder. "That's a hospital thing. I guess into their room. We don't keep it, ma'am. But we don't toss it."

"You've been great, thank you so much. I knew you would know." She looked at him, approving.

He looked down at his black sneakers. "Sure. Stay safe out there."

"You, too," she said. "Thanks for all you do." And she hurried toward the ER's sliding glass doors.

She heard a noise behind her, another siren, and within seconds it seemed, an arriving EMT crew bustled their way in, so quickly she had to jump aside to get out of their way. They were pushing a gurney with a blanket-covered figure on it, two medics, one on either side, one holding the patient's hand, the other holding up an IV bag. At the bottom of the stretcher, next to the patient's feet, was a bright green plastic bag. Full of something and tied at the top with a green plastic strip. That's what she was looking for, Monelle knew. And this patient's bag was coming with them, just as Nyomi's would have come with her.

Her purse, too, was probably in there. And her phone.

Her phone. She thought about simply calling her, imagining the phone ringing in her hospital room, imagining some clueless nurse handing it to her, and then . . . No. That would never work.

She scurried down the wide hospital corridor to the Atherton Wing, jabbed the button for 11. In the Uber, Monelle had handled three increasingly annoyed texts from Nolah, the first inquiring, the second insistent, the third demanding. Monelle hated to pull out the "where do you think the money for that dinner comes from" card, since Nolah could counter with the "who do you think takes care of the children" card, and that was a battle that had not been won since kingdom come, as Monelle's own mama used to say.

She pulled out her phone, texted Nolah. *At the hospital. Working. Missing dinner. And u. Sorry gorgeous. Love.* She hit Send. The elevator arrived.

The evidence—if it was evidence—on Nyomi's coat might be a turning point in the case against Ned Bannister, a career-saving case, and she and Nolah always patched things up when the time came. It all came from love, she knew that. They both knew that. *Get that coat,* she ordered herself.

She had eleven floors to decide how.

Stamoran might be a heavy-handed misogynistic pretentious lout, but he was smart, and savvy. She didn't have to like him, but he was the boss. And the more Monelle succeeded, the happier he'd be. And the safer Monelle and her family—a family that depended only on her for food, and insurance, and security—would be.

That coat was in this hospital. And she was determined to find it.

When her phone rang, she'd just stepped off the elevator. *Owulu,* the caller ID said.

"What?" she asked. The corridor in front of her was empty.

"Good news and bad news," Owulu said.

"Bad news first."

As he explained, she was glad she was in the hospital. In case she had a heart attack. Her eyes narrowed, and she tried not to be angry. She'd *told* him—

"And so by the time I got back, the car had been cleaned off. It's still there, but someone wiped it."

Monelle could not find her voice. Could not find any words. Had forgotten how to talk. "How the hell did that—"

"It was fast, gotta say. Couldn'ta been more than what, seven minutes?"

"Someone was watching us. Or ratted." *Ned,* she thought.

"Yeah," Owulu said.

"Well, we still have the photos. From before." She had told him to go get warm, after all, and no reason to rake the guy over the coals. She knew he was upset by this, and everyone makes mistakes. And it was true, they did have the photos of the salt. The missing salt. The missing and perfectly placed salt.

But not of who tried to destroy that crucial evidence.

"Wanna hear the good news?"

"More than anything."

"Before I got the car, I set up my backup phone to video the place. Record it while I was gone. Just in case. I hid it behind a water pipe, aimed at the car."

Monelle leaned against the hospital's tiled wall, an oil painting portrait of two nurses, one Black and one white, with an angel hovering behind them on one side of her, and a watercolor field of sunflowers on the other. Video. Owulu had video.

"Did it work?" was all she could think to ask. It had to be. *Ned.* It *had* to be. She knew it. *Got you, dude.* "What did you see? I mean, who? Can you tell?"

"Not now," he said. "Not yet. But the enhancing team is on it."

"How long—"

"I told them it was life and death."

Monelle listened to the undercurrent of the busy hospital, pings and alarms and murmured conversations. Where life and death decisions were made every day. Life and death was right, she thought. Nyomi Chang's life. And Ned Bannister's.

And her own.

PART FOUR

46

ARDEN WARD

The car remained motionless at the end of Georgianna Bannister's driveway. It could leave any minute now. Arden had her from-a-distance photos, and certainly Ned was watching on the surveillance camera, but they could not know who was inside. They could not see the license plate.

"Pip? Do you have a telescope up here?" Arden said. "For you and, um, Ned to look at stuff?"

"Yeah." Pip shrugged. "But in winter we take it in."

A random tan car. Parked on a street. Where cars are supposed to be. Where this particular car was *not* supposed to be. But no way to prove it.

"I'm wondering if you're right," Arden began, talking out the window, as if she were addressing the grove of trees surrounding them. "Maybe we should see if they need directions. Maybe GPS isn't working."

"GPS works here," Pip said. "Even though phones don't always. But maybe they don't have GPS."

That car could speed away much faster than they could get to it. If they didn't make a move now, they might lose their chance.

"Smart," she said. "How long will it take to get down there?"

"The front way or the back?" Pip asked.

Arden kept her eyes on the car. Still no lights, still no exhaust, still nothing. Parked.

"Front or back of what?"

"The front way is faster, but you gotta jump across a brook. It's not too big." He eyed her again. "You could probably do it."

"What about the back way?"

"The back way is like . . . It's longer, through trees, but you come in behind the car. They wouldn't know we were on our way to help them, so it's probably not as good."

"I'm not sure I could jump over that brook," Arden lied. "Let's go the back way, how long can it even take?"

"Not long, I guess, I could show you? And then like, we could try to call for help if they need it?"

"Exactly," Arden said. She seemed to have reached him, finally. He saw this as a game, an adventure. *A little boy,* she thought. She'd never do anything to put him in danger. But she was an adult, and she had a phone, iffy as it was, and his father—not his father, but Ned—was surely watching. "Their phone might be dead or something, don't you think?"

"Yeah," Pip said. Very serious. "Or maybe they're out of gas. We can be on like a mission."

"Good idea," Arden said. He seemed pleased with her approval, and she wondered how often his mother approved of him. Whether she told him so. His biological father was whereabouts unknown, his mother intent on a new life. What did an eleven-year-old know of life and desire? "Let's go check."

Wind at their backs and picking up, they began to climb backward down the ladder, Arden going first. This might be risky. But she couldn't leave him in the tree house. And if someone was looking for city girl Arden Ward, her current puffy persona in a weird hat, with marginal makeup and a young boy in tow, might not fit their description. Depending on how savvy they were.

"Are you a good tracker?" Arden asked, as they began walking through a dense patch of bare trees. The ice on the fallen leaves around them made the footing slick and treacherous, and the crunch of their footsteps seemed amplified in the rural stillness.

"We learned how to silent-walk in Scouts, in my other school," Pip said. "And we shouldn't whisper, just talk low. Like this. I'm talking low," he demonstrated.

"I get it," Arden said, matching his tone.

"Cool."

"Can I give you a secret job?" Arden said. "But you have to stay behind the trees."

"I guess so. What?"

"I need you to look at the license plate, and remember the state, and the letters and numbers."

"Sure," Pip said. "But what if I just take a picture of it?"

"You have a phone?" She'd never considered that.

"Sure, my mother doesn't like me to be without it."

"Cool," Arden said, thinking for a moment about his mother, and where she was, and why she had not called; not called Arden, or Ned, or . . . "Has she called you recently?"

Pip stopped, took his phone out of his pocket, and clicked on the power.

"She's out of town," he said. And began walking again.

His voice was still low, *kind of adorable,* Arden thought. He was really into this. She was, too. It was actually a benefit that he was with her. A camouflage.

"And she doesn't call you when she's out of town?" Arden asked.

"We usually FaceTime after dinner," Pip said. "But I guess she couldn't last night. Emma was sad, really sad. I guess that's why you came. So," he said, pointing. "See the big evergreens? We go around that, and then we're behind the car."

"Great," Arden said. "You ready to stay behind the trees? If you can't get a picture, that's fine, try to remember the state and some of the numbers. I'll go see if they need help."

Pip was silent for a few steps, then stopped, looked up at her. "You don't really think they're in trouble, do you?" he asked. "You just want to get their license plate."

Arden didn't quite know how to answer that. "Why would you say that?"

"I read books," Pip said.

47

She held her breath, concentrated on walking soundlessly through the icy leaves. At least her stupid hat, which Pip had told her actually belonged to him, kept her ears warm.

Pip, walking beside her, was just as quiet, his eyes focused directly ahead, his hands stuffed in his parka pockets.

"Almost there."

She smiled at his lowered voice.

"There's the trees, see? And the car is after that. You'll see it in a minute."

"You're a good mission partner." Arden used her Scout voice. "Let's stop. Get your phone ready."

The forest stillness surrounded them, the air crisp and smelling of the sharpness of change, and a mix of damp and dying. Sometimes leaves rustled around them; some woodland creatures, small ones, Arden hoped.

Pip pulled out his phone. "I have full batt," he said. "If it works. And camera is ready."

Arden couldn't decide whether to laugh or be impressed by his skills. "Good. I'll go first, see if they need help, you stay back, and get that photograph, then put your phone in your pocket. But stay back. I'll call you if I need you. I may say something like . . ." She thought for a beat. "Honey. Got it? Not your name. In this case, *honey* means you."

They had both kept their voices muted, and were standing close together again. Pip's hands had turned bright red with the cold, no sign of the excised splinter. His grandmother—*not* his grandmother, Georgianna—would have been annoyed to know he hadn't been wearing gloves.

"You can put your phone in your pocket for now, it's fine," she said, hoping he would. "Your hands, too. Until we get closer."

Was the car still there? She hadn't heard anything but rustles and flutters and birdsong.

When her phone buzzed in her pocket, the muted sound came out like an angry buzz saw.

Pip looked at her with widened eyes.

"Sorry." She hit ignore. Looked at the screen. *Cordelia*. At least the phone had worked.

The woman had impeccably bad timing. Arden tried to convince herself it was a coincidence. Tried to ignore the possibility that Cordelia knew exactly what she was doing. That maybe Cordelia was in that car.

In which case funny hat disguises or a nameless Pip would be valueless.

But Cordelia would not hurt her son, that Arden was certain of. So Cordelia in the car would be a good sign. A mysterious one, but a reassuring one.

"Doesn't matter," she said. "I'm sure the people in the car couldn't hear. But—"

"Count to ten," Pip said. "That's what my mother says to do when I'm making a decision."

"Right." Arden silently held up one finger at a time—not as effective under her mittens—ticking off ten seconds, and held up her hands when she was done. Still no engine sounds, still no motion from where that tan four-door was parked.

She tried to look confident, gave Pip a thumbs-up. "Stay here," she told him. "You know what to do."

The forest broke open sooner than she had imagined, and she stopped, behind a lofty bare tree trunk, to take one last look. The car had not moved. She took out her phone, and with the tree as cover, snapped a photo. If Pip got it, too, fine, but she couldn't take a chance.

A Vermont license plate. The numbers would be in the picture. The Vermont plate made it more likely that it was benign; someone making a phone call, someone who needed a nap.

Or, as her persistent worry nagged, someone who wanted Ned. Or her. Or both of them. Or the kids. But no, Ned had sent them—his own son—*wait*. Not his own son. Not.

It was still light enough to see, but promising deep shadows any minute. Her hat flaps dangled down her cheeks, and she pulled her borrowed muffler closer under her chin. Whatever it was, she had to know. No surprises.

No sound from the car. No window rolling down, or engine turning over, not a puff of exhaust from the back. No sound from Pip.

She widened her angle of approach, avoiding the rearview mirror.

Three steps away.

The driver's side window was rolling down.

A stranger in a knit cap, clean shaven but comfortable looking, eyed her from the front seat.

"May I help you, ma'am?" he asked.

What? She paused, regrouping.

"Thank you," she said, "but no, I was walking in the woods, and saw your car, and wondered if *you* needed help."

"Vermonters are good people," the man said.

"Are you lost?" She tried to look solicitous. "Do you need me to call for gas or the police?"

"Why would you call the police?" the man asked.

This wasn't how people talked. Arden hoped Pip had gotten his photograph, though she had hers. *If* it worked. She also hoped Pip would not join her here at the car. What this guy had said was—on the surface—beyond reproach. But it carried an undercurrent of aggression.

"Do *you* own this property?" He eyed her, amused. Then his expression shifted, almost imperceptibly. "I'm not doing anything illegal, am I?"

It took every ounce of her determination not to grab her phone and snap a picture of him. How could he stop her? *A million ways*, she thought.

"Illegal?" she repeated. "That's a surveillance camera, looks like." She pointed toward the two pillars at the driveway entrance.

"Why would I care?" the man said.

His expression remained infinitely easygoing; his posture, too. His right hand sat on the steering wheel, his other muscled forearm across the bottom of the open window. He wore no gloves. But there was a bulge under his jacket. A gun? And if Ned was actually watching the surveillance cameras, he would never suspect anything untoward. If he could see the man's face at all, it would look like they were having a pleasant conversation. Which meant this guy knew the camera was there. And didn't care. Which was either reassuring or terrifying.

And there was nothing Arden could do about that. Make a scared face at the camera? She had to pretend, just as this stranger obviously was.

Still no Pip. *What a smart kid.*

"I'm just watching the sun go down," the man finally said. "How about you?"

"As I said, walk in the woods."

Arden's phone buzzed with a text, insistent, in her pocket. She felt the vibrations through every cell in her body. But maybe this was good. It let this guy know her phone was powered on and worked. *Ned,* she hoped.

"Someone wants you," he said.

Arden smiled. If he could look amused, she could look amused, too. "Right," she said. "With these things, we're never out of touch."

"Lucky you."

"I'll just check to see what they want."

"Feel free."

Free was the last thing she felt. And certainly not lucky. But she took out her phone, planning to pretend she saw a text that made her happy. But the text wasn't from Ned. It was from Cordelia. And it did not make her happy. *New text. Says "BE CAREFUL." CALL!*

"I need to answer," she said. Pretending. She tapped at the screen.

His eyes narrowed for a beat, and she could have sworn he looked at the surveillance camera. Then at the bulge in his jacket.

Then she held up her phone. And snapped a photo of him.

His car door clicked open.

She turned and ran.

48

Wet leaves, she thought. *Slick*. She could fall. But she couldn't fall, she couldn't allow it. Arden had run back the way she came, her only ambition to get Pip, and get away from the man in the car. The stranger with a maybe-probably-gun whose photo she now carried with her.

Pip was gone.

She'd pivoted, putting the car behind her, and dashed blindly into the unfamiliar woods. Her cumbersome boots, half a size too large and not meant for running, seemed to drag her down at every step. *Wet leaves*, she thought, *icy leaves*. Pip had warned her about them, and she tried to go as fast as she could and not sprawl into the soggy cold treacherous woods.

Her first instinct had been to run back to the tree house—maybe Pip was there? But when she stopped, panting, caught in the gradual darkness of the November evening, she was completely disoriented. She tried to get her bearings, putting her mittened hands on her knees, trying to catch her breath.

Idiot. She'd been carrying the phone in her hand. She zipped it safely into her pocket. Call Ned? It wouldn't help, what could he do?

Where was Pip? Back at the house? Or taken? She hadn't gotten his phone number, dumb. *Shut up, Arden.* There was no way for him to be kidnapped. Now she was just—

She needed to find Pip. Get to safety. She listened, alert as a forest creature, on highest alert for footsteps or disturbance, but there was only silence.

And then, with a raucous screech, a huge black bird—a crow?—flapped up from a bare branch beside her. Her heart spiked in fear, and the bird disappeared into the night sky.

Keep going, she thought, putting a reassuring hand on her zipped-up pocket with the phone. It would be dark soon, except for the dim light of a partial moon. Which direction was the house? Which direction was the tree house? Where was Pip?

If she kept moving, it might be exactly the wrong thing. She might be walking right into the arms of Mr. Four-Door, although she had not heard him following her.

It would be stupid, she reassured herself. For him to knock her out, pick her up, stash her into the back of a car, and drive away.

He could probably manage it. But what would be the point? Why would they want her? Why would they—whoever they were—think she knew anything of value? Who was supposed to "be careful"? Of what? Or who?

If the man's quarry had been Ned, why didn't he drive to the house and knock on the door?

Because there was more to it. Because he was stalking, watching, brazen enough to do it out in the open, but not show his intent. He was a messenger. An emissary. A scout. Had to be.

In which case, she was safe.

But what about Pip? What if he found Pip?

She drew in a breath. *Keep moving,* she said to herself. *Keep moving.* Nothing looked familiar. There was only tree after massive bare-branched tree, their roots lumping to the surface like nature's own treacherous speed bumps.

A sound. That was a sound. And now here she was, defenseless and alone.

Come on, Arden, she thought. *There's nobody following you. And you're making yourself afraid when there is no reason to be.* She would feel embarrassed once she was home with a glass of wine. And at least there she knew who her enemies were.

She kept going, one foot in front of the other, trying to look down and out and around all at the same time. Trees, just trees. Should she be able to see the tree house? She took another step or two, and the ground felt different. Softer. Spongier.

Different.

She stopped, bouncing on the balls of her feet, wishing she had boots that fit. The ground beneath her feet looked damper. Slicker. She tried to remember what Pip had said. *There's a front way and a back way. The front way is shorter, but you have to jump a brook.* She followed the line of wet leaves glistening with ice, unlike the snow-covered leaves she'd just tromped through, a jagged line clearly distinguishable.

The brook. She'd hit the brook. If she had blindly gone forward, she might have stepped right into the water.

She closed her eyes, the reality of the dark and cold hitting harder. Her fingers were icy, even under her mittens, and she could not feel her face anymore. She hoped Pip had gone back to the house. And if he'd made it there, he'd tell his father—not his father, Ned—what happened. *Yes*, she reassured herself. *Exactly*. Ned must have seen her run, and knew something was wrong. Help could be on the way. As the sun faded, the cold became insistent, demanding attention.

And there was Pip.

He emerged, soundlessly, from behind a massive tree trunk, putting his finger to his lips.

She widened her eyes, questioning. Tilted her head, and pantomimed, hands to heart, *are you okay?*

He nodded.

She pantomimed driving a car, hands at ten and two. Looked at him questioningly. Then waved bye-bye. *He's gone?*

Pip shook his head. *No.* He pointed toward the woods. *Still there.*

Arden lifted her head, listening again, a panicked deer. She unzipped her jacket pocket, took out her phone. Signaled Pip to do it, too. Pip's safety was top of mind. She herself could handle whatever, probably, maybe, but he was a kid.

If she called Ned, that would bring him out here. And might be exactly what the man in the car wanted.

If Ned wasn't already on the way.

But maybe he did not plan to come at all.

49

A crashing now through the leaves, an unmistakable sound of someone approaching. Almost without thinking, Arden drew Pip closer to her, the boy not resisting Arden's protection. It could be Ned. Someone from the house. Or the man in the car. No way of knowing. The options raced through her mind, and she felt Pip trembling.

"It's okay, honey," she said. "Woods always sound weird when it gets darker. But you and I are here, and we have our phones, and everything is going to be fine."

"I know," Pip said.

"Did you call your—did you call Ned?" Arden asked.

The rustling stopped. Were they trying to lull them into dropping their guard? Or coming to help? If she yelled, she would give away their position. For better or for worse.

"The house is that way." Pip pointed, murmuring in his Scout voice. "Should we just go?"

It wasn't only the cold that was chilling her, it was fear of the unknown, and not only for her own safety, but for Pip's, who had innocently shown her his precious tree house. Under direction from his father. Not his father. Arden's brain slammed to a halt. Ned had *sent* them out here. He had seen that car. What if he recognized the car, and had sent them on purpose? Knowing the driver's intentions.

Pip was not his biological son. Not *his* son. But he was Cordelia's son. From another father.

Maybe this was Ned's . . . plan?

Jealous Ned. Jealous *Ned*. He could get rid of Pip, with Arden as collateral damage, and swear he was devastated, and guilt ridden, and a coward, and should have come out to see who was staking out his home.

He'd play the grieving parent, and it would all be a fraud. Was Cordelia warning *her*?

Whichever way Arden went, there was the possibility of disaster.

"Arden?" Pip said. "Do you hear anything now? Maybe that was, like, a raccoon."

"Maybe," Arden said. "So what do you say, we head back to the house?"

If this had been Ned's doing, and she and Pip could get back inside, they'd be safe. There was no way Georgianna was involved in this, whatever it was.

No sound from in the woods. She felt as alone as alone could be, alone with a little boy in a darkened wood, with danger, potential danger, on either side of them.

That way? Arden mouthed the words, and pointed.

"Yeah," he murmured. "But careful of the brook. We gotta keep on this side of it, so you don't have to jump over."

Pip took the first step, and Arden joined him. Without discussing it, both kept their footsteps as silent as they could. Arden had kept her arm around Pip for a beat, then let him go ahead. Leading the way.

The trees' branches laced together above them, and the moon, half-full or half-empty, shone weakly beyond them. They walked along the brook, its water still invisible under the icy leaves, and she trusted Pip knew his way. It seemed to take much longer getting back to the house than it had to get out here.

They had been out here for what, an hour? More? And, like the darkness falling, everything had changed since then.

Pip turned toward her as he walked, gave her a thumbs-up, then pointed forward and made an okay sign.

What a cutie, she thought. This was an adventure to him, she hoped, and hoped he would feel that way about it afterward. He'd probably been out here countless times; maybe it was as familiar to him as it was strange to her.

She touched the phone in her pocket. Certainly she could call now. And why hadn't Ned come out for them, if he had seen her run from the car? She frowned as she continued ahead. Ned would have yelled for them. Called out her name, or Pip's.

Maybe not, if he figured it would give away their location. Maybe he was being as cautious as she was.

The density of light seemed to lessen, and she sensed an opening in the stand of trees coming soon. Stars had begun to come out, the dark sky clearing and onyx hard. She could still see Pip, though the outlines of his body were fraying at the edges. When they finally, *soon* she hoped *soon,* hit the edge of the woods, they'd be in the open.

In the open.

Anyone tracking them could easily go around the woods, and head them off as they emerged. Pulling them back into the woods. And would anyone see that? If they did, would anyone care?

"Arden!" The harsh voice shot through the darkened woods.

She and Pip both stopped. Looked at each other. Looked for the sound. Arden saw Pip's widening eyes, the look of confusion and fear on his red-cheeked face.

Arden pointed ahead of them. "Let's go." She mouthed the words. "Keep going." She began to walk, then trot, shepherding Pip forward.

"Arden!" The voice again. "Stop!"

That voice—not Ned, but would she recognize him yelling?—came from far behind them, deep into the woods.

Arden jabbed a mitten to her right. Parallel to the house, instead of toward it. If they ran that way, maybe they'd hit the driveway.

"Go," she said and without questioning, Pip made a hard right turn and dashed toward where she hoped the driveway would be. She followed, matching his speed, and could tell he was slowing.

"Arden!" The call, now closer, was not Ned, no way it was Ned. Her brain raced faster than her feet, Arden gritting her teeth and hoping that they wouldn't fall, neither of them could fall, as they headed the way she prayed was correct.

Then another sound, from even closer, a cry of fear and surprise, an explosion of expletives and harsh swearing. She heard a watery splat, and a scramble, and a shuffling.

Got you, jerk, Arden thought. *Pretty good for a city girl.*

"Keep going," she called to Pip, "he's fallen into the brook." Her words came out panting, breathy, afraid. Relieved. "Great you told me that, dude."

Pip turned around as he ran, a grin on his face, then turned back to his path.

A sound from ahead of them. "Arden!" Her name again. "Arden!"

And *that* was Ned, she recognized him, Ned was coming from the driveway, not from the woods.

"Your dad," Arden told Pip. She ran toward him, caught up in three steps, and grabbed his arm, dragging him forward. "I mean, Ned. Ned is here. Let's go let's go let's go *go.*"

50

Arden, her arm linked through Pip's, emerged from the woods and onto the gravel driveway. Ned, holding a flashlight and cell phone, wearing a battered sheepskin jacket and heavy gloves, stood not a yard away from them. With the lights from the still-faraway main house and the rows of glowing ground-level lanterns lining the driveway, she could see clearly enough again. She hadn't noticed those lights before, they must have come on as the darkness increased. Arden moved in front of Pip, protective.

"Where the hell have you been?" The words came out of her mouth before she considered what to say.

"What's wrong? Are you okay, Pip?" Ned asked. He took a step closer, and Arden saw what might have been concern shadow his face. "Arden, are you?"

"I'm—" Pip began.

"Didn't you see me run away from the car?" Arden had to interrupt. Her heart was beating, fast, like the adrenaline was rushing in, or out, or both, and she felt unsteady. "Why didn't you come out when you saw that? You were supposed to be—watching us, me, at the car, weren't you? Wasn't that what this was about?" Had she misunderstood this whole tree house thing? *No.* She couldn't have. "Did you call anyone?"

"About what? The car?" Ned glanced at Pip, who'd stayed close to Arden. "Arden? I figured you were just going to the tree house, and that takes a while, and then Emma needed something, and I don't know, I'm so sorry, I—did something happen?"

Arden's heartbeat was almost back to normal, but her mind still revved on high alert. There had not been a sound from the woods behind them. Might he have fallen? Hit his head? Was he out cold, or dead? She was sure as hell not going to be the one to go find out. But someone had to.

"We can talk about this later, but there's a *guy*—you saw him, right?

Ned? The man in the car? And he's in the woods, and he was—chasing us." She paused, listening. Silence. "I think."

"He was," Pip said. "I think, too."

"He's back there?" Ned pointed.

"Ned!" Arden could not believe this. "Your son," she said deliberately, "is freezing. And so am I."

"I saw you, of course," Ned went on, as if replaying a memory. "I saw you talking to someone, but I couldn't see a face. And you seemed to be fine, you were just talking. And then I must have looked down and you were gone. So you *ran* away? Who was in the car?"

"Who? I have no idea," Arden said, "but he's probably listening to all this, and if we don't get out of here, we're going to find out pretty soon. He's in the woods, I think he fell in the creek. Brook. Whatever. Ned, call the police. He might be—" She didn't want to say "dead" out loud in front of Pip.

She saw Ned look toward the woods. "I'm sure it's nothing. Or a goon sent by Monelle."

"*Nothing?* You think? That seems unlikely. Monelle? Equally unlikely. They have no jurisdiction in Vermont, just saying. Come on, Pip," she said. "Show me how to get back to the house."

Still holding on to Pip's arm, she started toward the driveway. Then, despite her misgivings, she stopped. Turned back to Ned.

"Hey. Why did you come find us, then? If you thought everything was fine? Why didn't you call?"

"It was getting late. Dark. It was taking too long. I wondered about you. Worried." Ned frowned, peering at her, shining his flashlight on her. "And if there was a problem, why didn't *you* call *me*? Or Pip? You both had phones, I knew that. Was I supposed to guess? But when you didn't come back and didn't come back—well, I was—like I said."

Then they all whirled, turning, as thrashing came from inside the woods, the sound of heavy feet.

"He's coming. *Told* you," Arden whispered. She felt Pip trembling beside her. "Don't worry, honey."

"Shhh," Ned said.

A darkening November evening in the middle of rural Vermont, a house, a place of safety, not visible yet, on one side of her, and the road, not visible either, on the other. The darkness filled the space between them, charged with intensity, and the electricity of people making decisions. Arden could almost hear a clock ticking as they all played mental chess, parsing out the end games in the quiet seconds. Even Pip stayed silent, and not a creature chirped or hooted or fluttered or tweeted. The very air was motionless, stilled, it seemed, by uncertainty.

They stood, an awkward triangle, listening to the footsteps, then listening to them diminish, and then listening to nothing. Arden strained to hear the sound of a car engine starting, and thought she heard it, but maybe it was her imagination.

"I want to go home," Pip said.

"I know you do, Pipper," Ned said.

This was not a time for Arden to interfere, here in the unfamiliar darkness with an unfamiliar relationship unfolding in front of her. She felt protective toward Pip, but Ned knew his stepson better than she did. He was a kid, in a frightening situation. The danger, if it was danger, seemed to have passed.

"I know you had a weird experience," Ned went on. "Think hot chocolate might help?"

"With marshmallows?"

"Is there any other way?"

"Maybe." Pip fidgeted with the zipper on his jacket. Arden wondered what was going through that young mind. What he would remember tomorrow, when the world was—she hoped—back in equilibrium.

"Let's go," Ned was saying to Pip. "See if you can beat us. But don't run on the driveway." As Pip took off, Ned gave Arden a thumbs-up. "Now we can talk."

But Pip had stopped, and trotted back toward them, lined on either side by the yellow-white lanterns.

"What?" Ned said. "You giving up?"

"I have his license plate." Pip tapped his phone screen. "I took a photo of it. Arden said to."

"She did? You did? Let's see," Ned said. He tucked his own phone into his jacket pocket, the flashlight still on, and Arden could see the glow coming from inside.

He took Pip's cell. Stared at the bright screen. He yanked off one of his gloves with his teeth, then spread two fingers to enlarge the photo. For a moment Arden feared he would delete it.

"It's a Vermont," Pip said. "Like Gramma's."

"Good for you," Ned said, still looking at the screen.

Arden had a photo of it too, and of the man's face. But that was a secret she could keep, for now, for herself.

51

I have the number memorized, too," Pip began. "It's—"

The sound of concerned insistent barking interrupted Pip's recitation, and Ned handed his phone back. "Good," he said. "Bartok, stop!"

A flashlight beam cut through the semidarkness, Georgianna Bannister behind it. The barking dog paced in front of her as Georgianna approached, a fleecy cardigan wrapped over her turtleneck, and boots like the too-big ones she'd loaned Arden.

Bartok continued to bark, sharp and piercing.

"Hush, Bartok," Georgianna Bannister said. The dog instantly went silent.

"What on earth is going on?" Georgianna planted herself in front of them, fists on hips. "I had to leave Emma reading her book. What the—" She paused. Glanced at Pip. "Pip, you look unhappy. Arden, are you all right? Ned, it's time for you to explain."

Georgianna's benevolent face had toughened, her once-rambunctious dog now sitting, a sentry, by her side.

"I'm good," Pip said. "But there was a man. We saw from the tree house. He—"

"Let's go back to the house." Ned draped his arm across Pip's shoulders. "You can tell your grandmother about it inside. I think this young man needs some hot chocolate, Mother," Ned said. "With a marshmallow."

The boy leaned in as the two of them walked up the gravel driveway toward the house, Arden saw. Their relationship was more complicated than she had expected. Pip might be the product of an antagonistic divorce. Might be fragile. Emotional. Untrusting. His behavior not sullen preteen, but hurt.

Georgianna had stayed behind, and now, the dog padding obediently behind her, looped her arm through Arden's, escorting her back to the house.

"I want to hear it from you, Arden," she said. "Pip began to tell me about a man, and then Ned cut him off. Why? What man? If something was wrong, you would have called, would you not? When we were in the kitchen earlier, I understood from Ned's reaction that he'd seen something on the surveillance. Why didn't he go out himself?"

Arden had no idea what Ned had told Georgianna, and it was hardly her role to rat Ned out to his own mother.

"Let me ask you something first," she said, attempting to change the subject, though she feared Georgianna would not fall for it. "You said Cordelia told you she'd hired me. How did you feel about that?"

Hired. Not that she'd be an employee much longer. Her unemployed future unspooled before her, a map with no highways, a book with no words.

"My son would never have done what he was accused of," Georgianna was saying. "It was an accident. The jury was correct, and it is supremely unfair that his life is ruined as a result. I know he wasn't drinking. I know that firsthand. So yes, if you could help him, I heartily approve."

She stopped, and turned Arden to face her, clamping her leather-gloved hands onto Arden's forearms. Looked at her, intently. "Cordelia called about what happened to Nyomi Chang. Ned has not mentioned that to me." She swallowed, started again. "I was waiting for him to do so. Is he trying to hide something? I'm his mother, I can know."

"Mother?" Ned stood in the open front doorway. "Just checking on you two."

Arden, startled, blinked in the unfamiliar rural darkness. She could almost see the line of tension between mother and son. Or maybe it was fear. Or maybe disappointment. Or maybe all of the above.

"Come in," Ned said. "It's cold."

Once inside, Arden toed off her boots, and returned her parka and scarf and mittens to the brass hooks in the entryway, the chill coming off of the fabric. As they approached the living room, Emma and Pip jumped from their oversized flowered armchairs. Emma dumped an open picture book on the floor—puppies, Arden saw—and Pip carefully deposited his iPad on an expensively rustic side table.

"Can we have hot chocolate now, Grandma?" Pip said.

"I want it too," Emma said. "I'm cold, too."

"You are not," Pip said. "You didn't go outside."

"I don't care," Emma said. "I'm cold." She wrapped her arms around herself as if to prove it.

"Everyone gets hot chocolate," Georgianna said. "Come with me, children. And you don't need to be cold, Emma darling. Just say what's true. That's what we do in this house. Don't we, Ned?"

And with that, Georgianna bustled into the kitchen, kids trotting after, leaving them alone.

"What do you think she meant by that, Ned?" Arden kept her voice low as she asked. Such an unsettling conversation to be having here, in the midst of autumnal arrangements of chrysanthemums, an array of cornflower-colored candles lining the mantel of a redbrick fireplace, a crocheted afghan draped over every chair—luxuriously created to appear homemade, she thought. "And in any event, that man could not have been sent by Monelle. She doesn't know we're here. No one knows."

Cordelia might, though, Arden realized. What if she called Georgianna? If she had told Cordelia they were here, and then Cordelia had told—who?

"Honestly, Ned," Arden went on. "I can't control this, nor can you. You have some guy—who I think had a gun—possibly stalking you. Law enforcement is clearly after you, and a car accident victim on the verge of death in the hospital—"

"Do you know that?"

"We don't until we do," Arden said. "And until we do, until something exonerates you, there's no way to do this on your own. I'm only a—"

"Fine." Ned pulled out his cell phone. "A thousand reporters have called, by the way, I deleted them. But I have not heard from Jean Trounstine. Maybe she called while I was outside." And then his phone rang. "Ha. Speak of the—"

Ned held up his cell. Showed the caller ID.

"Monelle Churchwood," he said. "Crap. Unless—"

"I told her not to call you." Arden listened for footsteps from the kitchen. "Let it go to voice mail. I'll call her. It's about Nyomi, got to be. What did you tell your mother about that?"

Then Arden's phone rang, too, buzzing against her hip from inside her pocket. "See? Now Monelle's calling me." Maybe it was good news. Nyomi was awake, and recovering, and telling exactly what happened. That it had nothing to do with Ned. Although the last time, she had said that word. "Ned."

The phone rang again. She looked at her screen.

"Not Monelle. Cordelia," she whispered.

"Answer," Ned said. "Ask her why she hasn't called me. Or the kids. Why is she calling *you*?"

Good question, Arden had to admit. Her phone rang again.

Georgianna appeared across the room, framed by the circles of twinkling lights on the chandelier behind her.

"Come, Ned," she said. "We need to talk. I do not like the idea that a stranger was lurking outside my house. And arrived soon after you did."

At that moment, Arden's phone went silent, and she imagined Cordelia's annoyance after her frantic message about the newest text.

"Let me make a call," Arden said. "Then I'll be right there. We can plan."

"Thank you," Georgianna said.

And the two of them turned toward the kitchen; Georgianna glanced back at Arden over her shoulder, and a look passed between them. Arden recognized the woman was trying to tell her something—but could not for the life of her decode it.

52

The winding road back to the highway seemed infinitely more treacherous as they left, in the darkness, through the bleak tree-lined uninhabited expanse of rural Vermont. As she drove toward Boston, Arden half expected to see the blue lights of a sheriff's car swirling behind them. And would not have been surprised to be pulled over for some fictional transgression. Then hauled into the whatever-county-this-was sheriff's office, and stashed in a miserable cell, like something out of a Stephen King novel, held by some strutting backwoods cop who meted out his private and personal justice.

She half expected, too, to see the headlights of a tan Buick. And a driver who would not give up on whatever it was he'd wanted. Georgianna had a friend in the sheriff's office—who'd have thought?—and would ask her to run the license plate. But she wasn't there on weekends.

"It gets dark so early this time of year," Ned was saying. "I have no idea what time it is anymore, or even what I'm doing. I was tempted to hide in Pip's tree house, maybe stay there forever. It's still three hours back to Boston. I wish it were three days."

"Wrong. Sooner the better," Arden corrected him, keeping her eyes on the road. "What happens next depends on Nyomi Chang."

Everything had changed before Pip and Emma finished their second hot chocolate. Lawyer Jean Trounstine returned Ned's call, finally, and agreed to handle the next steps. She'd been at the hospital. "Get here," she'd told him.

Arden, hiding in the bathroom again, had quickly called Monelle, geared up to read her the riot act about her phone call to Ned. And to confront her about the man in the Buick. She couldn't resist looking again at the snifter full of perfume in the medicine cabinet. She'd never think of Joy the same way, the memories of her mother now tainted by the smear of an unfair accusation. And her own subsequent unemployment. But Nyomi came first.

"Monelle. I told you not to call—" she'd begun.

But Monelle had cut her off. "Yell at me when you get to the hospital," she'd said. "The nurses think Nyomi might wake up."

"Will she recover?" Arden had felt a wash of raw relief. Surely the district attorney's office would leave Ned alone the moment Nyomi exonerated him.

"And Nyomi's law partner refuses to leave," Monelle went on. "The hospital . . . they're stalling. Bureaucrats can never decide about anything."

Arden bit back a sarcastic reply. "We'll get there as soon as we can. It'll take some time though. Ned's—not home. I'm trusting you, Monelle."

"If your . . . client, do you call him? Makes himself available, we'll handle it as best we can," Monelle said.

"One more thing. Are you following him?"

"What? Following? Look. Just get here."

Emma's lip quivered when Ned said he had to go back to Boston, but he'd calmed her, somehow. Pip, too, seemed reluctant for him to leave. Arden had even gotten an acknowledgment from him.

"The tree house is cooler in the summer." He'd looked at the hardwood floor as much as he looked at her. "With all the stuff in it."

"Cool," she'd said. "You okay, dude?"

"Sure." Then a pause. "Are you?"

"Totally," she lied.

"Maybe Miss Ward will come back someday." Georgianna Bannister had put one arm around each of the kids' shoulders, Bartok nosing his way under Pip's other arm. "And Ned darling," she said. "I know you'll tell me when you want to."

"Tell you what, Mother?"

"Don't you have to get back, dear?" She'd handed them each a shiny red travel mug. "Coffee," she explained. "You're both exhausted. Take care of him, Arden."

Now Arden took a sip as she drove. She had returned Cordelia's calls, but Cordelia had not called back. Cordelia's latest text to her had warned: *Be careful.* Was—whoever it was—threatening Cordelia herself? Or was it about that man in the woods?

Cordelia. Cordelia was why she was on this dark road at nine o'clock on a frigid evening, driving an unfamiliar car. And sitting next to a person who was clearly a suspect in a hit-and-run, and whose wife did not trust him. Trouble seemed to find Ned, and cling to him. Or was he his own trouble?

"Thank you," Ned was saying. "Emma's better now, and that wouldn't have happened without you. I still don't understand why Dee hasn't called me."

Arden tried to figure out a way to ask about Pip. Wondered why Ned hadn't told her he wasn't Pip's biological father. Maybe it didn't matter. Like the cook didn't matter.

"Poor Pip," she began.

"He's tough."

"Takes after his father," Arden said.

"Could be."

Arden hoped Ned did not see her raised eyebrows. "So *do* you take him with you to get haircuts?"

"Huh?"

"Like your mother mentioned. Whether you still went to that same place." She tried to ask without asking.

"Oh, I've been going there for years. DJ's, it's called. Why?"

"That's famous, in Boston at least." Arden recognized it, and now she had a start for her research. *Good job, Arden.* Maybe there was more to learn. More to tell Cordelia. "All the muckety-mucks go there."

"Huh." Ned pointed. "The exit for 95 is coming up."

Good, Arden thought. Now she had to figure out why the barber mattered.

All the coffee in the world was not going to untangle her brain right now. She tried to concentrate on driving, seeing the off-green glare beside her as Ned scrolled through his phone.

"Anything?" She'd charge this time to her expense report, every minute. Even the trip to the tree house. Warren had voted her off the island. He owed her. "Messages? Calls?"

"Endless. Countless," Ned said. "I feel like Pip. I just want to go home. Though that's probably a terrible idea. The reporters are probably camped in our front yard."

"I hear you," she said. "Let's see what happens at the hospital."

She made the turn onto the highway, realizing she'd been almost subconsciously checking to see if anyone was following them, specifically that tan four-door. But so far, cars only sped past them.

"Ned," she began, negotiating her way around a hulking tandem big rig. "Your mother told me she knew, 'firsthand,' that you weren't drinking at your New Year's Eve party. How would she know that?"

Ned took a sip from his mug. "She was there. She always attends, and Father, too, when he was alive." He paused, and a mile marker flashed by in the darkness. "He loved the fireworks. So did she."

"Did the police talk to her? After?"

"Well, yeah. But so what?"

"Did Nyomi Chang talk to your mother, preparing for the trial?"

"Nyomi knew Mother was there. Mother insisted on testifying, in fact."

"Huh. I don't remember that," Arden said. "She took the stand?"

"No, in the end, she didn't. Because . . ." Ned settled his mug back into the holder and ran a thumb under his seat belt, maybe remembering. "Can you imagine? The headlines if my *mother* testified I wasn't drinking? How pitiful that would look?"

Ned was right. It wasn't difficult to imagine. *Big Time Biz Exec Relies on Mommy.* Or even *My Baby Boy Wasn't Drinking, Declares Parking Garage Murderer's Mom.*

"Yeah," she said. "But did *anyone* from the party testify?"

"No," he said. "I mean, everyone was gone when it happened, so that settled that. Their cars came in, their cars went out. My car was the only one left. The cops said they smelled alcohol on me, of course they did, I'd been serving drinks for hours."

"Who all was there?" Arden asked. "Is there a list? Who organized it?"

"The caterer drops off everything in the afternoon," Ned said. "Then it's serve yourself. Shrimp and oysters, champagne. Cheese. Funny hats. You know. Does this matter?"

Arden envisioned it, shiny people with rented champagne glasses and deely boppers, watching the fireworks and scarfing free shrimp. "Who cleaned up?"

"Oh god," Ned said. "My secretary arranges that. I know that sounds—male privilege. What does it matter, though? Randall Tennant . . ." He paused, as if the name caught in his throat. "Came into the garage at some point with his skateboard. But not in a car, clearly. There weren't any other cars."

"Yeah, I know. Did the police ask you about that, though? Did Monelle? Did Nyomi?"

Ned sighed, as if trying to remember. "I don't think so."

I'm not a detective, Arden thought, as they passed another exit. The sky was so dark and the lights so bright, the highway unspooling, dull and featureless.

But as the mile markers rolled by, and she dodged the zigzagging headlights of crazed drivers who thought speed limits were a suggestion, she kept envisioning that party, the cars leaving the garage one by one, past the broken security cameras, and out the gated exit. Leaving Ned's car there alone. The only car that could have hit Randall Tennant. No matter how many times she pictured it, what happened was always the same. Ned was lucky to have been acquitted.

"Ned?" She took a deep breath. What the hell. "Did you know Randall Tennant?"

"Did *I*? Why are you thinking about this?"

"Ned?"

"No. One hundred percent no. As I have repeated, infinitely, endlessly, to the entire universe."

"Okay, okay." Arden put up a palm. "Truce. But, well, did maybe Cordelia know him?"

"Same answer. As she has said, infinitely, endlessly, to the entire universe. Why are you *thinking* about this?"

"Because it's my job to think about it. Because—" She was about to tell him about the texts, but what if he was the one sending them? Why to Cordelia?

"Ned? I know she testified about it in court. But is there any possibility Cordelia wasn't home that night? Not that she did anything of course," she hastened to add. "Just asking."

"She was home with the kids," Ned said. "As she infinitely—"

"I know," Arden stopped him. "But . . ." She wished she weren't so tired. She knew from testimony that Ned had heard the thud of Randall Tennant's body as he hit it, that *his* car had run over him, that the tire treads proved it, that Randall Tennant, as a result, was dead on the floor of the parking garage.

"Just think about it," she went on.

"She'd never leave her kids," Ned said.

53

The happy people had all gone home, this time of night, and the hospital corridors held a silent buzz. Weary visitors, some with red-rimmed eyes, only glanced at Arden and Ned as they made their way toward their destination. No one wanted eye contact in this place of fear and worry.

The pale green of the tiled floor glared in the fluorescents. The scent of antiseptic mixed with the fragrance of coffee, and rubber-soled shoes squeaked on the linoleum. Maybe because Arden was exhausted, and so hungry she'd forgotten to be hungry, everything seemed edgy, impossible, insurmountable.

They waited for the elevator, both looking up at the numbers, not at each other. Only two answers mattered. What had Nyomi seen, and whether she could exonerate Ned.

"Just between us," Arden began, softening her voice. She unzipped her vest, felt the dirt of the highway on her face, her sweater and pants as rumpled and careworn as she was. She'd throw these clothes away, she decided. Stay in the shower for a year.

"Seriously, between us, and I'll die on this hill," she went on. "In the eleven floors before we face Monelle. Is there any chance in the universe, even a fraction of a shred of a possibility, that Nyomi would put you at the scene of her accident?"

"No," Ned said. "Not unless she lies. I don't know how many times I have to tell you. I was in my office, I never left. I never freaking left."

"Does anyone have keys to your car?" Arden struggled to find some alternative theory.

"No," he said. "Well, yes, sure. Cordelia has them."

"And let me ask you again," she said, as they entered the elevator and turned to face the front, watching the silver doors close them into the square box. "There's no way that she is *not* out of town."

"No," Ned said. "Where else would she be?"

"I'm just trying to think of every conceivable thing."

"Well, that's not conceivable. Nyomi saved my life." Ned looked even more tired than she did as he unbuttoned his wool overcoat, stubble beginning on his chin, she saw, dark with specks of gray, and his eyes lined with worry. "That's ridiculous."

The elevator doors opened, three floors below their destination. Two weary doctors, with stethoscopes and blue scrubs, entered, each studying their phone.

"And why would I want to harm her?"

Arden put a finger to her lips, signaling Ned to hush. It was a good question. All she could come up with was that maybe Nyomi knew something Ned didn't want her to tell. Or someone didn't want her to tell.

Or maybe it was an accident, and Monelle Churchwood was on an obsessive mission, with Ned caught in the middle. But you don't hit someone with a car without leaving evidence on the car. As of now, they had no idea what, if anything, the police had found on Ned's Mercedes. Or if they'd looked yet. Monelle would know. Still, the best evidence might be Nyomi herself. Ned's life, his future, depended on that.

Pip and Emma's future, too, Arden thought, her heart even more invested with them now that the two sweet kids were real people to her. And Cordelia's, whose future had already been devastatingly changed. That's why she'd hired Arden.

Warren, she thought. *What have you gotten me into?* She couldn't just dump Ned. What was she supposed to say? *You know, I'm sorry, Ned, and yeah, it's super-bad timing, but soon I won't work for the Vision Group anymore. And as a result, you're on your own, buddy.* Nope. She was stuck with this. Warren had held this job over her professional head—*handle this, or your reputation is ruined.* She was doing it as much for herself as she was for Ned, or Cordelia, really. And whether it was a good or bad thing— that ship had sailed. She had a week more on the job. She had to succeed.

The elevator stopped. The doctors got out, the doors closed again. Nothing between them and the answers now.

Of course, Warren could never have predicted any of this. Maybe now that Arden was stamped with Patience Swanson's scarlet letter, he didn't care what she did. If she succeeded or if she failed, Warren would spin it, so either way *he* would win.

The elevator doors slid open. Her eyes met Ned's, and she could not decide whether she was seeing fear or sorrow or regret or apprehension.

Or, like her, anger. A formidable businessman might be reduced to rely-ing on the words of one critically injured accident victim. The woman who had saved his life, essentially, and now could ruin it.

"Got to tell you, Arden," Ned said as they walked up the corridor, seeing, ahead of them, the dour oil-painted portrait that signaled the Atherton Wing. "This feels like a trap. They'd have told us good news over the phone. They'd have said all's well, go home. But they didn't."

"Maybe." Arden considered this, hoping she'd never have to be at this hospital again. "Monelle is all strategy and tactics, we know that. But your lawyer will be there, so follow her lead. She's probably already got a plan."

They were almost at the corner, ready to turn toward Nyomi's room, when a figure appeared at the end of the hallway and walked, quickly, toward them. A tall woman, Arden saw, hair slicked back, dark coat open over a white blouse and dark slim skirt, briefcase in hand, glasses on top of her head. She looked as polished as Arden was disheveled, and exuded twice the confidence.

She raised a palm, stopping them. Looked between them, assessing, lips pursed. "Ned, Arden? I'm Jean Trounstine," she said.

The harsh fluorescents lining the ceiling made a faint hum as one of the tubes crackled, dimmed, then blossomed back into bright.

"You made good time," she went on.

"Nyomi?" Arden began.

"Thank you for being here," Ned said at the same time. "What did—how is—?"

"She was awake," the lawyer said.

54

"nd?" Arden and Ned spoke at the same time.

"'Was'? Was someone in the room with her?" Arden went on.

Jean nodded. "She pushed the buzzer, and that nurse, Zuhrah, went flying in. And closed the door. Good job freaking out the hospital brass, Arden," Jean went on. "I tried to convince them I was Nyomi's lawyer, but that didn't fly. At least Monelle couldn't go in, either."

"And is she *still* awake?" Ned asked. "For god's sake, what did she say?"

Arden heard footsteps. Sharp and determined, high heels on a mission. "Someone's coming," Arden said. "Hurry."

"Got to be Monelle. The woman has barely left my side." Jean turned, looking at the still-empty hallway. The footsteps had stopped. "I don't know what the hell she thinks I'm going to do."

"Quickly. Nyomi."

"She said 'Ned.' Again. That's all. According to the nurse, at least."

"The nurse came out of the room, and just *told* you that? Both of you? Just—'Ned'?" Arden said. Arden felt all of her work, all of her precautions, come crashing down. Certainly the nurse knew the rules. Maybe she'd known exactly what she was doing. Was well aware she couldn't unsay it, and maybe had decided to provide her own personal "justice."

"Exactly. Before anyone could stop her. You can't unring the bell, but Monelle could never use that in court. It's the ultimate hearsay, what an injured patient may or may not have said to a nurse."

"Whether it was really the name Ned. Or bed. Or head. Or ten million other words."

Jean nodded. "The ambiguity could work in our favor."

"Or in Monelle's," Arden had to say. "If you decide the victim was revealing the name of the person who hit her. But it might have been 'Call Ned' or 'Tell Ned' or . . ." *Nyomi.* At least she was alive. For now.

"So we're back at ground zero." Ned shoved his fists into his coat pockets. "Will she recover? Crap." He cocked his head. The heels had started again. "Monelle."

Arden followed Ned's gesture, saw Monelle striding toward them.

"Ned, you don't say a word," Jean instructed. "Arden, you, either. I'll do the talking."

"Mr. Bannister. Arden," Monelle began. "And Jean." She stood in front of them, her back to the empty corridor. Behind her, hospital alarm bells pinged, one then two then three, and then went silent.

Arden cataloged Monelle's drooping silk blouse, her wrinkled pants. Mascara had smudged around her eyes. Arden probably looked just as exhausted. They both had jobs to do. Both had their goals. They were simply diametrically opposite.

Arden had no doubt Monelle would stop at nothing to nail Ned. And push the law to its very edge, or maybe even past it.

"Monelle," Arden said. Not fifteen seconds earlier Jean had ordered her to keep quiet, but Nyomi was her friend. "How's Nyomi?"

"Arden." Jean's voice was taut with caution.

Monelle shook her head. "Too soon to tell," she said. "But now that your lawyer is here to represent you, Mr. Bannister," she went on, "are you comfortable with Arden hearing what I'm about to say?"

"Ah—" Ned looked at Jean, and Arden felt his loyalties shifting. Maybe that was wise. Arden could not protect him, and Jean could. Better for her to leave. But—Nyomi. She lingered, needing to know.

"I think—" Jean began.

"Oh, by the way, your wife called me," Monelle said, looking only at Ned.

"My wife?"

"Stop talking," Jean said. "That is not a suggestion. Monelle, you know better."

"I'm simply informing him," Monelle said. "Would you rather I kept that from him? And from you?"

"Give us a moment. You stay right there." Jean took Ned by one arm, pulled him to the side of the corridor.

She'd turned them both to face the tiled wall, and they were framed on either side by a vast field of oil-painted daisies. Jean had leaned her head close to Ned's ear, and blocked her mouth with one hand.

Monelle raised an eyebrow at the two of them. "Excuse me," she said to Arden, then began scrolling through her cell phone screen. "One minute."

Arden's mind revved into overload. *Cordelia?* Had called Monelle? A million reasons why she might do that: wanting to know Nyomi's condition, wanting to know about Ned's theoretical involvement, maybe wondering if Ned needed a lawyer. Would she have called about the texts? Or that video?

Time had melted into a meaningless continuum, now Saturday night, pushing eleven o'clock, sleep seeming distant and impossible. She'd driven from Boston to Vermont and back, met a magazine-cover grandmother and two vulnerable children, and been threatened—possibly—by someone who meant her harm. Or not.

And at the center of it all, Cordelia.

Or Ned.

Or both of them?

You've been watching too many movies, Arden told herself.

"So." Monelle slid her phone into the side pocket of her tote bag.

"What did Cordelia want?" Arden couldn't resist asking, though Monelle would never answer.

"Do you think she loves him?"

Arden, startled, needed a beat to untangle the pronouns. "Cordelia? Ned?"

"Yeah," Monelle said.

"Oh, I—why?"

Both looked up as Jean and Ned approached. Ned hung back a step, eyes ahead, challenging, but silent. Arden wished she could be invisible.

"Monelle, is my client a suspect in Nyomi Chang's accident?" Jean said. "Right now, yes or no, now's the time."

"Everyone is a suspect," Monelle said. "And no one is. If Mr. Bannister can be helpful, we'd appreciate it. Like telling us where he was yesterday afternoon."

"In my office. The entire afternoon," Ned said. "Waiting for Ms. Chang, as a matter of fact. Ask anyone. Ask her assistant. Ask *my* assistant." Ned paused, and his expression hardened. "Ask my wife, the next time she calls you."

Which was, Arden remembered, still baffling, and still unexplained. But had to be true.

Jean gestured at Ned, glaring. *Stop talking.*

"I was waiting for her," Ned went on, persisting. "Why would I be anyplace but where I'd promised to be?"

"Monelle, do you know exactly what happened?" Jean interrupted. "*Was* she hit by a car? Ned tells me there's a video. Where did that come from? We need to have that. Are there witnesses? Who? You need to share that. Now."

Monelle's phone buzzed, the sound cutting through the corridor's silence. Then Jean's made a similar sound.

"What?" Ned asked. "Who's texting you? Is it my wife?"

Monelle and Jean exchanged glances, and Arden's stomach clenched. Something pivotal was about to happen.

Monelle spoke first. "It's the hospital lawyer," she said. "Ms. Thurau-Gray. Says if you are willing to release the hospital from any and all liability, in writing, you two can now speak with Ms. Chang."

They were in.

Arden searched Ned's face, wanting to connect, wanting to reassure him, flimsy as her reassurance would be. What must he be thinking now, at this Rubicon moment, where the next words out of Nyomi's mouth could result in his being charged with a crime? Nyomi might be wrong. She might lie. She might have no idea what happened. Why had she said "Ned"? Or had she?

They were about to find out.

"And Ms. Ward?"

Alarm bells went off, but in Arden's head, not in the nurses' station.

"Yes?"

"In order for us to proceed, you'll need to leave. It's now a private legal matter."

"What?" Leave? *Now?* She'd come so far, and it was not only about Ned's life, but about her own. Her career flashed before her eyes. Her empty future. All the lies about her that everyone would believe. "Ned," she entreated. "Jean. What if—?"

"I don't mind if she—" Ned began.

Ned's lawyer put a hand on his arm, stopping him.

"Go home, Arden," Jean said. "I'll take care of Ned. We'll call you tomorrow."

55

At least the fish needed her. Bleary from the past twenty-four hours, Arden remembered to tap some flakes into her burbling aquarium. Bella the firemouth swam gratefully toward her, if fish can be grateful, and gulped down her food. Arden had returned the rental car to an indifferent attendant, and taken an Uber home. There had been not a word from Ned or Jean. Or Monelle. Or Cordelia.

The sunflowers seemed to taunt her now from the dining room table; still perky, still golden, still utterly inexplicable. Cordelia had sent them to thank her for—what was it again? Because she had decided Arden, in some way, had gotten Nyomi to call Ned and tell him something. Something that made him upset.

Not true, and Arden had denied it. But Cordelia had thought she was being coy.

As long as she had been with Ned, Arden realized, peeling off her vest and tossing it on a chair, she at least had a mission, a job. She'd been part of this story, *his* story, his and Cordelia's and the kids'. Now, almost midnight on a Saturday, and she had never felt more adrift and alone.

She headed for the spiral stairway, planning to flop onto her bed, and maybe, never get up. A shower seemed too difficult, wine seemed too easy, and it was possible nothing in her life would ever be right again.

When the doorbell rang, she stared down the hallway toward her solid wooden front door. Her mind tried to recalculate the time, but no, she hadn't been wrong. It was almost midnight. No one, *no* one, would be at her door spontaneously or randomly. Or for any good purpose. What if it was the guy in the Buick? She'd recognize him, certainly.

The options raced through her mind. Ignore the doorbell. Look through the peephole but ignore the doorbell. As soon as she did, though, whoever it was would know she was home. Race up to the second floor maybe, undo the door connecting her to Olen and Mariah's apartment, race down their back stairs and out the back. Call 911. And say what?

She heard the lion's-head door knocker, and took two steps closer. Listening hard. She heard two beats of silence, followed by a sound. A clicking sound. A key turning in her lock.

Before she could do anything, the door swung open. And there was Luz.

"Oh dear lord, you scared me to death." Luz slapped a palm to her chest, took a step backward. "My hair probably just went totally gray. What are you doing home?"

"Luz," Arden said, unnecessarily. "What are *you*—"

Luz reached into the pocket of her wool coat and pulled out a purple packet. "Feeding the fish," she said. "Like you asked me to. I got held up on a thing, and then . . . well, it doesn't matter. I was worried Bella and her fish gang would be starving, and you'd come home to find them floating. But whew, you're home." She tilted her head, put the fish flakes back into her pocket. "I thought you were gone for the weekend."

"Long story," Arden said. Her heart was still pounding, even though it was clearly just Luz. Though—no. Through the open front door, Arden could see a car, idling, headlights on, exhaust pluming in the clear night sky. "Is someone waiting in the car?"

"Another long story," Luz said. "You look tired. Are you all right?"

"It's midnight," Arden answered. "And I'm fine."

Luz turned, looked out toward the street, then back at Arden. She eased the door almost closed. "Everyone ate your cupcakes," she said.

Arden had to laugh. So ridiculous, cupcakes. With Ned Bannister's future on the line, and Nyomi's life in the balance, and Arden's unemployment. Though poor Luz, poor optimistic Luz, had no idea about any of it. Except . . .

Whatever, she thought. *What are they going to do, fire me for asking?*

"Luz," Arden began. "Do you know why Warren sent Cordelia Bannister to me? To me particularly. He knew I would only be at Vision a little while longer."

"Oh, I don't really." Luz glanced out the front door again. "I mean, other than their being friends."

"Friends? Who?" She did not want to invite Luz in, nor did she want to let her leave. Not quite yet. "How do you know?"

"Ahhh." Luz seemed to be searching for the answer. "When I was his intern, you know, when I first arrived, I guess I . . ." She pursed her lips again. "Well, sure, yeah, the Bannister New Year's Eve party. That's it.

Warren went to it, was invited to it, at least, and his wife, too, when she's in town. He told me that's where he watched the fireworks. Had done for a few years."

"What? He never told me—what? He was at that party?" Arden tried to decide how angry to be. Freaking Warren. And Luz knew, too. "So Warren knew Cordelia from Ned? He'd met *her* at the party, too?"

"Guess so," Luz said. "Why?"

The fish tank murmured behind them, and a gust of cold air pushed the door open an inch or two. It creaked, complaining, as if admitting an unwelcome visitor.

"Just trying to figure out the connections, you know me." Arden frowned, ignored the cold. Pictured that party: New Year's Eve, with Warren now in attendance. But not Cordelia. Not last year at least. Not when Randall Tennant was killed. "How did the Bannisters meet Warren in the first place? He must have met Ned Bannister *before* the invitation."

"Ah," Luz said again. Then nodded. "Yes. Mr. Swanson? Could that be? I have half a memory from the calendar that—"

"Arthur Swanson?" Arden pictured the party again, adding Arthur Swanson.

"Yes. He and Mr. Carmichael—I keep forgetting to call him Warren now, since I'm working with him on the Swanson account. Were friends, I guess. They golfed, stuff like that. Did Mr. Swanson invite *you* to the party, too? Since you worked with him?"

"No." Arden heard the brittle edge in her own voice. Luz, of course, had no idea what Arthur Swanson and his venomous wife had done. She had one more question. With an answer that might change everything. "Did Ned Bannister golf, or whatever, with them?"

Luz shook her head. Shrugged. "Not that I know of, no. I mean. . . ." She shrugged again. "How would I know? But not that I ever heard. It was always just the two of them, Warren and Mr. Swanson."

What a suck-up, Arden thought. He probably let Swanson win.

"I'm so sorry, Arden," Luz was saying. "I have to go, it's late, and I have . . ." She gestured to the door. "Anyway . . ."

"Yeah, well," Arden said. "Might as well give me back the fish food, Luz. And my key. You've been so generous to fish-sit for me. I wish you all the best at Vision." She paused, couldn't resist. Tried to phrase her question so it wouldn't come out as hostile. "I hope they're giving you my office."

Luz nodded. "Aw. Yes, they are. You've been a real mentor to me. And you'll keep in touch, right?"

She pulled the package of fish food from her pocket, and then a single brass key with a length of red grosgrain ribbon for a key chain. "Here. Give my best to Bella and everyone."

Arden had promised herself this wouldn't happen. That one heartbreaking moment of having an elemental part of her life ripped away; unfairly, ridiculously, leaving her helpless and trapped by a mistakenly and bizarrely concocted story. Though on paper she had a week left, her life at Vision was essentially over, whether she'd walked out with a banker's box of useless notes and a cellophane-wrapped package of leftover cupcakes or stood in the doorway of her own townhouse taking back a key. Over was over. Now was now.

She wished she could warn Luz about it, the treachery and selfishness that came with success, and the soul-crushing decisions that people made to get what they wanted. Warren's soul had been crushed long ago, Arden decided. And his odious buddy Arthur Swanson. And that bitch Patience Swanson. Being evil must get easier with practice.

Taking a few steps closer to Luz, she accepted the key and purple package. Then, on an impulse, leaned in to hug her. "I'll miss you," she said into the shoulder of Luz's plush wool coat. She inhaled, deeply, preparing to say her final goodbye. "I'll come in next week and tell everyone—"

She stopped, and knew Luz was waiting for her to finish her sentence, to come up with whatever her valedictory words would be. But instead she pulled back, keeping one hand on each of Luz's shoulders.

"What?" Luz asked.

Arden narrowed her eyes, trying to think of a way she was wrong. She wasn't. She couldn't be. *Joy.* Luz was wearing *Joy.* Luz was working on the Swanson account.

"Luz? Who's waiting for you in that car?" she asked. "Anyone I know?"

56

Three hours ago, wearing a frayed and tattered Red Sox T-shirt, all she'd wanted to do was slide under the flowered comforter and sleep. Now, as the glittering stars filtered through the glossy white shutters over her bedroom window, Arden understood that was a goal she would not attain. She kept playing back that moment, her face buried in Luz's coat, the fragrance, unmistakable, of Joy perfume. And when she'd confronted Luz—she kept picturing it now—Luz had turned, propelled herself down the front steps, and leaped into the passenger seat of the waiting car. The car had disappeared in a plume of cloudy exhaust, big, dark, and anonymous.

The only people, the *only* people in the universe who could have been driving that car were Warren, a disgusting enabler, or his smarmy benefactor, Arthur Swanson. She'd bet her life on it. *Joy* was Swanson's signature tactic. And poor sweet Luz might be his next conquest.

Arden closed her eyes. She'd folded her hands protectively over her cell phone, the phone placed in the center of her chest on top of the comforter, charger attached to a power strip on her bedroom floor. Ned had not called. Jean Trounstine had not called. Monelle had not called. Something had happened, it must have, at that hospital.

Nyomi Chang had either talked or not talked, and she, Arden, was being kept out of the loop.

Which brought up the other frustrating either-or situation. Ned. Who, as a result of what Nyomi Chang did or didn't say, was either safely at home in his own bed, or under arrest and in custody.

And what could she do about any of it? She only had five more days at Vision. Warren had made it clear this job was key to her future.

She turned over, shifting her cell phone, putting the pillow over her head. That New Year's Eve party, she conjured it in her imagination. Started the movie in her mind.

Made herself *be* Ned, that night.

After midnight. Two in the morning.

Taking the elevator to his car on the lowest floor of the parking garage. The elevator door opens, the place is deserted. Maybe he's had a glass or two of champagne, maybe even more. He clicks open the door of his car, gets in, pulls out, drives up the ramp toward home, where his wife and sick children wait for him. They'd be long asleep, he might have thought. So he might not have hurried. Or he might have. Arden shifted, putting herself more deeply into the story. He might have been hurrying to get home to them, maybe Cordelia had *wanted* him home earlier. Okay, he's driving fast, Arden decided.

Up one floor, then another, no cars parked in the garage. Arden drew on her visit with Monelle, remembering the lack of windows, the gloomy lighting, the harsh bare concrete walls. One lane blocked off for painting new lines. The arrows for exit and entry.

Ned goes up. Fast. Knows there'd be no other cars, knows it's the middle of the night, knows no one will be in his way. Maybe he's distracted, thinking about the party. When suddenly—

Arden forced herself to keep her eyes closed now, not wanting to lose her mental movie. He testified he hadn't seen Randall Tennant. He'd testified he hadn't heard Tennant's skateboard coming down the ramp toward him, though he could have had his windows up, or radio on. It was winter. New Year's Eve. He testified he'd felt something under his wheels. He testified he felt his car lurch, bump over something. Had he ever used the word "hit"? Had he ever said *I hit him*?

At that, Arden sat up. The phone slipped from her chest and clattered to the floor.

She stared at her wallpaper, past the familiar fading green stripes, fuzzing her vision, transporting herself across Boston and into the Bannister parking garage.

Were there any other cars in the garage? Monelle Churchwood had been quoted as asking him that. No, Ned had responded. Well if you didn't run over him, who did? Monelle had demanded. I never said I didn't run over him, Ned had replied. Arden remembered the television news clips she'd seen, replayed them in her mind, Ned obviously holding back tears.

And that sneering newspaper headline. Her brain changed the picture as she closed her eyes. *I never saw him,* or whatever it said. *"What guy?"* In that huge font. Arden felt her heart beating faster, and tried to still it. Kept her eyes closed, almost as if meditating.

So no one, no accident reconstruction team or police officer or investigator in the district attorney's office had ever looked for another way that Randall Tennant had died. Ned had *admitted* his car had run over him. And Nyomi Chang, too, had to work with what evidence she had. An admission, essentially a confession, essentially the truth—that Ned's Mercedes, a two-ton behemoth, had flattened Randall Tennant, crushing his body beneath its massive wheels.

But maybe Ned hadn't *killed* Randall Tennant. Maybe Randall Tennant was already dead. Maybe Randall Tennant, *already dead* Randall Tennant, had arrived in one of the cars that came to the party earlier. And no one would have looked for evidence of that gruesome passenger, of course, because there was no reason to do so. And now, almost a year later, whatever evidence there would be of that would be long gone.

Ned Bannister may not have known Randall Tennant, but *someone* did. And because whoever that someone was could not have risked anyone else seeing what they did, that someone had to be the last person to leave the party before Ned.

She struggled to poke a hole in that story. Was that right? What was she missing?

But since the surveillance video was—chronically? Or conveniently?—out of commission, there was no way to know for sure. No way to know who was second to last to leave.

She struggled to name the emotion she felt. Not exhaustion. Not bafflement. Maybe—hope. Hope.

But Nyomi Chang was still gravely injured. By someone's car. A car that was caught on camera. A car that looked like Ned's.

Arden remembered, vaguely, with a teenager's memories, a teenager who was half-intrigued with her father's political life and half studiously ignoring it, remembered when her father had partnered with a persistent nemesis. Some truculent legislator who attempted to thwart her father at every turn, at least that's how it was presented at their dinner table conversations. Her mother had disapproved. "Darling, that man is a . . . ."

Arden remembered it, because her mother had clearly been censoring herself, and judgmental teenage Arden, rolling her eyes, had already heard raunchier language than her mother could even imagine.

"That man is a coward and a weasel," her mother had finally said.

Her father had laughed. "The ends justify the means, my dear," he'd said.

She remembered that, too, because he seemed to be trying to teach her something. And at that moment, her heart had been open to it.

"Politics demands unlikely allies," he'd told her, raising his glass of burgundy. "Never let your animosity distract you from a solution."

Politics, she thought. Like her own job—the one she used to have—politics was sometimes the science, the craft, the art of making things happen the way you thought was best.

Politics demands unlikely allies.

This wasn't politics. It was murder. She believed that now to the depths of her soul. And if someone—not Ned, definitely not Ned—had killed Randall Tennant, then that someone—again, not Ned, definitely not Ned—had tried to kill Nyomi Chang as well. Who would hate both of them that much? Or what one fact could they both have known that put them in such danger? And might that person be sending anonymous texts?

What's more, Arden herself might—unwittingly—know whatever it was, too. Which meant she might also be in danger.

She knew who she had to call. *Unlikely allies.*

But it was way too early now. She had to wait at least until seven. Maybe eight. She retrieved her phone, eased back under the covers, punched her pillow into submission, then sat up again. Set the alarm for 6:59 A.M. Put her cell phone on her chest again, just in case. And finally closed her eyes.

57

Arden felt ridiculous, furtively scanning St. John Street as she got out of her Uber across from Ned Bannister's brownstone. The affluent neighborhood seemed peaceful, with the particular stillness of a Sunday morning, a few determined joggers making their way through the snow-damp sidewalks, one weary guy in sweatpants battling a snuffling beagle who pulled at its leash. Cars slushed down the narrow street.

She caught herself peering in the windows of each passing car, assessing—*were they noticing her?*—and dismissing. Then she scrutinized the ones in the resident parking spaces along the other side of the street. Everyone's cars looked the same in the snow, colorless and shapeless. Anyone could be hiding inside, watching. This whole thing had made her paranoid, and now she hardly knew what to be afraid of first. The texts, the reporters tailing Ned, the obsessive Monelle Churchwood. The interloper in Vermont. *It's not me they care about,* she reminded herself. She hoped.

Ned had called her, not three minutes after her 6:59 AM alarm rang. She'd whapped it off, apparently, but not budged.

"You up?" Ned had asked, assuming she'd know who it was.

"You home?" A million questions had raced through Arden's mind, and, she realized with a heartbeat of relief, that she'd been asleep. For some amount of time, at least. She'd scooted herself to a sitting position, back against her headboard. "And it depends what you mean by up. Anyway, tell me everything. Are you home?"

"Yes. I'm home."

"And?"

"And what? Am I charged with vehicular homicide? No. Is Nyomi talking? No, she had some sort of medical thing, I don't know, event. They sedated her again."

"Oh, no." Arden put Ned on speaker, and wiped her hands across her eyes, hoping to clear her vision and her brain. "What's the prognosis?"

"She'll be fine, eventually, they think, thank god," Ned said.

Arden glanced at her ceiling, through the roof, and into the heavens. *Thank you,* she mouthed the words. "And what about Monelle?" she asked, back to reality.

"Listen, can you . . . meet me?"

"Why? Where? Is Cordelia home? Have you heard from her? Did she say why she called Monelle? That was so strange. And strange that Monelle brought it up."

There was another way to find out, but it was still too early to make a phone call. Unless you were Ned Bannister, apparently.

"Just come over," Ned said.

"Over?" Arden tried again to shake the sleep out of her brain, tried to bring herself back to life.

"To Brookline. My place. It's fine, there's no one here, no reporters, no anyone. And no one will care or notice you."

"I don't think anyone cares what *I* do." Arden hoped that was true. "But Ned, let me ask you something." She remembered her conclusion from the night before, her authentic-feeling theory about what might have happened in the parking garage. "Do you remember when—"

"Can we do it in person?" Ned interrupted. "I honestly can't talk on the phone for one more minute. I feel like I'm tethered to this thing. By the way. I had a message from my mother. She said to tell you that Pip thinks you're cool. So that's a life ambition filled, I'm sure."

"Aw, could be," she said. "But Ned. You're *home*. What happened?"

"Yeah, right? For now, at least, I'm not in handcuffs in the Charles Street jail. Look. Just come over. We need to plan. The front-front door is open, then buzz unit four. Or just push the inside door, someone always props it open. You can invoice me for your hours. Sunday must be time and a half, right?"

Arden laughed, then stopped herself. An invoice. Which reminded her of Warren, and Arthur Swanson, and Luz Ocasio, and whether her suspicious perfume meant anything except business as usual. Whether Luz was its next victim.

Now she put her hand on the brass front doorknob of the Bannisters' building, feeling the cold throb through her leather gloves. She'd been here once before, seemed like months ago, but had been only a few days. Cordelia had given her brownies. Which reminded her of their college-student cook. Which reminded her of Ned's lie about carryout pizza.

Every time she began to believe him, to trust him, to feel sorry for him or protective, his whack-a-mole lies popped up to remind her. She paused, considering, standing on the cobblestone top step of Ned's threshold.

She'd hear Ned out, she decided. Then go straight to her office—hoping her card key still worked, that'd be interesting—take her stuff, and leave a final invoice under Warren's door. And never talk to any of these people again. She'd be fine.

Ned and Cordelia would have to work things out on their own. Pip—and Emma—they seemed happy in their grandmother's care. Nyomi's recovery was not affected by anything Arden did. And whatever type of . . . justice, she guessed was the word, she hoped would happen with Ned's legal travails, she'd have to read about in the papers.

She was done with the Bannisters' lives. Done with trying to adjust their reality. She needed to work on her *own* reality. Her own future. Starting now.

"Arden?" The front door opened. Ned. Flannel shirt untucked, jeans, loafers with no socks, holding open a thick glass inner door with a massive metal latch that led to a glass-walled entryway behind him. "I saw you out the front window, saw you cross the street. Figured you must be at the door. Come in, it's freezing. Elevator's broken, we have to walk."

"Hey, Ned. I was lost in thought, I suppose," she said.

"Worried about more bad guys in Buicks?"

"I'm not worried about anything," she lied. "Except Nyomi, of course. And whatever Monelle is trying to do to implicate you. Did Jean get that video?"

"Let's get inside. It's cold."

He started up and Arden followed, trying to decide what to do. A sixteen-paned window let morning light onto the wide first landing, and as they turned the corner and continued upstairs, the upper walls were decorated with ultramodern lithographs, geometric and demanding attention. *Cordelia probably chose them*, the thought crossed her mind.

Ned opened the apartment's front door, allowing her into the hard-edged living room she remembered from her visit with Cordelia. It smelled like coffee and cinnamon now, irresistible.

Ned locked the door and held out his arm. "Let me take your coat."

"Can I ask you something?" She unzipped her parka. Paused. "Remember that night at dinner, at Salazar, when you talked about having to survive on carryout pizza?"

"Sure," he said, drawing out the word.

"I came here to visit Cordelia one day last week," she said.

"You did?"

Arden thought the surprise on his face was genuine. "Yeah. And I met your . . . your student. Your cook. Megan?"

"And so?" Ned still had his arm out for her coat.

"Megan cooks for you," Arden said. "Why did you tell me you were living on carryout pizza?"

Ned's arm dropped to his side. "I don't know," he said. A look crossed his face; embarrassed, or sorry. "I didn't want you to think I was . . . I don't know."

Arden tried to figure out what word he might mean; privileged, or pompous, or rich.

"Sorry," he said. "Yes, Megan cooks. Or cooked, she's not here anymore. School's out for Thanksgiving. And I sometimes prefer carryout pizza. I didn't mean to lie, Arden." His face turned serious. "That's not what I do."

"Like your mother told Emma." Arden handed over her coat, reluctantly. As if it signaled her acquiescence to being there. Which, she guessed, it did. "Remember? 'Just say what's true.'"

"Mother's motto," Ned said. "I've heard that a thousand times."

"Then why didn't you *do* it? Why didn't you tell her about Nyomi? And Monelle?" She worried about her wet boots on the Bannisters' expensive-looking carpeting, so she toed them off and tucked them beside the front door.

"I didn't want to hurt her." Ned was hanging her coat in a hall closet, talking to her over his shoulder. "Or worry her. I know, stupid, but she's been through enough. I just hoped you could—I could—we could—fix it. I don't mean *fix* it," he hurriedly added, "I mean make it go away. Since I did nothing wrong. I sat at my desk that afternoon, and suddenly I was a suspect again. It's bull. They'll find out. As soon as they stop hounding me and go after the real bad guy."

"Hope so." Arden rubbed her hands, trying to warm them. On New Year's Eve in the parking garage, Ned had not left the scene. The other night, whoever hit Nyomi *did* leave. If that mattered. "So did Monelle say anything? About the video, or—anything? Have they looked at your car?"

"Coffee's in here." Ned pointed to the living room, black couch, red chairs, not one sign that children lived there. A crumble-topped coffee cake, with two pieces cut by a silver-handled knife and placed on white plates beside it, had been set out for them. A coffeepot sat on a silver trivet. Ned held up a finger. "Napkins. I'm out of practice. Pour your coffee, have a seat, I'll be right back."

"So there *is* news."

"One minute." Ned turned his back and left her alone with the coffee cake and her own complicated thoughts.

58

"N ed?" Arden had heard something, not coming from the kitchen but from the hall. Clearly, unmistakably, the sound of a key in the front door. Fiddling with the lock. Like Luz last night, but this could not be Luz.

"Ned?" Arden stood as she called out again. There was nothing to do, of course, whoever was about to come in would see her in Ned's living room early on a Sunday morning, in her stocking feet, and with what was essentially breakfast in front of her.

It all happened at the same time. To her right, Ned appeared at the edge of the dining room, two white cloth napkins in his hand. To her left, the front door clicked open, and Cordelia, pink-cheeked and wearing a belted black coat and matching muffler, pulled a sleek black roller bag into the entryway.

For a moment no one spoke, and Arden could almost feel each of them trying to figure out what to say.

Cordelia's laughter broke the silence. "My, my," she said, spinning her bag into place just beside Arden's boots. "Oh," she said, seeing them.

"Dee," Ned said. "This is a surprise, honey."

"Apparently," Cordelia said. "Although this is my home. Where else would I be? I missed you, and worried about you, but—apparently I shouldn't have worried."

"Welcome back," Arden said, trying to diffuse the surprising—and scathing—animosity. She should never have come here, she should have stayed in bed this morning, she should have dropped Ned at the hospital yesterday and erased this whole episode from her life. But she'd played a different hand and now she had to stick with it. "Are you okay? We hadn't heard from you in . . ." *We,* she thought, *possibly not the best choice of pronouns.* "I—"

"So." Cordelia eyed the coffee and cake, pointedly looked at Arden's feet. Maybe at Ned's untucked shirt. "This is cozy," she said. "Am I interrupting?"

"What?" Ned, still holding the two napkins, looked like a baffled waiter.

"Cordelia." Arden decided to pretend—*not* pretend since it was true—that everything was aboveboard and professional. "I just arrived, and Ned was about to tell me what happened last night at the—"

"I'm sure." Cordelia eyed Arden again, up and down, almost as if amused. "I thought you had rejected these . . . tactics," she said. "Apparently not."

"Tactics?" Ned looked at Cordelia, frowning, then at Arden.

Arden opened her mouth, trying to figure out how to explain, but Cordelia kept talking.

"Didn't I hear from Warren Carmichael that this is why you were let go from the Vision Group?" Cordelia tapped a finger to her lips. "I suppose I'm not surprised, at you both, actually. Both of you have, shall we say, histories."

"That's ridiculous." Ned's face clouded with frustration. "Cordelia, you're overreacting. *You* hired Arden, and *you* asked her to help me. She's helping me. You left town, Nyomi Chang got hit by a car. And I'm being targeted for it. Meantime, you have ignored your children, and made your daughter miserable and worried, which sent us to Vermont to—"

"I heard about that chummy little outing, too," Cordelia said. "Arden, you were quite the hit. I'm sure you'll be very happy with Ned and his dear mother. Please sit down, Arden, where are my manners? You must be so . . . tired from last night."

Arden put up a palm, trying to stop Cordelia's sarcasm. She understood, from Cordelia's point of view, what this must look like, and did not want to belittle her feelings. On the other hand, Cordelia was extraordinarily wrong, and there was no need for her confusion or misunderstanding to continue.

"Cordelia, Ned is right, I'm doing what you hired me to do. Monelle Churchwood is focusing on your husband for what happened to Nyomi Chang. It's a public relations nightmare. So of course I was at Ned's side. Doing my job. No matter what time it was, or where. And a good thing, too. Monelle and two police officers were ready to pounce on Nyomi, question her even in her medicated and injured state, and what she might have said could have inadvertently incriminated Ned. Not to mention breaching lawyer-client privilege. *That's* why I'm here. To help you. Ned asked me to come, and, as you can see from my wet boots"— she pointed—"I did, indeed, just arrive."

Take that, she thought, but then tucked that emotion away. She was going to extricate herself from this, the sooner the better. These two people had problems, but not the kind Arden had expertise in solving.

"Ned? You think Arden is trying to help us?" Cordelia tilted her head, a cynical coquette. "When Warren Carmichael sent me to her, he warned me about her." She nodded, unwrapping the long black muffler from around her neck, but keeping it draped around her shoulders. "But you know, Arden, I'd heard so much about you, and your public relations prowess, and I thought, well, if she can help my darling Ned, it doesn't really matter about her personal life. And certainly after your sordid little escapade with—well, we won't go into it. I assumed you'd be more—professional. But apparently not."

"What?" Now it was Arden's turn to be perplexed. 'My darling Ned' was the last phrase she'd expected to come out of Cordelia's mouth. "Sordid? What are you talking ab—"

"I think you should know, darling," Cordelia went on, "that Arden here is hardly working to help us. In fact, she's working to harm me. And I'm afraid she has. Not only by . . ."

Arden squinted at Cordelia, baffled. Her voice had trailed off, and it looked like the woman's eyes were welling with tears. Arden could not for the life of her understand.

"I thought we could hold our marriage together. And I did my very best," Cordelia said, taking a deep breath. "But this"—she gestured toward Arden—"might be more than I can handle."

"'This' what?" *Talk about a nightmare,* Arden thought. *Darling Ned? Hold our marriage together?* Only a few days ago, Cordelia had told her she was afraid of Ned, and believed he was hiding something about the accident. That Nyomi Chang had known it, too. And moreover, Cordelia had told Arden that Ned and Tennant had some mysterious connection at a barbershop. But if what Arden had surmised last night about the parking garage was correct, all of that was wrong. Ned was innocent, just as the jury had decided, and that would mean—

"Cordelia, you're being unreasonable." Ned tossed the napkins on the couch, and approached Cordelia, palms up, pleading. "And I have to say, honey, out of line. Arden here has done her best to help me, and without her, I'm not sure what I would have done."

"Aww," Cordelia said. "That's sweet."

"Like I said," Ned began. "We'd both been at the hospital last night—why don't you take off your coat, Dee? And when I was finally allowed, with my lawyer, to talk to Nyomi, they sent Arden home. So I wanted to tell her what happened."

"And the phone wasn't good enough?"

"I'm not going to have you second-guess my decisions," Ned said. "Especially when you were not here to share them. Can we just move forward, please? And I wonder that you're not interested in what happened in that hospital room overnight."

"Oh, I know what happened," Cordelia said. "But Ned? How convinced are you that Arden here is trying to help you?"

"What?" Arden's protest carried the weight of utter confusion. Cordelia herself had suggested that Arden look into that night in the garage. And that's what she had done.

"You hired me to guide Ned through his reentry into society," Arden said, "and to help your children smoothly transition back to school. But my efforts were somewhat thwarted"—Arden tried to make her language as formal as possible—"when your husband became the focus in yet another serious pedestrian injury. I must say I'm baffled by your reaction."

"Are you?" Cordelia matched Arden's arch tone. "Ned, let me ask you two questions."

"Do I have a choice?"

"One. Did you know our Arden was the last person to meet with Nyomi Chang before the . . . accident? Did she tell you about that?"

"No." Ned glanced at her, perplexed. "But it would have been fine."

"And I met with her, Cordelia, because *you*—" Arden began.

"Question number two. Ned, has this very helpful Ms. Ward seemed curious about where you got your hair cut?"

Arden turned to Ned, who was looking at her. Curiously. Suspiciously?

"Why?" Ned finally said.

Cordelia loosened the belt of her coat, showing a black turtleneck and black pants underneath. A dangling gold pendant. She tucked the ends of the coat's belt into the pockets.

"I fed your Ms. Ward a quickly concocted and pretty far-fetched story about how you and Randall Tennant had been connected via some barbershop, that I had no idea what the name of it was, but that I suspected it was where you two had been involved in some nefarious scheme. And that if only she could find out the name of this barbershop, she could prove that you actually had killed Randall Tennant on purpose. That you were a killer. Of course that's ridiculous, and any law enforcement types worth their salt would have discovered such a thing, but your helpful Ms. Ward bought right into it. She agreed to investigate you, just as she was coddling and escorting—*ha*—you."

Arden felt her eyes widen. Cordelia had *never* said that, ever, about killing Tennant on purpose. Cordelia had simply confided she thought Ned was hiding "something." And, trusting her, Arden had pursued the haircut thing even to the point of asking Ned's own son about it. *Not Ned's son,* her brain reminded her.

"So," Cordelia went on. She smoothed her hair from one cheek. "What say you, Ned?"

A sophisticated predator, Arden thought, *toying with her prey. But who was the prey?* Arden eyed her boots, wondering how quickly she could grab them, and her coat, and get out of this place.

"Ned? I'm asking you again: Has Ms. Ward seemed curious about where you got your hair cut?"

"What?" Ned said. "I mean—"

"Ah. She has. So ask yourself, darling, is Arden really working with *me*?" Cordelia raised an eyebrow. "Working for *you*? Remember—you told me Arden told you there was surveillance video. How did she find out about that? Did you know she and Churchwood paid a little clandestine visit to your garage? Trespassing, I might add."

"It wasn't tress—"

"Might the truth be, Ned darling . . ." Cordelia had come closer to her husband, and wound her arm through his elbow, cat capturing canary. "That your Arden is actually working *with* Monelle Churchwood? And trying to bring you down?"

59

"What the absolute hell," Arden muttered under her breath, stomping to keep her feet warm as she waited for her Uber at the corner of St. John and Beacon Street. She supposed she could understand Cordelia's "woman scorned" conclusion, and even could admire her forthright confrontation about it. But nothing could be further from the truth, and the woman should have accepted their honest explanation. And not to mention the ridiculous idea that she had been working with Monelle all along.

But the barbershop was a fabrication? Why? Cordelia had turned on her, had come at her, hard, with wild attacks and wilder insinuations, and it seemed clear that she wanted to make Ned distrust and despise her. Could that *all* be from her noxious jealousy? Or had she gotten more texts? Cordelia had confided in her from the beginning, crying, and fragile, and fearful. And now—Arden was somehow the enemy.

She searched the gray sky, begging the universe for answers. They all should be drinking coffee and laughing by now, understanding that they had been through—and were still going through—an emotionally charged time. And everyone's nerves and judgment were frayed.

But the woman had turned even nastier, even mentioned Arthur Swanson by name. Why would Warren have spread such destructive gossip about her? Warren and Cordelia. *There* was a match made in the netherworld. She frowned, hard, jamming her fists into her coat pockets.

She'd confront Warren with it. And mentally increased the balance on the final invoice she'd present to him. Money wasn't the point, but the damage to Arden's reputation seemed to be increasing, and she was the only one who had not done anything wrong. She'd need to use her own crisis management techniques to manage—and repair—her *own* life.

"Gah," she said out loud. The list of people she'd like to kill was getting longer: the odious Arthur Swanson, his equally-odious Patience. Warren. Now Cordelia. The lot of them.

She'd finally said something to the Bannisters, she barely remembered what, and fled. Now, standing here alone on a street corner, she felt like a pawn in some chess game. People moving her across the board, using her to get what they wanted. And she, obedient, was not even playing a game of her own. She'd been trying to do her job.

She kicked a pebble, watched it make a path in the snow, then stop, defeated. What did she herself want from this? What would winning look like?

The Uber app showed two minutes left to wait. She imagined the Bannisters watching her out the brownstone window, and felt enough outrage to melt the snow beneath her feet. All she had tried to do, *all,* was to follow the instructions her employer—Cordelia by way of Warren—had given her. Cordelia's motivations were incomprehensible. What did winning look like to Cordelia?

"She's a complete nut job," Arden said out loud. She should let it go, but she had to know what happened. Not only to Nyomi Chang, but in that garage. The second to last person to leave that New Year's Eve party might have murdered Randall Tennant. It was such a logical explanation. Who that was, and why, *that* mattered. Because if it was true, that person had flat-out gotten away with murder.

No one was investigating that "accident" anymore. The case was closed. The clincher—the baffling part—was that *Cordelia* was the one who had wanted it reopened. Pushing Arden to investigate the texts instead of ignoring them. That meant she herself could not be involved.

This morning, after Cordelia had lashed out so bitterly and unfairly at her, Arden had briefly wished Cordelia *was* complicit. But in reality, a killer, a murderer, she could not be. Arden allowed herself a moment of unworthy disappointment about that.

The Uber arrived. The moment she got into the car, she'd make the call to her unlikely ally. *Thanks Dad,* she thought, *I hope you were right.*

Yes. Time for her to make a move. Pawns could move. Pawns could win.

The Uber pulled away. She dialed a number.

The gray morning had turned even more gray, making the Boston skyline a swath of steel, and icy drizzle now had pedestrians on Atlantic Avenue putting up their umbrellas and yanking hoods over their heads.

They walked cautiously, shoulders hunched, determined, probably watching for the inevitable pool of shoe-ruining dank slush disguised as solid pavement. And now Arden was about to do exactly what Cordelia had accused her of. Work with Monelle.

Monelle had initially been wary at Arden's call, brusque and dismissive. But Arden had pleaded with her. "Just hear me out. Truth is truth, no matter what side you're on. I know you believe that. Two minutes."

First she'd asked about Nyomi, but the prosecutor, sounding exhausted, had reported that Nyomi had suffered some sort of seizure, and was sedated again.

"And listen," Monelle went on. "I don't want to burden you with my personal problems, but my wife looks like she's about to kill me. I've only been home two hours, and now I'm on the phone again. Whatever you're calling about, can it wait?"

Could it? Arden considered that now, as the Uber threaded through Brookline and toward Boston, past Fenway Park, and the tree-lined allée of Comm Ave. "Well," she said. "Let me put it this way. Did you ever check to see whether Randall Tennant was already dead when Ned's car hit him?"

Silence. Then Arden thought she heard a child crying on Monelle's end of the phone, and then the muffled tones of another adult. "I'm sorry," Arden said, "but—"

"No, you're right to call. Hang on."

They passed Boston Common; a greensward gone brown, bronze statues of generals, and one lopsided snowman with a carrot for a nose.

"Okay." Monelle was back. "I'm going to have to do a lot of gift-buying to make up for this, but go ahead."

Arden told the rest of her story as fast as she could; her conjecture, her theory, how it all might have happened a different way. She finished while looking over Boston Harbor, the water so leaden that there was almost no seam where it met the sky.

"So what I'm wondering," she wrapped up. "Was there some evidence proving the Mercedes killed Randall Tennant? I mean, that car is a monster, and if Tennant had been, well, beaten up, couldn't that be hidden by being crushed?"

All Arden could hear on the other end was Monelle breathing.

"Nyomi Chang should have brought that up in court," Monelle finally said. "Could have. But because Bannister essentially confessed . . ."

"Exactly," Arden said. "It wasn't about *when* Randall Tennant died, because everyone accepted *how* he died, so the *when* was a given. Mercedes versus human, the human is going to lose."

Again, silence.

Arden thought of something else. "Hey. Remember I told you that Cordelia, that night she called from the closet? Said Ned got a call from Nyomi and it had upset him. But she didn't know—or *said* she didn't know," Arden corrected herself, "*what* Nyomi said that made him so unhappy. And so—remember that?"

"I guess." Monelle sighed. "My mind is pretty baked."

"Ma'am?" They'd arrived at Arden's office. Her once-office. The Uber driver twisted to look over the seat at her and spoke through a square flap opening in the Plexiglass barrier between them. "This it?"

"Who's that?" Monelle asked.

"Uber driver," Arden said. "One minute, Rick." Arden used the name on the plastic ID attached to the barrier. "I'm really sorry, I'll leave a huge tip."

Rick gave her a thumbs-up.

"Where are you?" Monelle asked.

"At my office. Outside."

"Want to meet at the parking garage?" Monelle said. "Bannister's, I mean. If it wasn't Ned Bannister who killed Randall Tennant, then the scene of the murder—crap, *maybe* a murder—seems like the first place to look."

"Sure," Arden said, wondering what could be left to see. "And remind me to ask you about the guest list."

"Guest list?" Monelle said.

Arden gave Rick the new address.

"And," Monelle went on, "what were you going to say about Cordelia telling you about Ned's call from Nyomi? If that sentence came out in English."

"Yeah, it did," Arden said. "Here's the thing. I wonder if *that's* what Nyomi called Ned about. How Tennant really died. Maybe she'd thought of the same theory I did. Or maybe got some new information. Not to reopen Ned's case, but that could open a *new* case. Against a different person."

"And whoever wanted us all to forget about Randall Tennant . . . ," Monelle began.

"Needed to have Nyomi stop talking," Arden finished the sentence.

They both went silent, Arden letting the threat inherent in that sink in, knowing Monelle was feeling the same way.

"So that might mean"—Arden needed to say it out loud—"that the person who *actually* killed Randall Tennant is the same person who hit Nyomi."

"*If* your theory is right, then yeah," Monelle said. "Possibly. Or someone who was in on it. And decided to keep Nyomi Chang from talking."

"Yeah," Arden said.

Arden sat huddled into the corner of the backseat, suddenly too cold, staring out over Boston Harbor as the Uber inched across the Moakley Bridge. The Boston Tea Party had taken place somewhere nearby, she always thought when she passed here. She could see, in the distance ahead, the red brick of the Bannister Building parking garage. The place where someone—not Ned, definitely not Ned—had taken Randall Tennant's already dead body.

If her theory was right.

"Arden?" Monelle finally said.

"Huh?" Arden brought herself back to reality.

"Did you tell anyone *else* what you figured out?"

60

rden saw Monelle standing on the sidewalk in front of the parking garage, waiting, wrapped in a calf-length black jacket, her braids poking from underneath a black knit cap. As she got out of her Uber, Arden saw the almost-noontime sun battling the continuing intermittent drizzle. She slipped on a treacherous patch of ice, righted herself just in time.

"Careful." Monelle raised a hand in greeting. "Not sure what's to find. But two heads are better than one."

"Two confused and exhausted heads," Arden replied. They both stood, facing the parking garage. "Did you go in yet?"

"Nope," Monelle said. "But I did scout the attendant's office." She pointed. "That glassed-in place? No one's there. The garage is apparently just open. Unattended. The gate thing is automatic. I punched the entry button, actually, and the metal arm went up. A ticket came out. But there doesn't seem to be anyone here to take the money."

"Good luck to drivers getting out," Arden said.

"When we were here before, there *was* an attendant. Orville Welling? Something like that. Ex-con, maybe. Tattoos. Smoking. Not happy in his job, I would say."

"Yeah, well, who is?" Arden wondered *when* "before" was, but Monelle had obviously investigated the case from the beginning. "Happy in their job, I mean."

"Orvath. That's it. Orvath Welling. And got that right, sister." Monelle raised an eyebrow, just visible under her cap. "*My* boss is a total jerk. He blames *me* for the loss of the Bannister case. Not the facts, not the jury. Me. Course if I'd won, it'd be *his* victory."

"My boss is a—" Arden stopped midsentence. "He's not my boss anymore, long story."

"Warren Carmichael?"

"Yes," Arden said. She pulled her collar up closer around her ears. "How did you know that?"

"Everyone does," Monelle said. "Anyway, you're right, if the attendant's not here, how will people pay?"

"Maybe he's sneaked out quickly to get more cigarettes."

"Let's go *in* quickly then," Monelle said, "while he's not there."

"Works for me."

She followed Monelle, edging past the entryway gate and toward the gloomy walls of the garage, Arden scanning for surveillance cameras. The place smelled like stale motor oil and lingering exhaust; and the light fixtures, attached to the low ceiling and coated with dust, struggled to illuminate the dank interior. Parked cars, the few of them Arden noticed as they walked down the circular incline, were not covered with wet slush, not beading with water, their windshields not showing the semicircular swipe of recent windshield wipers.

"These cars have been here overnight," Arden said, feeling detectivey. "So far, no new cars today."

Monelle nodded. "Because there's no rain on them," she said.

"Yeah," Arden said. "They all have dried salt, though."

"I saw that, too."

Monelle continued ahead without speaking, and Arden wondered what she was thinking about. Probably exactly the same thing as Arden. Randall Tennant, crushed to death on this parking garage floor.

"Monelle?" Arden began. She heard the sound of their boots— almost-duplicate tan leather lace-ups with thick rubber soles—squish on the pavement as they continued.

"Yeah?"

"Remember I told you to remind me about the guest list?"

"What about it?"

"Did your people question everyone who was at Ned Bannister's party?"

"Sure," Monelle said. "Ned said everyone else was gone at the time of the 'incident,' and the parking lot tickets, according to the records, confirmed it. Showed that no one else was in the garage."

"But you interviewed them? About how much Ned drank, for instance?"

"Yes."

"Did you know Ned's mother was there?"

"Sure. She told us her son had only two glasses of champagne. As any wise mom would have insisted."

"And a business associate of Ned's, Arthur Swanson. And his wife."

Monelle gave her a look. "Arthur Swanson, yes. We know about him. He and his wife actually left early."

"And Warren Carmichael," Arden said.

"Maybe that's where I saw the name," Monelle said.

"Anyway. What I wonder is, was there anyone at the party who could have *been* Randall Tennant? A crasher? A guest of a guest? Not on the list?"

"That's an interesting idea," Monelle said as they continued down the steady concrete incline. "But—"

Their footsteps matched, and Arden yearned again for coffee. Her brain was demanding caffeine and sugar. But maybe she'd found a clue.

"But, yeah, we checked, and everyone correlated with everyone," Monelle was saying, eliminating that idea. "There were no extra people, no gate-crashers, no strangers. You ever thought of being an investigator, though?"

"Good one," Arden said. "Let me know when you have openings. Anyway. One more thing. Do you know in what order everyone left?"

A fluorescent light hissed and sputtered above them. No other sounds but their soft voices, and the soles of their boots.

"Specifically who . . ." Arden stopped, and spread her arms to encompass the entire parking garage. "Whoever was the second to last to leave must have, might have, *could* have, put Randall Tennant's body in Ned's path, and then, left it. No one was there to observe them, and then they left, too. See? Left an already-dead person for Ned to run over, and 'kill.' I mean, Ned *might* not have seen him, a person on the ground. In the dark, going fast."

"And the skateboard."

"Yeah, and the skateboard. Which is . . . where is that now, anyway? Did Ned ever see it? Are there fingerprints on it?"

Monelle tapped her lips with one finger, and Arden could almost watch her mind at work. Finally, she sighed. "I don't think anyone looked for them," Monelle said. "We still could, of course, it's in the evidence room."

"It would have been wiped, anyway." This was all speculation. Hindsight. Second-guessing. "But one more thing. Did anyone put Randall Tennant's DNA into any of those databases? The genealogy ones?"

"No, why would we do that? We knew who he was. Randall Tennant. There was no question about that."

"Hear that?" Arden stopped. Listened.

"A car," Monelle said. "No one will care about us. Just move to one side, act like we're going to our car. It's a parking garage. Anyway, to finish. We didn't do DNA because Randall Tennant had ID. He just didn't seem to have any friends. Or family. But that happens, you know? It's sad, but it happens. His DNA wasn't relevant, or necessary."

"But now that it might be that Randall Tennant was killed on purpose—" Arden tried to decide how to phrase this. Whatever car was arriving was getting closer, Arden could clearly hear tires on pavement now, and the shift of gears.

She stopped, grabbed Monelle by her arm. "Wouldn't it matter more who he was? I mean I get it, Ned didn't know him, so it didn't matter. But now, maybe, it *does*. Maybe especially to the second to last person to leave."

61

The car's engine got louder. And Arden struggled to calm herself.
There was no reason to be nervous when a car came into a parking garage. Monelle had stepped into the shadows, between a stand of once-white heating pipes, their paint peeling and flaked on the ground. She beckoned Arden to come closer.

"Might as well not be seen," Monelle said. "I admit I've freaked myself out a little."

"I'm with you," Arden whispered. She saw the pierce of headlights first, penetrating the gloom ahead, then the lights turned the corner, and there was no way, not with the angles and laws of geometry, that they didn't blast Monelle and Arden full on.

"So much for hiding," Monelle murmured.

The car stopped, headlights glaring, and Arden heard a shift into park. The engine kept running. A car door clicked open, and Arden could only make out a blurred silhouette through the glare. And maybe the crackle of a two-way radio. *Police?* If it was police, the thought went through her mind at light speed, they'd be fine. Monelle was Monelle. Law enforcement.

Arden put up a hand to cover her eyes, a reflex, then quickly took it away, trying to put an innocent-looking expression on her face. Why two women were in a parking garage without a car was going to take some explaining.

"May I help you?" Monelle took a step forward, put herself in front of Arden. Her voice had toughened with authority. "I'm with the district attorney's office."

Good call, Arden had to admit, go hardass. She wondered if Monelle had a weapon. Probably not. She did wield power, though.

The man stepped closer. Arden did not recognize him.

"I know who you are," he said. He wore a work shirt and jeans. His car—more like a Jeep—had a dashboard placard saying BANNISTER PARK-ING showing through the windshield. "I saw you on the cameras. Did you find what you were looking for?"

"We're fine," Monelle said. "Thank you."

"Your cop friend stayed longer than you. Then he got too cold, I guess."

"All good," Monelle said. "Thank you, Mr. Welling. And so you know, our permission from last time is still valid."

This must be the guard Monelle had referred to earlier. Welling, she'd called him, had referred to Monelle and a cop being here yesterday. Looking for something. Monelle had not mentioned that to her. Monelle seemed to have secrets—and suspicions—of her own. Why would today be different than yesterday? The reason, Arden decided, was something had changed. And what *permission*? A warrant?

"I'll see you on the cams anyway." The guard pointed up. "Not much else to watch but you two ladies, being a Sunday. Place is closed."

"Cameras working today apparently," Monelle said. "When did they finally get fixed?"

"Huh? Fixed? Fixed from what?"

Arden frowned, perplexed. It was eleven months ago, that deadly New Year's Eve, when part of the reason for Ned's acquittal, part of the reasonable doubt, was that there were no surveillance cameras working. 'Intermittent,' Arden remembered them as being described.

"'Fixed' from when they were 'broken,'" Monelle said.

Arden heard the bitterness and suspicion in her voice. Each word carefully enunciated.

"'Fraid I'm not following," Welling said.

"I see." Monelle nodded. "Sure. We'll be in touch, then."

Don't leave town, Arden wondered if she'd say.

"At your service," Welling said. "Need me? Just wave at the camera."

Welling drove off, making a too-fast U-turn in his little Jeep. Arden watched Monelle watching him, waited to hear what the woman would say. How she would explain. Her visit here yesterday. The "permission." The guard's apparent confusion over the surveillance. Arden's eyes adjusted to the returning gloom.

"Fun guy," Arden finally said.

"Shall we?" Monelle motioned for them to continue.

"Um, Monelle?" Arden put up both palms, stayed where she was.

"You were here yesterday? With a cop? Why? And you said you had permission—did that mean a warrant? Why?"

"Let me ask you something, Arden."

"Sure."

"Cordelia Bannister approached you. I know that. You work for Ned Bannister. That's why you've been joined at the hip for the past few days."

Arden waited.

"Would you work for someone you thought was guilty? Of a crime?"

"Ned Bannister was acquitted by a jury," Arden said. "I know that wasn't your favorite moment. And yes, I was hired to help the world see that not guilty can truly mean not guilty. Not simply that someone 'got off on a technicality.' I actually hate that expression. But that not guilty means—Ned literally did not do it, and that he and his family should be allowed to live their lives without being ostracized."

"Not what I asked you."

"I know," Arden admitted.

"But here's the thing. You came to me with a theory that someone else killed Randall Tennant, at a different time, and put the body in a place where Ned could not fail to run over it. Who do you think that person was?"

Arden had considered this, endlessly. Constantly. "Well, we can't know until we know who Randall Tennant *is*. Was. Because motive, means, opportunity. Without knowing who the victim was, you can't discover motive."

"Motive, means, opportunity, the three tenets of a murder investigation." Monelle smiled. "You been watching *Law & Order*? But I agree with you. And we considered that. But Ned *confessed*. And there's no 'motive' in an accident."

Arden saw Monelle scan the garage, maybe looking for the now-working surveillance cameras. Arden could feel that guard watching them. He certainly couldn't hear them, and she knew the cameras were for protection, but it felt more like scrutiny. Who might Welling call to report the two of them?

"What about Nyomi Chang, Arden? Who do you think ran *her* down? Do you think the two things are connected? Remember we have surveillance of a car like Ned's leaving the scene."

"*Was* it Ned's?"

Monelle shook her head. "Not conclusive."

"Right."

"But since you brought up motive, Arden, who do *you* think might have one to kill Nyomi? If they needed to keep her from revealing something?"

"I feel like we're in court, and I'm on the witness stand," Arden said. "Wanna just tell me what you're getting at? Which I suppose is—finally— the *real* reason you brought me here. Isn't it?"

"It is. Guilty as charged. Because Arden? What if it *was* Ned who killed Randall Tennant? Ned, *himself*? Not within the garage with his Mercedes. But *before*. And then—made the murder look like an accident?"

62

Arden's mind could hardly keep up with itself as they walked, quickly now, to where Ned's car had been parked. The pitted concrete floor was striped with yellow lines, and scattered with scraps of paper and traces of road salt.

Cordelia had said that Ned had secrets. That there was more to this than he was telling. She constantly alluded to his unfaithfulness. His manipulation. That she was afraid of him.

It would make sense, in a hideous way, if Ned was truly that calculating. And truly a risk taker. All he'd have to do is disable his building's surveillance system, and, ironically, *not* drink very much, so he would not be guilty of drunk driving, a risk that almost backfired since the breathalyzer had been, coincidentally, miscalibrated.

And if Ned had done it himself, Arden's whole theory about the second to last to leave was moot. Maybe the body had even been transported in Ned's own car. By Ned himself. Who would ever have looked? Or maybe the body was hidden somewhere in the parking garage. Ned owned the building, after all.

Arden stopped walking, thinking it through. But the *trial*. What if he had been found guilty? That was the unmistakable flaw in Monelle's theory. To go to trial? To risk a devastating guilty verdict? But Nyomi Chang was smart. Brilliant even. And maybe later, after her victory, Nyomi found out.

Maybe Nyomi found out. And had threatened to tell.

Monelle turned, maybe realizing Arden was no longer next to her. "What?"

"I'll tell you in a minute," Arden said.

"Look." Monelle pointed to a black Mercedes. "This is Ned Bannister's car. The one he ran over Randall Tennant with was white, but this is his new one." Monelle gestured, like a salesperson in a car commercial. "What do you think when you see this?"

"What do I *think*? I think my brain is about to explode," Arden said. Had she been hanging out with a murderer for the past three days, driving him around, sharing junk food, bonding with his family? How had she been so wrong about him? *The guy in the woods,* she thought. But one step at a time. "Why don't you just tell me what *you* think."

Monelle nodded, acquiescing. "Sorry to go into lawyer mode. This is Ned's car. It's black and shiny. Perfectly clean. As you noted yourself, the other parked cars have been here at least since yesterday, if not longer. They're covered with road salt, aren't they? As you said."

"Ned's isn't," Arden said, examining it. "So . . ."

Monelle took out her phone. Glanced up to where the surveillance cameras might be, then went back to her cell.

"Who are you calling?"

"I'm not calling anyone." Monelle tapped on her screen, then moved shoulder to shoulder with Arden, holding the phone in front of them. Arden saw a video, a white triangle centered on the shot. Monelle touched the triangle. The video began to move.

It was this garage, exactly where they were standing, Arden saw; disconcerting because it showed this same car, Ned's now-shiny black car, whitened and covered with salt. The camera then zoomed in to the passenger's side front quarter panel of the car, where some of the salt had been swiped away.

Monelle touched the video again, pausing it.

"Cutting to the chase here," she said. "This cell phone video was taken yesterday. You saw the right front of the car is the only part with no salt." She turned and stood beside the quarter panel. "And if this behemoth hit me—" She gestured, pantomiming. "It would hit right in the hip. Definitely knock me over. Can you picture it?"

Arden nodded, wincing, imagining.

"And that salt would have been transferred to me. A person who, this time of year, was wearing a coat," Monelle said. She paused, looking expectant.

The realization dawned. The ramifications. "Oh. Last night at the hospital. Did you check Nyomi's coat? Did you see the salt?"

"I wanted to look, but we didn't have a warrant. And if I had looked anyway . . ." Monelle shook her head. "We wouldn't have been able to use it. So there it remains in that hospital closet, the coat with salt, or without salt. The piece of evidence we need. Nyomi, of course, is not able to tell us anything. Not yet, at least."

"Crossing fingers. But . . ." Arden pointed, frowning. "The salt isn't there anymore. On any of the car."

"Exactly." Monelle nodded. "Let me show you another video."

"Of what?" Arden said.

"Long story, but yesterday I left a detective here to guard the car. And whatever, he had to leave, but fast forward, he, luckily, had set up his backup phone to roll video. In case something happened."

"Did it?"

"It did," Monelle went on. "Someone cleaned off the salt. And there'd be no reason to do that except to cover up the evidence. Once that evidence is gone, salt on a coat means nothing. Whoever did this was helping Ned get away with it."

Arden looked at the car again. "Wow. But so many possibilities. Even a person we don't even know."

"Right. And the original video was . . . rocky. But our tech team came through. And late last night—one reason I'm so exhausted—they finished the enhancement. So now we know exactly who cleaned off Ned's car. Someone who was trying to get rid of evidence. Someone who *knew* what happened. Knew what the missing salt would irrefutably mean."

"Ned?" Arden asked. Could that be? But no, she'd been with Ned the whole time.

Monelle tapped the phone again, then held it up, like a mini movie screen. "Watch."

Arden heard recorded footsteps, then saw the light change, a faint almost-shadow. And then a figure came into view, full view, holding what looked like a roll of paper towels. There was no question who it was.

"Cordelia," Arden whispered.

"You can watch the rest, if you like," Monelle said. "She takes a squirt bottle out of her bag, see? And sprays the quarter panel first, then does the rest of the car. She has on work gloves. Those are probably long gone, wherever she stashed the paper towels."

Arden watched Cordelia step back, as if admiring her work. Unsettling that they were now standing in almost exactly the same place, looking at the exact same now-clean car. She'd been holding her breath, she realized, and let it out with a sigh.

Maybe Ned had called Cordelia from Vermont. With instructions. And that's why she'd flipped out this morning. Not from jealousy. From fear.

Monelle tucked her phone into her tote bag. "My office has a copy of this, as does my investigator, so you know," she said. "As to why she did it, that we have to explore. But here's what worries me. She might be in danger. Might be the next 'accident' victim."

"Exactly what I was thinking. And that explains why she was so upset about the verdict. Because she knows. Because she knew all along. And that's why, the day she came to my office, she asked *me* to find out the truth about Randall Tennant."

"She did?"

"Not right away," Arden said, remembering. "I had to drag it out of her. But finally she admitted that, yeah, she was afraid her husband was hiding something." Something nagged at Arden's memory, and she struggled to retrieve it. *Oh.* Right. "But wait, that night in the hospital. Didn't you say Cordelia called you? Why? What did she tell *you*?"

Monelle broke eye contact for a moment, then looked at her with an expression Arden could only describe as embarrassed.

"No. Ah. I mean, just between us. I made that up. The phone call."

"You made that *up*?"

"It's a tactic, what can I tell you? I wanted to see how Ned would react. But then that lawyer, Jean, grabbed him, and took him away."

"Remind me never to trust you," Arden said.

"Too late now," Monelle said. "But back to Cordelia. Did she specifically tell you she thought Ned killed Randall Tennant on purpose?"

"Not . . . really. Maybe that's why she sent the kids out of town?" Arden put her head in her hands for a moment, thinking. "But she sent them to be with Ned's mother. Which . . . does that make sense?"

"Might have been her only option, short-term," Monelle said. "Especially if she didn't want to spook him."

"She was supposed to be—"

"In Palm Beach, I know," Monelle finished her sentence. "But clearly, she wasn't. At least yesterday. Listen. We know she's at a hotel near Mass General. My investigator got her info after she was careless enough to use her own credit card at check-in. Not that she would be worried anyone would look for her."

And that's why Cordelia had not FaceTimed her children to show them the palm trees, Arden decided. There were no palm trees in Boston. Monelle's phone made a *text-received* sound.

In the gloomy silence of the parking garage, Monelle looked at her phone. Arden could not shake the feeling they were being watched. And she wondered, as a rash of goose bumps prickled her neck, who that security guard might be calling. Might be warning. They'd have to walk right by him to get out.

"Honestly?" Monelle's voice sounded bitter, and she focused on her message. "Can you not do your *job*? Are you *totally* incompetent?"

Arden's eyes widened.

Monelle made an exasperated sound, stashed her phone. "I was just yelling at the text," she said. "But so much for Cordelia. She checked out of the hotel this morning. And my guy lost her. Moron." She paused. "Arden? What?"

"It doesn't matter if he lost her," Arden said. "I know where she is."

63

I have to run this by my boss," Monelle told her.

Arden clicked on her seat belt as Monelle started her car, a beige four-door that looked government-issued. The parking lot attendant's desk had been empty as they hurried away from the garage, whether that was lucky or sinister there was no way to know.

Monelle had parked on Atlantic Ave., in a prohibited parking zone, but a fuchsia SUFFOLK COUNTY DA placard on her dashboard provided all the permission necessary. "I can't simply go to the Bannisters' condo," she went on, "and ask Cordelia why she wiped the salt off Ned's car."

"Got you." Arden nodded. "One step at a time. But that video is pretty convincing."

Bundled-up kids were ice skating on a makeshift rink in a street park, adults in bulky jackets with coffees held in mittens watching from the sidelines. A fluttering kinetic sculpture towered over the winter scene, purple and yellow against the wintry sky.

"I see, though, what you mean," Arden continued. "She could say she did it because the car was dirty. And you can't even prove that car was involved. Or that Ned was driving."

"We will," Monelle said. "Just you wait. Calling Stamoran now." She bullet-pointed the story for her boss on speakerphone as they headed for the district attorney's office.

Stamoran always works on Sunday mornings, Monelle had told her. *No one knows what he does.*

Arden made a quick check of her own phone for messages as Monelle talked, but nothing from Ned, nothing from Jean Trounstine. Nothing from Cordelia, no surprise. Or from Warren. Nothing from Luz, either. *Poor Luz.* But she didn't have time for that, not now, no time to decide how to warn Luz, or even confront Warren. This morning had not turned out the way she had planned.

The guard at the district attorney's reception desk, scrolling through her phone, barely looked up, and waved Monelle to the elevators. They made their way to Charles Stamoran's top-floor office. Glass double doors, then an empty beige-on-beige reception room, a long carpeted hallway. Monelle knocked on a door that was already open.

The district attorney's office was masculine-luxurious, supple-looking hunter-green leather, and an expanse of carefully arranged black-framed photos; a gallery of Charles Stamorans, confidently arm in arm with a diverse array of A-list politicos and sports heroes, heavy on baseball and golf.

Arden had seen Stamoran on television and was aware of his courtroom successes. His statehouse ambitions. His almost-patronizing attitude, though, surprised her. He actually eyed her up and down as Monelle introduced them. Arden tried not to squirm, and looked him square in the eye.

"Arden Ward." He pronounced her name as if it had a taste. *Ahden Wahd,* he called her, the Boston coming out. As their conversation unfolded, he raised an eyebrow when she explained how she knew where Cordelia was.

It made Arden wince to think of it. Maybe she'd miscalculated entirely, jumped to exactly the wrong conclusions. Cordelia had trusted her, confided in her, worried she was living with a liar. Arden had not believed it. Maybe Cordelia wasn't crazy. Maybe she was—understandably—stressed and tormented. And telling the truth.

Stamoran was typing on his computer now, and Monelle watched, her phone in her hand, dividing her attention between her boss and her phone screen. Arden was merely a spectator, but Monelle had insisted she tell Stamoran in person about where Cordelia was.

Cordelia. At one point, Arden had secretly wondered whether she was actually involved in Randall Tennant's death, but she had the perfect alibi. She was home with the kids. And . . .

"Oh," Arden said. Then she covered her mouth, embarrassed to have spoken out loud.

"Yes?" Stamoran said. "Do you have something to add to the preparation of my grand jury subpoena?"

"Sorry," Arden said.

Stamoran went back to typing, and Monelle gave her a questioning look. But she wasn't ready to share her realization.

Cordelia was not frightened. Cordelia was in on it. And she was covering up.

If Randall Tennant had not been killed after midnight that New Year's Eve in the parking garage, if he had been killed somewhere else and moved to the garage, then Cordelia Bannister's alibi for the time of the party wasn't the point. Because they might have staged the whole "accident." Together.

Maybe the savvy Nyomi Chang had theorized the same thing. Arden tried to remember—in that last conversation at the courthouse, had Nyomi said anything that might have indicated she knew the truth? She'd gotten a phone call. Talked briefly, tersely, to the caller. Definitely. Arden bit her lower lip, dredging up the memory. *It's critical*, Nyomi had said that day. *It's in the records.* Something like that.

Monelle herself had told Arden that now, legally, "it wouldn't matter" what really happened, because Ned had been acquitted. Nyomi must have known that, too.

But maybe *Ned* didn't know. And decided to keep Nyomi quiet.

And if Cordelia knew what Ned was planning for Nyomi, that's why she dumped the kids and pretended to leave town.

Arden's heartbeat spiked faster than she thought was imaginable. Should she tell the DA and Monelle what she had figured out? She had solved it. Absolutely solved it. These two were working to connect Ned with Nyomi Chang's case, not with Randall Tennant's. But the reality was that Cordelia and Ned were *both* involved in *both* crimes. They had done this together. And completely misled everyone in their path. *Including me*, Arden thought.

"Excuse me," she began. There was no way to justify it if she didn't tell them. Not just Ned. Ned and Cordelia.

"Do you *need* to be excused?" Stamoran's voice couldn't have been more dismissive.

"Are you okay?" Monelle asked.

Arden opened her mouth to reveal her theory. Then closed it.

Oh. No. Her brain skidded to a halt. No. She was totally wrong.

"Just wondering if you need any more from me," she said, trying to paper over her stupid interruption. "Or, even if you'd like me to go get coffee?" They must think she was a complete idiot, and, in fact, at that moment she was.

Because Tennant's body could not have been on the parking garage pavement before the party began. Or as people arrived, or even as the party ended. And the medical examiner would have noted a body that had been dead for a much longer time. Cordelia's home-with-the-kids alibi was still solid.

So it was either Ned—and an accident, the way he'd described it. Or Ned—on purpose. Or the second to last person to leave. On purpose. Not Cordelia.

I'm sorry, Cordelia, Arden thought. *I just suspected you of murder. I have failed you in every way.*

Stamoran had given Monelle a skeptical look, then gone back to his computer.

"We're fine, thanks," Monelle said, flipping phone screens. "No need for coffee. Would you mind . . ." She gestured Arden to the leather couch along the wall. "We'll be another minute." She turned back to Stamoran. "Owulu just checked in. They're 10–8."

"Finally. They have eyes on her? She's inside that building? And Bannister, too?"

"Owulu confirms," Monelle said. "So in my opinion we should—"

"Yes, of course." Stamoran stood. "Now here's the plan."

.   .   .

"So—you clear? We need to keep Cordelia in that condo. So you're going to just . . . drop by," Monelle told her as they waited for the elevator outside Stamoran's office. "Make sure she stays there until we can finalize the paperwork. It's fine, it's legal, the district attorney's office will stand behind you if need be, but there'll be no problem. PJ and Owulu are aware of the deal, they'll watch from their car. Remember, Ned and Cordelia are your clients. You have a perfectly good reason to be visiting them."

"You think?"

They—Monelle and Stamoran—had decided Arden would go in first, a stalling tactic, under the pretext of an apology. Withdraw from the case, they'd told her. Offer them anything they wanted.

"Including their money back," Monelle had suggested.

"They haven't paid anyway," Arden had said. "Not that I know of at least." She'd always thought it was unusual that Warren never mentioned money, but she'd planned on talking to him about that. So much for that idea.

"We're grateful, Arden," Monelle said now. She jabbed the elevator button again. "The district attorney and I understand about the risk you may be taking. Professionally."

"I have no profession. I won't be working for Vision anymore, at least."

"I'd love to hear about that." Monelle looked authentically curious, even sympathetic.

"In another lifetime, maybe," Arden said. "So I'm supposed to stall until you arrive with the subpoena. In case you need it."

The elevator pinged its arrival.

"Yes, as long as it seems safe." Monelle touched Arden's shoulder bag. "We've set your phone so you can notify PJ and Owulu, and me, if you need help, but again, that's unlikely. When I arrive, PJ or Wu will be with me, and you'll be—surprised."

"I sure will be." Arden tried to picture it.

"Arden?" Monelle's face had changed. "Did Ned ever talk about a gun? Or Cordelia?"

Arden grimaced. "You think—?"

"It'll be fine." Monelle put a hand on Arden's arm. "We simply need to ask Cordelia why she cleaned the salt off her husband's car. If she won't answer, and we have to actually serve the subpoena, then she'll get a lawyer and we're doomed. So, we'll see."

The scratchy brown doors of the elevator shuddered open, and Arden felt the presence of a passenger emerging. As she stepped into the elevator, she moved to her right to allow him to get out.

Monelle held the door as she followed Arden inside. Arden looked at the man, the casual glance of a random encounter.

He turned, and looked at her, too. Stopped, for a fraction of a beat. Then turned on his heel and headed toward the glass door of the district attorney's office.

"Monelle," Arden said. Her voice came out a whisper. "Do you know who that is?"

Monelle shook her head. "No idea. Why?"

He's the man in the four-door, Arden wanted to tell her. The man with a maybe-gun who had frightened her, scared Pip, and chased after them in the Vermont woods. And now he was visiting the district attorney.

"Long story," she said. "We have to go. I'll explain in the car."

64

The front door is always open, Arden remembered Ned had told her. If a door was open, she rationalized, she could go in. She walked up those wide interior steps again, jewel-toned carpeting, mahogany banisters and lathed newel posts, the lacquered wall with the modern paintings.

When was the last time she'd shown up at someone's house, uninvited? Or without asking first? Like, never. She took a deep breath. Knocked on the door. Silence. She waited a beat, then another. Knocked again.

"Arden?" As he opened the door, a thousand questions crossed Ned's face, Arden could almost translate them. *Why,* then *what are you doing here,* then *what the hell is going on.* "What—"

"I'm so sorry," Arden began, and at least that was true. "I went back to my house," the lies began, "and I just couldn't get over this morning. I feel so terrible that—"

A sound came from behind Ned, a clatter. "Ned?" Cordelia's voice.

"I'm so sorry," Arden said again. Her assignment was to stall, she knew that, so any way she could make things take longer, she would. Excruciating as it was. "May I come in? Seriously, I need to apologize to your wife. I really cannot—"

Soft as a gathering wind, Cordelia appeared behind Ned. She had changed from her black turtleneck, and now wore a gauzy white tunic over black pants. Bare feet. Her usually styled hair cascaded long over her shoulders. Arden had never seen it like that, out of control.

"My my," Cordelia said.

The three of them stood, an uneasy triangle, two people inside, Arden still in the hallway.

"Where are my manners?" Cordelia swept one hand toward the living room. "Do come in. I'm afraid you've missed brunch."

Arden, wishing she were anywhere but here, followed Ned and Cordelia into the living room; soft music, she noticed, classical, came from hidden speakers. An empty champagne bottle, top down and stashed in a silver ice bucket, sat on the coffee table next to the remnants of the now-demolished coffee cake, a sharp knife on the edge of the decorative plate. Coffee cups, one with lipstick stains, sat empty. The pillows on the couch had been disarranged. Ned looked disarranged, too, Arden noticed. Arden could almost smell the lust in the room, disturbed now by her, the uninvited and unwelcome intruder.

"You were saying?" Ned had his hands in his jeans pockets, and his flannel shirt was fully buttoned. He too, was barefoot.

"I am so sorry," Arden said for the millionth time, "but Cordelia, I'm here to talk with you. Honestly. Thirty seconds. I'm haunted by—"

"You are quite the piece of work, Arden Ward." Cordelia curled up on the couch, tucked her bare feet underneath her. The collar of her white tunic gapped, showing a curve of pale skin underneath. "Did you leave underwear here, or something? Ned, you said you'd never see her again."

"I had nothing to do with this visit, obviously, Dee," Ned said. "I'm as shocked as you are. But—"

"Let me talk, I'm so sorry, Ned," Arden began, remembering her assignment from the DA. *Stall.* "Cordelia, you just so deeply have the wrong impression of me, and all I have is my reputation, and I know this whole thing is complicated, but I never, we never, there's never been any—"

"Never been any?" Cordelia draped an arm across the back of the couch. "Never been any what?"

"Well, when you arrived this morning, it was a surprise." Arden waited for Cordelia to make a snide remark, like 'obviously,' but she didn't, so Arden went on. "I had gone home after I got thrown out of the hospital last night, and was so frazzled that I got no sleep, and when Ned asked to talk to me, as any client would, I came over. And there was coffee, and this coffee cake . . ."

"Megan's special," Cordelia said.

"And I know how it must have looked, but it was nothing like that. We were trying to figure out what to do about Nyomi. And how Ned seemed to be targeted by the district attorney's office."

Arden saw Cordelia's face shift, saw her chest rise and fall with a deep breath. "Is there any word from Nyomi?" she asked. "Please tell us Nyomi's fine and told you it wasn't my Ned."

"Ned would know more than I do. He's talked to Jean." Cordelia had

changed the subject, for better or for worse. It was probably true, ironically, Arden thought, that Ned and Cordelia knew more about Nyomi's
accident than even Monelle did. How could Arden have been so thor-
oughly duped? Especially by Ned? "He was going to tell me about it this
morning. But he never got a chance, because—"

"I was going to tell you, Arden, that Jean Trounstine hadn't heard
from Monelle. Or the hospital. I haven't either. Have you?"

Arden scrambled to lie as little as possible. She wasn't getting suspicious vibes from them, or feeling as if she were in danger. But things could
change, and quickly, she knew that. Was Ned a murderer? And Cordelia
his accomplice?

"Well, I'm only here to say that we should . . . end our business relationship. You know I'm not going to work for Vision anymore, and it
would be strange to continue to represent you, to help you, even though
I want to, of course, when I have no portfolio. Possibly you could talk to
Warren"—the words almost stuck in her throat—"and he can connect
you with a more appropriate partner."

Cordelia blinked at her now, and Arden felt the intensity of her scrutiny. It felt as if Ned was waiting to see what Cordelia decided, and then
follow her lead.

"I'm sorry too, Arden," Cordelia finally said. "I'm on edge, and stressed
out, with the kids away, and poor Nyomi, and everything we talked about
before . . ." She looked at Arden, narrowing her eyes. "You know, everything we talked about before."

Arden wondered about that shorthand. *Everything we talked about
before* . . . Cordelia might be trying to remind her how suspicious she'd
been of Ned. And the text messages. And the relentless and intensifying
scrutiny. Of course she couldn't say that with him in the room.

"I understand," Arden said. "I hear you. It's been a difficult time."

"So let's keep working together," Cordelia said. "I love my husband so
much that I would do anything for him." She paused, as if struggling to
come up with her next words, but Arden wondered if it was actually to let
what she'd said sink in. *I would do anything.*

"And the idea that there would be someone else," she went on, and
wiped a manicured finger below one eye. "I am so sorry. I'm a mess. A
total mess. Arden, I apologize, too. I know you're a professional. I'm so
sorry for my meltdown earlier. I went a little crazy. I was just—flailing.
Confused. I am *so* sorry. I know you would never . . . Truce?"

"Truce," Arden said. "I know it's easy to make a wrong decision under pressure," she went on, choosing her words carefully. Seeing if Cordelia would communicate. "That's why you came to me in the first place. It's difficult when it seems like the whole world is against you. That you have no control."

Cordelia picked up her coffee cup, seemed to realize it was empty. She looked at Ned. "Could you . . ."

Ned reached for the cup, then stopped. "Would you like some water, maybe?" he asked. "Arden, how about you?"

"That would be wonderful, darling." Cordelia uncoiled her legs, as if to stand. "But I could get it myself."

"Nope," Ned said. "I'll be right back."

Arden watched Ned walk toward the kitchen, and Cordelia shifted on the couch again, leaned forward, arms on knees, beckoning her closer.

"Arden," she whispered. "We have about thirty seconds. Can you get me out of here?"

65

Not a chance. She could not get Cordelia out of there, not unless she wanted to send her into the waiting arms of the police and Monelle Churchwood. She could imagine that, Cordelia with Arden in tow, blithely leaving the Brookline condo as if it were any other chilly Sunday afternoon. She also imagined them colliding on the sidewalk, or the glassed-in front lobby. She could *almost* hear footsteps in the hallway.

"Too long to explain," Arden said, "but it might be better, if you want to talk, to get *Ned* to leave."

"No. He'll never leave us," Cordelia said. "He'll insist that—"

Now the footsteps were real, and coming from the kitchen. Ned carried two stubby crystal glasses with ice and water, a wedge of lemon tucked into each one.

"Here you go," he said. "Room service."

"Thanks, honey." Cordelia darted a glance at Arden, and Arden wondered whether that was the go-ahead signal. Couldn't hurt to try.

"Ned? I was thinking. Has your car been in that parking garage since . . . the other night?" Arden began. Risky territory, but she'd racked her brain for some reason why this would be a problem, and couldn't think of one. Monelle and her cops had their video, and hadn't impounded the car. Arden needed to appear to be on Ned's side. This might be a way to show her allegiance. And introduce the topic she needed to probe. She needed to find out about the salt. And Cordelia's motivation for removing it.

She couldn't decide whether she wanted Monelle and crew to hurry or not. It was more unsettling that she had no control over it.

"Well, you didn't move it, did you, Dee?" Ned was asking. "You're the only other one with keys."

Cordelia flinched. "What?"

"Teasing, honey," Ned said. "I know you were in Palm Beach. But no, Arden, I haven't been at the building since . . . since Nyomi."

Ned still referred to Cordelia as being out of town, Arden noted. What was that about? Was he performing, or did he really think so?

"And the police haven't asked for access to your car?"

"No," he said, "but would they have to ask?"

"Above my pay grade," Arden said. "But maybe . . . go get the car. Maybe it looks bad if you leave it there. Like you're trying to stay away from it? After all, if they think it was involved in the accident . . . Well, it seems like you should keep an eye on it. Which you can't, when it's in that parking garage."

She was wildly making this up, but now she couldn't take it back.

Ned tapped his fingertips together, considering. "Sure. I might need it, anyway." He picked up his cell from the coffee table. "I hate to ask you to drive me, Dee. I'll Uber."

"Brilliant," Arden said. *Go,* she thought.

"I will if you want me to, of course," Cordelia said, "but . . ." She waved an arm languidly and nestled herself closer into the corner. "I'm so tired from travel and everything, and I'd love to collapse. And I'll have Arden, luckily, because I need to apologize. To both of you. I'm just—it's a lot."

"You good with that?" Ned tapped his phone. "We'll talk when I get back?"

"Sure," Arden said. She wondered if one of the police officers would follow him. PJ and Owulu were in separate cars. They'd report to Monelle that Ned had left. And that Arden was still inside. *Go,* she thought.

"But, honestly"—she needed to remember the rest of her script—"I'm still fine with leaving you two to handle this on your own. Warren can find a replacement, and—"

"We'll talk later," Ned interrupted. He'd pulled a black jacket from the front closet and patted himself for keys. "The Uber will be here in one minute. And I'll be back in less than an hour, max."

Cordelia stayed on the couch, pantomiming kisses, and fluttering her fingers. "You're the best," she said.

The door to the apartment closed Ned away. Arden had a discomfiting memory of Monelle asking about guns, and with Ned gone she had to admit she felt safer. Something desperate had happened to the Bannisters, and Arden could not figure what.

"Arden?" Cordelia took a sip of her water. "Let's make sure Ned's in the Uber and gone before we do anything. And, since you brought it up,

I've been wondering. Do *you* know whether the police have looked at Ned's car?"

Arden shook her head, avoiding a direct answer.

"If they did," Cordelia went on, "do you think it was right after the . . . accident? Or would they wait? That Churchwood woman set her sights on Ned the minute it happened. She's still insanely bitter about the verdict. She'd do anything to put Ned behind bars."

"Seems like it. Awful for both of you, and your poor children." Arden sat across from Cordelia, on one of the red wing chairs, and shrugged off her coat, draping it over the curved back. She still had her boots on, maybe a good thing. "When we were in Vermont—" Arden paused, dangerous territory. But Cordelia did not react. "Emma would not leave his side," she went on. "And Pip, well, typical mercurial preteen, I guess? Though Pip seemed to care about him."

Pip. "You know, Cordelia," she went on. She picked up her own water glass, stared at the lemon for a beat. "Pip mentioned that Ned wasn't . . ."

"Ned is his stepfather. He's doing the best he can."

"Ned? Or Pip?"

"Both of them, I guess."

"So you were married before?"

Cordelia widened her eyes. "No. Things happen, and that's the world. Pip's father is—dead."

"I'm so sorry," Arden said. "Does Ned know who he was?"

"He knows—that I'm not quite sure who the father is. Was. But neither possibility is still alive."

"That's very difficult," Arden said. "I'm so—"

"Thank you," Cordelia said, dismissive. "So, the car?"

"Oh, right," Arden said. So much for the subject change. "I don't know when they would have looked at it."

"I wish I knew," Cordelia said.

"Why?"

Cordelia's face changed, and her eyes welled with tears. Her chin seemed to tremble. She picked up her glass again.

"Cordelia?"

"Never mind," she said.

66

rden recognized this tactic. The reluctance to tell, coupled with the obvious yearning to do just that. Cordelia had worn the same expression on day one, when Arden had to persuade her to reveal her suspicions about Ned. Now she was hedging again, about Ned's car. *Never mind,* Cordelia had said.

"I do mind," Arden said. "Because I need to protect you. My whole goal is to protect you."

"I know." Cordelia nodded. "I trust you, Arden."

Arden thought of Monelle and her two police officers outside, their arrival imminent. She looked out the front window. No police in sight. But. "Ned's still waiting for the Uber," she said.

"Good thing we didn't leave yet," Cordelia said.

There was not a sound in the elegant apartment, not the hum of a heater, or the crackle of a fire, and Ned had turned off the music as he left. The ice in the silver bucket clattered then, melting, and the upturned champagne bottle inside dropped deeper into the cold water, only its molded green bottom now showing.

"Look," Arden began. "We're alone. Just us. Cordelia, when was the last time *you* were in that parking garage?"

"Why would you ask me that?" Cordelia whispered.

"Because, as I've told you *so* many times, I cannot be surprised. If I don't know the truth, I can't help you. My father always told me the best defense was a good offense." Arden leaned forward. "So. When was the last time you were in that garage?"

"He *made* me do it, he made me." In an instant, Cordelia crumpled. She put her hands to her cheeks, wiping away tears, and, inelegantly, sniffled. Arden handed her one of the cloth napkins from the coffee table.

"Who did?" Arden matched Cordelia's whisper. "Made you do what?"

"He made me pretend to be out of town. He made me stay in that hotel. Oh, I stayed in a local hotel, you don't know that. It was supposed to give me an alibi, and him an alibi, so I could do whatever he told me and then he would be with you, you know? So you were his alibi, too."

"You're saying—Ned. He made you do *what*?" Arden asked again. "Something about the car?"

"He worried there was a mark on it. Or some evidence of . . . you know. So he shut down the surveillance cameras and drove into the garage. Then he went back to his office, and turned them on again. You know he could always control them from our phones." Cordelia paused. "Don't you? They revamped the whole system after . . . New Year's."

"Go on."

"I can't say any more, I really truly can't." Cordelia's words tumbled over themselves. "I've already said too much, so so *so* too much. Ned can never know. You *promise* me, right? This is my life we're talking about. And my children's."

So much for the script Arden had been given. And Cordelia's story matched Monelle's video.

"The only way," Arden began, trying to decide what to say. "The only way you'll be safe, and trust me on this, is for you to talk to Monelle Churchwood. You were coerced, you were abused, you were threatened with—"

"He threatened my children, too. Can you believe that? Emma has no idea, he's such a good actor. But I know Pip doesn't trust him. That boy is so smart, he—"

Arden put up both palms, stopping her, trying to calm her. "We'll handle this," she said. "That's why you have me. I need you to talk to Monelle. Now. Before Ned gets to her. His lawyer would tell him the same thing, but to blame *you*. So *you* need to be the first to tell the truth. Will you do that for me? For your children? I can get her here very quickly."

She couldn't allow the DA's storm troopers to come barging in. Arden needed to get Cordelia away before Ned could interfere. Ned would silence her, Arden predicted, and she'd never tell the truth again.

"You promise it's the thing to do? I'm so lost, my only options are to pretend, pretend that I still love him, and it's incredibly difficult, Arden, the most difficult thing I've ever done, but I did it for my children."

Arden pulled out her phone, tapping out a message to Monelle.

Cordelia was still talking. "Ned even told me to hire you."

Arden paused her typing. "What? No. You specifically said he didn't want me."

"Oh, come on. Of course he wanted you. He wanted you to get him out of it."

"What? No. He told me—"

"Arden?" Cordelia looked almost pitying. "Don't you get it yet? How he works? He knew you could do it, he said you were the best. He also told me that if we presented it to you as if he *didn't* want you, then you'd take the job. You'd want to prove how good you were. He duped you, Arden, just like he dupes everyone. I warned you."

"Oh, I don't think . . ."

Cordelia shrugged. "It takes people awhile, sometimes. He's handsome, I know that. You're . . . single." She paused, as if allowing the subtext to sink in.

Was she right? Maybe the bias for "handsome sensitive guy" was so deep-seated, so pernicious, that sometimes we don't recognize it, Arden thought. To the detriment of our sisters. *I'm sorry*, Arden silently promised. *I'll do better*. She glanced out a front window.

"Ned's gone. And I'm contacting Monelle," she said, hitting Send. "She might be here quickly. Put on some warm boots, get your coat. And purse. We're leaving. We have just enough time."

Cordelia got to her feet, almost ran out of the room. Arden finished her text, saying they'd meet Monelle at the front door. Ned would still be on his way into Boston. They'd be fine.

Cordelia reappeared wearing a long camel coat, the one she'd had on to meet Arden outside her own office. "Oh," she said. "My phone. Two seconds."

"Hurry." No response yet from Monelle.

Arden put on her own coat, rueful and sad and worried. Almost ashamed. She'd gotten it wrong, completely wrong. But it wasn't too late to remedy this. She felt such regret about her initial assessment of Cordelia, seeing her as a good mom, sure, but needy and oversensitive. 'Nut job' she'd actually called her. She herself had been swayed by Ned, she admitted it. Enjoyed his reliance on her, his confidence, his eventual deference to her—supposed—proficiency. She'd always known something was off about him, and tried to talk herself out of it.

"I'm ready," Cordelia said.

"Good." Arden looped her muffler around her neck. "You have house keys? Let's go. And hey." She pointed. "Bring that suitcase, too. Just in case."

67

Their departure had been swift and efficient, surprising but logical. Monelle had arrived within three minutes, heard the latest, then hustled Arden and Cordelia toward a waiting black car. They were introduced to Detective Owulu, the driver, who put Cordelia's roller bag in the trunk.

"I've got to go to the hospital," Monelle said. "I have no idea what's happening, I just got a text from my team outside Nyomi's door. I'll let you know. Meanwhile. Arden, you and Cordelia are going to your house."

"Wouldn't it be safer to go to your office?"

"It would," Monelle said. "But Stamoran's gone for the day, and it's closed. I've called him, no worries. We're under way."

"How about the guy in the elevator? Like I told you in the car." Arden asked. "Why was—"

"Tell you later," Monelle said.

Arden noticed Monelle scanning the street.

"You sure?" Arden asked. Babysitting a potential key witness in a hit-and-run case—if that's what she was—when her husband, the suspect, was still out there did not seem like the wisest way to spend a Sunday afternoon. Not to mention the Buick guy.

"It's our only option." Monelle was clutching Arden's arm. "Listen. Your place is close to the hospital. I'll come as soon as I can. Detective Owulu will stay outside. You'll be fine." She opened the back door for Arden. "Don't worry. Thanks."

"I guess." Arden climbed in, skeptical.

Monelle thumped her hand, twice, on the driver's side door. "Go," she said. "You know the address."

Arden rolled down her window. "What about Ned and the Mercedes?"

"We're on it," Monelle said.

Cordelia, her arms wrapped around herself and staring straight ahead, had not said a word all the way to Arden's building. Arden caught the detective eyeing her in the rearview once, but he looked away as soon as he noticed.

"I'll be watching," Owulu said when they arrived. "You have my number, but nothing is going to happen."

"A lot of people seem to be reassuring us that nothing is going to happen," Cordelia muttered, as she yanked her roller bag up Arden's front steps.

"I hear you." Arden unlocked her front door and showed Cordelia inside. "But they're right. I'll build a fire, I'll make some—tea?"

"What will Ned do when he finds out we're gone?"

"That's what I was thinking about all the way here," Arden said. "I suppose it depends on Monelle, and what her people do. I'm sure she has a plan." Arden hoped that was true. But a cop was guarding the house, and they were safe inside.

"Wait," Cordelia said. "You told me something earlier about the best defense?"

"Yes." Arden smiled, hanging Cordelia's coat and tucking her suitcase into a corner. "A good offense."

"Exactly," Cordelia said. "Let's just . . . call Ned. Let's tell him exactly where we are, and that we came here because . . ."

"Because we saw the cops outside," Arden finished her sentence.

"So we sneaked out the back, and called an Uber, and fooled them."

Arden thought about this as she hung up her own coat. "There's a back exit of your condo?"

"Sure, it's the building code. Remember me, real estate?" Cordelia half smiled. "Anyway, we'll say we'll meet him at some point. But that he should stay at his office until we let him know. Nice fish," she said, pointing. "It makes the room kind of blue."

"Thanks. And see, your sunflowers still look so pretty. Take the couch or sit anywhere, I'll go get tea and cookies or something. I'm starving."

"Lovely. Thank you, Arden." She paused. "For everything. Understanding."

Arden hoped Cordelia would never know how much she'd doubted her. "Just doing my job."

Cordelia was sitting cross-legged in the armchair when Arden returned with tea and chocolate chip cookies. "From a box, I'm afraid." She set the tray on the coffee table. "I still have your brownies, though, from the other day. Maybe we should have those."

"You've been busy," Cordelia said.

Arden took a seat on the couch, and picked up her mug. She noticed Cordelia's eyes were rimmed with red, and wondered if she'd cried while Arden was in the kitchen. Then tried to hide it.

"You have, too," she said. "Been busy."

"Only because of Ned." Cordelia's eyes welled again. "Damn it. This is very difficult for me. I know I'll have to tell the whole story, to that . . ." She shook her head. "Churchwood person. But I can't handle it any longer. This is not the kind of person I ever thought I'd be. I can barely look at myself in the mirror. Sorry for crying," she said. "But I think of that dear woman in the hospital, and I know what Nyomi knew about Ned, and I just keep thinking . . . if I don't do what he says, I'll be the next victim. Everyone who crosses Ned gets hurt, that's how it goes. You're his friend until you aren't. You're his ally until you're not. You're his lover until you're not. I found out too late way too late."

The fish tank hummed and bubbled. Arden waited.

"He ordered me to wipe the car, Arden. And I did. And now I'm in trouble."

Arden narrowed her eyes, thinking about that. "Why didn't he do it himself? That night?"

"I know! I asked him that!" Cordelia's voice tightened. "He said he was too upset, and then it was too late for him to go back and do it. So he waited until he was with you, you the alibi, and then sent me in. I told you about Ned. I told you."

"Weren't you worried about being seen?"

"Well, it was my husband's building. I'm always there. And it only took a minute or two. But that's not the point. The point is he knows he hit her. And left the scene. And he's covering it up, and making me be complicit. And what if she dies?"

"I hear you, I do. It'll be fine, Cordelia. You're doing the right thing." Arden looked at her phone, wishing for a text from Monelle. "So your idea of calling Ned—"

"I did that, while you were getting the tea."

"You did?"

"He said we were smart. And that he would deal with it. He's staying at his office, exactly what we wanted him to do. So I told him he was smart, too. He loves that."

"Wait," Arden said. "A minute ago you said you knew what Nyomi knew about Ned. What does that mean?"

"That he's hiding things, like I told you from the moment we met. And what he's hiding is that he got away with hitting Randall Tennant, and now he's trying to make sure he gets away with this, too. But I won't let him. And you can't, either."

68

W e've got him," Monelle whispered to Arden before she'd even closed the front door behind her. Two black cars were idling outside.

Monelle had texted *I have news. Be there in two.*

Cordelia had clapped a hand to her chest at the text, wide-eyed. "That's got to be good. Don't you think? I hope she's not coming to arrest *me*."

"I'm sure she's not," Arden had said. "You'll need a lawyer too, of course, but you were coerced and in danger. That will make a difference."

"My poor children. We'll have to leave. Or move again."

Pip, Arden thought. "Cordelia? Why did you make up that thing about the haircut? And tell Ned you were trying to trap me? Did you make up the text messages, too?"

"I have no idea about those awful texts! But the haircut, no, I *didn't* make it up, Arden. The barbershop thing is totally true. I was letting Ned know that you knew. It was better for me to tell him than for him to find out I'd told you earlier."

"So . . . he *was* connected to Randall Tennant?"

"It doesn't matter now, does it Arden? It doesn't matter. Ned dug his own grave, hitting poor Nyomi Chang. Sometimes karma just works. Have you heard anything about her, anyway?"

Arden shook her head. Remembering the coat Monelle was so eager to examine.

"*He'll* say he never told me to do it. You know he will. Can any of us ever be happy?" Cordelia sniffled again, dabbed at her nose with a napkin.

"We can only do our best," Arden said. "Pip and Emma will need you."

"Pip will lose two fathers now," Cordelia said. "Poor kid."

Now Arden showed Monelle inside, remembering the last time she'd been here. Monelle even sat exactly where Ned—a satisfied lion, she remembered—had been that night. Arden had trusted him. Protected him. Now she was another of his victims.

"We got him, Mrs. Bannister," Monelle said again. "Hit-and-run, leaving the scene, vehicular homicide if Ms. Chang dies. I told him we had him dead to rights about wiping off the car."

"Did he deny it?" Cordelia said. "Where is he now? Can he get to me? Can he get to the kids?"

"How's Nyomi?" Arden asked quietly.

"Looking good, Arden, fingers crossed," Monelle told her. Then she straightened, changed her demeanor. "Ms. Bannister, we'll need to take a formal statement. May I call in Detective Owulu, and do that now? Here? Arden, do you mind?"

"Sooner the better," Cordelia said. "Oh, sorry, Arden, if it's all right with you."

"You sure?" Arden wasn't. "My advice would be to get a lawyer first." Seemed like she was always telling people to get lawyers.

"No," Cordelia said. "And I don't need that. I did nothing wrong."

With Arden still wary and Cordelia clutching her hand, and with Detective Owulu and Monelle in separate chairs across from the couch, two cell phones recorded as Cordelia told her story.

That the night of the verdict, Ned had argued with Nyomi on the phone. That he had been upset, and would not tell her why. That late that night he'd ordered her to cancel her trip, and to stay at the hotel by Mass General Hospital.

"Why that particular hotel?" Monelle asked.

"He gets a deal there, I think. Ned knows everyone and can work anything."

Arden wondered about that, remembering what Monelle said about Cordelia using her credit card.

"But you used your own credit card," Monelle said.

"Of course. It was all about making it look like it was *my* idea. *My* deception. Not his. Don't you even see?"

"It's all good," Owulu told her. "Go on."

Cordelia described how Ned had used Arden, too, as an alibi. Even gone to Vermont, probably to get money from his mother.

"Were the two of them ever alone?"

Cordelia turned to Arden. "Did they send you on some invented errand?"

"They—" Arden began, remembering the tree house. And Buick guy.

"We'll talk to Arden later," Monelle said. "Go on, Ms. Bannister."

Cordelia described how Ned had ordered her to clean the car. That she had done it, and stashed the cleaning materials in a dumpster. "He told me I didn't have to hide them," she said. "But I did."

"Were you in fear of your life at any time?" Monelle asked.

"Every moment of every day that I knew him," Cordelia said. "And for my children."

Arden wished she had told Monelle about Ned not being Pip's biological father, but she couldn't do it now. In ordinary life, having a stepkid wouldn't matter. But in this case, it might.

Monelle did not bring up New Year's Eve, nor did Cordelia. Arden watched the counters click by on the recording cell phones, and as Monelle and Owulu wrapped up their inquiries, Arden knew Cordelia was right: karma did prevail.

"It'll be so complicated," Cordelia said, sniffling again. "Is Ned . . . free now?"

"He might be," Monelle said. "His lawyer was with him. Do you have a place you can stay? Where you'll feel safe? Where Ned might not look for you?"

"I—" Cordelia began. She looked at Arden. "I have a suitcase from . . . before. Arden told me to bring it."

"No. You can't stay here," Monelle said. "This is the first place he'd come."

Cordelia nodded, agreeing. "I have a friend. I'll call them, they'll pick me up. I'll get my car, and go to a hotel. Park in their downstairs lot. Ned won't see it."

"Not the hotel by—" Monelle began.

"Of course not."

"And you need to tell us where you are."

"Of course."

"I can take you," Arden said. She had all the time in the world. "You don't have to call anyone."

Cordelia shook her head. "No, you've done so much. I don't know how to thank you. But Ms. Churchwood? What should I say to the kids? They're with Ned's mother now."

"That's a good place for them. I'll text you with the latest, very soon,"

Monelle said. She signaled Owulu, and they both stood. Owulu picked up the two still-recording phones.

Monelle took a deep breath. "Look, Ms. Bannister. You should know we have a video of you wiping the car."

"You do?" Cordelia pressed her palms together, as if in prayer. "Wonderful. That proves I'm telling the truth."

"It's good you owned it," Monelle went on. "And told us why. It'll matter. I promise, it'll matter. But you'll need to be available."

"And now you'll find a lawyer," Arden said. "Cordelia, seriously."

"I'll trust you, Monelle," Cordelia said.

"Recording ends at three twenty-two P.M.," Owulu said into the phone mics. Then handed Monelle's back to her. "Thank you, Mrs. Bannister," he said. "You did the right thing."

Cordelia nodded. "I had to."

"Yes," Monelle said, tucking her cell away. "You did. This was brave of you. I know you've had a difficult time. But we're all trying to do our jobs."

"I know," Cordelia said. "And this time, I'm glad you are."

69

For the first time in however many years, so many she could not bring herself to think about it, Monday morning at nine-thirty, not a holiday, not a day off, just . . . Arden, aimless and unattached and without plan or portfolio.

She'd spent the rest of yesterday in a blur of alternating rage and depression, alternating tea and pinot noir, wishing she liked Scotch. Her fish had not been the best of company, and she felt as trapped as they were.

Technically she still worked at Vision until Friday, she thought as she walked toward the ring of the front doorbell, and she didn't want to lose the severance and recommendation Warren had promised as incentive for seeing the Bannister job through. Well, screw Warren. Whatever the Bannister "job" was now, she could "see it through" from home.

It would never leave her, the rancor and bitterness at Warren, at Arthur Swanson, at Patience Swanson. What earthly good had it done to fire her? Just so Arthur Swanson's wife would leave him alone? Arden had been ruined by false suspicion, and what was so frustrating, it was just what she herself had almost done to Cordelia Bannister. There was some irony in it, but no consolation.

"We have to stop meeting like this," Arden said, as she opened her door to see Monelle Churchwood.

She tucked her thin T-shirt into her ratty sweatpants, conscious of her dishevelment compared to Monelle's professional polish.

Now Monelle gestured toward the living room. "May I come in?"

"Is it about Nyomi?" Arden said, her heart flaring. "Or Ned? Or Cordelia? What's—"

"All of the above." She took off her gloves, took a step forward. "Can we sit down?"

What? Arden frowned. "Sure. You know the way. Is Nyomi . . ."

"She'll be fine," Monelle said, smoothing her black coat under her as she sat in the center of the couch. She loosened the buttons, folded her fingers together in her lap. "First, I have a confession."

"Confession? About what?" Arden took the chair across from her. She pushed her hair away from her face, wondering if she had combed it, and grabbed a cashmere throw from the back of her chair to cover her tattered white T-shirt. "Is it a good thing or a bad thing?"

"The man we saw by the elevator. The one you told me about in the car? Who chased you and Pip in the woods?"

"Yeah, what about him? That's been driving me crazy. You said you'd—"

"I know," Monelle interrupted. "I'm sorry about that. I didn't know him, but Stamoran does. He's an investigator, a Boston cop, who Stamoran assigned to follow Ned. Turns out that rental car you had? As they all do now, has a tracking device. Stamoran wanted to nail Bannister from the moment Nyomi said 'Ned.' And decided Ned was fleeing the jurisdiction. Which, in fact, he was."

"What? There was nothing illegal about going to—"

"I know. I *know*. That's why I'm confessing. Stamoran's guy got out of hand, all hyped up with his belief in Ned's guilt. Thanks to my boss."

"But that man called *me* by name."

"Stamoran told him all about you. I wasn't supposed to tell, but I know it upset you, as well it should. And that's not necessary."

"What a jerk." Arden remembered their fear. "Pip was terrified. And I wasn't much better."

"Stamoran, again, will deny it. But there you have it. He's got a lot of power. And, it seems . . ." She shrugged off her coat, let it fall behind her on the couch. "He was right about Ned."

"Seems like." Arden stood, leaving the throw on the chair. "I need coffee. You want some?"

"Bad me. I should have brought it. But sure. Speaking of Ned," Monelle said as they crossed the dining room. "He was briefly in custody, but his lawyer's about to get him released on personal recognizance. Of course he denies telling Cordelia to clean the car. But we knew that would happen."

"And you're coming to what, warn me?" Arden paused, grimaced, envisioned herself as a target. Ned Bannister, who had apparently run down Nyomi Chang because she knew something, whatever it was. And Cordelia herself had said *you're his friend until you aren't.* Maybe Arden's time was up.

"So." Monelle pulled out one of the kitchen stools.

"What?" She fussed with the coffee filter.

"Cordelia. She's at the Knightsbridge, you know that hotel?"

"Sure, super ritzy, super exclusive." And owned by Arthur Swanson, Arden didn't add. Her skin crawled at the name.

"The owner is a client of your office, isn't he? Arthur Swanson?"

"I don't *have* an office." Arden poked the coffeemaker button. Heard the gurgle of the heating water. "But yes, he's a client of Vision. Warren Carmichael."

"Okay. Anything else you want to say about that?"

"No."

"Have you heard from Cordelia?"

"No, though I guess I didn't expect to," she said, wondering if that was true. "Monelle? What's going on? You're interrogating me."

"Well, I have news. I just came from the hospital. And two things. Nyomi is awake, and recovering. She's in complete control of her faculties, it appears, she'll eventually be fine, it appears, and asked to speak to the police."

"She *what*? Fine? Appears? Police?"

"Let me finish. The cops outside her door called me. I went to the hospital; I went into her room. I'll skip all the legal maneuvering stuff, Arden, and tell you that what Nyomi had been trying to say—was not 'Ned.'"

"I told you that. I *told* you." Arden had said, from the beginning, that Nyomi wasn't saying 'Ned.' But now everything had changed. If Ned actually *had* hit her, then—well, what did that mean now? "So what *was* she saying?"

Monelle took a deep breath. "She was trying to say 'Ned's *wife*.'"

70

She said—'Ned's wife'? 'Ned's *wife*'?" Arden's mind raced as the fragrance of brewing coffee bloomed into the kitchen. "There's only one person that could be, right? There are no other 'Ned's wifes.'"

"Nope," Monelle said. "Just the one."

Arden stared at the coffeemaker, and the dark liquid dripped into the red ceramic mug.

"So *Cordelia* hit her? And wiped off the salt marks to cover up for herself? And then blamed it all on Ned?" Arden actually closed her eyes, trying to envision that. "Because, as we know, she wasn't in Palm Beach. And . . . she took the car, Ned said she had keys. Have you arrested her?"

"So here's the thing." Monelle took a deep breath. "The salt on the coat."

"Oh, right right right." Arden nodded. The proof. "You got the coat. And?"

"And—no." Monelle shifted on the stool. "There was no salt on the coat. It's black, and there's not a speck on it. Dirt, yes. But no swath of salt. If that car hit her, it would be there. And Owulu says there's not one bit of body damage on that car, the results are in. As for our video snippet—a bystander shot it, but even my fancy tech guys say it's irretrievably inconclusive."

"I *told* you—"

"I know, don't give me that look. But, once they plowed through the corporate red tape, they finally acquired clear video from a Dunkin' Donuts cam. It doesn't show *any* black Mercedes in the area. It wasn't . . ."

"Ned's car." *It wasn't Ned's car.* Was she—relieved? But then why would Ned tell Cordelia to clean *his* car off? Something was wrong here. She pushed the button to brew the second cup of coffee.

"Nope, it wasn't." Monelle shook her head, slowly. "And Nyomi didn't recognize the driver. White, was all she could come up with."

"So. Cordelia? Hit Nyomi using a *different* car?"

Monelle sighed. "Nope. Like I said, she has no idea who hit her. But Nyomi had discovered 'Ned's wife' was being—she suspects—blackmailed."

"What? How? Why?"

"Let me finish. And whoever is doing it, the blackmailer, may *know* that Nyomi had figured it out. *That's* why Nyomi was meeting with Ned, that's what she'd warned him about on the phone, that's why he was upset, that's why he didn't explain to Cordelia. We're moving Nyomi to safety now, I cannot even tell *you* where."

"Good thing you had the guards outside her room," Arden said.

"Well, yeah. And that's because of your edict, Arden. There'd be no reason to monitor her otherwise. We'd have pulled them, and waited until she woke up. Who knows who might have gotten to her by then. You thought you were protecting Ned, but you were also protecting Nyomi."

"Whoa." Arden took a squat green glass pitcher from a cabinet, imagining. "But blackmail? How'd she discover it?"

"Ned's bank records. Nyomi was closing out her files after the verdict, and still had the account records from the case. She saw Cordelia had repeatedly transferred funds. To a separate account."

In the records. She'd heard Nyomi say that on the phone at the courthouse. She'd been talking to *Ned*. Arden had already known that. But it still wasn't the only explanation.

"Women do that," Arden said. "The greedy ones. Or the frightened ones."

"Yeah, well. But now that Cordelia's cooperating, we were able to pull the more recent records, too."

"Maybe she has too close a relationship with Saks. Or maybe she's skimming for herself. D'you want milk?"

"Arden? The transfers stopped after the Randall Tennant accident."

"The transfers *stopped* . . ." Arden paused, hand on the refrigerator handle, and tried to play the movie in her mind, but there were too many possible pictures, going by too fast. "So Randall Tennant was the blackmailer? And Cordelia convinced Ned to—how would that have worked?"

"Those are the questions, all right. And Nyomi was looking for the answers. And sure, milk, thanks."

As she filled the milk pitcher and got out two spoons, something nagged at Arden, a thought she couldn't quite retrieve.

"Listen, Monelle." Got it. "If Randall Tennant was the blackmailer, *if*, and now he's dead, who hit Nyomi to stop her from talking about it? Someone else knows. And that's got to be—"

"Cordelia. Or Ned. I agree. But Nyomi didn't recognize the driver. So it wasn't. Although seems like Cordelia was trying to make it look like it *was* Ned."

"I wondered about that. She said Ned told her to clean the car. Maybe someone else told her to say that? Wait—you saw the patch of missing salt. But there's no salt on Nyomi's coat. Maybe Cordelia made that swipe in the salt, left it for the police to see, and then wiped it off." Arden thought back. "She was pretty interested in when the cops saw the car. But why—?"

"Welcome to my life, Arden." She poured milk into her cup, stirred.

"You have to find out what Cordelia was being blackmailed about," Arden said. "But hey. If Nyomi says it wasn't Ned who hit her—doesn't that let him off the hook?"

Monelle took a sip of coffee. "Not . . . quite yet. Because both Ned and Cordelia know more than they're saying."

"Do you think—they're in it together? Whatever it is? Or!" She pointed a forefinger at Monelle. "Was *Ned* being blackmailed, too?" She thought about Pip, and little Emma.

"I don't know." Monelle pressed her lips together. "So we'll handle Ned. But Cordelia still trusts you, Arden. And that's why I'm here."

71

No. No no *no*. Arden was half a block away from the Knightsbridge, loosening her scarf in the unusual November afternoon sunshine, and stopped when she saw him. She'd have recognized that swaggering walk anywhere, the plaid muffler, the bespoke overcoat. Warren Carmichael was walking toward her on Huntington Avenue, eyes on his phone, glancing up from time to time as if to check his progress or avoid other pedestrians.

The deep red awning of the Knightsbridge, fluttering in the stiff breeze, canopied the sidewalk between them, and a patent-capped doorman, hands clasped behind him and gold braids looped through his uniform's epaulets, stood sentry in front of the hotel's famous brass revolving door. If Warren Carmichael was on his way to the Knightsbridge, too, there was no way for Arden to avoid him.

Arden watched him as he walked her direction, oblivious to her. She felt the flames of her own animosity, her disappointment, the embers of her trust. He had taught her, and mentored her, like some bossy big brother who, she'd always believed, had her best future in mind. And then he'd sacrificed her. Betrayed her.

A police car, siren blaring, careened by, and as Warren looked up, he saw her, too. And stopped. He was two steps from the hotel awning.

Her first instinct told her to ignore Monelle's assignment. To turn tail and run. One flash of anger later, and that's exactly what she decided not to do.

She lifted her chin, tossed her head, and pretended she was fine. Absolutely fine. "Well, Warren," she said, coming closer. "What a coincidence. Are you headed inside?" She paused. What the hell. "To meet your friend Arthur Swanson? You're not dressed for golf, I see."

"Arden." He blinked at her, stashed his phone. "I, uh—"

The doorman took a step forward, tipped his hat at Arden, then turned to Warren. "Good afternoon, sir. May I—"

"Thank you, Mike," he said, putting up a palm. He tried to pull out his phone again, fumbling.

She reveled in his confusion, this supposedly unflappable spinmeister who always knew exactly what to say. "Yes? No? Cat got your tongue? Are you late? Am I interrupting?" She was being rude, she knew it, and it felt great. "I was planning on visiting you at the office today, imagine that. If I'd gone there first, I'd have missed you."

"Coming to the office?" The massive brass revolving door began to move, one glass triangle, empty, then another. Warren took a step back. The sun glinted on one more panel of glass, then an elegant woman, holding the hand of a mop-haired little boy, revolved out into the afternoon. Mike, touching his hat again, went back inside.

"Well, of course, the office," Arden went on. An Uber pulled up, and the mother and son climbed inside. "You assigned me a client, correct? Promised me a big payout?" She smiled, her super-nicest smile. "You're all about the money, right? You taught me well. In fact—"

The revolving door started again, and this time Warren stepped away so quickly he almost stumbled. But no one emerged.

"Warren? You look a bit green, I have to say. You have a tough night? Are you expecting someone?" She was shocked with her own audacity, and knew burning bridges was never a good idea. But Warren had certainly burned hers.

"I am, in fact." Warren's shoulders squared. "So I'll need to say goodbye. But indeed, we should talk about your final invoicing. Give my office a call at—"

"I know the number," Arden said.

"So." Warren had finally extracted his phone.

"One last thing before you walk away," Arden said, moving toward the still-revolving door. "Aren't you wondering about the clients you sent me?"

"Well, that's why I'm here," Warren said. "Cordelia and—" He stopped.

Arden raised her eyebrows, encouraging and oh-so-interested. *Cordelia.* Was here at the Knightsbridge. But no one, *no one*, except for Monelle and Arden, was supposed to know that.

"Yes, Cordelia," Arden went on, trying to keep a poker face while her mind played out the rest of the hand. How would Warren know Cordelia was here? "What about her? I know you're friends, of course, you sent her to me. Are you two keeping in touch? Are you taking over the Bannisters' case? Is Ned meeting you, too?"

Trick question, to see if Warren knew Ned was in custody. She remembered the possibility of bail. So he might be out.

Warren's phone rang, a jangle Arden recognized from happier days.

"I'm making you late," she said. "I only need thirty more seconds."

Warren held up a forefinger, put the phone to his ear, and turned his back on her.

72

Arden fingered her own phone, now, as Warren continued his sidewalk conversation. Wondered if she should call Monelle. Let her know that Warren Carmichael knew where Cordelia was. And was planning to see her. He was not the blackmailer, because she'd reached out to him when she needed help. *After* the payments had stopped. And had anyone actually told Cordelia not to reveal her whereabouts? It was Ned she was hiding from. Warren had protected Cordelia before, sending her to Arden.

Maybe Warren was protecting her again.

Warren turned, faced her, his demeanor warm and cordial. "Speak of the devil," he said, holding up his cell. "Guess who?"

"Cordelia?"

"You got it in one." Warren held up the phone as if it were a prize. "We were about to have lunch. You're right, I am taking over her case. But we'd love you to join us. We can pick your brain. You can bring me up to speed."

Outrageous. Talk about audacity. He'd fired her. And now he thought he could take her to *lunch*? Pick her *brain*? Arden felt her blood simmering, and was grateful for the two sleek women, wearing identical black jeans and furry boots and tousled hair, who bustled through the door. They gave her a chance to think. Maybe she could use this.

Monelle had sent her here to see if—by drawing on their relationship—she could find out more about the suspected blackmail. Tell Cordelia that Ned was in deep trouble, and that the police were about to examine his bank accounts. Maybe even use the safety of the kids as leverage. Arden had balked at crossing that line.

"Did you know," she'd finally had a chance to tell Monelle over coffee this morning, "that Pip Bannister is not Ned's biological son?"

"What?" Monelle had pursed her lips, thinking. "No, I didn't. Who *is* his father? And where?"

"Pip's father is—" Arden had realized how two different people had told her two different things. "Huh. I'm not sure."

She'd sketched out all she knew about that; Ned's affection for the boy, Cordelia's admission that she and Pip's father had not been married, that she wasn't even sure who the father was, and that in any case he was dead. Then Pip's awkward revelation, with the indication he was alive. She tilted her head, considering. "How can someone be both alive and dead?"

"Do you know the possible father's name?"

"Nope. I thought about asking Pip, but it seemed too—" Arden had put down her coffee cup. Listened to the aquarium gurgling in the living room, saw the winter sun filter through the kitchen curtains and cast soft shadows on Monelle's face. "Monelle. What if—"

She propped her chin in her hands. "What if Randall Tennant was Pip's father. And the blackmailer? Because of—well, because of something about Pip?"

Monelle tilted her head. "And then Cordelia got Ned to kill him? Really?"

"Well, I'm just theorizing. Neither of them said anything to me about Pip's father. Only Pip did. They were consciously keeping it from me."

"And me, too," Monelle said. "And everyone."

And then it hit her, one little crazy idea. It might work, it might not. It might matter, it might not. Just like everything else in the world.

"Monelle," she'd said. "Listen to this."

Now, in front of the Knightsbridge, Warren wore his please-the-client face, his earlier annoyance erased. But Warren was the king of "seeming," Arden had known that from the beginning. From the beginning when "seeming" was skill, and persuasion, and power. Now she knew it was simply cynical manipulation. A way for Warren to get what he wanted.

But Arden had been a very good student. And now *she* wanted something.

"Wonderful," she said. "I'd love to join you. And I won't even bill you for my time."

"I'm so sorry, again, Arden," Warren began.

Arden shook her head, almost flirtatiously. "I totally get it, Warren. And now I'm going to order the most expensive thing on the menu."

The elevator had one button only, marked PH.

"Aren't we going to the restaurant?" Arden asked as the polished wood doors closed them in. The Armory was on the first floor, outside, on a specially enclosed and heated plaza, decorated with garlands of hydrangea to mimic constant summertime.

"Special treat," Warren said. "Cordelia has ordered in, room service. She has a balcony."

"Penthouse," Arden said. "Very nice."

"I always get a special deal from—" Warren paused. "I mean Cordelia—"

Arden swore he almost blushed. Even Warren could not finish those sentences, the words that would certainly explain that Arthur Swanson was paying for this room. Some things even a boa constrictor could not swallow.

The elevator door opened into the foyer of the suite. Cordelia stood there, welcoming, looking soft and vulnerable in white cashmere and white pants. Bare feet, on the plushy carpeting.

"Arden," Cordelia said.

73

Cordelia was holding out her arms as if for a hug, but Arden pretended she had not seen that. She entered the room, Warren behind her. The elevator door slid closed.

The suite was a study in luxury, high ceilings and flooded with natural light, dotted with curvy almost-Victorian lettuce-green damask couches and curlicued chairs puffed with velvet. A fireplace held a crackling stack of real wood, flames popping and spitting against a coppery screen. A sleek coffee table was scattered with glossy magazines. Sliders to the balcony patio were open, and Arden saw tall triangular stainless-steel heaters glowing on either side. *Arthur Swanson's world.*

"What a treat to see you. Do you have news?" Cordelia brushed her hair away from her face, perhaps to cover her unreturned and now-awkward attempted embrace.

Warren had unbuttoned his coat and laid it across a velvet chair. His black turtleneck the mirror opposite of Cordelia's white.

"You don't need your coat, Arden. Throw it anywhere." Cordelia gestured to a silver ice bucket holding an open green bottle. "Chardonnay?"

Arden glanced at Warren, as if trying to send a private signal to Cordelia. "No thanks. And I do have news. But . . ." She pretended to wince. "It might be a little bit private."

"Oh, Warren doesn't care," Cordelia said. "We've known each other forever, haven't we, War? Since high school."

"That's so fun," Arden said. "And that's why you came to him in the first place. After Ned's incident."

"And have you heard from him?" Cordelia stood in front of the sliders to the terrace, her back to the white clouds reflected in sleek glass buildings.

"That's the thing. . . ." Arden let her voice trail off, hoping it felt portentous yet protective. "What I meant by private."

"Whatever you can say to me, Warren can hear."

"No no." Warren raised a palm, dismissing. "I'll leave you two. Run down to the bar, have coffee. Make calls. You talk." He pulled open the door to the hallway. "Text me when you're ready."

They text, Arden thought. Friends since high school. Confidantes, clearly. New Year's Eve partiers. Which no one had bothered to mention. A relationship which, in fact, Cordelia had actively dodged, and Warren flat-out omitted.

Cordelia slid her bare feet into black velvet flats, then gestured to the balcony, where a round table was surrounded by four white chairs. Over the waist-high wrought iron railing, the sweep of the Boston Public Garden. They were so high, Arden could see the crisscross layout, the bare trees dotting the expanse of snow lined with shoveled star-patterned pathways.

"Amazing," Arden said. *Like a tree house for rich people,* she thought, and Pip came to mind again. She smiled, crossed her fingers. Monelle had said her idea could work. All they had to do was wait.

Cordelia scooted two chairs side by side. Set her phone on the tabletop. "Come sit. See the view. What's so private?"

Arden made a show of looking hesitant as she put her phone down, too. The warmth from the heaters embraced her, the orange coils glowing behind mesh grids.

Cordelia blinked, and Arden imagined what she might be thinking. Cordelia couldn't say anything, Arden knew, for fear of saying the wrong thing.

"There's salt on Nyomi's coat," Arden lied. She almost smiled again. Critics said people like her lied for a living, even Ned had said so. Now she was essentially unemployed, and doing it anyway, but in the pursuit of truth, not power. There was nothing as tempting as a secret, a tenet of her profession. Even a secret that wasn't true.

Cordelia's eyes seemed to fill with tears. "Which means Ned did it. They know it."

"And they . . . ," Arden said. "Listen, you cannot tell anyone this—"

"Of course not," Cordelia whispered.

"They're pulling your husband's bank accounts, honey. They say—oh, this is so difficult. I don't know whether it's worse if this is a surprise to you, or worse if it's not."

"I told you Ned was hiding something." Cordelia crossed her arms over the delicate knit of her white sweater. "And I'm so grateful to know whatever it is. Maybe it'll be a relief."

"Did he ever tell you that someone was—I can't even say the word." Arden was in full acting mode now, though it wasn't the first time it had been necessary in her job. Clients wanted things, wanted things to be the way they wanted them to be, that's what she'd been paid to do over the last eight years. Now *Arden* wanted something. And she knew how to get it. "That someone was blackmailing him. Did you know?"

A tentative breeze fluttered the white tablecloth, and branches swayed in the faraway trees. They were cocooned up here, a different world.

"Blackmailing? Of course not," Cordelia whispered, leaned closer to Arden. "Oh, no. All his business things . . ." She sighed, dropped her shoulders. "And it was Randall Tennant? Who was blackmailing him?"

"Could that be?" Arden asked, as if Cordelia had a brilliant idea.

"Oh, wow, my mind is so full," Cordelia said. "How do they—why do they—think that's what happened? Blackmailing him for what?"

"Monelle told me—ah, this is awful. But Nyomi, I am sorry to say, told the DA's office she'd seen . . ." She waited a beat to see if Cordelia would remark on the breach of confidentiality, but the woman only leaned forward, eager to hear more insider information, no matter the source. "Seen suspicious withdrawals from your husband's account. And those withdrawals stopped after the . . . accident."

She paused again, dramatic. "If it *was* an accident. Problem is." Arden sighed, looked disappointed. "If Ned killed his blackmailer, there's no way to prove it. None. Monelle's office is at wit's end. They'd love to charge him, I hear, but . . . Are you sure he never mentioned it?"

Cordelia's chest rose and fell. She touched her coral-glossed lips. "He might have—mentioned something."

Arden waited.

"What was Randall Tennant threatening to tell?" Arden had risked the leap of casting Tennant as the blackmailer. See if Cordelia would bite.

"I don't *know*." Cordelia looked devastated. Anguished. "I tried to find out, but—Ned told me it was none of my business. Oh, Arden, that's what I'd hoped you'd discover. It was, it really was. I am incredibly grateful. You saved me. I knew you could."

"I do what Warren sends me to do." *I should get an Oscar,* Arden thought. Cordelia had just confirmed the blackmail. And that Tennant was behind it. But why? What information was so volatile? "Protect you. And I'll continue to do that."

"Thank you," Cordelia whispered. "Oh, Warren just texted. I'll tell him ten minutes?"

Arden nodded. "He must care about you very much."

Cordelia's face changed. "Did he tell you that?"

"But before he gets here, Cordelia. You have to tell me everything. Like I always said."

"About—"

"About what happened on New Year's Eve. And why."

Silence.

"Cordelia? Now or never. Time's running out."

"Ned said he'd make it look like an accident," Cordelia said. "Insist he hadn't seen him."

"How did he get him to the garage?"

"He'd offered a final payoff. A big one. And said it had to be in person."

"Pretty dumb to show up in a deserted parking garage," Arden said.

"What can I say?" Cordelia's eyes narrowed as she turned in her chair, put her hand on Arden's arm. "It's all about money. People will do anything for money."

Arden nodded. "You are so right."

"So you'll—tell Monelle? Make sure she knows what Ned did?"

"That's what I'm here for, Cordelia," Arden assured her. And that time, she was telling the truth.

PART FIVE

74

MONELLE CHURCHWOOD

Y ou're hearing this, right?" Monelle pointed to the cell phone on her desk. The FaceTime video showed only blurry Boston sky, but the voices of Arden and Cordelia came through perfectly. Like listening to an old-time radio show, or a master class in persuasion. "I have to say Arden knows her stuff," Monelle went on. "That's as shrewd a cross-examination as I've ever heard."

"I love that she ratted me out for giving you information," Nyomi said. She was stretched out on the county-issue couch in Monelle's office, propped up on three throw pillows, with Nolah's crocheted afghan pulled up to her chin, only her face and arms showing. A wheelchair was folded against the wall. "The Board of Bar Overseers is going to pounce on me."

"I'll protect you," Monelle said. "Got to admit, we're the unlikeliest of allies. Don't tell. It'll ruin my reputation."

"Warren should be back in ten minutes." Nyomi shifted on the couch. "And sounds like Cordelia is getting wine. Always a good sign. Of worry, or complacency. Either one works for us." Nyomi shifted again.

"You okay?" Monelle asked. "Lisa Gray insists I call the hospital if you need—"

"I'm more than fine, even though I've got wheels for a few more days. I'm sore, I admit. Has Stamoran texted you yet?"

"He's just next door," Monelle said.

"Yeah. It's just . . . listen." Nyomi picked at the afghan, poking her fingers through the lacey spaces. "It doesn't make sense that Randall Tennant, no matter how ruthless a criminal, would show up in Ned Bannister's garage at two in the morning. That's just—"

"But it does make sense," Monelle insisted. And she knew she'd been right. The murdering Ned Bannister had gotten away with it. And, if she had to face it, it was her fault. No matter why Tennant had been in that garage, to murder a blackmailer was still murder. "Ned lures him to the garage, and greed outweighs caution."

Nyomi shook her head, and picked at the blanket again.

"Hey, careful with that. My wife made it."

"It's beautiful. But here's the thing about the 'Ned in the parking garage with the Mercedes' theory. If Randall Tennant was coming for his payoff, what, he brought his skateboard? I mean . . . who decided he was skateboarding anyway? If somebody is a big skateboarder and they're celebrating on New Year's Eve, fine, who knows what people do and who are we to judge. But if he's coming to meet Ned Bannister, then he's *not* coming to skateboard. And the whole story falls apart. Maybe some kid's skateboard was simply left in the garage."

"You're still defending him?"

No sound from the phone.

"You're still prosecuting him?"

Monelle had to laugh, shook her head. "Got me. Let's just see if we can find the truth. Which I bet will lead to your hit-and-run driver. And then, boom, we'll prosecute *him*."

"Or her."

"Right," Monelle agreed.

She recognized the footsteps in the hallway. *Charles.* Monelle mouthed his name, held up crossed fingers on both hands. Nyomi mirrored her gesture.

Stamoran entered the room, suit-and-tie immaculate, as confident as if he'd had a no-knock warrant. He held a single piece of paper. "Hey you two."

"Is that it?" Monelle felt her heart race. It always did, times like these. Pivotal. "And?"

"Obviously it would be simpler to email this to you. But not as much fun." Stamoran held up the paper. "You don't know how many—" He paused, looked at Nyomi on the couch. "'Favors' I had to provide to get this, Monelle. How are you feeling, Ms. Chang?"

Monelle stood up so quickly her swivel chair banged into the wall. "And?"

"And?" Stamoran held the paper between two fingers, dangling it. "That wad of Kleenex Ms. Ward gave you from her vest pocket, with the spot of Pip Bannister's blood and the splinter, provided a good sample

for the lab. And here is young Pip's DNA profile. Before you see it, I should tell you they also ran Randall Tennant's sample. That one I had requested long ago, but we never needed it. Now we do. And they finished it just a couple of days ago. Your tax dollars at work."

"You didn't tell me that," Monelle could not help saying, even though her voice came out a little petulant. It had been her case, after all.

"I didn't have to," Stamoran said. "It was need to know."

"Well, now we need to know." Monelle still felt annoyed. But he must have twisted some arms, hard, to get the results. Usually DNA testing took weeks.

"Any last guesses?" Stamoran said.

"Pip's father has *got* to be Randall Tennant," Nyomi said. "He was blackmailing them, Cordelia certainly. Whether Ned knew it or not. That's my guess. Cordelia transferred the money, remember, not Ned. Clearly Cordelia did not want Tennant to tell Ned about Pip's parentage. Ned had no idea who he was killing. By 'accident.'"

"Always the defense attorney," Monelle said. "Or maybe Ned found out about the payments, and was so mad that he killed him. Doesn't that make just as much sense? Ned lured him to the garage for a final payment, then ran him down on purpose. I agree, though. Randall Tennant is Pip's biological father. They kept it hidden from Pip. Somehow."

"Both persuasive arguments," Stamoran said. "Both of you should be lawyers."

"Ha ha." Monelle pointed at her phone. "Remember Arden Ward is FaceTiming us right now from Cordelia's hotel room. We're muted of course, and the warrant we got covers us. But we need to listen. So come on. Tell."

"Nothing sadder than a lawyer who is wrong." Stamoran handed the paper to Monelle. "Bottom line, what the results prove is that Randall Tennant is not Pip Bannister's father."

Monelle scanned the report, wide-eyed. "What? *Not?*"

"Ow," Nyomi said. "Sorry." She waved off Monelle's concern. "I forgot, and tried to stand up. But *what?* He's—"

"Impossible," Monelle said. "They did it too fast, they did it wrong. DNA samples are sometimes wrong."

"I'll remember you said that," Nyomi told her.

Monelle rolled her eyes. "But Charles—"

Stamoran held up a palm. "However. Because of my infinite connections, and the power of the Suffolk County DA's office, we were able to convince two DNA ancestry finders to run little Pip's sample. He's what, eleven years old? Ten?"

Monelle nodded. "And?"

"Sadly, his father's sample was not there."

Monelle could almost feel the oxygen go out of the room. Nyomi's eyes closed for a beat, and Monelle shared her disappointment.

"But." Stamoran pulled a folded sheet of paper out of his pocket. "Others in his father's lineage were there. One of a relative's mothers was a Deborah Linda Hightshue. Who, according to our crack research department, married, in 1971. And soon after had a son. Her spouse was one William, middle initial *W*. . . ." He paused.

Monelle would not give him the satisfaction of yelping again.

"William, middle initial *W* for . . . Warren. Carmichael."

75

W arren Carmichael was their son? And so *he's* Pip's father?"

"Looks like," Stamoran said.

"So what did Randall Tennant have to do with . . . *what*?" Nyomi shook her head. "I think the painkillers are scrambling my brain."

Monelle came to the front of her desk, trying to rearrange puzzle pieces in her mind. There was a life-changing picture to be created, she just didn't know what it showed. Yet. "How does Randall Tennant connect with Warren Carmichael or Cordelia, then? Or Ned?"

"Your turn to do some work," Stamoran said. "Randall Tennant's DNA comes back with his name, Randall Tennant. That's who he is. Was. He's simply not the boy's father. So we've gotten the answer to something. Question is, what was he doing in that garage, and why. But maybe it doesn't matter. Ned Bannister was acquitted."

He looked at Nyomi, then Monelle, crossed his arms over his chest. "And that case is closed. As you both well know. And we're not going to prosecute a dead person for blackmail."

Monelle remembered Arden's theory. "What if Tennant was murdered *before* he got to the parking garage? Then we'd prosecute someone else."

"Bring 'em to me," Stamoran said. He seemed to consider. "We'd take a hit, but we could spin it. Good thing Bannister was acquitted. Never thought I'd say those words."

"So. Warren is married, and Cordelia is married," Nyomi was saying. "Warren for longer."

"And therefore, ripe for blackmail." Monelle felt odd, collaborating with Nyomi. But the truth was worth any collaboration. "Maybe Tennant— however he found out about it—was threatening to tell Ned, or the entire world, including Warren's fancy wife and family and Cordelia's wealthy in-laws, that not only had Warren and Cordelia been carrying on behind their spouses' backs, but that the adorable Pip was the result not of a long-bygone relationship with a mysterious or dead person, but of an affair. *While* Warren was married, and probably ongoing."

Stamoran raised an eyebrow at Monelle. "And we know all about Warren Carmichael and his buddies, don't we?"

She knew what he was talking about, but could not answer in front of Nyomi.

"What?" Nyomi frowned, seizing that morsel.

"What's more important, that's what may have happened to *you.*" Monelle took two steps to the couch, edged in beside Nyomi's feet, patted the intricate afghan, woven to comfort and protect. "You told me in the hospital, you *suspected* the blackmail. And mentioned it to Ned. Who probably told Cordelia. And that was the beginning. They—Warren, or Cordelia, or both of them—could not risk having you investigate any further. Could not have you find the truth about them. And they—Warren or Cordelia, or someone they control—hit you on purpose. And meant to kill you."

Monelle wished she had a blanket, too, for comfort against these cold realities.

"Because now," she went on, "we not only *suspect* the blackmail, we know about Warren and Cordelia. Meaning—Pip. But here's the bigger threat. *We* know. But Arden Ward doesn't. And she's there with both of them now."

Stamoran looked down at her, with an expression she'd never seen before. Approval. And then, maybe, worry.

"I'll send a guy to the hotel. Just in case." Stamoran turned toward the open office door. "Luke!" he bellowed. "Hannaberry," he said, as if that explained who it was.

Monelle almost laughed, then, when the "Luke" arrived. Luke Hannaberry was the zealous investigator who'd terrorized Arden and Pip in Vermont.

"I'm coming with you," Monelle said. "Arden will hit the ceiling if she sees you, Luke. She thought you were out to kill her."

"I'll try to make up for it," Luke said. "If I get the opportunity."

A sound came from the FaceTime. Monelle, startled, whirled to look at the phone.

"*Warren!*" The voice on the FaceTime was high-pitched. Intense. The voice was Arden's.

76

ARDEN WARD

I'm simply poking the fire, Arden." Warren had raised a black cast-iron poker, but stopped, turned, and jabbed it into the fireplace flames, then added two more split logs from an elegant burlap-covered container by the fireplace. He'd returned to the suite, looking like he'd had something stronger than coffee to drink, and poured a glass of white wine from the open bottle.

"The fire was almost out," he went on. "Can't let that happen, right?"

Arden had left her phone on the table on the balcony, wished she had brought it with her.

"What were you two talking about, anyway?" Warren asked.

Arden decided to let Cordelia take the lead. See how she characterized their conversation.

"Girl stuff." Cordelia pushed up the sleeves of her sweater. "Arden was just leaving."

"Before lunch?" Warren asked. "Or perhaps you have some job interviews, Arden."

Arden looked at that fireplace poker, wishing it was in her own hands. She clenched her fists, put them behind her back so Warren would not see.

"You know that ridiculous story about Arthur Swanson and me wasn't true." Arden didn't try to keep the bitterness out of her voice. Warren had clearly gossiped about that with Cordelia, since she'd already taunted Arden with it. "I don't know what Patience Swanson's game is, or Arthur Swanson's. Or yours. But you hired me to do a job, you sent me Cordelia, and I did my best."

Arden regretted it, then, not the sentiment but the personal tangent. She was here only to get Cordelia to reveal the reason for the blackmail. Minutes ago, Cordelia had implicated Randall Tennant, and certainly Monelle had heard it on the FaceTime. Nyomi, too. At least they hadn't heard this Arthur Swanson remark. Still, she needed to get her phone back into closer range. She edged toward the balcony door.

Warren continued to poke the fire. Sparks flared into the elegant room, and settled, smoldering, on the plush carpet.

"Arthur Swanson is not going to be happy that you're singeing his expensive carpeting," Arden said.

"Don't worry about Arthur." Warren poked again.

"I told her everything, Warren," Cordelia said.

Warren paused, poker in mid-jab. "Everything what?"

"Well, Arden told me *Nyomi* knew about Randall's . . . financial demands."

A gust of wind hustled through the room, lifting more sparks from the open fireplace. Arden had to get her phone. Between her and the door were Warren with his poker, the open fire, Cordelia hovering at the entryway to the room's kitchenette, with its glistening knives in a stainless-steel holder. She knew she was making too much of this, it was a ritzy Boston hotel, and her only threat was her overactive imagination. *Get the phone, say goodbye, leave,* her brain instructed her.

Arden looked at her Apple watch, feigning surprise. "Oh, I'm getting a phone call," she said, holding up her arm.

"Better get it," Warren said. "But answer it in here, Arden."

"Right. It's cold." Arden pretended to misunderstand, trotted to the balcony, picked up her phone. She tapped off the picture, just to be safe. At least Monelle and Nyomi could still hear everything she said. She hoped they took the cue.

"Oh hello, Monelle," she said, pretending the line hadn't already been open. "I was just going to call you, so funny. I'm here with Cordelia."

"Can they hear me?" Monelle had kept her voice low. *Her Scout voice,* Arden thought.

She clamped the phone closer to her ear to prevent the sound from leaking. "Oh golly, no," Arden said. "I'd wanted to see if I could meet with you. It's important. Do you have time soon? Wait, first, what were you calling about?"

She smiled, signaling conspiratorially to Cordelia.

Monelle was quickly bullet-pointing what they'd discovered. Warren and Cordelia. The affair. The splinter. The DNA. Pip's true father. "You were so brilliant to save that splinter. And brilliant idea to have it tested. And now we're hearing everything you all say," Monelle whispered. "But stall, okay? Stall."

"Really?" Arden pretended to be intrigued. And tried not to look at the two clandestine lovers, the two who were pretending they had no illicit past. And no incentive to kill Randall Tennant and blame Ned Bannister for it. "Wow. I believed every word he said. Well, I guess justice is done. All the more reason we should talk." She paused, making sure Cordelia and Warren were listening. "Let me know when he's in custody again. So Cordelia can feel safe."

She made a show of hanging up, even though the line was still open. She put her phone on the coffee table, then put one of the glossy magazines on top of it so the others wouldn't see it was still on. She and Monelle had experimented. Good thing.

"Believed every word of what who said?" Cordelia asked. "Who's in custody?"

"There's no way out of it for Ned this time," Arden lied.

Warren turned, still holding the poker.

"The DA's office is going for it, Cordelia." Arden tried to look concerned. "The blackmail, the payments, luring poor Randall Tennant, exactly as you said, to the garage. It's risky, since the evidence is so circumstantial. Since you're married, you can't be forced to testify against him. Unless you want to?"

"Do they know *why* he was blackmailing Ned?" Cordelia's voice was a whisper.

"He's dead, Cordelia. They've decided they'll never know. I mean, Ned certainly won't tell. And Nyomi—well, she's not long for this world. So they'd charge him with vehicular homicide for that. Because of the salt on the coat. And you cleaning the car."

"He made her do it," Warren said.

Confidantes, she thought. "I know. And now I need that wine."

She half turned, poured the Chardonnay. She felt more than saw Cordelia move closer to Warren, then out of the corner of her eye, saw, for a fraction of an infinitesimal second, Cordelia's hand link with Warren's.

Cordelia and Warren.

"The weird thing?" Arden said, pretending to sip her wine. "Monelle says they're suspecting Ned killed Tennant *before* the parking garage. Maybe stashed him in the trunk?" She shrugged, as if it were absurd. "And then made it *look* like an accident. Of course there would be evidence of that in Ned's car, but they never looked."

"Why do they suddenly think that?" Warren asked. "The case is closed."

"Come on, Warren. It's bureaucracy, how long have we worked with government agencies?" Arden toasted him tipsily with her still-full wineglass, hoping he wouldn't notice she hadn't taken even one sip. "Some autopsy report was lost somewhere, I was on the phone with Monelle for two seconds, I have no idea."

"Will they look for his car to see—well, it's long gone now," Cordelia said. She fussed with her hair. "Even if they found it, it'd be too late."

"Oh no," Arden said, "if there was a body in the trunk, or whatever, you could clean the car a hundred times and it would still be there." She had no idea if this was true, and hoped the other two didn't either. Hoping that Monelle, listening, would not howl with laughter. "Science, you know. DNA. DNA is always the clincher. Don't you watch TV? Good thing he wasn't using *your* car, Cordelia. *If* he did it."

Cordelia nodded, and Warren turned back to the fire. Seemed to be intent on the flames, stabbing at the wood.

"Bathroom?" Arden said to Cordelia, a little louder than perhaps necessary. "This wine is going right through me, I'm afraid."

Cordelia pointed. "Back there," she said.

77

MONELLE CHURCHWOOD

Yes," Monelle said. "Good girl. Sounds like she's leaving them alone. With the line open so we can hear."

"I wish we could see them," Luke said. He'd pulled their car out onto Congress Street, headed toward the financial district.

"Too risky. She's covered the screen, looks like, hiding it. Turn here."

"I know where it is."

"Now we cross our fingers. But listen. Sunday at Arden's, Cordelia told us she'd park her car in the hotel garage. Our records show it's the same one she had before, a white Audi. If she actually did kill Randall Tennant and stashed him in her car, and then Carmichael drove the body to the Bannister garage, then, exactly as Arden warned her, there could still be evidence."

"Unlikely," Luke said.

"She doesn't know that. Shhh. Listen."

"I told you to clean that car, Cordie." Warren's voice. Low. Menacing.

"I did. Of course." Cordelia's voice. "*I* told *you* we should have gotten rid of it."

Monelle looked at Luke, gave a thumbs-up.

"Right," Warren was saying. "And how suspicious would that have been? The only way to keep the focus on Ned was—"

"I know."

"Randall just . . . came at me for more," Cordelia said "At my *house*. He wouldn't leave me alone. Oh, I just want us to be—"

"Stop talking," Warren said. "I know what happened. We don't need to talk about it. This is what I do for a living, you know that. You asked me to make it look like an accident. So I did. I always make the world be the way my clients want it to be. And now it is. Almost."

Monelle drew one finger across her throat. "Toast," she whispered, even though she didn't have to. What would they all do without their phones?

"But, my dear." Warren's voice again. "I'm afraid your car is about to be stolen. You can't trust parking lots these days. Insurance will get you a new one. And no one will be able to test *yours* for DNA evidence in the trunk. Or whatever."

"Sweetheart, I—"

"Get everything out of it you might want. Don't do too good a job."

"Now?"

"Now."

"I can't do it alone. What if—"

"Go, Cordelia."

"Arden will wonder—"

"I'll tell her Arthur Swanson called. Wanted to come up and see you. She'll be grateful you kept her out of that, trust me. I'll give her more wine. All of that—sisterhood abused-wife bullshit. I knew she'd do her best for you. I knew she'd get Ned implicated, and get us off the hook—and now she has. And she has no idea. And don't worry, one wrong word from her and I'll unleash the Arthur Swanson story to the world. She knows that. She's neutralized. Harmless now."

"Got that wrong," Luke said, making the final turn to the hotel. "She's—"

"Hush. Listen. Sounds like Cordelia's leaving. We have to get to that car before she does."

"No way. We wait. Wait for whoever Carmichael sends to steal it."

"Wish you could do it," Monelle said.

"Damn. Red light." Luke stopped, drummed his fingers on the steering wheel. "You know what? I could. Make her think Carmichael sent *me*. Tell her to get her stuff. Get her to give me the keys, you know? Just to start it."

"Think she's that dumb?"

"You're asking that now?" Luke accelerated through the intersection, made the turn into the Knightsbridge garage. "She's nervous. Off balance." He rolled down his window, pushed the button to open the garage gate. Took the ticket. "You'll expense this, right?"

"Drive," she said. "She has a white Audi, we'll find it, easy. It's not like she's driving away. She'll recognize me, though. I'll duck. And keep an ear to the FaceTime. So far, no one's talking. She's gotta be on the way. Arden's gonna have some explaining to do, why she took so long in the bathroom. But good thing she did."

Monelle kept watch as Luke drove them into the darkened garage, gloomy and sparsely occupied, one winding narrow lane providing space for only a few dozen cars—many hotel and restaurant guests, she knew from experience, used the valet parker.

"There's just one elevator bank." She pointed ahead. "See it? She'll never use the stairs so . . . Luke." She sat up straighter, pointed again. "There's the car. End of the row. And a spot right by it. Back in. Leave the windows open. Give me the keys. Since you're a car thief you wouldn't have driven here. I'll duck."

"Do you see her?"

"Nope, nope, nope, just park. I'm watching the elevator. Back in. We arrived first. Great. You ready?"

Luke maneuvered the car into place. "I'll take the car to—"

"Play it by ear. Go. Hide."

Luke clicked open the door, slid out, disappeared around the corner. Did he look like a car thief? To Monelle he looked hip. Confident. Arden, though, had been afraid of him. Maybe Cordelia would be, too.

"Where's Cordelia?" Arden's voice on the FaceTime.

There'd be no way to warn her they were in the basement. *Go home, Arden,* Monelle tried telepathy. *We got this.*

"Your friend Arthur Swanson called." Warren's voice. "While you were apparently indisposed. He wanted to come up. I decided you might not want his companionship, so Cordelia went to see him. You can thank me later."

"I'll never thank you," Arden said. "You believed Patience Swanson. And not me."

"Way it goes, I'm afraid."

Monelle heard rustling, maybe Arden getting her coat? And her phone. She kept watch on the elevator doors. Nothing.

"Could I just ask you before I leave . . ." Arden's voice was louder now, maybe she'd picked up the phone. Was signaling her intentions. "Where did Ned get that skateboard, do you think? Did he use it as a prop to make it look like Randall Tennant was skateboarding?"

"Huh? Don't they have a kid? A boy?"

More silence. What was Arden doing? *Get out,* Monelle thought. *Leave it.*

"They do, yes," Arden said. "But you know? I'm thinking . . . mulling this over. Their 'son'"—she paused. "Looks a lot like you. So strange, right? And I'm wondering what your wife would think if you were required to take a paternity test?"

Shut up, Arden, Monelle thought. Carmichael thought Arden was speculating. Being spiteful. But Arden knew Monelle was listening. So what was she doing?

78

ARDEN WARD

What the hell are you talking about?"

Warren's face had turned red. Good.

Arden widened her eyes, all innocence. "Oh, Warren, I'm so sorry, I didn't mean it that way," she lied. "I just meant . . . if *I* thought of it, you being Pip's father, who knows who else might have thought of it. Maybe Randall Tennant. Maybe Nyomi Chang." Arden shrugged. "Not that she could tell anyone. So I hear."

"That's insane."

"Oh, I *know*. Insane."

Arden stalled, swirling her wine. She knew Monelle and Nyomi were listening, and maybe Charles Stamoran himself, waiting in the DA's office to see how deeply Cordelia and Warren would implicate themselves in the murder of blackmailer Randall Tennant—whoever he was and however he knew about Pip—and in the attempt to silence Nyomi Chang. Now they knew Cordelia was away, with Arthur Swanson. And that she had Warren alone.

So far, Cordelia and Warren had admitted to the blackmail, but insisted the target was Ned. Arden herself suspected that Tennant's targets were Warren and Cordelia. Forcing them to pay to hide the paternity of Pip from their wealthy spouses. Not to mention their ongoing—she remembered their surreptitious touch—clandestine relationship.

Now that Cordelia was off with the vile Swanson, maybe Arden could clinch the case. Take Warren down. Just like he'd done to her. Thanks to Pip's splinter and Stamoran's DNA tests, Arden knew the truth. Now she had the power.

"But thing is, and I cannot believe I'm saying this to you, Warren, but I understand that you did what you had to do for the good of Vision. You taught me well."

"Got that right." Warren poured himself more wine, did not offer her any.

"But I think . . ." Arden paused, as if she was considering what to do. "Since Monelle Churchwood knows about the blackmail, and knows Ned is not Pip's father—"

"She *knows* that?"

"It's not a secret, right? Pip told me himself."

"He did? Did he say who his father was?"

Arden winced, tried to look sympathetic. "Well, not in so many words. But . . ." She shrugged. Lied again. "You really do look alike."

Warren took a slug of wine.

"And knowing how Monelle Churchwood operates . . ."

"How she operates?" Warren's wine was almost gone.

"I'm just saying, and I should bill you for this, ha ha, but let's say Monelle decides it's not *Ned* that Tennant was blackmailing, but Cordelia. So Monelle goes to Cordelia. Confronts her with that."

"With what?"

Arden could almost see his mind at work. "I mean, listen, between us. Monelle Churchwood is a monster. She blew the Bannister case, and she's out for blood. I mean, talk about revenge." *Sorry Monelle,* she thought. She pictured them cozily in her office, laughing about this.

She watched Warren processing her words. He probably knew Cordelia better than anyone, wondered how quickly she'd turn on him. Arden needed to keep at him, not give him a chance to think too hard. Classic PR strategy. She poured more wine for him, then some for her, just for show. It was all a show.

"I'm worried about you, Warren. If Monelle can't get *one* Bannister, she's gonna go after the other. And hiding a love child is a pretty classic motive for murder." This made no sense, and she couldn't believe she'd said "love child," like some forties movie. But she was gratified to see Warren drinking even more. Becoming even more upset. Arden was simply making the world the way she wanted it to be. She'd had a very good teacher.

"Does Ned know? About you, and about Pip, the boy he's now raising as a son?" She whispered, pushing him, conspiratorial. "If I know the truth, I can help you with him. You set me up to do that, right? Take him down? I can. But only if I know the truth. You taught me that, right?"

79

MONELLE CHURCHWOOD

Monelle had to hand it to her. *Go Arden*. And hoped her telepathy worked. She peered up through the passenger side window of the car, allowing only her eyes and black knit cap to show. No sign of Cordelia in the garage yet. Back at the office, Nyomi and Charles, without the FaceTime, were waiting for her report. She could no longer see Luke, who'd hidden around the corner from the white Audi.

Nothing but rustling sounds from the FaceTime now, and it was hard to tell what was going on in that penthouse. She had to mute it, though, in case the sound carried through the silent garage. If Arden got Warren to tell the truth, it would all be on the digital recording. It was down to the final key questions: Who knew Randall Tennant, and which of them killed him. And who had tried to kill Nyomi.

Monelle could not help but smile. She loved a good conclusion. This would be fast, and unassailable. The moment Cordelia handed over the car keys. "Toast," she whispered to herself.

Cordelia would not be looking to see if she was being watched. Would only be focused on getting her possessions out of the car. And then disappearing while Warren's emissary stole it. Probably, Monelle theorized, the same goon he'd sent to hit Nyomi Chang.

Money. Money and greed. And making the world be the way you wanted it to be. But she, Monelle Churchwood, wanted the world a different way. She wanted justice.

The elevator doors opened. Monelle had a perfect view as Cordelia, dressed in white like a pristine ghost in the dusky shadows of the garage, paused briefly as they closed behind her. She took a key fob from her pocket, clicked it in the direction of the Audi. Monelle heard the distinctive click-beep. Saw the lights flash. Knew that Luke was seeing it, too.

He'd wait, Monelle figured, for her to begin her mission. Cordelia walked toward the car, silent, furtive, the keys in one hand and the other in a fist.

Cordelia clicked open the trunk, took out a canvas tote bag. She kept one hand on the trunk lid, seemed to be deciding. Monelle saw her select a pair of running shoes, put them in the bag, then stand for a moment, motionless, her hand on the trunk. She slammed it closed. The sound seemed to startle her, and she looked, quickly, back and forth.

She opened the passenger front door, leaned in, went out of view. Monelle imagined her rummaging in the glove compartment, taking out the insurance information perhaps, or the registration.

Luke's approach was so stealthy, Monelle did not notice when he first came out of the shadows, but she watched him, then, striding confidently toward Cordelia.

Cordelia looked up, wary, but Luke walked on by, as if he weren't interested. *Good,* Monelle thought. *Let her start to walk away.* Cordelia closed the door. Did not lock it.

As Cordelia walked toward the rear of her car, she paused again, now-bulging tote bag over her shoulder. Maybe she was saying goodbye. Luke had stopped by a nearby black Lexus. Waited.

Crap. Was there surveillance? Should have thought of that. But, hey. Wouldn't matter—unless someone was monitoring live. But she was the DA's office. Cross that bridge if they came to it.

Luke began walking toward Cordelia. She looked at him, and Monelle saw the joy in her eyes. Not fear. Not hesitancy. Relief.

"Mr. Carmichael says to ask for the keys," Luke said, smiling. "It'll make this faster."

"He didn't tell me that," Cordelia said. "Won't that make it look like—"

"Happy to hot-wire the car." Luke shrugged. "But if there's surveil-lance . . ."

"There isn't."

"All the more reason to make it easy." Luke held out his hand. "Ma'am? Standing around yammering is probably not the best idea. If you take my drift."

"Whatever." Cordelia handed him the keys. "We just want this car gone."

Luke took the key. "We know you do." He put the fob in his pocket.

Cordelia adjusted the tote bag. Took a step toward the elevator.

"Mrs. Bannister?" Luke took a step closer to her. Glanced at Monelle.

Monelle, phone in hand, clicked open her car door. Slid out, ducked behind it. Waited. He put the keys in his pocket. He'd played it by ear, as she'd suggested. She'd follow his lead.

Cordelia turned, frowned. "How do you know my—"

"We know everything, Mrs. Bannister," Luke said.

"What?"

"Not so fast, ma'am." Luke reached out, grabbed one of Cordelia's wrists.

"Help!" she screamed. "What are you doing?"

Monelle hurried toward her, holding her black-walleted DA credentials in front of her. "Nice to see you again, Mrs. Bannister. You remember me, right?"

"You have the right to remain silent," Luke began.

80

ARDEN WARD

Hell. I bet she'll leave," Warren was saying.

Arden had watched him pace in front of the fireplace, silent, glass in hand. He'd taken a bottle of bourbon from an artfully concealed liquor cabinet. Slugged one glass, poured another. She knew she simply had to wait. And hope that Cordelia would stay with Arthur Swanson long enough to give Arden time to convince Warren to tell the truth. She was close. She knew she was close.

"We have to stop her."

"What do you mean, she'll leave?" Arden was honestly perplexed. "Leave with Arthur Swanson? Stop her from what?"

"There is no Arthur Swanson. I mean, he's not here." Warren's words slurred. Lunch had never arrived, and Arden wondered if maybe it was never planned. They'd just wanted to pump her for information. Well, *she'd* done the actual pumping. But now something had changed.

"You're losing me, Warren."

"She's bolting. She told me when you were in the, uh, bathroom. She'd left something incriminating in her car, and she had to destroy it. In the hotel parking garage. But she's been gone too long now, and—I think you're right. After you told her the DA was onto something, she decided to turn on me. Tell. But I'm too smart for that. We have to stop her."

"We? Whoa," Arden said. "You mean, tell the cops? Or Monelle? Tell them what?"

Warren stood. Hit the elevator button. "You have to come with me. Convince her. She'll listen to you. You can have your job back. Water under the bridge, all is forgiven. Yes, I only pretended to believe Patience, but let's go, for god's sake, let's go."

Arden grabbed her phone. Saw the counter numbers clicking forward. Monelle was hearing this. Knew where they were going, knew Warren was about to intercept Cordelia. Not that Monelle could stop them from her place in the DA's office, but at least she knew they were going to the hotel garage.

The elevator took them down. Arden kept her phone rolling in her pocket, but Warren was silent, fuming, as they descended. When the doors opened into the garage, he stepped out. Arden began to follow, and almost ran into him when he stopped.

"Shit. Shit," he hissed. "Go back go back go back."

"What?" Arden peered around him, and saw—the guy from Vermont? But Monelle had said he was a cop who—

But there was Monelle. *What?* And Cordelia. Cordelia was sobbing. And in handcuffs.

"Arden!" Cordelia cried. "Warren!"

"Carmichael!" Monelle called out. "Stop!"

At that instant, Warren grabbed Arden's arm, twisted it behind her. Held it, tight.

She flinched, surprised. A shiver of fear shot through her.

But Warren only leaned closer.

"Do not say a word," he whispered. "Do not. Say a word. I have people who can hurt you. And I have people who can help you."

All Arden could think of was the FaceTime in her pocket, audio still recording. *You can't hurt me anymore;* Arden almost said it out loud.

"I told you, I told you," Cordelia was wailing, her face awash with tears. "Warren made me do it, he made me come down and allow the car to be stolen. That's who I thought you were! That's why I gave you the keys!"

"Like Ned made you wipe off the car," Monelle said. Arden saw the quiet triumph in her face. "Don't you have a mind of your own? Cordelia?"

"Arden, Arden," Cordelia, her face red and blotchy, now entreated. "Please come tell them. Come tell them the truth."

Warren was pulling Arden's arm tighter. "I'm warning you," he murmured.

"The truth? That you told me Warren Carmichael was Pip's father?" Arden said. "And that Randall Tennant was blackmailing you to cover up your affair?" Totally not true, but Arden lied for a living. That's what she did. Ned was right.

"You idiot," Warren yelled. "You told her that? Why in hell would you do that?"

"I never—" she began. Then she paused. Arden watched the woman's face change, in the dim light of the garage, saw her entire posture straighten, her shoulders square, even with that Vermont guy holding her.

"*He* killed Randall Tennant." Cordelia cocked her chin toward Warren. "*He* did. Yes, I have a mind of my own, Ms. Churchwood." Her voice had gone bitter. Imperious. "And yes, now, delighted to tell you the truth. Warren always loved me, and still does, and when Randall threatened to tell his wife? He's a pathetic henpecked rabbit, and . . . well. We knew Ned would be gone that New Year's Eve, so Warren came over. But Randall had followed him. Confronted us. Said he had pictures. Warren hit him with one of Pip's skateboards—his own son's skateboard! And then . . ."

Monelle had moved closer to Cordelia. Grasped the cuffed woman's arm. "Luke," she said.

The man—Luke—stepped toward Warren.

Warren had not loosened his grip on her. He held Arden close, so close she could feel the motion of his breathing. He might be enraged, and betrayed, and trapped, but he could not actually hurt her, could he? Not with Monelle and this Luke person here. Who was still scary, but apparently on her side. Unlikely allies.

"Kidding me?" Warren's voice came out like a wasp, a viper. "You came to me, you bitch, you told me what you'd done, bashed him with one of *our* own son's skateboards, stashed him with it in your trunk. You turned to me, like you always do, to clean up your mess. 'Make it look like an accident,' you whined. Not anymore, Cordie. Not anymore. I admit, I do, Miss Churchwood, to helping her. But she forced me. And I did it for our son, and his future."

"That's ridiculous!" Cordelia's face twisted, her eyes blazing. "Ask *him* who sent those fake texts. Look at his phone. Ask *him* who took that video of the car that hit Nyomi. How well did all *that* work, Warren? I told you it was going too far. But no, *you* had to—"

"Right," Monelle said. "You'll each have a long time to work on your stories. Separately. And good luck with that."

Luke took another step toward Warren.

Warren pulled her arm up higher. She would not let him know how much it hurt. This would be over soon. And then she felt the metal against her head. *Warren had a gun?*

"I'm getting in that elevator," Warren said. He hit the button with his elbow, and the doors obediently opened. "Do not come one step closer. Or I will shoot her. I'll let her go when you let me go."

Arden saw Luke and Monelle exchange looks. There was no way they could communicate, decide what to do. Arden saw the triumph on Cordelia's face. *Hell with that.*

"I don't think so," Arden said. Before she could even think about it, she smashed her elbow into Warren's gut, then stamped his instep, a skill every woman needed to know. *Thank you, kickboxing.* In a fraction of a second, Luke was at her side, wrestling Warren into handcuffs. Grabbed the gun.

"You and your *words,* Warren," Arden could not resist saying. "This is real life. This is the truth. And the truth wins." *Asshole,* she didn't say out loud.

"You—" Warren began. Cordelia had dissolved into even more tears, which seemed to amuse Monelle.

"Arden?" Luke said as he led Warren away. "This moron called you 'harmless,' by the way. That's wrong. I knew that the first time I met you."

81

A rden and Monelle had collected their coffees at the Howell's on the corner, and walked in the brilliant Boston sunshine, heading to the district attorney's office. City Hall Plaza, the vast brick and concrete expanse, was now decorated for the season, sprays of bittersweet tied with fluttering orange and brown ribbons attached to the rows of trees.

"The *doorman*? At the Knightsbridge? *Tennant*?"

"Yup," Monelle said. "And we have your friend Arthur Swanson to thank for that bit of information."

Arden wiped a fluff of latte foam from her lips. "Why were you talking to him?"

"It's, well, just listen." Monelle looked at her phone, stashed it. "Swanson says Tennant was the hotel's 'overnight guy.' His phrase. Doorman, desk clerk, whatever was necessary, basically the only one there after midnight. No day workers knew him at the hotel, he was under the radar because of his shift, and . . . get this. There are no employment records, because Swanson was paying him under the table. Tennant had noticed Warren and Cordelia meeting there, late night, a rendezvous courtesy of their buddy Swanson. But then Tennant got some moneymaking ideas of his own. Meaning blackmail. So Cordelia and Warren certainly weren't going to ID him for police, or at the trial. And Swanson couldn't own up, since it would reveal his illegal business practices."

"Money and power," Arden said. "It's terrifyingly easy to convince people the world is how you want it to be. For a while, at least."

They stopped at a crosswalk, watched a Duck Tour bus trundle by, its wide windows framing faces of gawking tourists. The district attorney had called the two of them in, Monelle had explained—half an hour, max—for a final debriefing. "He just wants to make sure he has all the info."

Arden had nothing else to do this morning. She was unemployed. Nyomi was recovering at home, then taking some downtime in Costa

Rica. Arden's life, her different life, would go on. Eventually she'd be able to think of Warren's betrayal as "job experience." She thought about Paris maybe, someplace far away. There was just one bit of unfinished business. Couldn't even decide if it *was* her business. But her conscience kept nudging her.

"We'll get Warren for hiring the rent-a-thug he sent to try to kill Nyomi," Monelle was saying. "And Cordelia for killing Randall Tennant. Both trials are going to be a mess, with all the finger-pointing. They won't have Nyomi to defend them, that's for sure. But who knows what a jury will think is reasonable doubt."

Their light turned green. "But Warren's extramarital secret is out," Arden said. "Cordelia's, too. Whatever the jury verdict, their lives are ruined. And they did it to themselves. They're toast." The coffee seemed even better than usual.

"My very words." Monelle lifted her steaming paper cup. "And you, my dear, were right about the second to last to leave. Warren had driven Cordelia's car. Toted Randall Tennant's body with him. Waited until everyone else had left the party, and put the body and skateboard in Ned's path. You should be an investigator, sister. Much more virtue in that than PR."

"Kind of a risky plan, though," Arden said.

"Yep. They all are, when you come to think of it. Crime is a razor's edge, you know?"

"I mean, Ned might have seen Tennant, might have stopped. Might have, might have, might have. But that's not how it happened."

"Never thought I'd see the day when I was happy for an acquittal," Monelle said.

They walked in silence for half a block, Arden remembering that drive to Vermont. Ned's genuine bafflement about Cordelia. His affection for the kids. His comforting little Emma, and embracing Pip. Even his endearing relationship with his mother. And goofy Bartok.

"Ned seems like a genuinely good person, under all that veneer," Arden finally said. "I know he loves those kids, I talked to him last night. He's moving to Vermont. The kids, too. I'll go visit, someday. Pip and Emma are terrific, but I worry about them a bit. They have quite the hurdle. Still, Ned loves them, and Georgianna, too."

"Ooh." Monelle's eyes twinkled. "Do I detect a budding romance?"

"Nope, nope, nope. Too complicated for me. And for him. And for

the children." She shrugged. A personal relationship with a client? *Never.*
That's what had started this whole story. "Life is unpredictable. We'll
see."

A wash of briny air from Boston Harbor puffed by them, and in the
distance, a lone airplane blazed a white contrail through the pristine blue
sky. A wave of commuters from the Government Center T stop hustled
across Cambridge Street. Arden and Monelle paused to let them all by.

One thing still didn't make sense.

"Why didn't they—Warren and Cordelia—leave well enough alone?"
Arden asked. "I know they tried to frame Ned for Randall Tennant's
death and get rid of him altogether, but even when they failed, they still
kinda pulled off the perfect crime. They'd killed their blackmailer. And
got away with it. I mean, even though Plan A didn't work—to get Ned
convicted and out of their lives—they should have just called Plan B, the
acquittal, a win."

"Yup. And it almost worked," Monelle said. "Warren's rich wife
traveling, rich Ned back to his all-consuming business, and a willing
babysitter in the grandmother—all of which would have allowed Warren and Cordelia to continue painting the town. Or whatever people say
these days about affairs. Even with Ned free, they could still use their
marriages to get what they wanted. But then Nyomi, wrapping up her
paperwork, found the blackmail, and the cover-up had to continue. So
they conscripted *you* supposedly to make Ned look good—while they
were actually setting him up to take the blame for Nyomi. Who they'd
hoped would die."

"Talk about domestic violence," Arden said.

"Got that right," Monelle said. "Till greed do us part."

They arrived at the redbrick building. A yuppie pizza place occupied
the first floor, the DA's offices above. It smelled like oregano, and Arden
always wondered how anyone got any work done.

Monelle reached out to open the glass double door, but Arden put her
hand on Monelle's arm, stopping her.

"But speaking of violence. Before we go in. One thing I need to tell
you. I didn't quit at Vision, I was—"

"I know," Monelle said.

"You do?"

Monelle nodded. A teenager with two flat pizza boxes barreled out,
and Monelle had to step back to let him go by.

"Well, there's a woman at my office—used to be my office—Luz Ocasio," Arden continued. "I'm worried about her. I think she may be vulnerable. And I need your advice on what to tell her. *How* to tell her. Without—"

Monelle cocked her head toward the door, pulled open the thick glass. "Let's talk to Charles first. He wants to see you in person, he insisted, like I said. Then you and I can confer."

Monelle obviously had an agenda, or at least the district attorney did, and Arden understood obeying your boss. Probably wants to thank me, Arden thought. She had a moment of unworthy pleasure, imagining Warren stewing in the Suffolk County House of Correction. Cordelia, too. Neither would do well at being corrected.

"It's sad," Arden began. "Pip, and Emma . . ."

"We all make decisions at some point, don't we," Monelle said. They opened the door into the DA's office hallway. "One step, and then another, all trying to get what we want," she said as they walked. "Some people do it to make everyone's lives better. Others do it for themselves. I see that every day."

"And that's why I wanted to talk to you about—"

"Two minutes," Monelle cut her off again.

Charles Stamoran sat behind his desk. "Come in," he said. "Right on time."

Arden scanned the wall of trophy pictures, impeccable leather-bound books lined in built-in bookcases, the lofty cloud-dusted view out the tall window over City Hall Plaza and on to the Boston skyline. Stamoran himself, pinstriped and paisleyed, almost looked benevolent.

"Arden Ward," he said. *Ahden,* she remembered his accent. *Wahd.* "Monelle says you were quite the investigator."

Exactly what Arden had predicted. And it was classy of him, generous, to acknowledge that she'd accomplished what his office hadn't. "Thanks." She gestured to Monelle. "Unlikely allies, I guess."

"Yes, indeed." Stamoran stood, waved them to the leather couch. He pulled up a visitor's chair, sat closer to them. Leaned forward.

"Arden? So. Arthur Swanson."

This seemed out of left field. "What about him?"

"Listen. Please." Stamoran put up two palms, maybe sensing Arden's flare of anger. "Because of your personal situation—"

"We don't *have* a personal situation." *What the hell?*

82

Your personal situation," Stamoran went on, "in that your former employer dismissed you because there was some gossip about you and Mr. Swanson."

Arden felt the blood drain from her face. Looked at Monelle in betrayal and disbelief. "I *never*—"

"We're not doing this very well, are we, Monelle? Arden. *Listen*. We know there was nothing between you and Arthur Swanson. Absolutely nothing. We've been watching him. He's not only engaged in illegal business practices, he's a predator. And there's a whole string of victims."

"Your colleague Luz Ocasio?" Monelle said. "We know about her. She came to our office at some point after he'd approached her. Because she knew, when she was at your house one evening? Is that correct? That you suspected as well. Something about perfume? Anyway. Mr. Swanson will soon be out of the picture, we wanted you to know that."

"And Luz?"

"Luz is fine, Arden," Monelle said. "Swanson's mostly about conquest and power tripping. But not always. I couldn't talk to you about it until we'd made our final case. But now you know. No wonder Patience Swanson was antagonistic. Her husband was disgusting. And Warren Carmichael allowed it to happen. More than allowed. Enabled. 'Cost of doing business,' Carmichael told us. 'Keeping the paying clients happy.' Probably figured that'd help him in court."

Stamoran made a sound, contemptuous. "It won't. Those two are done."

Arden felt tears of profound relief come to her eyes. Warren's scarlet letter, that's how she thought of it, would have followed her wherever she went. She'd have been guilty in the court of professional opinion. One wrong word, if that lie had stuck, and Arden's life would have been forever changed. She even felt sorry for Patience Swanson, who was only trying to protect her marriage.

Words have power. It seemed like a glib and persuasive thing when she'd say that to her clients. A pitch. But now she knew, intensely, how devastating the wrong words could be. She'd be even more careful. More compassionate. Words had almost ruined her.

"Thank you," was all she could think to say. She'd have to work out her feelings, that would take awhile. Valuable things often did.

A knock on Stamoran's office door. Luke Hannaberry.

"You buzzed?" He said he looked different in a suit, Arden thought. No longer the thuggy mysterious stranger in Vermont, or the stern-faced plainclothes cop in the Knightsbridge hotel basement. They'd been formally introduced after Cordelia and Warren were led away.

"Yes," Stamoran said. "Something you want to say to Miss Ward?"

"You go ahead," Luke said.

They all looked like they were hiding a secret. With Arden the only one not in on it. And she hated surprises.

"You handle it, then, Monelle," Stamoran said.

"Handle *what*? You're scaring me here."

"Geez, you two. Arden. We have a job for you," Monelle said. "If you're interested. Being an investigator for the district attorney. It won't pay as much as your PR job, but it will be all about finding the truth. You'll work with Luke. He's on loan here from Boston PD, but he'll teach you the ropes before he's reassigned."

"I'll still be in Boston, though," Luke said.

"Monelle said you knew your stuff," Stamoran said. "And she's the best there is. By the way, if you want to lead this investigation, Ms. Churchwood, from here on, it's yours. You deserve it."

Arden heard a quiet sound from Monelle, saw her put her hand to her chest, surprised.

"Thank you," she said. "I'm—thank you." She took a deep breath. "Arden, too? On the team?"

"Takes a village," Luke said. "Especially a village with skills. And brains."

"And heart," Monelle said.

"You're killin' me here," Stamoran said. "Doesn't anyone have work to do?"

That image of her father came to Arden's mind—the one with him and her mom on the steps of the statehouse, that first day he was elected. The one framed on her nightstand. She'd been what, seventeen? Dad had opened his arms to her, and she'd walked up the marble steps to join them. Her father had embraced her and whispered in her ear. "Follow your heart," he'd said. "And you will never go wrong."

"You know I'm so grateful," Arden said. "Being your unlikely ally, Monelle. And Luke, I've never been so terrified as when you were chasing me in the woods."

"Doing my job," he said.

"Right," Arden said. "But I was frightened, and so was Pip, and even now I know you're a good guy . . . Well, that was a crisis moment in my life, and Pip's, and I had to figure out how to handle it. It makes me think about all the people who are frightened like Pip, and frightened like me, and have nowhere to turn."

"You're saying no," Monelle said. "I can't believe it."

"I admire you, Mr. Stamoran. Charles, okay," she amended at his look. "And your devotion to your job. And you Mo, and Luke. You somehow know what side you're on, and go for it, passionately, and that's admirable."

"But?" Monelle asked.

It felt like the atmosphere in the room had softened, the once pompous Charles Stamoran had moved to look out the window at the intensifying snow. Luke had stuffed his hands in his pockets.

"I'm not so sure I know what's right, or who's guilty, with as much certainty as you do. I can see both sides of things." Arden thought about what she meant. "What gives me joy . . ."

She paused, realizing what she'd said. *Joy.* The thing that had changed her life, for the worse, and then for the better. She started over.

"What brings me joy," she went on, "is guiding people through their tough times. Sometimes we have disasters not of our own making. And I know, sometimes . . ." She shrugged. "We have a hand in it. But like a nurse who guides us back to health, or a lawyer who zealously stands up for a client, I want to be there for those who need help."

"You're actually saying no." Stamoran had turned back to her.

"He's not used to that," Monelle said.

"I'm saying . . . ," Arden went on, deciding as she spoke. "I'll start my own agency. Maybe get Luz, and a few others from whatever's left of Vision, those who want to help change the world for the better, and keep people's lives in equilibrium. Things happen that we cannot control, and sometimes we need help. That's who I want to be."

"We can still be friends though," Monelle said.

"We could hang out," Luke said. "Have some fun."

"Doesn't *anyone* have work to do?" Stamoran made a show of opening his computer. "I certainly do."

We all do, Arden thought. Her own future, no longer bleak and empty, now seemed full of possibilities. With new allies, and new opportunities. Friends, even. And, with luck and hard work, some justice.

"Earth to Arden?" Monelle waved a hand in front of her face. "You with us?"

"I am indeed," she said. "With endless joy."

ACKNOWLEDGMENTS

Do you read the acknowledgments? I remember, in my before-author times, I would read the ones in other people's novels, infinitely curious about the mysterious and special worlds they hinted at. Writing the acknowledgments could only come when a book was finished, couldn't it? And it seemed like such a profound signal of success and completion and teamwork and hope and . . . whatever the magical journey was. I couldn't imagine writing acknowledgments without tears coming to my eyes, and I wondered if the authors felt that way, too.

The other thing that fascinated me back then was how many names were often included. Names, and specific titles, hinting at teamwork and relationships, and skill and expertise and cooperation. Who are all those people, I wondered? What do they all do?

Now I know. Now I truly deeply know. Those names in the acknowledgments—they are the lifeblood. They are the electricity. They are the power and the joy that is behind every novel. My beloved team at Forge Books—I am constantly impressed with your knowledge and brilliance and constant perseverance, and honored by your support and friendship.

My total genius editor, Kristin Sevick. Readers, every word you read in this book, she has read two, three and four times, always gently and brilliantly shepherding me in exactly the right direction. Without her this book would be so different, and I would be, too. The wise and patient and incredibly organized editorial assistant, Troix Jackson. The indefatigable Alexis Saarela, who will make sure everyone knows absolutely everything about *One Wrong Word*. I am incredibly grateful. It's probably the artistry of Katie Klimowicz who tempted you to buy this book—can you believe the gorgeous cover?

And please give a massive round of applause for copy editor Debbie Friedman—you are a complete rock star. Thank you for protecting me from career-ending errors. And proofreader Marcell Rosenblatt, whew.

Thank you! And sorry for the battles over the hyphens and commas—readers, Marcell was so patient with me. My style is my own.

So many thanks to managing editor Rafal Gibek, production editor Jeff LaSala, and production manager Jacqueline Huber-Rodriguez. And whoo-hoo for marketing—thank you Julia Bergen and Jennifer McClelland-Smith. Sales, yay, ever fabulous, determined, persistent, and knowledgeable. Every one of you is a complete professional. Linda Quinton—your impeccable and visionary leadership has me in awe every single day. And the powerhouse combination of Lucille Rettino, Eileen Lawrence, and Laura Pennock is a force to be reckoned with. Love you so much. And Devi Pillai, you are a genius, and continue to make my dreams into reality.

And everyone at Macmillan Audio. Oh, you are life-changing! And whenever I hear this book read so beautifully by one of your brilliant storytellers, it again brings tears to my eyes.

Agent Lisa Gallagher. Standing ovation. My dear friend, and a treasured heroine and fierce protector, you are utterly brilliant. I always say I love everything you do, and every decision we make—long may we decide things.

The artistry and savvy of Madeira James, Charlie Anctil, Mary Zanor, Andrea Peskind Katz, Pamela Klinger-Horn. Ann-Marie Nieves, Suzanne Leopold, Keri-Rae Barnum, Christie Conlee, Nina Zagorscak, Mary Lou Andre, and Jon Stone. You are all so fabulous. Kathie Bennett! You are such a powerhouse. Karen Bellovich and Margaret Pinard at A Mighty Blaze, you are perfection. Maxwell Gregory and Mary Webber O'Malley, I am in awe. Jenna Blum, you are a rock star.

Sue Grafton, always. Mary Higgins Clark, ditto. You are both still with me. Shari Lapena. Mary Kubica. B. A. Paris. David Baldacci. Lisa Jewell. Ruth Ware. Thank you for everything. Heather Gudenkauf. Lynne Constantine. Valerie Rees. Lisa Scottoline. Lisa Unger. Erin Mitchell. Barbara Peters, Kym Havens, and Robin Agnew. You are amazing. James Patterson, you are a treasure.

My incredible blog sisters at Jungle Red Writers: Rhys Bowen, Hallie Ephron, Roberta Isleib/Lucy Burdette, Jenn McKinlay, Julia Spencer-Fleming, and Deborah Crombie. And my Career Authors posse: Paula Munier, Dana Isaacson, Jessica Strawser, and Brian Andrews. What would I do without you? And Ann Garvin and the Tall Poppies, standing ovation. Thank you. My dear friend Mary Schwager—we have been through it, right?

And my darling sister, Nancy Landman.

Speaking of life-changing: Bookstagrammers! If I list you, I will forget someone, but you know who you are. I am grateful every single day.

And also life-changing: my partner in fictional crime, the brilliant bestseller and treasured friend, Hannah Mary McKinnon. There would be no First Chapter Fun without you, and my life would be significantly different. You are incredible in every way. And the amazing Karen Dionne—our collaboration on The Back Room has been a constant joy! And you are a dear and brilliant pal. And to all of you, Funsters and Blazers and Back Room attendees, it is always a joy to see you. Thank you.

Jonathan is my darling perfect wonderful husband, of course. Thank you for all the driving, and carryout dinners, and your infinite patience, and your unending wisdom. (And for being my in-house counsel.) Love you so much.

Do you see your name in this book? Some very generous souls allowed their names to be used in return for an auction donation to charity. To retain the magic, I will let you find yourselves.

My true inspirations are you, darling readers, and those who helped this book become a reality. It's not fully realized until you read it, and I am so grateful to you for keeping it alive. And yes, indeed, tears came to my eyes writing this.

Sharp-eyed readers will notice I have tweaked Massachusetts geography a bit. It's only to protect the innocent. And I adore it when people read the acknowledgments. Keep in touch, okay?